The Melting Queen

NEWEST
PRESS

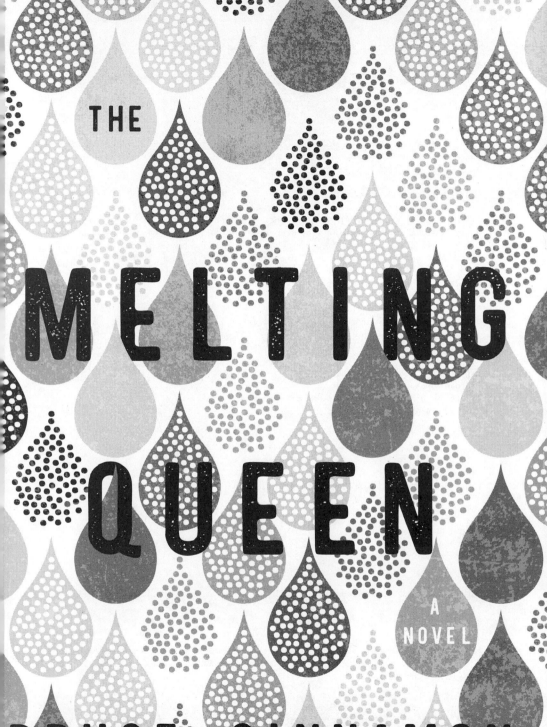

THE MELTING QUEEN

A NOVEL

BRUCE CINNAMON

NeWest Press wishes to acknowledge that the land on which we operate is Treaty 6 territory and a traditional meeting ground and home for many Indigenous Peoples, including Cree, Saulteaux, Niitsitapi (Blackfoot), Métis, and Nakota Sioux.

Library and Archives Canada Cataloguing in Publication

Cinnamon, Bruce, 1991-, author
    The melting queen / Bruce Cinnamon.

(Nunatak first fiction series ; no. 48)
Issued in print and electronic formats.
ISBN 978-1-988732-50-3 (softcover).--ISBN 978-1-988732-51-0 (EPUB).--
ISBN 978-1-988732-52-7 (Kindle)

    I. Title. II. Series: Nunatak first fiction ; no. 48

PS8605.I56M46 2019   C813'.6   C2018-904440-3
                                         C2018-904441-1

Board Editor: Thomas Wharton
Cover and interior design: Michel Vrana
Cover images: istockphoto.com
Author photo: Joanna Włodarczyk

NeWest Press acknowledges the Canada Council for the Arts, the Alberta Foundation for the Arts, and the Edmonton Arts Council for support of our publishing program. We acknowledge the financial support of the Government of Canada.

NeWest Press
#201, 8540-109 Street
Edmonton, Alberta T6G 1E6
www.newestpress.com

No bison were harmed in the making of this book.

Printed and bound in Canada

1 2 3 4   21 20 19

To Edmonton—a city I have loved, hated,
left, and returned to many times.

Table of contents

The ice has broken.
The river runs on again.
Winter is over.
—Old Melting Day haiku

After a long winter

I go to the river every day to see if it's finally free.

Before the sun rises—before daylight comes to illuminate a miserable world, before dawn chases away the endless possibilities of night—I shuffle out onto the barren streets of this godforsaken city.

Edmonton. A prairie town, crushed flat by huge, heavy skies. A northern outpost, encased in ice for months on end. Its houses huddle together against the cold wind, which digs its claws under doors and around window frames. Its roads are lined with mountain ranges of dirt-encrusted snow, painted orange by weak sodium streetlights. Its people sleep, dreaming of summer. Dreaming of somewhere far away.

I dream of green grass and running water as I walk to the river. My boots crunch on the salt-stained sidewalks. The dry air scratches at my skin, flaying my nostrils for daring to inhale, trying to force me back to bed. But I bow my head against the winds and soldier on, driven by the tiniest ember of hope.

When I reach the stairs that lead down into the river valley, I close my eyes and look out at the landscape. I let my desperate dreams flare up, projecting my desires onto the world. I imagine myself looking out on a shattered river, freed from its icy prison. I say a prayer to all the ancient gods of the earth and the river:

Please. Let it be today. Let the ice break. Let winter end.

But every day for the past six months I've been disappointed. The world defies my dreams. I stand on the top step and open my eyes and see a solid ribbon of dead white ice. The river is held captive, its waters locked in place. The skeletal trees along its banks stretch their brittle branches toward the sky. Tufts of blanched grass poke up through heaped snowbanks. The whole river valley—emerald green in summer, golden yellow in fall, blossoming pink in spring—is trapped in grey stasis.

I swallow my disappointment and start down the stairs, to search the ice for signs of fracture.

Edmonton is a typical grid city. It sprawls out over the flat, wheat-stubbled prairie like a smashed egg oozing across a crumb-covered kitchen floor. Its perfect, rect-angular blocks are completely interchangeable. They stretch to the horizon like the world's easiest and most boring jigsaw puzzle. Apartments and restaurants and office blocks. Schools and houses and strip malls. Every part of this city looks the same: short, squat, and square.

But the river valley is different. The river rips this city in two. It carves a wind-ing path through the heart of Edmonton, pulling the paved-over prairie down into a deep crevasse. The orderly grid of streets unravels into nonsensical curves. The structured metropolis gives way to a wild urban forest. Two dozen bridges stretch across the river, pulling the two halves of the city together like stitches trying in vain to close a wound.

I've walked across each of them, inspecting the ice from above. I hunt for some hint of a crack, some hope of an imminent collapse. But the ice is flawless, pristine, spread from shore to shore like a starched white sheet. It's just as strong today as it was yesterday, and it was just as strong yesterday as the day before that. And the day before that. And the day before that.

It's been six months since the First Snow fell. Six months since that grim fall day when frosty lily pads started to clog the river. The longest winter in living memory. It should've been spring weeks ago, but still the ice locks the river in place. It's the middle of May, and there are still no signs of summer.

After a while, my inspection of the ice becomes too depressing. The sun comes up, my dreams of spring evaporate in the pale white light, and I start to believe that the river will never be free. Winter will last forever.

I stand on the High Level Bridge, stare down at the thick white ice, and wonder what it would take to break it. Would an object, falling from a great enough height, have enough force to shatter the river and free us all from the tyranny of winter? I've flirted with the idea—hauling a bunch of rocks up to the bridge deck and throwing them down with all my strength. Or dragging one of the historical cannons from the Legislature grounds and tipping it over the railing. Or just taking a tiny step forward...

"Adam?"

A familiar voice rips my reveries apart. An icicle of fear and dread and panic slams into my gut, slides up under my ribs, bursts both my lungs. I turn to face him breathlessly, with the wind knocked out of me. I've been asleep for too long, I know. But this is not how I wanted to wake up.

"Oh my god. Oh my god, Adam."

The look on Brock Stark's face is more honest than any mirror ever could be. I can see in an instant what I've become, and I feel the icicle of panic vaporize into red-hot, burning shame.

"What happened to you?" asks Brock. "Where have you been all winter?"

He steps towards me. We're the exact same height, but that's where our resemblance ends. Everyone used to joke that Brock and I were twins—or at least we would've been, if not for my bright red hair. His hair is more gold than blond. His jaw could cut diamonds. If he flexed he would probably rip his coat apart at the seams. He looks like a Greek statue, but his flawless white skin glows with a bronze radiance even now, after all these months of winter.

From the moment we met pledging Delta Chi Upsilon in first year, we were a pair. Brock and Adam. Adam and Brock. Like salt and pepper: never one without the other. My best friend. My mirror-image. But not anymore.

His model-quality green eyes are wide pools of emotion. I see a whole synchronized swim team of feelings splashing around in them.

"Adam. Say something! What's wrong?"

I have lockjaw. I have no idea what to say. I have no way to explain away the past six months. I couldn't explain it then and I can't explain it now. I just had to leave. It was easier to just make a clean break with everything and everyone. Even him.

"Oh, hi Brock," I manage to croak out. It's hard to remember, but I think it's the first words I've spoken in six months. "I've just been, you know, around. Long winter, huh?"

He stares at me, mouth agape.

"Long winter? Are you kidding me? Where *were* you? You just disappeared. I tried to call you. I tried to *find* you. We all thought you'd left town or something."

"I'm sorry," I say. "I didn't mean for you to worry."

I owe him more than this. But there's nothing to be said. That life is over now.

He just stares at me with those wide, horrified eyes, taking in my sunken face, my exhausted eyes, my tangled hair, tumbling halfway down my back. I know I could never explain what I felt in a way that would satisfy him. I can barely explain it to myself.

Seeing him right in front of me, with his bulging muscles and his close-cropped hair, it's hard to believe that I looked just like him once. I used to be everything that a man is supposed to be. But now this body—once so virile and vigorous, once so strong and solid—is a husk of its former splendour. All I do is sleep, and check the river, and fantasize about spring. I've been surviving on saltines and peach yoghurt for six months. I haven't been to the gym since I stopped going to campus in the fall. I've become addicted to walking—up and down the river valley, back and forth across bridges—and every step erodes my body further. I'm wasting away, dissolving a little more each day. My life with Brock feels like a distant memory now.

"Tell me what happened," he says. His voice is thick and rich, like a knifeful of butter on a big slab of toast. "Tell me everything."

"Things changed. I changed. That's all."

"Why didn't you answer my texts or calls? Why did you disappear off Facebook and Instagram and everywhere?"

"I threw my phone away. I deleted everything, all my profiles."

"Why?"

"I just couldn't have them anymore. They were wrong. They were all lies. They weren't me."

I turn my face away from his. I don't want to see myself reflected in his eyes. I don't want to hear my own weak explanations

"You shouldn't've cut me out like that," he says. "I'm your brother."

It took Brock a year to come out to me, and another year before he was brave enough to tell all the other Delta Chi Upsilon brothers. But he wasn't the first gay Dixie and he won't be the last. I can't stand there like he did and say, "I like guys, but I'm still one of the guys. I'm still your brother." I'm not some frat brother anymore. I don't know what I am, but I know I'm not that.

I look past him, to the end of the bridge, then force myself to meet his eyes.

"I can't be a brother, Brock. I'm not Adam Truman anymore."

He shakes his head.

"What does that mean?"

"I don't know. Never mind. It means nothing. I have to go."

"Adam—"

"No. Not Adam. Not anymore. Forget about him. Forget about Adam and Brock. Forget about Delta Chi Upsilon. Forget about the past four years. Please. Please just forget that I ever existed, okay?"

His jaw sets in that stubborn, familiar way.

"Never," he says. "No matter what. You're still my best friend. You're still my brother. And clearly you need me right now."

"I'm sorry," I say. "I have to go."

He makes no move to stop me as I walk past, but he calls out after me.

"We're not done yet, Adam! I'll find you!"

"I'm sorry," I mumble under my breath as I walk away.

I go off the south end of the bridge, up the hill, past the Garneau Theatre and Antidote Café. My heart thunders in my chest. I know he's not following me, but I can still hear his voice ringing in my ears. I walk down 109th Street, turn onto Whyte Avenue, weave through the afternoon crowds. I feel my cheeks burning, hot and red against the cold winter air. I wish he hadn't seen me this way. I wish he could've just remembered the good times we had and left it at that.

I have to get out of this city. I've known it for a long time, deep down, but my fantasies of spring have made me too complacent. I've been wasting time here, walking in circles. I should've gone the moment the First Snow fell. If I stay I'll just run into more Brock Starks, more ghosts from my past life. No more walking. No more waiting for the river to break. It's time to go.

I grit my teeth and take a confident step forward, finally resolved. And then my bootlaces explode.

It's a coordinated effort, like two samurai lovers committing seppuku side by side. My laces spill out over my toes, unravelling like steaming intestines, and I go crashing to the pavement.

I force myself to get right back up, tripping over the carcasses of my boots, ignoring the bug-eyed stares of the strangers around me. I push past the couple who are asking if I'm okay, ignore the stinging in my knee, open a door and stumble into the nearest shop. A bell tinkles above me. Heat washes across my face and my pores sigh in relief.

"We're closed."

An enormous woman with a bad slouch sits behind a messy desk. She wears a fuzzy green cardigan which makes her look like a moss-covered boulder. Her black hair is cut short and shot through with wiry bristles of grey and white. Her skin is brown and speckled, as are her eyes. There are dark, puffy circles under them, but they stare out at me with sharp focus. She looks like a big brown bear who's just woken up from hibernation—still sleepy, but she might spring into action if provoked.

The big bear woman dominates the space so much that I barely noticed her surroundings at first, but now reality seeps back in. Worn, stained carpet. Cardboard boxes stacked throughout the room. Faded posters on the walls: the Sydney Opera House, the Pyramids, Machu Picchu.

It's a travel agency. Of course it is.

"I'd like to book a trip," I announce.

"I told you, we're closed," she says. "As in: Closed Forever. Going out of business. There's a sign."

She gestures and I look over my shoulder at the bare glass on the door.

"Oh. I guess I forgot to put it up," she says. She grabs a piece of paper and starts writing out a sign. My sudden burst of energy is just as suddenly snuffed out.

The travel agent walks around me and affixes the sign to the door. She returns to her desk, picks up a stack of brochures, and throws them into a swollen blue recycling bag. I notice a huge pile of bags filled with shredded paper in the back corner of the shop, under a sagging Stonehenge poster.

"You don't have any last-minute deals?"

"That was last month," she says. She continues emptying out her desk for a moment then looks up at me.

"Why are you still here?"

"Oh. Right. Sorry."

I turn to leave and the husks of my boots trip me up. I stumble into a rack of postcards and it crashes over beside me. The travel agent just watches me flail as I struggle to keep my balance.

"I'm sorry!"

She swats my apology away.

"Whatever. I'm gonna throw all that shit out anyways."

"All these postcards? Why? They're beautiful."

The travel agent gives me a look that's either disgust or pity or a mix of both. I blush and stare down at the mangled remains of my boots.

"I'm sorry. I'll go now. Just, do you have any tape I can borrow?"

The travel agent folds her arms across her chest. I feel her really looking at me now—her gaze scratches across my surfaces, prying at the grey layers that I've cocooned around myself as insulation. She's noticing how thin I am, how translucent my skin has become. The long red hair spilling out from under my toque. She's frowning now, probably wondering what the deal is with this guy. Looking up and down my body, imagining what she would see if she peeled away my bulky winter coat.

"Never mind," I mumble. I turn away and shuffle toward the door. I'll walk home in my socks.

"Wait," sighs the travel agent as I reach the exit. "I have tape. Just give me a second."

She lumbers away, into the back of the shop. I wait a moment, then shuffle over to one of the chairs in front of her desk. It coughs out a little plume of dust when I sit down.

As I wait for her to return, I look at all her dated, faded travel posters. All winter, as I've been walking back and forth across bridges, I've been dreaming of the new person I'll become when the ice breaks. I've dreamed that the ruins of my past life will crumble away, and a glorious new me will rise from the rubble. Sometimes I close my eyes as I walk, and imagine this shining new self in a more lustrous city. In my mind's eye, Edmonton's drab streets are transformed around me into the sun-soaked alleyways of Paris, the neon-drenched avenues of Tokyo, the fluorescence-flooded streets of New York City.

I dream that my new, glorious self will be born on the first day of spring. When the ice breaks and the river is freed, the whole city will celebrate Melting Day, Edmonton's most important holiday. The sun will boil off the snow and the city will rise from its slumber. The people will flood into the streets and ascend into revelry. Everyone will laugh and drink and feast and dance and cry with joy that the Long Winter has finally ended after all these horrible months. And I will be made new again.

I'm staring at a poster of the Trevi Fountain when the travel agent clears her throat. I jump—it sounds like a shotgun blast—and she seems almost amused.

"Found the tape."

She walks over to me, holding a thick roll of duct tape.

"Did you know that they collect over three thousand euros from the Trevi Fountain every day?" I say, gesturing at the poster. "They have police guard it so nobody steals the money and they give it all to charity."

"Neat," says the travel agent.

"And did you know that it's illegal to chase stray cats out of their habitats in Rome? The city council passed a law saying that they were part of Rome's cultural heritage and couldn't be moved. Now there are over two hundred feral cats living in the Colosseum."

"Wow. You know a lot about Rome," she says. "Have you been there?"

"No," I say, studying the posters to avoid her stare. "I haven't been anywhere. I just like to read about other cities. There are so many interesting places in the world, aren't there? Like Seattle—they have a famous wall covered in gum and people make pilgrimages there to stick on their own pieces. Or Tokyo—they have a spa resort where you can soak in pools of wine and coffee and green tea. Or Uyuni, Bolivia—they have a Great Train Graveyard of abandoned locomotives at the edge of the world's largest salt desert."

"What about Edmonton?"

The travel agent's words cut through my fantasies of these faraway places. They pull me back to her coffee-stained carpets and the snow-choked street outside.

"What *about* Edmonton?"

My words come out with a sharper edge than I intended. She looks at me with something verging on desperation.

"Do you know any stories about Edmonton? About the High Level Bridge or the Muttart Conservatory or West Edmonton Mall?"

"Edmonton isn't that kind of city," I say.

"Why not?"

I stare at her. Surely she must understand, if she lives here.

"The High Level Bridge is just a bridge."

She nods slowly.

"I heard that twelve people throw themselves off every year," she says.

"Really? I thought it'd be more than that."

"Yeah, about one a month."

"Not in the winter though," I say. "They wouldn't want to hit the ice. They wouldn't want anyone to have to see that."

"No. I guess not."

"And even in the summer, the river is shallow there. You'd hit the bottom for sure. But maybe that's a good thing. Maybe you'd just get absorbed into the silt of the riverbed, and no one would ever find you."

"Maybe."

She stares out the window distractedly. I study her creased face, but I can't imagine what she's thinking. After a moment she looks back at me and says nothing.

"Well, I should go," I say.

I start to stand up from my chair.

"You didn't get any tape," she says.

"Oh yeah."

I sit back down. Rather than handing me the tape as I expect, the travel agent kneels next to me. She lifts up my heel and proceeds to wrap the roll of duct tape around and around, looping up and down my calf.

"Are these women's boots?" she asks.

"No. They're mine."

The travel agent raises her eyebrows but says nothing. She tapes up my other boot and then gives it a pat.

"Should be good to go."

"Thanks," I say, standing up and walking to the door.

I look around the desolate shop. Everything here makes me sad: the broken coffee maker, the faded posters, the dusty brochures. I can feel all the energy draining out of my body just from being here. No wonder the travel agent seems so exhausted.

"Have you ever been to Rome?" I ask, hoping to lift her spirits a little. "I'd love to hear what it's really like. If you know about any hidden gems, or anything like that."

The woman looks irritated by my question, but her voice is sad.

"No," she says, lifting herself off the floor with a grunt. "I've never been to Rome. I've never been anywhere."

She looks down at a shoebox on her desktop, then back at me.

"You said you like postcards?"

I nod. She picks up the box and brings it over to me.

"Here. I have some old ones you might like. You seem like you could give them a better home than I can. Or just throw them out. I don't care."

I take the surprisingly heavy box from her—she held it like it weighed nothing. My hand touches hers for a second as she passes it to me. Her fingers are warm.

"Thank you."

The travel agent nods. She seems uncomfortable and I don't know how to say goodbye. But she clears her throat again and turns back toward her desk and I guess our interaction is over.

I look outside and see that the sun has come out. Not the pale white sun of winter, but the rich golden sun of summer. It visits us sometimes in the depths of winter—peeking through the ice-particle clouds, spreading its yellow radiance across the city. The people walking by are all standing up straighter. It's amazing how the right kind of sunlight can change your whole day.

I look over at the travel agent, packing up her failed business. I wonder how long she's been waiting for spring, whether she's been watching the river like I have. I wonder how many people in this city have been huddled in their homes, taking shelter in their dreams, cursing the calendar for its betrayal. Waiting.

"Happy Melting Day."

I say it without thinking, surprising myself.

The travel agent looks up from her desk, startled.

"It's not Melting Day, is it?"

"No," I say. "Not quite yet. But it will be soon."

She stares straight into me, and for a moment I feel like she might flip over her desk, break into a rage, charge at me. But instead a small, reluctant smile appears on her face.

"Happy Melting Day," she says.

{2}

Far from the world, here at this bend in the river

The sun has sunk below the horizon by the time I get home. Not that I can ever see the sun from my room. I live in a basement bachelor suite in a prewar bungalow, perched on the border between Little Italy and Chinatown. At night, the red neon light from the Gate of Happy Arrival spills through the tiny window beside my front door. But other than that, it's a dark little cave.

I've plugged in half a dozen lamps around the room, probably too many for the old wiring to handle. I never turn on all the lamps at once because I'm sure it will start an electrical fire. And I have plenty of kindling.

Over the last six months, I've covered every last inch of my walls with postcards. Every day, after the sun sets, when I'm making my way home after inspecting the river ice, I steal another postcard from the convenience store down the street. They're only ten cents apiece and I buy overpriced yoghurt there every once in a while, so ethically it all comes out even. I can't resist the bright, colourful scenes of famous landmarks and tropical beaches and crowded streets.

When I moved into this place, the walls were decorated with a dozen artsy, black-and-white photos of Edmonton: the palm trees in the Legislature dome, the tangle of waterslides at the West Edmonton Mall waterpark, the high hedges of the Infinite Maze in the Sky Harbour Gardens. I tried to take them down, but the previous tenant had hot-glue-gunned them to the drywall. So instead I just plastered my walls with scenes of the world's great cities, surrounding these Edmonton landscapes like the hungry sea eroding an archipelago. I've been waiting all winter to cover them up. And now, with the travel agent's gift, I finally can.

I sit on the corner of my bed and open the box of postcards. There are hundreds of them. Enough to finish my project, and wipe out the Edmonton scenes for good. I lift a handful of them out of the box and they slip through my fingers and scatter across the floor—all face down, like peanut-buttered toast. I notice that they've all been written on. They've all travelled from across the world, back here to Edmonton. I pick one up, an Amsterdam canal scene:

> *Dear Clodagh,*
> *Thanks for arranging our trip.*
> *Wish you were here!*

I pick up another, the Carnaval in Rio:

> *Dear Clodagh,*
> *I can't believe how much fun we're having.*
> *Wish you were here!*

A big pink palace in Hungary:

> *Dear Clodagh,*
> *You were right! We love Budapest.*
> *Wish you were here!*

And on and on, dozens of them, hundreds. Messages from around the world. From satisfied customers. To a travel agent who never travelled.

I feel my heart breaking for her. Is that what I'm going to become? Just another beaten-down Edmontonian, snowed in and miserable? Hating my life but too exhausted to escape?

I look from the travel agent's box to my walls of postcards, this weird shrine which has brought me so much comfort throughout the winter, and something inside of me shifts. Some load-bearing beam collapses, and I finally see my postcards for what they really are: a lie. A false promise. They're not airline tickets. They're not even memories. They're just a sad consolation prize. They're trapping me here, giving me just enough false hope to keep me alive, just enough solace to stop me from leaving.

I feel my cheeks burning with shame. Poor, pitiful creature. Stupid, naïve child. I can't believe I ever loved these pictures. Now, I hate them with a burning, all-consuming fury.

I rush to the closest wall and tear down as many postcards as I can. The Eiffel Tower. The Burj Khalifa. The Tokyo Skytree. They all go tumbling down.

I try to rip one of the Edmonton photos off the wall but it's still stuck there completely. I pull and I pull and I claw at its edges but the picture isn't going anywhere.

Just like you.

I collapse in a heap on the floor, in a dirty little nest of the world's great cities. I want to burn them all. I want to scream and cry and wail. But nothing comes. My eyes are dry. My heart is hammering, my breath heaving. I start to crawl toward my bed, so I can at least escape into sleep.

No. Not today. Not anymore.

No more mopey bullshit. No more sleeping. No more dreaming. I'm done with waiting. I'm done with praying for the world to change. It's time someone took matters into their own hands.

Before I doubt myself, before the spark inside me dies, I head for the door. I'm tired of overthinking it. I know what I have to do. What I should've done weeks, months ago.

I go to the river. I don't stop at the top of the stairs this time. I don't say a prayer. I thunder down the wooden steps, through the empty park, deserted at this hour of the night. I race up to the promenade along the river's edge, heave myself over the railing, down onto the snow-covered stones they've used to shore up the crumbling riverbank.

I grab the nearest stone, ripping it out of the frozen soil, and I hurl it at the ice.

"Come on!" I shout.

The stone smacks the ice and skitters across the river, barely leaving a mark. It slides towards the big white hull of *The Edmonton Queen*. The indolent riverboat stands trapped in the ice, moored on the far bank.

I grab another stone—bigger, heavier, more jagged—and throw it as high and far as I can.

"Come on! Break goddammit! Fucking break already!"

The stone hits the ice and tumbles away. The ice shines, immaculate in the moonlight.

I try to grab a larger stone but I'm too weak to lift anything else. Fine. Fuck it. There's only one way to do this and I'm going to fucking do it.

I walk out onto the ice, to the middle of the river. I pick up the jagged stone and slam it down, over and over.

"COME ON. COME ON!"

I abandon the stone and start jumping up and down, throwing my full weight onto the ice. It's as hard and resistant to me as it was to the rocks. I hammer down on the river with the heels of my taped-up boots.

"COME ON YOU PIECE OF SHIT, BREAK! BREAK!"

I slam my feet down one more time and the ice gives way beneath me.

I scream and twist around but it's too late. The last thing I see is the glittering image of downtown Edmonton, perched smugly up on the high riverbank like a useless lifeguard. And then I'm under, in the darkness of the river.

Every cell of my body is set on fire. My skin is peeled off. My muscles are ripped apart. My bones are ground to dust. I'm colder than I've ever been, and I burn.

Everything slows down. Everything fades away except for me. I'm in this wet, dark place and I'm alone in the universe. I'm holding my breath. My lungs are going to explode. I start to breathe out, getting ready to breathe in and flood myself with icy cold water.

This is it. This is okay. This is how you leave.

No.

No. Fuck that shit. I'm not fucking dying here, in a shallow silty river in fucking Edmonton. I kick and pull myself in what I hope is an upwards direction, until I can feel the irregular underside of the ice above my head. My lungs are on fire, but I resist the urge to breathe in with every ounce of willpower I have left. I grasp at the ice until my hand finds an edge, sharp as a knife. I feel like I'm slicing deep into my palms, down to the bone, but I pull my way up through the hole and my head breaks the surface of the water.

I gasp in the dry winter air and I cough and cough. I claw myself out of the hole and crawl on my stomach across the infinite desert of ice before me. Finally I reach the riverbank. I pull myself up onto the rocks. I'm trapped in soggy, freezing clothes that weigh a thousand tons. I tear them off until I'm naked, standing on the river-bank, steam rising from my skin. I don't feel cold at all. I feel as warm as a blazing pyre. I blink at the blurry world before me, where a big black pool of ink seeps out across a white piece of paper. I takes me a second to understand what I'm seeing.

The ice is breaking. Cracks are spreading out from the hole I created. I hear the crunching sound, and see the stress-lines forming—titanic force being released, stasis giving way to motion. As I watch, the river begins to run.

The first day of spring

Finally.

Finally, winter is over. Finally, spring is here.

My face aches from smiling, but I can't help myself. The ice is broken. It's Melting Day. I started the spring, and now I can finally leave. And I know just how I'm going to celebrate my last day in Edmonton.

Over its long history, Melting Day has shamelessly absorbed the customs of a hundred other holidays. At first it just stole its traditions from spring festivals around the world: dancing around the Maypole, blowing up the Böögg, rolling giant wheels of cheese down the hills in the river valley, tying Martenitsi yarn dolls to trees to welcome Baba Marta, eating eggs in every possible configuration. But now there are Santas and leprechauns, cupids and calaveras, firework displays and lanterns released into the sky.

One of the first non-spring traditions that Melting Day absorbed into its grand pastiche was Hallowe'en costumes. Not everyone dresses up on Melting Day—some people are too busy kissing under mistletoe or searching for chocolate eggs or drinking shamrock beer—but a significant number of Edmontonians seize the opportunity. You can be scary. You can be sexy. You can be whatever you want to be. And I want to be a brand new self, resplendent and glorious.

So as the sun rises over Edmonton, revealing the shattered river to an overjoyed city, I sit at the centre of my room and build a paper gown. I pick the postcards off my floor, connecting them with tape, staples, safety pins—anything I can find. I've never made a dress before. I've never worn a dress before. But that doesn't matter. It's Melting Day. I can do anything. I can tame these postcards and take on the power of the places they represent. The whole world will cover me, stretching out in a grand flowing train behind me.

When the gown is done, I lower it over my body and look at myself in the mirror. My eyes travel from my feet to my face, sweeping across a dozen landscapes: the Ganges and the Nile, the Danube and the Rio de la Plata. I look truly magnificent, the Angel of a Thousand Worlds. I rein in my wild red hair with a regiment of strategically placed barrettes. I pull on my last pair of back-up boots. And then I'm ready to go.

The sun has risen, but it doesn't shine. It spills pale yellow light down onto the mounds of snow, the denuded trees, and the grey patches of grass. The impotent sun cannot melt the snow. This is an artificial spring.

But it doesn't matter. The Bacchanalia has begun.

The streets are packed with people, each living out their pent-up fantasies and personal traditions. Cars have been banned on Melting Day for as long as I can remember, except for the police officers who patrol the city and try to maintain some semblance of order. Melting Day is uncontainable chaos—hundreds of festivals happening all at once, everywhere. There are vanilla Melting Days happening in church parking lots and kink Melting Days happening in nightclub dungeons. There are family-friendly zones with face-painting and three-legged races, and adult-only areas with orgies and fight clubs. Melting Day is a grand buffet, an elaborate smorgasbord. All you have to do is choose your feast.

Thousands of people flood the streets, marching from far-flung suburbs into the city's core. I join the great parade, a bright speck in a tumbling kaleidoscope. Under the Chinatown Gate I see a group of revellers dressed in nineteenth-century naval uniforms. They're loading an historical cannon—a relic of old Fort Edmonton—with confetti, firing it off to cries of glee from the crowd. Little pieces of paper settle in my hair like technicolour snowflakes, land in the snow and dissolve into mush.

I leave Chinatown and pass through Little India, where people are racing around, showering each other with handfuls of riotous rainbow powders.

"Happy Melting Day!" a sari-sporting woman says. She dabs a bright yellow bindi on my forehead before hefting a Supersoaker filled with pink dye and blasting it off into the crowd.

Dozens of costumed revellers fill the streets around me. Some are wearing homemade projects like my postcard gown, but most of them are recognizable characters. There are Harry Potters casting spells and Chewbaccas growling at snarky Han Solos. There are Cruella de Vils luxuriating in their fur coats and James Bonds drunk out of their minds on vodka martinis. There are Marie Antoinettes and Terry Foxes, Frida Kahlos and Lady Gagas.

And so it is that I eventually walk into Sir Winston Churchill Square, Edmonton's civic centre, arm in arm with an elderly Chinese-Canadian woman dressed in an Optimus Prime costume. She doesn't seem to speak English very well but she laughs uproariously whenever I say "What?" She hands me a lime Bacardi Breezer from a compartment inside her costume, then kisses my cheek and tromps off into the mass of people.

I walk across the square, toward the statue of Winston Churchill himself, and see that his stooped figure has been festooned by pink and green crepe streamers. A pigeon wobbles from foot to foot on his head, takes a shit, then keels over as a Katniss Everdeen shoots it with an arrow.

At the statue's base, someone has used bright pink spraypaint to cross out Churchill's famous quotation from his World War II Christmas address to the Canadian Parliament:

"We have not journeyed all this way across the centuries, across the oceans, across the mountains, across the prairies, because we are made of sugar candy."

The clever vandal has replaced the words with another quotation:

"To improve is to change; to be perfect is to change often."

Under the statue's surly pout, a group of revellers are congregated—mostly small children and their young parents. They're sitting, nibbling on brownies, watching a trio of drag queens tell stories.

"Who wants to hear about the first Melting Day?" coos the lead queen into her microphone. She's a fabulous creature in a dress made out of fresh green leaves all stitched together. A hundred children squeal with delight and stretch their hands towards the sky.

"Well," purrs the lead queen, sweeping her black eyes back and forth across the crowd, "it all started over a hundred years ago, just down the hill from where we are now, on the banks of the river. Who can tell me what happened to the river today?"

"The ice broke!" a hundred voices cry in unison.

"And what does that mean?"

"Spring is here!"

"Ooh you kids are smart! That's right, and that's exactly what they thought way back in 1904. Back before Edmonton was even a city. Back when there were only eight thousand people in the whole town. Look around, there are probably more than eight thousand people in Churchill Square right now!"

The wide-eyed kids swivel their necks around, climb up on their parents' shoulders, and try to count the ever-shifting crowd of Charlie Browns and Beatrix Kiddos and bumblebees.

"Well, all those people were feeling blue after the Long Winter. It was almost as long as this year, and even colder! So when they saw that the ice had broken, they rushed out into the streets and started to celebrate. All their stuffy old prejudices melted away, and everyone—poor and rich, Indigenous and settler, woman and man—came together. And what did they do?"

"They danced!"

"That's right! Come on, let's dance!"

The children jump up and start gyrating along to an electropop beat.

"Come on Cherry Poppins! Come on Mary Cone! Show us what you've got!"

The two other drag queens—a matronly white governess with a bedazzled umbrella and a fabulous Latina peacock in an extravagantly feathered Carnaval costume—bust into a choreographed number. The lead queen belts out some gay diva anthem and the kids go wild.

When the song is done and the hyperactive, sugar-high kids have calmed as much as possible, the main queen resumes her tale.

"Spring is here! It's 1904 and we're partying like never before!"

Suddenly she leans in, frowns, lowers her voice.

"But children! The day is almost over! The ice is almost gone! We're just going to go back to our boring, humdrum lives tomorrow and forget all about our big special day. Aww..."

She slinks away, and the kids moan in disappointment with her.

"But wait, Magpie," says Mary Cone, the Carnaval peacock. "Isn't there someone who can make sure we don't forget this day?"

"Yeah," chimes in Cherry Poppins, the prim governess. "Isn't there someone who keeps the spirit of this special day alive, all throughout the year? Well?" She looks at the kids. "Isn't there?"

"Yeah!" shout the kids.

"Who?" asks Magpie innocently.

"The Melting Queen!" five hundred people shout in unison.

"Of course!" cries Magpie, smacking her forehead theatrically, "I forgot to tell you about the Melting Queen, and she's the most important part! Mary, Cherry, why don't you tell the kids about the Melting Queen?"

Magpie retreats to the back of the stage and her two back-up queens shuffle forward to take up the story.

"Those eight thousand people knew that if they did nothing, then they might forget the true freedom, the happy anarchy they felt on this day," says Mary Cone.

"So they held a grand council on the riverbank, beneath the sizzling northern lights overhead, which had come to bless them all," says Cherry Poppins.

"They started arguing about the best way to preserve this special springtime spirit, and soon they weren't happy anymore, they were mad!" says Mary, turning towards Cherry, shaking her feathers with rage. "They were fighting and dividing back into their old groups, forgetting the merriment of their unity."

"It looked as though this glorious festival would die, and never come again," says Cherry, facing down Mary, brandishing her umbrella like a sword. "But then a pure, clean, solitary voice cut through the argument."

"STOP!"

Everyone's eyes flash to Magpie, who steps forward between Mary and Cherry. They're much taller than she is—their shoulders are broad and their chests are wide and their jaws are thick and masculine compared to her strawberry-shaped face—but they give way as she takes command of the scene.

"A woman stepped out of the forest," says Mary Cone, "clad in a gown of fresh green leaves, with a wreath of wildflowers on her head."

Cherry Poppins lowers a woven crown, blooming with pink roses, onto Magpie's head.

"And what was this woman's name?" she asks.

"May Winter!" scream the kids, mesmerized.

"That's right," says Mary Cone. "A woman named Winter saved spring that year, and for every year to come. She'd only arrived in Edmonton a few months before, but already she knew that this was a special place and she wanted to help it thrive. So she said…"

"Let me be your Melting Queen," declares the goddess in green. "Let me take in this moment in time, preserve this glorious vitality which has vanquished our Long Winter, guard this spirit of spring for a year, until the next Melting Day."

"And then they watched in awe as the aurora shimmered down from the heavens and May Winter breathed it all in with one deep breath," says Cherry Poppins.

The leaf-clad queen mimes gulping down the northern lights, the kids copying her.

"From that day forward, Edmonton has never been without a Melting Queen," says Mary Cone. "She protects us. Nurtures us. Announces when spring has sprung. She's our eternal mother, our city's First Lady, and no other city has a woman like her. One hundred and fourteen women have had this honour, from May Winter to Saoirse Beltane, from Organza Grant to Alice Songhua. You can breathe out now," she adds, and Magpie and all the kids release their pent-up breath in one big burst.

"And who can be the Melting Queen?" gasps Magpie.

"Any girl who wants!" shout the kids.

"That's right!" says Magpie. "Whether she's a grandma or a little girl like some of you, any woman can be Named. All she has to do is put a leaf with her name on it on May Winter's statue."

She leans coyly toward the kids and raises her exquisitely plucked eyebrows.

"Maybe I'll be the Melting Queen this year," she says.

"Nooooo!" giggle the kids.

"I can't be the Melting Queen?" she asks with mock outrage.

"Nooooo!" repeat the kids, loving it.

"Why not?" she pouts.

"Cuz you're a boy!" some of them shout, and Magpie folds her hands over the front of her dress suggestively, a faux-shocked look on her face.

"Who told?"

The kids laugh and the drag queen ruffles haughtily.

"Well I don't need to be the Melting Queen to have a great party today and to be thankful to May Winter for starting this tradition! And what's the most fun thing to do on Melting Day?"

"Dance!" shout the kids, and on cue another song kicks off, the drag queens and the children and their parents all jolting along to its spasmodic beat.

Once the drag queens are done performing, the crowd rushes in to take selfies with them and get a lipsticked kiss on the cheek. I watch parents posing their children for photos, and as my eyes flick around the crowd, I notice that Magpie, the lead queen, is staring straight at me. Our eyes lock together. She's surrounded, but solitary, like a statue. Her giddy performance face has slid off for a moment, and she looks at me with piercing, omniscient intensity—at my wild red hair, at my postcard dress, at my pale thin body, underneath it all. I smile at her, imagining that she's May Winter reincarnate, come back to wish me bon voyage. Then a little boy with a red cape and a Thor hammer launches himself onto her, and the light in her eyes comes back to full brightness.

I glance at the City Hall clock tower, but of course its hands are waving madly in every direction. Clocks are profane on Melting Day—a tradition that began one year when the ice break-up coincided with Daylight Savings Time and everyone rioted about losing an hour of the festival. Still, I have somewhere I need to be.

Café Fiume is one of the strangest places in Edmonton. Ten years ago, the city decided to replace the one-hundred-year-old Walterdale Bridge with a brand new link across the river. They built the gleaming new structure right alongside the rusting old arches, which were scheduled to be torn down the following summer.

But before the wrecking barges could come to haul away the old girders, the Walterdale Bridge was granted a reprieve. A group called ECHO, the Edmonton Civic Heritage Organization, fought against the city government, halting the demolition by designating the bridge a special historical landmark.

Eventually the city sold the bridge to a private company, set up by the deep-pocketed ECHO board members. They slapped on a bright white coat of paint, ore up the metal bridge deck, and replaced it with six-inch-thick plate glass. A few months later, they opened a restaurant and lounge, ten metres above the ever-flowing waters of the North Saskatchewan River.

When I go through the door, I see that the restaurant is empty except for one patron. He sits at a table at the exact centre of the long dining room, his face buried deep in a menu. As I go to meet him, the solid riverbank gives way beneath my feet. I levitate above a flotilla of icebergs. No matter where I look, I can see the river. The doors and walls and tables and chairs are all made of glass or transparent plastic.

"Hello, Sander."

He lets the menu drop and looks up. Our eyes widen at the sight of each other. Sander is a naturally small and wiry person, and he's always thin and gaunt after his long slumber. But this year he seems more cadaverous than ever, drowning in his saggy pyjamas. His fingers are short splintery twigs. His cheeks are sunken and hollow. His black hair is dry and lustreless. He's half-Korean, but he's almost as pale as my ginger skin after six months locked away from the sun. His black eyes are rimmed with sleep, but they're still sharp and bright and intelligent.

I can feel them inspecting my body, taking in my own transformation and my unexpected style, my postcard dress and extravagant hair. He offers me a weary smile as I pull up a chair.

"Hello, Adam," he says. "You look colourful. Like a Klimt painting."

"And you look hungry," I say. He has sauce on his lips and crumbs in his lap.

"I ate some appetizers already," he admits, nodding to the stack of a dozen licked-clean plates beside him. "And I've ordered a few more things. You like shrimp, right?"

"I don't know," I say. "I used to, but who can say anymore?"

"Did you know that peppermint shrimp are all born male and then become hermaphrodites as they age?" asks Sander idly, chewing on the end of his fork.

Sander Fray is always sharing such facts. A devoted Wikipedian, he spends hours every day reading, researching, writing, and building up his vast hoard of knowledge. He told me once that everything in the world will one day have its own dedicated Wikipedia article, and we will all be both readers and contributors. His contributions have so far involved nearly a thousand pages about Edmonton: geography, architecture, history, you name it. Everything I know about Edmonton I've absorbed from him, by a sort of reluctant osmosis.

I met Sander in my first year at the University of Alberta, where he was a TA for my mandatory history class. I went to his office hours to ask him about a paper and he just never stopped emailing me further reference materials. He's still in the middle of his History PhD, searching interminably for the perfect thesis topic. But since he can only work until the First Snow falls, it's taking him forever to finish his degree. I have no doubt that he'll one day be a respected authority on Western Canadian history. Just not in the wintertime.

"So tell me," he says, knitting his bony fingers together. "What day is it?"

"It's the 18th of May."

His eyes already look like two full moons in his emaciated face, but now they swell even wider.

"Is it really? That's surreal. The latest Melting Day on record is May 2nd, 1942. That was a rough winter, with huge blizzards."

"There were some storms this year, but mostly it was just really cold. And dark. And long. But now it's over!"

I grab a dinner roll and rip off a chunk of bread with my teeth. It's the most delicious and flavourful thing I've ever tasted. My appetite is back, and I'm prepared to go head to head with Sander to see who can eat more. I know I'll lose, but just the fact that I'm excited for a contest makes me smile. Winter is truly over, and I'm done with sulking.

"Well hopefully it doesn't snow in August again this year," says Sander. "I can't afford to lose any more time."

Now that he's out of hibernation, Sander only sleeps an hour or so every day. It's not uncommon to get a 4 a.m. phone call from him, eager to tell me about his latest discovery or ask for my advice with an article. He works at a frenzied pace, all too aware that the First Snow will send him back into slumber.

Sander always wakes up on Melting Day and comes to Café Fiume to reunite with me and our mutual friend Odessa Steps. She spends her winters travelling the world, but she never fails to arrive back in Edmonton on the first day of spring. The three of us live our lives in harmony, diverging on the day of the First Snow and converging again on Melting Day. The Long Winter moves us all differently: She migrates. He hibernates. I endure. But we always come together in the end.

This has been our tradition for many years, and like most traditions it becomes more permanent with every repetition. We meet at noon at Café Fiume. Sander's always early, Odessa's always late, and I'm always right on time. As we eat, we share stories of our winters. I hear about Odessa's travels and Sander's dreams, and I tell them that Edmonton in winter is a harsh place that they're wise to avoid with travel and with slumber.

But not this year. This year, for once, I have good news.

"Do you like my postcard gown?" I ask Sander. "I made it this morning."

"I do," he says. "What inspired you to create this costume? I've never seen you dress up for Melting Day before."

A waiter comes and pours a glass of water for me. Sander orders six more dishes and asks if we can have another basket of complimentary bread.

"I made it because I'm going to visit all these places soon," I say. "Today is my last day in Edmonton. Melting Day is kind of like my farewell tour."

"Oh really? That's so new for you! I always thought you didn't like travelling."

"I just never had the chance to before now. But I'm turning over a new leaf, Sander. I'm going to travel the world, just like Odessa. But I'm going to go in the summer and the winter. And, to be honest, I'm not sure if I'll come back."

He stops chewing at a hangnail and gapes at me.

"Leave Edmonton? Forever? But you'll come back for Melting Day, right? Like Odessa does every year. You have to."

I smile at him. I know it probably makes me a bad person, but I'm kind of enjoying his shock. Adam Truman never would've left Edmonton. And in a sense, Adam Truman never will. I'm free from that life now.

"Maybe I'll come back for Melting Day," I say. "Or maybe we can start a new tradition. You can wake up and come to the airport and fly and meet Odessa and me in a Tuscan villa or a Mongolian yurt."

"Where are you going to go first?" asks Sander. "Are you really leaving tomorrow? Did you find an urban planning job somewhere? Or are you just going to travel for the summer and then look for work in the fall? You must've just graduated, right?"

I'm surprised by the spike of irritation I suddenly feel towards Sander and his incessant questions. Fortunately, the waiter returns with two bursting basketfuls of bread, and just as Sander starts tearing into them, the restaurant's glass door opens and Odessa Steps enters.

Whenever she comes into a room, the words *Odessa Steps enters* float into my head like stage directions. Her entrances and exits always transform an entire room. The world rearranges itself around her in a more artful way, bending gracefully to flatter her like footlights in a theatre. With only a few very remarkable people do you feel the weight of the air that they displace with their bodies, the universe making way for them. Odessa is one of these people.

The clouds part as she strides across the restaurant, and a spotlight of blinding white sunshine falls across her face. She's cut off all her hair since the fall, and her bald head gleams. Like every other style, she's mastered it effortlessly.

"Hello boys," she says, sliding up to the edge of the table and throwing herself into a chair beside Sander. Her grey eyes flick back and forth between us.

"You both look starved to death. What are we eating?"

She sticks her finger in the olive oil and balsamic, takes a lick. Picks up the wine lists, flicks through, decides she doesn't want any. Picks up the dessert menu, beckons the waiter over, orders one of everything. All the while, she never stops talking.

"Your hair is gorgeous, Adam. How did it grow so long in six months? It must be down to your waist! It's almost as if you've stolen mine. I cut if off on a whim in Nha Trang. Do you like it? I do. I think it looks great. Sander, you clearly need to eat something, like right now. Why don't you have food in your mouth? Are you finished with that bread already? Here, eat these Earl Grey Kit Kats I got for you in Japan."

Odessa Steps tears through the world like a tornado, stirring up dust that most people would rather keep settled. I met her on the LRT, where she was performing an unauthorized one-woman Fringe show that she called *The Clitoris Monologues*. I've never been so deeply uncomfortable and hilariously entertained at the same time, and I've seen every one of her shows since. She describes her work as feminist performance art, and her most infamous pieces include painting guerrilla murals with her menstrual blood and wearing her used tampons as jewellery. It's a mark of pride for her that she's been banned from a dozen public buildings. Last summer her big project was called "Please do not feed the animal." She sat at the head of a long feast table in a public park and invited people to come eat while she starved herself, occasionally reading out quotations about female body image. She was almost as thin as Sander by the end.

The waiter arrives with heaping plates of pasta. Odessa dishes out some fettuccine for me and some linguine for herself and lets Sander sort out his own food. His appetite is actually a little frightening on Melting Day, when it seems like he could unhinge his jaw and swallow us whole, along with the table and chairs. We nibble. He gobbles.

I chew my pasta and look between my two friends. One in grey pyjamas and one in a seemingly infinite loop of scarves. One the picture of frailty and one the image of robust health. One listening and one speaking.

When you're part of a trio, it's tempting to go through every group of three and assign each person a part. Sander is super-ego; Odessa is id; I am ego. Sander is rock; Odessa is scissors; I am paper. Hermione, Harry, Ron (the ginger always gets stuck with Ron). Sander loves Edmonton; Odessa doesn't seem to care; I hate this city. We're three sides of a triangle (equilateral, scalene, isosceles), the strongest shape in the world.

"So I know you're both dying to know where I've been," says Odessa. "And I've got to say I'm a little disappointed with myself: only six countries this time. I got stuck in Luang Prabang for months, learning how to weave scarves."

"I had some excellent dreams," says a barely comprehensible Sander through a mouthful of lasagna. "In one of them, a convoy of barges carrying confetti cake mix crashed into the High Level Bridge and the hot afternoon sun baked the whole river into a birthday cake. People walked out onto the spongy river and gobbled up handfuls of the cake and jumped on it like a trampoline."

I'm usually as hungry as Sander to sit back and feast on their stories. But this year I finally have a story of my own to share.

"I had something happen this winter," I announce.

They look up from their plates, surprised. Sander stops eating. Odessa stops making faces in the back of her spoon.

"You did?"

"Yes."

I look through the tabletop, down into the river, at the swiftly flowing chunks of ice. I take a deep breath.

"Normally I stay inside all winter. I only go out to attend lectures, or go to the gym with Brock, or go to parties with the Dixies. But not this year. This year I walked in circles every day. Outside. For hours. I went down to the river, waiting for it to break, praying every day for spring to arrive. I slipped into a mind-numbing routine of sleeping and waking and walking and waiting. And after a while, I realized that I didn't exist anymore."

Odessa's eyes narrow, then start roving over me, picking apart my postcard dress. Sander holds a dinner roll up to his open mouth, frozen in concentration.

"I felt like I'd walked down into the ocean, and the waves covered me up bit by bit. For months I was down there, on the ocean floor, where no light could penetrate. I knew who I was when I left the shore, but I didn't know who I was at the bottom of the sea. I knew I wasn't Adam Truman anymore, but I didn't know what would happen next, where I would surface again or who I would be. I didn't know when I'd reach the other shore, and be a person again. But yesterday, I finally did."

I smile. Telling the story makes me realize how lucky I am to have escaped my winter doldrums once and for all.

"Yesterday, I realized that I'd become addicted to being on the ocean floor. It felt good to be numb. It felt good to be nothing. But it was also killing me, slowly and surely. So yesterday, *I* broke the river. *I* decided to end winter, to end my sleepwalking, and to finally become the new person I'm meant to be."

My cheeks are hot, burning red yet again, but this time with pride. I look between my two last friends, the traveller and the dreamer. Odessa looks mildly impressed. Sander's eyes bulge.

"*You* broke the river?" he says. "Is that even possible? That doesn't seem right. I mean, is this really spring at all then?"

"Of course it's spring! You're awake, aren't you? Odessa's back. And I'm finally feeling alive again! To think that all these years it was possible, but nobody ever did it! We always just waited and waited for the ice to break. But I *made* winter end. I *made* spring come. Because that's who I am now: I *am* Melting Day!"

I stand up, high on my newfound confidence, ready for a blinding white sunbeam to spotlight me just like Odessa. My friends look up at me, dumbfounded.

"Seriously?" I say, almost laughing but also irritated. "Nothing? Not even a *bravo*, Odessa?"

She leans back in her chair and folds her arms across her giant beard of scarves.

"Oh yes," she says with a knowing smile, "you deserve a *bravo—brava, bravi*! You've finally started your secondary succession."

"What does that mean?" I ask, sinking back into my chair.

"It means that sometimes you have to burn everything to the ground so that a new life can grow from the ashes."

She rests her elbows on the glass tabletop and stares at me with her penetrating grey eyes.

"Primary succession is simple. You're born, you grow up, there's not much there to begin with. Everything is new and it's easy for your first identity to take root. But your second self, well, that's trickier. Your second self is the hardest to make. It's a painful process. It helps if you have some sort of disaster to clear away your old life and make room for the new. But don't worry. The third self is a bit easier. And the fourth is even easier after that."

Odessa reaches across the table and takes one of my hands in hers.

"Everyone needs a catastrophe to intervene every once in a while—to burn everything down so that new life can bloom."

She looks between Sander and me, then lays her hand across her belly.

"Which is why I'm pregnant."

"Uh, what?"

"Four months along, or something like that. I'm going to give birth as a piece of performance artwork in the fall."

She looks back and forth between us with familiar energy coursing across her face, flushed with the excitement of a new venture.

"It's going to be the ultimate performance. An act of pure artistic creation. I'm going to do it all myself."

"Is that safe?" asks Sander.

Odessa shrugs glamorously.

"True art is never safe."

She gives a toast to her own words with her glass of sparkling water.

"Thank you for not asking who the father is, by the way. Most people would've. But that's why I like you two best. To me it really doesn't matter. I'm going to be a kickass single mom. I'll raise my kid in a hundred different countries. Maybe I'll call her Pangaea. Or wait to find the right name during our travels. Or let her name herself."

She brings a spoonful of tiramisu to her mouth, tilts her head at me as she sucks the sweetness off the spoon.

"*You* should pick a new name," she says. "If everything about Adam Truman is dead and gone, then it's time for you to kick the name as well. That's one of the first steps of secondary succession, if you really want to have a new identity."

"I don't know enough about my new self to have a name yet," I say. "Except, well, I guess there is one thing—"

"A name could be a good place to start," carries on Odessa. "The name you choose is a promise you make to yourself. A statement about who you intend to be. 'Odessa Steps,' for example, is my fifth name. I chose it because I love *Battleship Potemkin*. It was the first movie to popularize montage, which I think is the greatest artistic technique of the past hundred years. In a montage, hundreds of shots come together to make something big and powerful. Slips of images are cut up, realigned into a deliberate order, to make something new—something that didn't exist in any of them until they were brought together. That's how people are really made."

She pauses, and picks up an individual grain of risotto with her fork. She repeats this as she speaks, until she has a dozen grains artfully arranged along the edge of her plate.

"We all sift through all of our life experiences—everything we do and see and say and feel—and we use this raw material to build narratives for ourselves that make sense. Most of our lives end up on the cutting room floor, even in our own memories. We take a bunch of random shit, and we make it meaningful. We can even manufacture false memories if we have to, or use fictional ideas about our-selves to build our real identities. Like how there never actually was a massacre at the Odessa Staircase. Eisenstein made it up. But the images were so powerful that the Potemkin Stairs became a real historical memory. That's the kind of art I want to make. Art that turns lies into truth. Art that redefines reality."

I try to cut back into the conversation, but Sander snaps back at Odessa.

"I think that's incredibly dangerous," he says, again through a full mouth. He swallows his ravioli and wipes the sauce from the corners of his mouth. "History needs to be true and accurate. If we start saying 'anything goes' for history and mem-ory, then how will we ever know what's real anymore?"

Odessa shrugs.

"How do we know if anything is real now? How do we know if 'real' really means anything anyways? 'Real' is whatever version of reality that the majority decides to agree upon, and it changes all the time."

I see Sander struggling between the competing desires to argue back or to finish off the heaping bowl of pesto fusilli. Fortunately he opts for the latter.

"*Anyways*," I interject, not bothering to hide my irritation at having my big news railroaded by another one of their philosophical debates, "I was just trying to tell both of you that I'm not Adam Truman anymore. I'm starting a new chapter of my life."

I turn to Odessa.

"I told Sander already that today is my last day in Edmonton. I'm going to leave tomorrow, and start fresh somewhere new. Maybe I'll pick a new name. Maybe... maybe other things will change too. I don't know. But I just wanted to know that you've got my back."

Odessa smiles.

"Of course we do. Always."

Sander lowers the plate of carbonara that he's been licking clean and gives me a nod.

"If you have to go, you have to go. But I hope you'll come back. Edmonton isn't as bad as everyone thinks it is."

He wolfs down one last spoonful of ribollita and then leans back and puts a hand on his belly.

"I think I'm full," he says. "For a couple hours anyways. What do you say we check out the party?"

He waves his hand up the hill at downtown Edmonton, where jubilant cheers ring out.

"I thought you'd never ask," says Odessa, waving to the waiter. She whips out her global elite platinum card.

Odessa's grandfather, Ludlow Spetnik, is a hundred years old and the rea-son she hasn't moved to New York or London or Los Angeles. Her mother died when she was very young, so he's all the family she has left. He invested in oil sands development in the mid-1950s, so he's incredibly rich. Odessa manages his invest-ments, and they make enough money for her to travel and fund all her art projects—not to mention buying us lunch every Melting Day.

The waiter hands Odessa her receipt, builds a teetering tower of plates—glan-cing warily at Sander all the while—then skitters back to the kitchen.

We spend the rest of the afternoon wandering through a dozen decadent debauch-eries, greeted at each with open arms and free drinks. We sip piña coladas at a luau where fat men in grass skirts drape huge leis made of fragrant flowers over our shoulders. We drink margaritas at a fiesta and smash at an army of piñatas until candy pours forth and a pack of children swarm around our ankles. We pound back vodka shots at an ice bar and watch in awe as a magician uncorks a set of reverse Matryoshka dolls—a larger one springing out of each smaller one, until he opens up the final doll like a cello case and out walks a woman in a pink ball gown.

By the time we get to the parade route on Jasper Avenue, we're well caught up to the million drunken Edmontonians who bumble around us. I try my best to forget my earlier irritation at Sander and Odessa, and I throw my arms around their shoulders. I love these two weirdos, even if they weren't as enthusiastic about the new me as I'd hoped they would be. Jostling for a place at the curb, we're squeezed in between a Totoro with a tiny umbrella and a Gene Kelly with a giant one.

It doesn't take long for the parade to arrive. A mop-haired cover band belts out "Here Comes the Sun," the unofficial Melting Day anthem, from the first float. A deluge of dancers—small children dressed as sun sprites, acrobats and fire-blowers—flows down the avenue. They pull people into the parade with them, swelling its ranks. The crowd shouts out the lyrics incoherently, but with such utter enthusiasm that their lack of tone or rhythm doesn't matter. The three of us join in, laughing at how bad we are, waiting for Her to appear.

And then there she is: Alice Songhua. The Melting Queen. Glowing like a bea-con with some internal fire. She wears an open-backed pink gown. Legs spread, she rides a giant blue horse, train trailing on the slushy street behind her. She scatters candied wild roses into the crowd. Her smile is so wide it stretches past her cheeks and scrapes against the windows of the office towers on either side of the avenue. The massive emerald in her crown glints in the sunlight, surrounded by peridots and pink sapphires. When she passes us, a frangipani fragrance settles over our hair. I smile as wide as she does, high on the delirious joy of Melting Day.

After Alice Songhua has ridden past, Sander and Odessa and I hoist ourselves up onto the shoulders of three people in rubber sumo wrestler suits who offer us a lift. We flow into the street with all the other revellers. A papier mâché hot air balloon skids down from above, firing off pieces of candy from on-board cannons. People wave and cheer from the roofs of the buildings around us. I wave back at them, imagining that this parade is just for me, a grand send-off for a famous adventurer.

"Look!" cries Sander.

I follow the line of his finger. A wing of huge silver airplanes sweeps across the sky, flying towards the setting sun in goose formation. I try to count them—one, five, twelve—but then the sky is obscured by a white haze, trailing from the planes. It starts to rain down around us—snow, hail, sand!

"Sugar!" shouts Odessa. "See if you can catch some on your tongue!"

I do as she suggests, and I'm instantly overwhelmed by the flavour.

"It's salt! Oh god!" shouts Sander, scraping at his tongue.

"Bleh! This is awful! Why did you say to do this!?"

"I thought it'd be fun but it's not! Oh god!" Odessa retches.

I heave. I need water.

"Grab some snow," I command the sumo wrestler, pointing at the dirty curb crusts. But the snow is doing worse than we are, dissolving under the lethal powdering of salt. The months-old ice crackles and fizzes as the salt burns into it. People all throughout the parade are brushing salt off their shoulders, shaking it out of their hair. After a stunned moment, the mob roars with joy to see the end of the snow.

After plenty of spitting and a couple of fresh coconuts from a nearby vendor, we carry on with the parade to its end point at the front steps of the Alberta Legislature, where Alice Songhua dismounts her mighty blue steed.

"Edmonton!" she cries, standing in front of the Legislature's huge sandstone pillars. "You have waited with great patience for the end of this Long Winter! I have stoked and tended the fire, worked hard to maintain the spark of life within our city. But now the sun has risen! The ice has broken. The river runs on again. Winter is over. Spring has returned. And with this new light comes new life!"

The crowd cheers, and then a group of DJs takes to the stage and a huge rave begins on the Legislature Lawns. The Melting Day playlist blasts through a disorienting array of musical genres. Baroque harpsichord segues into Ariana Grande then bounds on through Elvis and Edith Piaf. "Orinoco Flow" blends into "You Only Live Twice." The playlist is decided by popular submission, and nobody's suggestions are turned away. Like all else on Melting Day, the result is a lovably terrible hodgepodge.

As a Stravinsky concerto blares out, jolting the merrymakers into euphoric leaps, Sander suggests we go around to the gardens behind the building to see Her statue.

Years ago, someone decided it was a good idea to haul the statues of all the famous Edmontonians from across the city to the Legislature gardens, where they could stare at each other for all eternity and be stared at in turn by picnickers and pigeons. As we walk through the statue park, Sander points out this important Edmontonian and that one, jabbering on about their contributions to the city.

I tune out Sander and look around at the crowd. People keep glancing at me, admiring my postcard gown and my mane of ginger hair. I straighten my back and hold my head high, enjoying their attention. I'm glad someone appreciates the effort

I put in. Odessa and Sander sure don't seem to care. They're back to debating each other again, arguing about whether some of the statues of old racist men should be taken down and destroyed or left up with signs explaining their true histories. I sigh, wishing my friends cared more about discovering my new self and less about winning arguments with each other.

We arrive at the centre of the vast gardens, where a sacred rite of spring is taking place. At the heart of the Legislature Statue Park stands a larger-than-life sculpture, the most important Edmontonian of them all. May Winter is over six feet tall, and her features are impossibly serene. Unlike most of the other statues—whose bronze has blackened and whose marble has chipped—the first Melting Queen is made of bright burnished copper that glows like a pyre in the night. Sander told me once that the statue is polished every day by the devoted followers of the Cult of the Melting Queen, who revere Her as a goddess—the fertility queen who breathes life back into Edmonton every spring. Two white-robed acolytes stand on either side of the statue now, handing out green pieces of paper.

On Melting Day, a special ceremony takes place at the statue. Women and girls of all ages write their names on "leaves" and affix them to the copper foliage of May Winter's famous dress. Just after dawn, the thousands of names will be harvested by the people who select the next Melting Queen, and Melting Day will end with the Naming of the new Melting Queen tomorrow morning.

Women and girls have been adding names all day, and the statue is covered by several layers of green paper leaves. I watch as a mom lifts her little girl way up over her head so she can affix her leaf to the statue. May Winter's smiling face shines down on them.

A stooped old woman has been waiting behind a group of teenage girls for the past few minutes. When they've finally stopped taking selfies and stuck their leaves to the statue, the old woman approaches the statue and reaches up with a frail, trembling arm. She presses her leaf onto May Winter's dress—quickly, self-consciously. She turns away and hobbles off through the crowd, and a moment later her leaf tumbles off the statue and onto the ground. One of the acolytes sees it, looks after the old woman for a second, then steps slightly to the side, covering up the leaf with his foot. Neither Sander nor Odessa seem to notice.

"We only started this tradition fifty-eight years ago, you know," says Sander, staring up at May Winter's shining face with reverence. "Before then the Melting Queens were chosen by a committee of prominent women called ELLE, the Elite Ladies League of Edmonton. For a few years in the thirties the city even tried to have a vote, but that ended straight away after Saoirse Beltane was voted in and led the Hunger March against the government during the Depression. And at one point in the fifties the outgoing Melting Queen just chose a name out of the phonebook."

"I've always wondered how the current Melting Queen has time to look up all the names in the city directory," I say. "It seems impossible."

"Of course it's impossible," says Odessa, leering at the statue and the massive crowd of Melting Queen hopefuls. "Clearly this leaf thing is a big sham. They obviously just have pre-approved list that they choose from."

"That's not it at all!" says Sander. "They have an automated system that sorts and ranks all the leaves, and then a huge team of researchers reviews all the submissions and selects the best choice."

"And they've been doing that for fifty-eight years?" says Odessa, eyebrow arched to the heavens.

"Yes, as a matter of fact, they have," says Sander. "Maybe not with the computerized system, but they—"

"That's bullshit," says Odessa. "Okay, sure, maybe they get someone to stick up the name they want every year, to keep up the charade. But when do they ever pick someone who actually makes a difference or does anything to upset the status quo? Never."

Sander looks ready to either launch into a long lecture or duel to the death to defend the honour of the Melting Queen, so I cut in.

"Have you ever stuck your name on the statue?" I ask Odessa.

"Of course not," she says, practically spitting out the words.

"I think you'd be a great Melting Queen."

"Are you serious? What a horrible job. You'd have people telling you what to do all the time, fitting you into this little box of picture-perfect femininity. It would be a good platform for performance, sure. But still, not worth it."

"You're wrong," says Sander. "Melting Day is unique in the world. I've read quite extensively, you know, and nowhere else is there a festival like this, where a whole city—rich and poor, gay and straight, every race and religion—comes together truly as one. Getting to embody this tradition is an incredible privilege. I think it would the greatest honour to be Named as Melting Queen."

"Well it's too bad you'll never be Named then," laughs Odessa.

Sander's cheeks flush red and he looks away.

"Oh Sander," says Odessa in a sing-song voice, "don't be like that. Trust me, you don't want to be the Melting Queen. When are you going to realize that Melting Day is all a lie? I mean sure, it's fun. But it's not as freaky or liberated as everyone thinks it is. It pretends it's risky, but really it's safe. It promises subversion, but it exists within the confines of a controlled system—all these backwards, intolerant, timid people can point to this one day they were bold and open-minded, as if that excuses them from being boneless assholes the other 364 days of the year. Look around you—do you think all these people are really filled with brotherly love of their fellow Edmontonian? Melting Day is just a big pressure release valve. Without it, the stress of our insane way of life would build up and burst in violent revolution. And on top of that, it's all just an excuse to sell costumes and booze and limp green onion cakes."

I want to believe in Sander's version of Melting Day. It's true to a certain extent, or at least for a certain percentage of Edmontonians. Lots of people truly do let their wild sides out on Melting Day, and do daring things that would never otherwise be permissible. But Odessa's version is just as true. She turns to me expectantly.

"Back me up on this, Adam."

I just stare back at her for a second, but she doesn't seem to notice my sour expression.

"Not Adam," I say. "I told you."

"Oh. Right. Sorry. But you agree with me, right?"

I sigh.

"I have to pee," I say. "Will you two wait here? I won't be long."

"Sure," says Sander.

I set off towards the Legislature, making my through a mob of people who are increasingly indistinguishable from their costumes. Sailor Moon pushes a very intoxicated FDR past in his wheelchair. Anne of Green Gables and Pennywise the Dancing Clown run by, giggling and playing tag. A badger with a paintball gun chases a whole khalasar of Daenerys Targaryens.

I have a headache. I thought that my two strangest friends would want to celebrate my going away. But Sander and Odessa are just making me feel crabby, weighing me down on a day when I should be flying free. I'm sad to admit it, but I need a break from them.

Escaping the undertow of the crowd, I climb up the main steps of the big sandstone building. The doors of the Legislature are wide open. The crowd has burst inside, filling the halls with laughter and song. The Legislature Rotunda is built out of ammolite, an iridescent gemstone harvested from the Rocky Mountains, made from the fossilized shells of prehistoric crustaceans. The glittering rainbow surfaces reflect the flickering light of fire breathers, who spit flames down from the dome and into the cavernous rotunda below.

Walking through the palace of Alberta's government, I see the best and worst of freed impulses—the twin faces of Melting Day, both exhilarating and horrifying. Acrobats hang from strips of silk, performing intricate manoeuvres while suspended from the palm trees in the dome. A ninja fights a pirate in the Rotunda fountain, cheered on by a crowd of bloodthirsty spectators. Captain Jack Sparrow smashes a display case and hefts the province's royal golden mace, leading a mad parade of security guards through the building. Fine oil portraits of Premiers past stare down on the depravities with mute horror. The Lieutenant Governor himself is swaying drunkenly through the crowd, slamming back tequila shots with anyone who'll accept a lime wedge. I see a pair of duelling jugglers trying to one-up each other by chucking more and more *pysanka* into the air, the fragile Ukrainian Easter eggs blurring together into dark circles.

Tomorrow all these transgressions will be forgiven. People will gather sheepishly in Churchill Square for the Melting Queen's Pardon, and all the drunk and disorderly revellers who got themselves locked up will be released. The Melting Day Fund, which claims a penny from every financial transaction in the city, will be used to pay for any damage incurred in the course of the carnival. Everything will be set right. Back to business as usual. Everybody will hide away their costumes and their kinks. Edmonton will go back to being a grey, bland, introverted city for another year.

I have to go down to the basement to find a bathroom that people aren't having sex in. One cramped little men's room is mercifully empty, and I amuse myself by peeling back a couple postcards like a little door as I stand in front of a urinal.

I've just started to pee when I hear the door swing open behind me and music spills into the room.

"Whoa, sorry!"

I glance over my shoulder and see the back of a man in an Oilers jersey, exiting the bathroom at top speed. A moment later he pokes his head back in the door.

"Wait. Uh, is this...?"

He looks at the sign on the door, then at me. He finally connects the dots, realizes I'm standing at a urinal.

"Oh man, I'm so sorry. I thought you were a chick."

He shambles up to the urinal beside me in a looping walk.

"It's fine," I barely say.

"Yeah. Whoops! Fuck. I'm sorry dude. Just your hair. You know. My bad."

"Don't mention it," I say.

"Yeah. Sorry. I didn't mean—you know? Nice costume though bro. I dig it. It's cool."

"Thanks."

Everybody loves a man in a dress on Melting Day, when inversions and perversions are queen. Come tomorrow it'll be a different story. Come tomorrow the candy-coated veneer of tolerance will be shattered just like the river.

But come tomorrow I'll be gone, and this humdrum city with its once-a-year splendour can do whatever it likes.

I finish peeing and go wash my hands as quickly as possible. The guy leans against the wall as he pees—he's already forgotten about me and seems on the verge of falling asleep.

I look at myself in the mirror and cringe. I don't look magnificent or resplendent or glorious. My postcard dress is tattered and ratty. My face is the same gaunt mask with dark-circled eyes. Is this how I've looked all day? Like some awkward, gangly man in a cheap homemade costume? So much for my new beginning. I'm so far from the person I want to be, but it seems so impossible for me to get there.

I leave the bathroom in a slump, trying desperately to maintain the guttering fire of my spirits. I feel so tired, and cold, and ugly. I return to May Winter's statue, but I can't see Odessa and Sander anywhere. All I see are more characters, more revelry, more pandemonium. I can't stop seeing it through Odessa's eyes now, and it all seems like such an embarrassing, empty farce.

I go around the grounds looking for my friends, trying to stamp out these dark thoughts that nip at the edge of my mind. I search for them at the Periscopes, at the Holodomor memorial, in the cherry tree grove whose pink blossoms still haven't bloomed. I go back into the Legislature building and check every room, accepting more drinks from strangers along the way, trying to stem the tide of these depressing thoughts. A sweet one, a salty one, a sour one, a bitter one. The cocktails have imaginative names, but eventually they all taste the same.

After what feels like hours of searching, I finally find them on the roof of the Legislature, looking down on the vast party below. Odessa has collected a little audience around herself as she does her own interpretive dance to Beyoncé's "Girls." Sander is having an argument with John Diefenbaker and Cookie Monster about the viability of the welfare state in the twenty-first century. Diefenbaker has just said something about the healthcare costs of aging Baby Boomers, and Cookie Monster ripostes by talking about Tommy Douglas and the cornerstones of Canadian identity.

"Where've you been?" I shout. I notice my words slurring together. How many drinks did I have? It doesn't matter. "I looked all over for you!"

"There's an all-you-can-eat egg buffet in the Legislative Chamber," says Sander. "And a fairy with turquoise hair is granting wishes from the Speaker's Throne."

"Cool. Great. I wanna leave."

"What!?" gasps Sander. "We haven't even seen the fireworks yet!"

"Who cares? This is all a sham anyways, right? This is all a big festival of lies anyways, right?"

Sander looks aghast. Odessa stops her dance and puts a hand on my shoulder. "Adam—"

"No! How many times do I have to tell you!?"

"Ugh, yes. Christ, sorry, I forgot. I'm sorry. It won't happen again."

"Yeah, okay, sure. Whatever. I just want to go. I wanted today to feel special and I don't feel special and I wish I'd just left last night when I broke the river and what am I even doing here?"

"If you want to go, then let's go," says Odessa. "Sander. Come on."

"Okay," says Sander reluctantly. He shakes hands with Cookie Monster and hugs Diefenbaker, who slaps him on the back and pins a "Keep the Chief" campaign button on his pyjamas. We're just heading towards the stairs when a hush falls over the crowd.

"They're announcing the Melting Day Baby!" says Diefenbaker.

"COOKIE!" says Cookie Monster.

The Melting Day Baby is like a New Year's Baby, only instead of being the closest born to midnight, the winner is the baby that's born nearest to sunrise on Melting Day.

Odessa shrugs apologetically, then follows Sander back to the roof's edge. Down on the steps of the Legislature, the parents hold the squirming infant up to Alice Songhua. She kisses its forehead and the crowd roars its approval.

"Is it a boy or a girl?" asks Odessa, peering down.

"Boy, I think I heard," says Sander.

I feel a thin tendril of nausea snaking up my throat, and I turn away from the roof's edge.

"Does it matter?" I ask.

"Well no," says Odessa, "but it's always kind of nice when it's a girl. It feels like a real moment of sisterhood with the Melting Queen."

I look at her and Sander, and all the other men and women leaning out over the building to see the new child. They're all asking each other the same question.

"You know what, I think I'm just gonna go," I say. "You two stay here, enjoy your night."

I turn towards the stairs. Odessa grabs my arm and pulls me back.

"Nope! You're not going to leave like that. No way. Tell us what's happening. Why are you in such a mood?"

"In a *mood*? Okay, how about this: I told you that I'm not Adam anymore but you keep on saying it over and over—"

"I already apologized for that."

"—and I told you I wanted to use Melting Day to celebrate the start of this new chapter of my life but you just took a shit all over it and made it seem like the worst festival in the world and the stupidest idea to think that today could be special."

"And *you*," I turn to Sander, who shrinks back. "You've just basically ignored me all day. Like, thanks for the history lesson, Sander. But do you even care about me?"

Sander just stands there looking uncomfortable, looking self-conscious that I'm making a scene even though none of these drunk assholes in the crowd cares at all. Odessa is even worse, with that typical all-knowing, ever-patient smile on her face.

"And you know what else?" I say, not holding anything back anymore. Fuck it. I'll probably never see them again anyways. "You're the only two people I chose to keep. I had to cut everyone out, start fresh. Our friendship has always existed in its own little pocket universe, though, outside of my regular life, so I thought I could keep you two. I thought: 'Oh, I can keep Odessa and Sander. They're cool. They'll understand.' But you're just like Brock. You're just like everyone else."

"What don't we understand?" says Odessa.

"Can you just let someone else talk for once, okay Odessa? Fuck! This was supposed to be my going-away party, the new beginning of my new life. But you both had to ruin it with your arguing and your shitting all over Melting Day and the fact that you care more about statues and trivia than about me. Haven't you noticed that there's something else? I've been trying to tell you all day, but I don't know how to say it. It doesn't make any sense. I don't have a good explanation. It's just a feeling, deep and impossible to get rid of. Like, I'm not Adam Truman anymore. But, like,

I'm not a guy at all anymore. Right? That doesn't make sense. Like every time some-one looks at me and says 'Hey man' and is all like 'Yeah bro I got you,' it feels wrong. It's not me. I'm not that anymore. I'm not a woman either. I'm just nothing, some other thing. That makes no sense. That's not something that just happens one day to people. I don't want that. I don't get that. So there, I told you, there you go."

"We should go somewhere and talk about this," says Odessa.

"No. No, I don't want to talk to you. I don't want to hear you explain everything to me about how you know better about everything. I was wrong before. I shouldn't have come today. I should've just left right away, right after I broke the river. So that's what I'll do."

I push through the crowd and head for the stairs before Odessa can grab me again. Whatever. I need to go and they aren't going to help me go. Melting Day is almost done and what have I done with my day? I need to get home and pack, start making a plan to go. I don't have much money left or a passport so that'll be a prob-lem but maybe I can borrow a car from someone, hitchhike even. But first I've got to go. Just get going, like I should've done last night. I can't believe I've wasted the day like this.

I shove past a bunch of people who are all wearing a stupid Scooby-Doo group costume. I hurtle down the stairs, to the ground floor, crash out a side door into the Legislature's statue park. And then I begin to run.

{4}

As sundown claims
the melting city

My postcard dress is disintegrating, scattering Parthenons and Pantheons across the dead grass. I race through the statue park, toward the river. I run out onto the High Level Bridge. Its black girders are studded with lights which glow pink and green for Melting Day. I sprint along this tunnel of light, only stopping when I'm in the exact centre of the bridge.

I look down. It's too dark to see the water, but the white icebergs are lit up by the bridge's pink and green emanations. Every so often a huge piece of ice will slam into one of the pillars and shake the whole structure. Good. I hope it shudders apart and all comes tumbling down.

The light changes and I look up. I might be imagining it, but I think I see a faint blue light on the horizon.

Soon the sun will come up.

Soon it will be spring.

And then summer.

And then fall.

And then winter again.

And I'll still be here. With people like Brock and Sander and Odessa remembering my old self. With the ghost of Adam Truman haunting me wherever I look.

I notice with detached curiosity that I'm on the other side of the railing, looking down at the dark waters. They seem at the same time far away and too close. How easy would it be to take a little step, and fall, and vanish into thin air—to finish what I should've done yesterday, the easiest way to leave.

"NO!"

A voice cracks out into the cold night air, dry and hard and sarcastic.

"STOP!"

I twist my head around, but there's nobody on the bridge deck behind me.

"Don't do it!"

The voice is loud, clear, right next to me. I must be going crazy.

"You have *sooooo* much to live for!"

I cling to the railing, feel the wind slapping at me and making my postcards dance.

"Who's there?

I hear a tinkling sound, glass on glass, and then the voice drawls out again, mocking me.

"If you're really going to jump at least cut off your hair first and give it to me. It would make a fantastic wig."

I hear a rustle of movement and then I see her as she stands up. She's not on the pedestrian path behind me—she's on the bridge's upper level, on the train tracks where the streetcar runs in the summer. Up close I can see that her green leaf dress isn't fresh or living like in the story, but made of scratchy green synthetic leaves like an office fern. She's got a bottle of sparkling wine in one hand and a champagne flute in the other. Her black hair is streaked through with shocks of phosphorus white and iridescent blue. Her eyes are dark, leering down at me. Magpie. The Melting Day storyteller.

"You! What are you doing here?"

The drag queen adjusts her dress and takes a swig of champagne.

"I came to watch the sunrise," she says. "I'd ask what you're doing, but somehow I think I know."

I look down at the river again and suddenly feel very self-conscious.

"So what's really your plan here?" she says. "You're not actually going to jump."

"You don't know that! Maybe I will jump! Maybe I'll land on an ice floe and sail away to a more exciting place than Deadmonton."

"Well you'd flow east, so you'd go to Saskatchewan," says Magpie.

"Oh god, never mind. I'll aim for the water."

The drag queen cackles and plops back down on the train tracks. She dangles her legs over the edge and kicks her feet back and forth, high heels swinging wildly from her toes.

"It's a long way down. Look."

She drains her champagne bottle and then heaves it over the edge. It arcs through the air and smacks dead centre into an ice floe, shattering it into a dozen pieces. The shards bob up and down in the water, spiralling off and crashing into other floes. I imagine what it would be like to hit the water, from this height. I probably wouldn't even feel it.

"So you're really depressed, aren't you?"

The drag queen's voice breaks into my thoughts.

"What? No I'm not."

I snap back this automatic answer, despite the fact that I'm hanging off the edge of a bridge.

"It's okay," says Magpie. "I can tell."

"Oh really? How is that?"

"I'm really perceptive," she says. "It's my superpower."

I roll my eyes.

"Wow. You can tell that someone is depressed when you find them hanging off the edge of a bridge? What a gift."

"You don't have to be ashamed of your depression," she says. "At least not in front of me. The real reason I can tell is because I'm depressed too. And there's no way you're as bad as me. I'm catastrophically depressed."

She says this with such obvious self-satisfaction that I can't help but groan.

"So what? Everyone has depression in the winter. You're not special. You're just not taking enough vitamin D supplements."

Magpie drains her champagne glass and tosses it after the empty bottle. She flips down off the railway tracks with a surprising lack of grace and lands in a heap on the bridge deck. She clambers to her feet and skitters over to where I'm hanging off the railing.

"Can I show you something really personal?" she asks.

"No," I say. "But I have a feeling you're going to show me anyway."

Up close I'm amazed at how feminine her face is. If I hadn't seen her with her two other drag queens before I might've thought she was just a historical performer. Her eyes catch mine picking her face apart and I turn away and look back down at the ice lily pads flowing away.

"I know I saw you before, at Churchill Square," she says.

"Oh yeah," I say, not looking up. "Quite a performance."

"It's all bullshit, isn't it? The people of Edmonton all coming together in peace and harmony and brotherly love. Please. But still, my girls and I have gotta eat. The city pays us well."

"I should hope so."

"I trust you for some reason," she says. "Have you ever had that before—people just naturally trusting you?"

"I don't think so."

I watch two icebergs converge, producing a dozen smaller floes.

"It makes me suspicious but I can't seem to help it," says Magpie sharply, clearly irritated that I'm not looking at her.

"Is that so?" I respond, for some reason very satisfied by her frustration.

"So here it is," she declares.

Magpie holds her hand out beside me and I see that she's holding a black, kidney-shaped stone. Blacker than anything I've ever seen. Black like a black hole, so black that not even light can escape its pull. It looks like it ought to be burning through her hand, falling to the riverbed, eating its way down to the earth's core. Its weight warps everything around it. The girders above our heads buckle in and shred themselves apart. The revellers on the Legislature Lawns are ripped to pieces as the world is sacrificed to the stone's evil hunger. It feels like the stone is looking into me, plotting how it will erase me from existence along with everything I've ever loved. I tear my eyes away and look up at Magpie's face. She's staring at me with a neutral expression.

"What the hell is that!?" I ask, dry-mouthed.

I clutch the edge of the bridge, gripped with wind-whipped terror. Magpie rubs her thumb across the surface of the stone and looks down at it affectionately.

"I've only ever shown this to one other person," she says.

My heart begins to slow down, and my sense of reality returns. The buzz of activity resumes from the party at the Legislature. I don't want to look at the stone directly.

"*Where did you get that?*"

"I made it," she says. She flips the stone over. I can't shake the sense that it's watching me—that it's the pupil of the world, and everything I've ever seen has just been the vast, colourful iris around it.

"This stone was white when I pulled it out of the river," says Magpie. "I used it to absorb all my negative thoughts and feelings. It's not a special stone at all. I chose it at random. I thought, if I can have one small point to concentrate all these dark feelings, maybe I can purge them out of me and get rid of them forever."

She hefts the stone in her hand. It smacks her palm with audible weight. It seems heavier than anything its size has any right to be.

"It was a good receptacle, for a while. I felt a bit better. But now it's full. Overflowing. I guess I could go find another one. But then I'd be pulling stones out of the river for the rest of my life. And what do I do with the ones I've used up? Throw them back? Is there anything more toxic than this?"

She holds the stone out to me and I tense up. She laughs.

"Calm down, it won't hurt you."

"You don't know that," I say. My shock has abated, and now I find myself surprisingly angry. "You have no idea what you've made, do you? You can't even feel it anymore, can you? That thing is *wrong*. And you say that it's only an echo of your own negativity. How can one person be that horribly negative?"

Her heavily made-up face twists into a grimace. She bites her lip, looks away.

"I'm dying," she says. "I have cancer."

I feel like an asshole.

"Shit. I'm sorry."

Magpie shrugs.

"How could you have known?"

She drapes herself across the railing, looking out at the river valley.

"This is my disease," she sighs, lifting the stone to her lips. "My externalized tumour. This is what grows in me, eating me from the inside."

"Wait, what? So you don't have actual cancer?"

"I have depression, like I said," mewls Magpie. "It's an emotional cancer."

"Wow, are you kidding? That's horrible. You can't just pretend to have cancer."

"It's just as serious as a physical cancer. Or no, actually you're right. Cancer is easier. At least there are effective treatments for cancer."

"People can treat depression. There are solutions."

"Says the man hanging over the edge of a bridge. You're just oozing stability."

"Well you have bad breath."

"I have diabetes, I can't help it."

"Just like you have cancer? Is it emotional diabetes?"

"No, this time it's real diabetes."

I snort and look away from her flushed face.

"Yeah right. Emotional cancer. That's minimizing the suffering of—"

"Yeah well what about *my* suffering?" she says loudly.

"What do you have to suffer about?"

She stares at me for a long time. The silence is unnerving but I'm determined not to speak first. I shift my weight on the railing. My muscles are sore from being in the same position for too long.

"You're not going to throw yourself off this bridge," she says at last. "I know you're not. We both know you're not."

We stare each other down for a few moments, then she holds out her hand. After a moment's hesitation, I take it. She helps me climb over the railing and I plop to the bridge deck with no more grace than she did before.

"Did you make this dress?" she asks, tapping the Golden Gate Bridge with her toe as I climb to my feet.

"Yeah, this morning."

"I like it."

"Thank you."

We stand there, face to face finally, me towering over her.

"What's your name?" she asks.

I feel the words come automatically to my tongue, like they've done for twenty-two years. But I stop myself.

"I don't know."

"Okay. That's not a weird answer at all."

"I mean, I had a name. But my friend said I should pick a new one. And I think that makes sense to me now."

She turns away and leans against the railing. I lean next to her and look out at the river. The old metal feels sturdy, strong, powerful from this side.

"Is your friend a drag queen?"

"No. Well, I guess she sort of is. But not really."

"I've had lots of drag names. Right now I'm Magpie, because I'm obnoxious but also very beautiful. For a while my drag name was Tara Nullius, because I'm Métis and also very clever. Not as clever as my friend Andrés—you saw him earlier, he's Mary Cone now, but he used to be Panama Canal, and before that he was Marianas Trench. He's really obsessed with his fictional vagina. But anyway, my name is René Royaume."

"René?"

"It's French. *Je suis francoalbertain.*"

René Royaume offers his hand again, and I shake it. A second later, there's a pop and a whistle and huge green and pink fireworks start exploding above the Legislature. The soundwaves bounce off the bridge, booming across the valley. We watch the fireworks display grow larger and larger until it's one huge stuttering explosion. Then smoky silence. A chorus of cheerful screams rises up from the Legislature Lawns.

"I've had an idea," says René when the voices have died down and the smoke has drifted away.

"What?"

"Do you have your CIRCLE? Give it to me."

I have to rip apart one of my postcards (sorry, Ponte Vecchio) to get at the pocket of the pants I'm wearing under my gown. But the dress is in tatters anyways at this point, so I don't mind. I pull out the ID card and hold it out to René.

Citizen Identity Registration Cards for Living in Edmonton were established two years ago, an initiative of that year's Melting Queen. Everything—the transit system, the library, fitness centres, homeless shelters, the art gallery and museum and conservatory, complimentary city-wide Wi-Fi—is available if you're in the CIRCLE.

"You keep it," says the drag queen. "I have two suggestions. One, you could throw it over the edge. A symbolic suicide. Much less permanent than your last idea."

René looks down at the ice floes.

"Or two," he says, "you use this."

He rummages around in his cleavage for a moment then pulls out a permanent marker.

"Why do you have a permanent marker?"

"Vandalism. My enemies aren't going to write their own names in gas station bathroom stalls."

"Okay."

"I should've kept my champagne bottle," says René. "We could've smashed it over your head and rechristened you. But this'll do."

He hands me the pen.

"I'm René Royaume," he says. "What's your name?"

I look down into the little square photo where the sharp-angled face of twenty-year-old Adam Truman is imprisoned. I twirl the card through my freezing fingers, out in the empty air above the abyss. I look down on Edmonton's river valley, the grey salted city. Far on the horizon I see the true colours of dawn emerging—a lick of pink and orange swooping up from the land to join the light blue and deep navy sky.

"Is it lighter or is it just me?"

"It's almost dawn," says René. "Sunrise. Spring."

Spring. New life.

If I don't leave now I'll never leave. If I stay in Edmonton any longer I'll get stuck here like so many people have gotten stuck in lives they hate. Melting Day is over now.

I put a thick black line through that old name. Adam Truman, redacted. I look down at the icy waters, and I write a new name for this new self. It flows right into my mind. It's obvious. The name you choose is a promise you make to yourself.

René tilts his head toward me, reads my CIRCLE.

"I like it," he says.

So do I. My name is River Runson.

The Melting Queen shall Name a successor

Dawn drapes itself over the city, lighting up the shattered river, the snow-free streets, the wreckage of the carnival. I walk through the barren cityscape and watch the remnants of Melting Day being cleared away. Cleaning crews repair the damaged property, sweep up the shattered glass, pick up the soggy streamers and the hundreds of people passed out in the street. Opportunistic magpies feast on the discarded confections of the revellers. People peel off their bright costumes, fold them up carefully, and hide them away for next year.

Every year, on the morning after Melting Day, the city gathers at City Hall for the Melting Queen's Pardon and the Naming ceremony, where the Melting Queen speaks the name of her successor. I'm hungover, dead on my feet, but Churchill Square is on my walk home to Chinatown. I might as well go see this one final ritual before I start packing my bags.

I wonder if I'll see Odessa and Sander at the ceremony. I feel somewhat guilty for the way I blew up at them, and I want to make things right before I go. I tried to find them, back at the Legislature, but I gave up after what felt like hours of searching. I'm unlikely to find them here either. Churchill Square is packed. Thousands of hungover revellers cling to each other, trying to hold themselves upright so they can see Melting Day through to the end. Even if Sander and Odessa are here, I'll never be able to find them.

I walk into the square just as Alice Songhua has finished giving her royal Pardon for all the night's sins. Behind her stand the six big green marble pillars of City Hall. On the three to the left of the main doors, they've projected the number 114, and on the other side there's a massive 115. This morning, Alice Songhua will name Edmonton's 115th Melting Queen.

But for now she steps aside. A grizzled old man in a three-piece suit steps forward, standing behind a lectern. His name is Kastevoros Birch, and he's the head of the Edmonton Civic Heritage Organization, the group that organizes the Office of the Melting Queen. He stares out at the crowd until a hush has fallen over Churchill Square.

"Life."

The word echoes out over ten thousand heads. Birch lets it hang in the air until the sound has faded from everyone's ears.

"The Melting Queen is nothing less than this. New life, sprung forth from sleeping earth. The spring wind, come to breathe away the winter. The spirit of Edmonton, embodied. Our eternal mother, inspiring fire, defending us against the cold."

I shuffle through the crowd, mumbling "excuse me" at sporadic intervals.

"Today, we choose one woman to carry on our city's noble tradition. One woman. To bless us with a long and fruitful summer. One woman. To keep our fires burning in the darkest depths of winter. One woman. To follow in the footsteps of this year's spectacular Melting Queen, Alice Songhua!"

Birch's rasp is drowned out by the roar of the crowd. Alice Songhua walks to the lectern and leans down for a kiss on the cheek from Kastevoros Birch. The old man steps back as she takes the microphone. The applause continues for several minutes as the Melting Queen repeatedly thanks the audience.

"Thank you, everyone. It's been an honour to represent you all over the past year. I can't believe it's gone by so quickly."

She brushes her hair back from her face, reaches up and adjusts the crown on her head. Its magnificent emerald glitters.

"Being the Melting Queen isn't always easy. When my name was called fourteen months ago, I had no idea what was in store for me. But no matter what challenges we faced, the people of Edmonton never ceased to amaze me, inspire me, and make me laugh. I am humbled to have been your Melting Queen. I love you."

Her voice is full and rich and pure and I believe every word she says.

"But my time is over now. A new Melting Queen is coming, and I can't wait to Name her and to Crown her. May she be as strong, kind, and giving as May Winter.

May she carry on our noble tradition with grace, grit, and goodness of heart. I wish her a warm spring and a mild winter."

Alice Songhua pauses. Everyone in the square holds their breath. I study the faces of the women close to me as I continue to push through to the other side of the square. Will it be the young mother next to me, toddler balanced on her hip? Or the muscular woman in the wheelchair next to them? Or the woman in the green gown next to her?

In any case, I'm sure she'll be a new, fresh, invigorating young queen. And once they pick her the spring will really start, and River Runson will bloom, just like the city.

I have a wild and sudden fantasy that Odessa will be named as Melting Queen— the feminist performance artist who ditches Edmonton for months at a time, who impregnated herself on a whim. I'd love to see the bland people of this grey city react to that. A real shit disturber. A real Queen after so many pliable princesses.

Alice Songhua looks up at the sky—I half expect the northern lights to be waving down from on high, but of course the mid-morning sky is pale white and barren—then back down at all of us. She touches the emerald in her crown, brings her fingers down to her lips and kisses them, and stretches her hand out towards the crowd.

"This year's Melting Queen is River Runson."

{6}

Endowed with a marvellous vision

It can't be me.
But she just said your name.

There must be some other River Runson.
But no one else is springing out of the crowd to take Alice Songhua's hand.

I didn't put my name on the statue.
But somehow they knew.

Even if I had put up my name, they'd never pick me. They'd do a search for River Runson and find no one in the CIRCLE directory—unless another River Runson already exists. So it must be someone else.

But you know that's not true.

46

As the disappointed mob disperses, I try not to look like a criminal fleeing the scene. I trust my feet to carry me home as my heart thunders, overhearing conversations that make me blush.

"River Runson," says one woman. "Are you serious? That's the perfect name for a Melting Queen. It's almost too good to be true."

"So was May Winter," observes her partner.

For the rest of the day, I hide inside my basement cave, peeking out through my small window every time I hear someone passing by. I wait for a team of police commandos to break down my door and drag me out in front of the city and interrogate me about how I tricked Alice Songhua into Naming me.

The Office of the Melting Queen issues increasingly urgent requests for River Runson to present herself at their headquarters. But if they can't find me, they can't do anything about it. They'll just have to find themselves another Melting Queen.

In the middle of the night, I remember my scratched-out CIRCLE—an incriminating piece of evidence. I jolt out of bed and rip my room apart, determined to destroy it for good. But when I find it, and see my new name, I think of Odessa. *The name you choose is a promise you make to yourself.*

Odessa has a car. Odessa has money. Odessa will help me escape.

I draw curious glances as I walk down Jasper Avenue the next morning. I know I must look like a crazy old cat lady, with unbrushed hair and huge, sleep-deprived eyes. But people's gazes linger longer than they would for a regular Jasper Ave eccentric. Almost as if... *You're just being paranoid. They don't recognize you. How could they?*

But when I stop at a crosswalk to wait for a light, a woman with a screaming toddler stares straight at me and won't look away. I glance at her a few times, and on my last peek I see her marching toward me, tugging her child along by the hand.

"River?" she whispers. She falls forward into my arms and I give her an awkward, terrified hug.

"I hate my daughter," she whispers into my ear. "I know that makes me a bad person, but it's true. She just never stops."

Her daughter yanks on her arm and screams and pulls the mother off me. I look down into the girl's scrunched-up face. She looks so angry in a very grown-up way, enraged at being led around by the hand and then ignored. On impulse I lean down and look her in the eye. I reach out my hand and put it on her shoulder. She blinks in surprise, then smiles at me like she can barely comprehend her own changed mood.

"Thank you," says the mother, tears in her eyes. "I'm sorry. But you're... How is that possible?"

I remember myself, feel a molten vat of fear pour over my head. I pull away from the child and her mother, push past them and into the crosswalk.

"River!" the mother calls after me. I run.

In quick succession, four more people recognize me, call me by my name. They stop me on the street and start telling me stories of misery and guilt—their dog ran away after they kicked him, they were passed up for a promotion at work, they cheated on their boyfriend, they found out their sister has brain cancer. All I can do is listen. I'm exhausted by having to woodenly console them in exchange for the hope that they'll keep my secret.

I'm ducking away from another person who's stomping toward me when I hear the name "River Runson" come out loud and clear behind me. I flinch, expecting yet another person who recognizes me. Instead, I see a TV screen in a nearby bus stop. It's broadcasting a live episode of *EdmonTonight*, the city's most popular local news show. Rosemary Silt, Edmonton's public-access Oprah, is interviewing Kastevoros Birch.

"I think the real question on everyone's mind now is: who is River Runson?" says Rosemary, sipping tea from a fancy cup. She always eats extravagant meals on her show and shares them with her guests.

"We understand that it can be quite a shock to the woman who suddenly finds herself Named," says Birch. "But we want her to know that we're here for her, and we're excited to meet her, and that a highly trained team of people, who are soon to become her very good friends, is eager to help her."

"If you're just joining us," says Rosemary, "we're continuing coverage on the new Melting Queen, River Runson. So far we've been unable to locate River, or learn anything about her from friends or family, so it's quite a mysterious start to her reign!"

A visibly irritated Birch looks straight into the camera.

"If you're hearing this, River, you are asked to present yourself at the Office of the Melting Queen as soon as possible."

I turn away from the TV and jump. René Royaume is standing right next to me.

"I should turn you in," he says. He's wearing a green Tashtegos Coffee apron and holding a matching visor crumpled up in his hand. The other is in his pocket, no doubt fondling his stone. His long, black-blue-and-white streaked hair is tied up in a messy bun, but otherwise no trace of the drag queen Magpie remains on his epicene face.

"Why would you do that?" I ask.

He shrugs.

"Isn't it my civic duty?" he asks mockingly. His lips are chapped. He has acetone breath. "Isn't it *your* civic duty to be the new Alice Songhua?"

"It isn't me," I say weakly. "There must be another River Runson."

"Oh yeah," he says, "I'm sure it's a super common name. Just like Tara Nullius and May Tea and Magpie."

"Whatever," I say, in no mood to mince words after being waylaid so many times. "It doesn't matter. I'm leaving."

"I thought you were leaving yesterday," he says. "You said that Melting Day was your last day in Edmonton. And yet, here you are. It's almost as if you're not actually going anywhere."

He smirks at me. I glare at him.

"Why are you being such a jerk? And why are you even here? Are you stalking me or something?"

"I'm not stalking you, you egomaniac. I just happened upon you. I just got fired."

"I don't care. The last thing I need right now is another tale of woe. And coming from you it's probably not even true. And besides, it doesn't matter what you tell them," I say, turning to leave. "You don't know anything about me other than my name. Goodbye."

"I wasn't going to turn you in anyway," he says, matching pace with me. "Can't really be bothered. I've got things to do."

"Oh yeah, I'm sure you're really busy."

"As a matter of fact, I am. I have a bunch of dresses to sew for our next show. And later tonight I have to go dramatically stop a wedding."

"You know, maybe you wouldn't need a horrible stone of condensed darkness if you weren't such an asshole to people."

"Or maybe I wouldn't be such an asshole if I didn't have this emotional cancer."

"Sure. Whatever. I don't care to argue the point."

René shoots back some snarky statement, but I don't hear it. In between two determined steps, I feel an atomic blast of panic explode through my body. My heartbeat spikes, my pupils swell, every hair on my skin stands on end. The world goes dark.

I'm running, sprinting, desperate to get away. Tree branches smack me in the face, leaving deep scratches on my arms and chest. I trip and almost fall but I keep going, hurtling through the forest. The moon shines down from above. An overpowering smell of wet rot floods my nose, making me gag.

"YOU CAN'T RUN FOREVER! WE'RE GOING TO CATCH YOU!"

A voice booms in my ear, but it's not René's. It's not any voice I recognize. I sob and gasp for air and try to run faster.

And then, just as soon as they appeared, the voice and the forest and the fear are gone. I'm lying on the ground with René peering down at me, the hints of a curious crowd gathering behind him.

"So that was really weird," says René. He offers me a hand up and I ignore it. "You didn't tell me that you had seizures. Shouldn't you have a golden retriever or something?"

My cheeks are on fire. I push past René and the few bystanders.

"Hey!"

He races after me.

"What was that? Your eyes were all bulgy!"

I don't answer. I wouldn't know what to say anyway. My skin is unmarked, but I feel lingering scratches along my arms and across my face. *What the hell was that?*

"Please just go away!" I yell. "I'm leaving town. You'll never see me again. Good luck to you and your stone and finding another job, preferably not in customer service."

"Seriously, you should probably go to the hospital, don't you think? Or are you worried that they'll know you're the Melting Queen?"

I stop and round on him.

"What do I have to do to get rid of you? Seriously! Back off!"

René smirks and throws his Tashtegos visor into the garbage can next to me. We're under the marquee of the haunted house that used to be a church that used to be a movie theatre. Thankfully there are no more people trying to tell me their miseries. But as I'm about to turn and run away from René, I hear the violent burst of an infant's cries tear through the air. I jerk my head around but I can't see a baby anywhere. It stops as suddenly as it began.

"Did you hear that?"

"What?"

"The baby crying."

"No," René shakes his head. "I didn't hear anything. Are you having a stroke? You look like—"

His voice is drowned out by renewed shrieks.

"There it is again! Where is it coming from?"

"I can't hear anything. You're definitely dying."

I look around and frown. There's something wrong with the sky. It's behaving strangely, flickering through several different shades of blues and yellows and whites. I'm about to point this out to René when the world splits in half.

Through my right eye I can see everything as it is, where I am now: the pale grey sky, office towers, the salt-stained sidewalk, René's arched eyebrow. Through my left eye, the world has gone insane. Every second a new image takes hold. I see dozens of Jasper Avenues, flickering in and out of existence. Brick buildings become steel-and-glass storefronts, then are replaced in the blink of an eye by empty lots. People in fancy Sunday clothes become ravers dressed in neon tights. Parking meters turn into horse posts, then sprout up as tall trees with knitted cozies on their trunks. The marquee of the haunted house is bright with lights, announcing movie screenings for a dollar—*Revenge of the Jedi* at 11:30—then dark with peeling paint. The street is a muddy rutted track, then a cracked and patched boulevard, then a smooth concrete thoroughfare with a clanking trolley running along its tracks.

Everything shudders between the world as it is and all the myriad others. They meld and blend—the solid, stable mid-afternoon and the dozens of encroaching images, racing by faster and faster. I feel an inescapable force grab me and start pulling me out into the street, where people are flickering in and out of existence. I hear their cheering cut in and out, a terrifying staccato. I hear cars honking and tires screeching.

And then the world I know is gone, replaced entirely by another.

I walk down the centre of the avenue, surrounded by cheering people in all sorts of costumes. I'm wearing a pink dress and holding the reins of a big blue horse. Confetti streams through the air. I look up at the movie theatre marquee:

HAPPY 92ⁿᵈ MELTING DAY
WE'LL MISS YOU VICTORIA GOULBURN!

Victoria. Yes. That's my name.

I start to feel my body. It feels different. Foreign. Alien. Everything is of unfamiliar proportions. The way I move is strange. The colours I see are all a bit off. The odours in the air are things I've never smelled before. The dimensions of my body alarm me. I feel knobbly, bony, angular. My eyes are dry. My joints are loose.

But this brief dysphoria is like a wave crashing to shore—it washes over me, drowns me, then retreats. I feel myself settling into this new body as though I was playing musical chairs. The music stopped and I sat upon a strange chair—a straight-backed, hard-seated, long-legged piece of furniture. At first it felt odd, but I got used to it. The shock dissipates, and I hear the noise that has drawn me here. A baby is crying, wailing.

I spot the bundle in the crowd, in the arms of its mother. I pass the reins of the blue horse to someone nearby, cut a swath through the marchers. Approaching the baby, I recognize the two parents and their children, younger than I've ever seen them.

"Is this a potential Melting Day Baby?"

I feel my mouth forming the words, the bizarre coordination of tongue and teeth and lips and gums. I'm not sure if I'm choosing to speak, or just following some pre-ordained script. I want to say these words, I feel them rising up to the surface of my mind, and then I hear myself speaking them.

"I'm afraid not," says the father. "He was born yesterday, in the morning. On the last day of winter."

"Well look at you!" I say to the mother. "What a trooper, up and about the very next day!"

"I never miss the parade," says the mother. She bobs the baby up and down in her arms, trying to console it, trying to make it stop, already at her wit's end with the crying. She smiles grimly up at me.

"I'm sorry. He hasn't stopped crying since he was born. I don't know what's wrong."

"What's his name?" I ask. I look down at his face for the first time. Scrunched up in rage, in inconsolable fury. As if he wasn't ready, and his gestation has been interrupted by this frenzy of spring. As if he never wanted to be born at all, affixed to the tracks of time.

"We haven't decided yet."

"May I?" I hold out my arms.

The mother nods at once, instantly trusting in the superior motherly powers of the Melting Queen. She passes the bundle over to me. I cradle it in my arms. Bump it up and down.

"Hey," I whisper into the baby's ear, so quietly that no one else can hear us in this din.

"Hey. You're okay. It's going to be okay. Shhhhhh. It's springtime now, and you're healthy, and you have a mom and dad who love you, and everybody can't wait to find out who you're going to be. So be strong. Don't cry. Be brave. And you'll grow into a big strong man, and make your mommy and daddy proud."

I kiss the baby on the forehead and he stops crying. He unscrunches his little face and looks up at me. Our eyes meet. For an instant, I recognize myself.

"How about you name him Adam?"

The moment I speak the name, the world collapses, and everything is dark. I feel cold hard earth pressing against my back. I have a pounding headache and my ears are ringing. My muscles ache and for a minute I can't remember my name:

Adam?

No.

Victoria?

No.

River.

Yes. River Runson.

I sit up and look around. I'm in Beaver Hills House Park, a couple blocks away from the old movie theatre. There are always a few homeless people lying on the grass next to the pond, so no one has come to check on me. After a moment, I notice the note pinned to my chest:

You passed out and were mumbling and making baby noises so I got bored and left. Text me some time. RR.

I don't even bother reading René's phone number before I crumple up his note. I stagger to my feet and the world spins around me but I start walking west again, out of the park and along the avenue. Odessa. I need to get to Odessa's.

Odessa lives in a handsome brown bungalow in Belgravia, just south of the university. Bursting at the seams with artifacts that stand guard in the same dust-bordered positions they've held for decades, it's less of a house and more of a museum. And the museum's subject is Ludlow Spetnik, Odessa's grandfather, whose century of travel brought him to every continent and nearly every country (those that still exist and those that have predeceased him). Every room is full of curios: a huge kaleidoscope with a crack running along its side, a snow globe showing a cityscape of Rome, decorative medals for a hundred forgotten accomplishments.

Marching up the driveway, I go past Odessa's car. She drives a giant Chrysler New Yorker the exact colour of a copper penny with a white canvas roof. Like everything she owns, it's is a relic of Ludlow Spetnik's life, very old but perfectly maintained.

I don't bother knocking at the back door, but barge in and call out Odessa's name. She calls back to me and I find her in the bathroom, immersing a hundred Canada Dry bottles in the bathtub like she's bobbing for glass Granny Smith apples.

"Hey!" she looks excited as I come inside, but frowns at the look on my face. "Are you okay? You look awful. Did you just throw up?"

"I just saw myself as a baby," I stammer, losing control of my tongue. "I was myself but I was someone else. I was running through the woods. And then I was marching in the Melting Day parade."

"Sit down," says Odessa, taking my shoulders in her strong capable grip and plunking me down on the closed toilet seat. "What are you talking about?"

"I was the Melting Queen. But I was a baby too. At the same time. There were hundreds of times. I saw them all but then it was just one time. It doesn't make sense, but it was so real."

My eyes lock on to Odessa's and I remember my purpose.

"I need to leave," I say. "Can I have your car? You can come too, if you want. We can drive south. To Phoenix, maybe. That's a good place to start a new life, right? They would never find us. Not if we leave now, straight away."

"Hey!"

She shakes my shoulders, brings her face close to mine.

"Stop freaking out!"

She kneels in front of me and puts her hands on my knees.

"Tell me what all this is about. Then we'll decide what to do."

I dig out my CIRCLE and hand it to her. She examines it, saying nothing. I watch her eyes slide across the letters printed there, the ones I've scratched out and the ones I've written. A frown makes a tiny crease appear between her eyebrows, but just for a second. She passes the card back to me, for once at a loss for words.

"What...? When...?"

"You told me to rename myself. I did."

She looks at me like she's seeing me for the first time, for an uncomfortably long time. For a second I think I see something dark flicker through her eyes, something cold and hard and cruel. But I must be going crazy, imagining things, because I blink and it's gone, replaced with a warm, affectionate smile. She stands up and takes my hands and pulls me to my feet.

"Let's go for a walk," she says. "Let's go to the End of the World."

The End of the World is the popular name for a collapsed road with a spectacular view of the river valley. Odessa leads me out onto the only bit left standing, a curve of concrete pilings, and we sit at the very end. Beneath us, the mangled remains of a scenic road—chunks of concrete and iron rebar sticking out of the ground, being slowly digested by the riverbank—are wrapped up in dry prairie grasses that rustle in the wind. There are still no signs of green in the vast grey valley.

"I have really clear memories of riding my bike along Keillor Road when I was a kid," says Odessa. "I remember the huge cracks opening up in the pavement all the time. Workers would constantly come and fill in the cracks with black tar. And then one day we came along and the road had just slid down the hill into the valley. We knew it was coming. It was inevitable, doomed ever since they built it. They constantly had to repair it, and shore up the supports."

Odessa lines pebbles up along the edge next to where she's sitting, like a battalion of toy soldiers. After every available scrap of rock has been lined up, she moves her hand slowly along their ranks, flicking them over the edge one by one.

"One day the whole thing is going to collapse. Any day now, according to the Belgravia Community League. Which is why they put up those No Trespassing signs. As if anything could stop us."

We watch the river flow by. There are still stray chunks of ice being carried along by the current, but soon the silty brown water will become pea-soup green, running free and clear.

"What are we doing here, Odessa? There's no time. We need to go."

"You need to calm down," she says. "And nothing beats this view."

She smacks the concrete outcropping with the palm of her hand and rubs it back and forth affectionately, like a faithful horse's rump.

"What I need to do is leave. I've been wanting to leave for months and I keep finding excuses not to go. But now I need to leave. Like, *right now*. No more excuses."

"Because you're the Melting Queen."

Odessa runs her hand over her smooth, bald head and fixes me with an intense stare.

"I'm not going to do it," I say.

"Oh?"

"It's insane. I need your car. We can leave today. Then they can just Name another Melting Queen. Or get some woman who wants to change her name to River Runson. It's not hard. Apparently all you need is a permanent marker."

The sun beats down from the bright blue sky even as a cold breeze slams into us, carried all the way down from the mountains by the river. Odessa is silent. She puts her elbows on her knees and stares down into the valley.

"You think I should do it," I say. "Is that what you're saying? You think I should be the Melting Queen. That's crazy."

"I'm not saying anything," says Odessa.

"Well what would you do?" I ask her.

"It doesn't matter what I'd do. I'm not the one they Named."

"You'd do it though, wouldn't you?"

"You're not me."

"No. But you would do it."

She looks me up and down, from my booted feet to my mess of ginger hair.

"Yes. I would do it."

"Why? Then you'd have to stay in Edmonton a full year."

"I haven't spent a winter in Edmonton since I was seven," sighs Odessa. She gazes back down into the river valley, where a speckled horse is grazing on the salty grass. Eighty years ago some guy released a bunch of horses into the valley, and the City has never been able to catch all of the offspring. "Maybe the daring thing for me to do would be to stay. Not invent another adventure for myself."

"And you're saying that the daring thing for me would be to become the Melting Queen?"

"You're not me," repeats Odessa. "You don't have to do the daring thing. You do whatever's right for you."

"What do you think I should do?"

Odessa takes a battered cigarette case out of her pocket, opens it up. There are only two cigarettes inside, which she contemplates for a moment before sealing the case and putting it back in her pocket. I know that these old, stale cigarettes are Ludlow Spetnik's, and Odessa smokes them very rarely, and fears that when she's done the last one her grandfather will die.

"I've always thought that this whole idea that they Name a random woman as the Melting Queen was a total sham," she says. "There must be some sort of secret powerful cabal that chooses. They'd never want to name someone who really challenged their values, who questioned their institutions and their hierarchies. Overturning the status quo is okay for one day, but not for a whole year. That's why they always Name these bubbly cheerleader-types to trumpet how great everything is, how wonderful Edmonton is. Because being the Melting Queen means having a huge platform to advance whatever agenda you want. In the right hands, it's an amazing opportunity for resistance."

She glances over at me.

"Every Melting Queen has some token project or initiative that she undertakes, right? It's always reminded me of all the different Barbies. Like, instead of Flight Attendant Barbie and Zookeeper Barbie we have Chinese Heritage Barbie or Youth Homelessness Barbie. But none of them every make life better for people in a large-scale, lasting way. None of them really challenge the fundamental structures of power that govern our unequal society. They're still just women cutting ribbons and kissing babies in a man's world."

Odessa stretches out backwards. I worry that she might tumble off the outcropping, but she hooks the heels of her grandfather's overlarge cowboy boots under the ledge's concrete lip.

"I think that you have an opportunity to change things. To take this stupid beauty pageant and turn it into something meaningful."

I shake my head, wishing she'd just give me her car keys and wish me bon voyage.

"I'm not brave like you, Odessa. It's easy to imagine myself as brazen and shameless, but to actually not care what other people think? I don't know if I can do that. I'm not cut out to go up there in front of everyone."

I look down at the valley and see pine trees rustling in the wind. Out of nowhere, the feeling of panic rises along the back of my neck again. I shiver and gasp, shaking violently and almost falling off the End of the World.

"Hey!"

Odessa's arm is around me, sitting me up straight. The fear lessens into a low throb.

"What was that?"

"That happened right before, last time. When I had that vision. When I was in that Melting Queen's body."

Odessa shakes her head.

"We need to talk to the Melting Queen people. They'll know what's happening to you."

"No! We need to just go. I can't do it, okay? Stop trying to convince me."

Odessa growls with frustration. She lets go of me, stands up on the narrow outcropping, perched above the precipice.

"You need to do this! I'm more certain about it the more I think about it. I don't know why they chose you, but you are not some mindless bimbo who's just going to follow the script. You're going to have to fight really hard, harder than you've ever fought for anything, to make all this matter. But you have a responsibility. Think of all the expectations you can overturn! Think of all the people whose minds you'll be expanding. Think of all the genderfluid, nonbinary kids whose parents have no idea what those words even mean."

I look up at Odessa, hands on her hips, bald head haloed by the sun.

"Nonbinary," I say, testing the weight of the word on my tongue. It doesn't feel wrong.

"Yes," she says. "That's what you are. Isn't it? That's what you were trying to say on Melting Day."

"I'm sorry I lashed out at you and Sander," I say. "I just thought Melting Day would be this bright new dawn and everything would just be resolved and I'd feel great."

Odessa sits back down.

"I'm sorry for misgendering you and using your old name," she says. "That was really careless of me."

She reaches out and takes some of my hair in her hand. She brushes out the tangles with her fingers and starts braiding as she speaks.

"To be honest, I was kind of annoyed when I first saw you in Café Fiume. I hate when straight men wear dresses as some kind of audacious costume. They get all this attention and applause for being so brave, for daring to demean and lower themselves with femininity—always saying shit like 'I'm secure enough in my masculinity to wear this dress' like it's some big accomplishment. That's what I saw when I looked at you. But I was wrong."

She lets the braid drop and I turn to face her.

"I don't know how to explain it," I say. "I just have this feeling that sometimes I'm far more than what I used to be, and sometimes I'm nothing at all. Does that make sense?"

Odessa nods.

"You're not a man. You're not a woman. You're a bit of both, or even something else. You can flow between genders or not have one at all."

She looks out at the valley.

"I spend a lot of time thinking about gender, and challenging it in my performances," she says. "A gender is like a language. You learn to speak one since the moment you're born, so you never even notice its complexities, its weird rules and nonsensical exceptions. You don't pay attention to how it works, you just use it every day. In every interaction. Even silently, in your head, when you're alone. Everything is instinct. I imagine that being genderfluid is like learning a second language, or a third or a fourth or a fifth, and then speaking a hybrid pidgin version of all these different tongues, depending on which one has the best words to express how you feel. And right now you feel like you're using a different language for every sentence, don't you River?"

It's the first time she's called me by my new name. I look into Odessa's cool grey eyes. I feel an intermingling of joy and despair.

"That all sounds so beautiful. I wouldn't be able to say it half as nice as that. I want to be strong and clear like you, Odessa. But I don't think I can be. I think I'm going insane."

Odessa smiles at me.

"You are strong," she says. "Sander sleeps through the winter, and I fly away to greener pastures. But you stay here, in the frozen wasteland. You endure. You're a survivor, River Runson. That's what I've always admired most about you. That's why I love you. And even if you change your name, and become this bright new self you've been talking about, I know that will never change."

She looks at me with warm, radiant love, and I feel myself blush. Odessa has never said she loved me before.

"I love you too," I say. "And I admire your creativity and your total self-confidence and your fearlessness and your fighting spirit and your don't-fuck-with-me attitude."

"I know," she laughs. "I'm amazing."

She leaps to her feet.

"Now let's go throw some bottles against a wall," she says, yanking me up beside her. "Destroying things is amazingly cathartic when you're stressed."

I glance back at the river as we tightrope walk back off the concrete pilings. The colour of the water leaps quickly between several shades of blue and brown and green, and I can see Keillor Road flicker in and out of existence. I shut my eyes tight and take a deep breath to fight off a wave of nausea.

We arrive back at Odessa's house and she tells me to wait on the back patio next to the garage. She comes out a minute later with an old-fashioned gramophone and a stack of vinyl records. She pulls one out of the stack at random and puts it on, then goes back in the house. The Glenn Miller Orchestra bursts out in blaring brass. As the music crescendos, Odessa comes back outside with a sagging cardboard box full of old Canada Dry bottles, sticky labels now peeled off from their soak in the bath.

"Give it all you got," she says, handing me a bottle.

She hefts one of her own, then heaves it with as much force as she can at the garage wall. The bottle explodes, sending little pieces of green glass showering down on the cracked concrete patio.

Her garage walls are beige cement with small jagged white rocks plastered into them. I pick a particular rock, which sparkles in the reflected light of the sun, and with a grunt I send my Canada Dry bottle straight at it. The bottle strikes just above my target, shattering into a hundred pieces.

"Nice," says Odessa, handing me another. "I've got probably five hundred of these. So don't hold back."

She sends another bottle to its demise with a karate-like cry of force.

"Why are we doing this?" I ask, drawing back my arm and unleashing the bottle with as much power as I can muster. It disintegrates splendidly against the wall.

"I'm going to use the shards to build my birthing dome," says Odessa. "My Womb Room. I'm going to create a mystical ritual for my birth performance."

She adds a spin to her next throw, and her bottle tumbles end over end before smashing spout-first into the rough wall. I shake my head and can't help but grin.

"I envy you, Odessa. You always know exactly what you want and exactly what you need to do."

"It's easy," she says, heaving another bottle. "Just do whatever you want and ignore everyone."

After finishing off all the bottles and collecting all the pieces of glass, we sit down at the kitchen table and sort the shrapnel. Odessa show me how to pick out correctly sized pieces, and to put the larger ones in a pile for further disintegration with a hammer. She starts arranging pieces on the tabletop, finding configurations so perfect that they're almost seamless.

"I'm going to glue these all together with a special craft bond that makes them hold completely. The glue is very thin, but you can still see the lines of fracture everywhere, even when the surface feels totally smooth."

She pushes a piece of glass into the mosaic she's building, then flips it around the other way and it fits better. But then she flips it back again, so that the dissonant edge is against the others, standing out, drawing the eye.

"Because if you can't see the cracks, then what's the point?"

She continues to pluck out pieces of glass for a moment, then stops and looks up at me.

"I'll go with you, River. Sleep over here tonight and we'll go tomorrow. Either to Phoenix, or to the Office of the Melting Queen. Either way, we'll go together."

{7}

Nothing in Heaven or Earth shall prevent it

I walk through the cavernous lobby of the Stalk, in between Odessa and Sander. Odessa's high heels click on the green marble floor. Sander prattles off facts about the building in a transparent attempt to distract me.

The Stalk only opened two years ago, but it's already an iconic feature of the Edmonton skyline. The tallest building in the city, it stands twice as high as any other skyscraper—you can see it from miles away across the prairie in every direction. Like any huge, dominating building, its construction polarized the public. Some people say that the Stalk is a triumphant addition to an otherwise woefully unambitious cityscape. The other side says that this glitzy monument looks like a big horrible piece of celery. The pale green windows, the curved tubular design, and the leafy public park on its roof all contribute to its notorious nickname. After a vicious editorial by an *Edmonton Bulletin* columnist, the cries to tear it down grew rabid. But really the debate had been over before it had begun. The thing was simply *there*, and every day it kept standing, its presence became more inevitable. The rooftop

park has since become known as Top of the Stalk, and every floor has been ten-
anted—including Floor 85, the Office of the Melting Queen, just beneath the park.

"You look great," says Odessa as she pushes the brass elevator button.

I nod, feeling my cheeks pinken, not quite believing her. Odessa helped me
assemble a killer outfit from her closet, a scarlet power blazer with lipstick to match.
She washed and brushed and braided my hair into what she called a Tymoshenko
Crown—a long woven strand, wrapped around my head so I look like a chess piece,
an agile and powerful red queen.

We step into the elevator and it rockets up from ground level, compressing my
vertebrae. Odessa tucks a stray stand of hair behind my ear.

"You're doing the right thing, River."

I nod again, not entirely convinced, but committed. It's too late to back out now.

The elevator doors slide open and we step into the Office of the Melting Queen.
I expected to see a busy reception desk and a dozen panicked assistants flitting about.
But the vast lobby is eerily quiet.

On either side of the long hall, two rows of green marble pillars stand sentinel.
Each pillar houses a circular, pneumatically sealed display case. Little brass plaques
under the displays identify the historical artifacts that they contain:

The first degree granted by the University of Alberta.

Ancient stone knives from the Rossdale Flats.

Wayne Gretzky's five Stanley Cup rings from the Oilers' dynasty period.

A grapefruit-sized chunk of hail from the Great Tornado.

I hear Sander suck in his breath as we approach the end of the lobby and look
up at the final display case, lit by a spotlight. Under its thick glass casing hangs an
extraordinary dress made from fresh green leaves. Jets of moisture spray down onto
it, just like on lettuce at the grocery store.

There are a few chairs and couches assembled beneath the leaf dress, but no
indication that anyone is here.

"Hello?" calls out Odessa, looking down the hallways that curve out in either
direction.

"Maybe we should just go," I say.

Odessa ignores this comment.

"Come on," she says. "We're bound to find someone eventually."

She heads down one of the hallways. I follow. Sander stands in the lobby, mesmerized by May Winter's leaf gown.

"Sander."

With visible effort, he tears his eyes away from the gown and turns to look at
me. Odessa called him in the middle of the night when I had another vision—running through the forest again, terrified of being caught. She figured his encyclopedic
knowledge of Edmonton would include something about the Melting Queen's
visions. But when I regained consciousness and asked him to explain everything, he
was forced to say his three least favourite words: "I don't know."

Now, he looks at me with an uncomfortable blend of emotions: the awestruck devotion of a fanatic meeting their goddess, the rabid attention of a scientist looking at a research subject. Whenever he looks at me he bores his gaze into my eyes, as if he's searching for some trace of the other Melting Queens in there. I hope it will pass.

"Come and look at these portraits," I say.

Giant oil paintings of all the former Melting Queens hang along the hallway. Alice Songhua is the most recent, standing on an outcropping above the river valley, surrounded by a crowd of people all releasing paper lanterns into the night sky. A Chinese dragon is coiled above her, breathing fire. Her hand is guiding a young child's as he lets go of his glowing lantern.

As we carry on down the hall we go backwards in time. Next comes Louise Morrison, who stands in front of a multicoloured transit map holding out a CIRCLE towards the viewer. Then there is Tegan Stornoway, planting the hedges that will become the Infinite Maze in the huge public gardens which replaced the decommissioned City Centre Sky Harbour. Then comes Summer Johnson, skating down the Freezeway ice lane which loops around downtown, a group of smiling children in tow. Each Melting Queen's portrait shows off her signature initiative.

We come to a portrait which features a tall angular woman with short black hair. Her portrait is very dark. Her pale face stands out against the thick, shadowy forest behind her. I recognize her immediately, and read the plaque beneath the portrait frame:

Victoria Goulburn
Melting Queen 92
08 April 1995 – 27 March 1996

I look up into Victoria's thin face. Unlike most of the other queens, she isn't smiling. She looks sombre, serious, and tired. I understand. I felt that fatigue, that heaviness, when I was her. I looked out of those eyes. I inhabited that skin.

"Over here."

I look up and see Odessa standing just beside a door, craning her neck around to peek inside. I come up beside her and peer into a huge room whose far wall gives a panoramic view of the river valley far below.

In front of this spectacular vista, a dozen people sit around a big crescent moon-shaped table, elevated on a dais. They're arranged like a tribunal, with one woman sitting at a table before them, on a lower level. The elderly man at the head of the committee is on his feet, shouting, spraying the room with spit and banging his fist on the table.

"Where is Alice Songhua? Where has she gone?"

"I don't—"

"Of course you don't know! You know nothing!"

Kastevoros Birch shakes with fury. His voice is hoarse and dry, like the sound of a winter tree creaking in the wind. He wears a faded suit that might've been in fashion fifty years ago, and waves his arms around with remarkable flexibility for such an old man.

"Where is River Runson? Why doesn't she exist in the CIRCLE directory? Why isn't she here, right now? Why can't you *do your job*?"

"Kastevoros," begins one of the other people at the table, but Birch holds up his hand and silences them.

All of the ECHO board members look exactly the same as their leader. Thinning white hair sits feather-light upon their heads. White skin sags and quivers under their chins. They have rheumy eyes and expensive clothes and frown lines carved deep into their faces.

"Do I need to remind you what will happen if River Runson is not found?" says Birch, his voice a low growl. The woman in front of him hasn't moved the whole time, but now she shakes her head.

"*Psst.*"

I look across the doorway at Odessa.

"I'm going in," she whispers.

"No!" I try to grab her arm, but it's too late.

Odessa pirouettes into the room and clears her throat. Everyone's eyes flash to the door, drawn magnetically as Odessa Steps enters. The woman at the low chair turns in her seat.

"How did you get in here?" snaps Birch.

He looks down at the woman in front of him.

"Where is Barbara? Have you lost her too? What's the point of even paying her? I swear to God, Kaseema, if she's down there on the 68th floor again, hunting for a husband, I'll—"

"Can we help you?" interrupts the woman in a steady, measured tone which makes the old man seem all the more shrill. Her brown face is framed by a navy blue hijab which matches her jeans. She cradles a tablet in the crook of her arm like it's a baby.

"Yes," says Odessa. "My friend—"

"Wait."

The old man frowns, pulls out a pair of glasses and rams them on his face. His eyes widen as if he's looking at Odessa for the first time.

"It's you! Finally! Where have you been?"

He pushes back his chair and stomps down from the high table, marching across the room toward Odessa.

"There's no time to waste. We must begin at once. Kaseema, call the tailors and schedule a gown fitting. Then call Rosemary Silt and schedule an interview. Then call City Hall and tell them we'll be ready to go by the first of June. A full week behind schedule, but better late than never! We've got a lot of work to do."

Odessa towers over him, but he seizes her shoulders all the same.

"River Runson!" he cries. "Not quite what I expected—she's bald, we'll have to find a wig-maker Kaseema, make a note, I'm thinking blonde—but definitely we can work with this. Where are my manners?" He takes her hand and pumps it up and down. "Kastevoros Birch! Official Advisor to the Melting Queen. Alice Songhua caught us off guard by Naming you. We had a substantial list of well-vetted suggestions. But there is a precedent of chaos, as I well know."

"Pleased to meet you, Mr. Birch," says Odessa with a radiant smile. "But I'm afraid you've jumped to the wrong conclusion. I'm not River Runson."

The old man's face droops.

"What?" he says flatly. "Are you sure? Of course you are. Look at you."

"No," she says. "This is River."

I'm too slow to slip away. Odessa lunges out the door and pulls me inside. I feel every eye in the room rake over my body. The combined force of all their gazes undoes my woven crown, smears off my lipstick, tears off my scarlet power blazer and strips me naked.

Odessa takes Birch gently by the shoulders and turns him so he's looking at me.

"Hello," I say, dry-mouthed.

The old man says nothing. His face is frozen. He isn't even breathing.

"We were hoping you could give us some explanations," says Odessa, who seems to be enjoying this immensely. "River here has had a couple of weird, out-of-body experiences."

The woman in the hijab stands up and comes toward us.

"The Melting Queens often have memories intrude into—"

"What are you doing?" Birch interrupts. "Don't humour this insanity, Kaseema. This is impossible!"

He rounds on Odessa, unwilling to even look at me.

"Is this some kind of joke?" he says.

"I know it's unusual," she says. "River was terrified when they heard Alice Songhua call their name. That's why they didn't come at first. But now something even more terrifying is happening to them. They had a vision and travelled in time, or something. They were Victoria Goulburn, in the 1996 Melting Day parade."

"I saw tons of things," I say. "All these different eras of the city, old streetcars and horses and a dark forest."

The old man looks at me with horror and revulsion on his face, the way you'd look at a compound fracture that's bursting through your skin.

"What did you say?"

"I was Victoria Goulburn, and I saw the city changing over and over, and I was running through a forest."

Birch shakes his head.

"This is impossible," he whispers. "This is very, very bad."

"Kastevoros," cautions the woman.

"No. No, this isn't possible. There's been a mistake."

Birch stares at me with the coldest, most merciless look I've ever seen.

"Get out of here," he hisses, his voice barely a whisper. "*Get out.*"

"Kastevoros," repeats Kaseema, stepping between us and the old man. "Once one is Named, she cannot be changed."

"Yes, Kaseema: she. *She* cannot be changed."

He turns to look at the ECHO board members for a moment, but all of them seem completely useless without his direction.

"I'm getting security," he says. "They will see you out. Don't you ever come back here."

"Kastevoros, please sit down."

But Birch ignores her and marches out the door. After a moment, all the ECHO board members stand up and file out after him, not deigning to even look at us.

Odessa and I stand awkwardly near the door, unsure of what to do. Kaseema glances up at the empty table, then gives us a tight smile.

"Well," she says, "you had better come with me."

She leads us out the door where we find Sander standing frozen against the far wall, mortified. Kaseema seems no less fazed by his appearance than she was by Odessa and me. She leads the three of us further down the hall of portraits.

"I'm going to explain what's happening to you as best I can. Kastevoros can explain better, but he's…"

"Being a total diva?" says Odessa.

"A little rattled. He's been the Melting Queen's Official Advisor for over sixty years."

We arrive at the end of the hall, where the first Melting Queen's portrait hangs under a spotlight.

"She doesn't look the same as her statue," I mutter to Sander as we walk by.

"It's just artistic licence," he says. "Unfortunately, there aren't any photos of May Winter, just drawings and descriptions."

Kaseema opens the door across from the portrait, leading us into a small and meticulously organized office. Our host settles behind her desk and gestures at the chairs across from her.

"I'm Kaseema Noor," she says as we sit down. "Executive Assistant to the Melting Queen. I coordinate the schedule, talk to the media, plan public events, and help execute whatever project the Melting Queen takes on for the year. I've been working for this office for fourteen years. I'm very good at my job. And I work for the Melting Queen. Not ECHO."

She looks straight into my eyes. Her voice is slow and calm.

"I don't know how much attention you pay to the Melting Queens every year, but you're young so I'll assume it's not that much. But even the fanatics who follow her every move don't know this: when you're the Melting Queen, you have a connection to all the others, throughout all of Edmonton's history. From the moment your predecessor speaks your name till the moment you crown your successor, you're connected to a noble tradition of women.

"The current Melting Queen has memories fall into her mind from all the others, stretching all the way back. We call them Intrusions. They can either be complete, full-body experiences, or small, isolated sensations—tastes, smells, sounds, feelings. Sometimes this happens often, sometimes only once or twice throughout a Melting Queen's full term. I've never experienced it myself, so I don't fully understand. Nobody really understands this position except for the women who've held it. Even Kastevoros. There are stories, old myths that may or may not be true. I don't know."

Kaseema leans forward, elbows on her desk.

"What I do know is that once you are Named it cannot be changed. It's in the Old Lore, Article Six. You are the Melting Queen. The Intrusion you experienced proves this. Birch knows this, no matter what else he says."

"He's an asshole," says Odessa.

"Yes. But that doesn't matter. We don't need him."

I sit in the chair, trying to process what I'm hearing. On the one hand, I'm not crazy. On the other hand, mental time-travel magic exists. I still remember being Victoria Goulburn. If I close my eyes I can still see that parade, hear baby Adam Truman crying. Her memory is part of me now, part of *my* memories, along with the hundreds of different Edmontons and the terror of the dark forest.

"So what now?" asks Odessa.

Kaseema stands up.

"I need to make some preparations for the Coronation," she says, spreading her hands confidently across her desktop. "And to be frank, you probably shouldn't be here when Birch gets back. But that's fine, because I'm sending you somewhere else anyways. There's someone I think you should meet."

8

A lush oasis in a desert of ice and snow

Odessa pulls her big glugging tank of a car up to the conservatory's main entrance.

"You're sure you don't want us to come with you?" asks Sander from the back seat. I can hear the longing in his voice.

"I'm sorry, Sander. I have to do this alone."

I turn to Odessa, sitting there behind the white plastic wheel, her grandfather's giant glasses perched on her nose with effortless style.

"Thanks for everything, Odessa. Thanks for being here for me, and being decisive when I'm so doubtful."

Odessa gives me a small smile.

"You'd do the same for me."

I lean over and give her an awkward car hug over the gearshift, then clamber out of the big copper boat and into the crisp afternoon sunlight.

The grass is still grey, and the trees show no signs of budding greenery. But inside the conservatory it's like I'm on a different planet. The moment I walk inside

I'm hit with a wave of humid, fragrant air. I smell the rich mossy soil, giving life to thick roots and colourful blossoms.

Stepping into each of the Muttart Conservatory's glass pyramids is like entering another world. Each one is a little oasis of life and warmth in the cold winter city. Four splotches of green on a sterile white canvas. Four terrariums, offering a taste of spring to those of us without the means to escape to Hawaii in the depths of winter. An arid desert in a valley of ice and snow. A temperate grassland sheltered from howling winds. A burst of blooming flowers under a perpetually dark sky. A tropical rainforest on the banks of a frozen, locked-up river.

I ask for Victoria Goulburn at the front desk and a volunteer directs me towards the Seasonal Display pyramid. I expect to be greeted by a majestic array of colourful flowers. Instead, I see that the flowerbeds have been completely torn up. A concrete path snakes its way around the room, past scattered patches of dirt.

Somewhat devastated by the lack of flowers—but never surprised by Edmonton's ability to disappoint—I make my way over to the tall woman who's unloading trays of orange-yellow flowers from a trolley.

"Hello," I say as she sets down a tray next to the flowerbed. "I'm River."

She unfolds herself and slaps her hands together, brushing off stray dirt. She holds a hand out to me.

"So you are. I'm Victoria."

She looks even thinner than she does in her portrait, if that's possible. She has moody black eyes and a long straight nose and her black hair is pulled back sharply from her thin face. She turns away from me, toward one of the trolleys.

"I'll be honest with you, River. It's always been uncomfortable for me to meet another Melting Queen once I've been inside her head or she's been inside mine."

She hands me a pair of blue coveralls to match her own, then kneels down next to the garden and pats the soil, as if for reassurance.

"But if you help me plant some marigolds, then we can talk a little. I know you must be very upset. So was I, when I had my first Intrusion. The least I can do is help."

"Then the least I can do is help you plant."

I pull on the coveralls and stand there, uncertain. Victoria gets up, hands me a flowerpot. I run my fingers over the petals of the nearest flower. It's dark orange in the centre, fading out to brilliant yellow around the sharp-lined edges.

"It looks like molten metal."

"Marigolds are our spring feature. Edmonton's official flower. Guess who decided that?"

We share a look and I can tell we're going to get along. She kneels back down and starts digging a shallow hole in the soil.

"I suspect the others feel the same way about being around each other," she says. "Which is why there's never been a Melting Queen reunion. When I'm around one of them I feel like I'm fraying at the edges. Like part of myself is pulling away, trying to leap back into that other woman's body who I've been for a while. It's not a pleasant feeling."

I sink down next to her and notice that this is exactly what I've been feeling. I can faintly feel my fingers patting against the soil. Except they're not my fingers, they're Victoria's.

"Does it stop?" I ask as I start planting my own flower. "Does it end once you're not the Melting Queen anymore?"

"Yes. Except when you're near another Melting Queen. A connection like ours doesn't just go away. It's something that you'll have for the rest of your life."

"I don't want it for another day, let alone the rest of my life."

Victoria looks at me from under a heavy brow.

"As much as I wish that this wasn't true, you don't have a choice. They're going to tell you lots of things that are just silly old meaningless rules, but that part is real. You're having Intrusions now. I'm willing to bet that you're having people recognize you, come up and share their grief with you too, right?"

I nod.

"That's part of it too. You get memories invading your mind all the time, and people confessing their sins and insecurities to you."

Victoria settles back on her heels for a moment and looks outside at the blasted barren moonscape beyond our pocket of greenery.

"The Melting Queen is Edmonton's perfect mother," she says. "And Edmontonians are all children in Her presence—clutching at her skirts, wanting to be heard, wanting to be forgiven. It's not important what you say to them, just that you listen to them. Just that you provide them with an excuse to hear themselves speak. Coo in their ear. Tell them it'll all be okay. Give them comfort. Absolve them of their guilt or grief or whatever they need."

She plunges her hands into the soil.

"The Cultists say the Melting Queen is the incarnation of fertility itself. She brings the spring. She is the new life. So it's best if she's a young, fertile woman. Or else the magic won't work and Edmonton won't bloom."

"That's crazy."

"So is having memories from a hundred years ago erupting through your mind."

"So that's why Kastevoros Birch was so upset," I say. "I'm not a fertile woman."

Victoria gives me a weary look.

"Look, I don't know what your situation is. Whether you're transgender or gay or one of the new ones I can never remember. But there's one thing you need to understand. The Melting Queen is more feminine than any real woman ever can be. *None of us* are good enough. We're all trying and failing to be May Winter. No woman can ever be the angelic mother that we're supposed to be. You just have to do it when you're Named. Even if you're not the ideal. There are consequences if you don't."

"Like what? Everybody keeps saying that, but nobody says what will happen."

Victoria shrugs.

"I don't know how much of this is true, but they say that some kind of natural disaster always happens. There are a few examples of Melting Queens in the past who have refused the call. Aloise Pennant refused in 1915, and there was a big flood. Opal Pearson said no in 1942, and there was a giant blizzard. Invidia Straum wouldn't do it in 1987, and then there was the Great Tornado. Something bad always happens, a catastrophe for the city. And we always end up doing our duties in the end anyways."

"What could be more catastrophic than a nonbinary genderfluid Melting Queen? A Melting Monarch, I guess I should say."

Victoria stands up and stretches, then goes to the trolley with the trays of flowers.

"It's not just about the city," she says. "It's also about your sisters."

She looks up at the fogged panels of glass overhead.

"I lived in Australia, you know," she mutters from across the room. "For twelve years. I built a life there, in Perth. I was vice-president of a successful company. It was beautiful. It was warm, all year. I was as far away from Edmonton as anyone can get."

"Then why would you ever come back here? If I escaped from Edmonton I'd never come back."

She brings another tray of marigolds over. She unpots one and settles it in the hole she just dug. She massages the earth around its roots and takes a deep, meditative breath.

"They contacted me. Birch and ECHO. They told me I had been Named as the Melting Queen. My mother had stuck my name on the statue, you see, just as she'd done every year since I left. And now I needed to come back here, to the city where I had grown up, the city I had fled at the earliest opportunity. I refused. I told them they were crazy. That I didn't care."

"So what changed? What got you to care?"

Victoria looks up at me with a pained expression on her face.

"I had an Intrusion."

She takes another flower from the tray and brushes her fingers gently across its petals.

"Shishira Sarasvati was the Melting Queen before me," she says. "She was young, only seventeen when she was Named. Everyone was so excited for her to be Melting Queen, because her mother Vasanta had been the Melting Queen many years before. It was the first time that two Melting Queens came from the same family. And even more special was the fact that Vasanta had given birth to Shishira during her reign. It seemed like it was her destiny to be Melting Queen."

Victoria puts the flower down and looks at it sadly.

"Shishira wasn't a great Melting Queen. People had high hopes for her, because her mother started the Heritage Festival and they all expected her to do something even better. But she didn't go out in public much or make many appearances. The ECHO people say it's because she was sick, that she was fighting off the cancer which eventually ended her life, sending the whole city into mourning. That's the official version."

She looks at me now, with her sharp-eyed raven's gaze, angry and sad and bitter.

"The truth is that Shishira killed herself. Because of me. Because I didn't come back. Because I ran away from being the Melting Queen. There was no coronation, there was no way for her to pass on the power of the Melting Queen to me. So it ate her from the inside. It drove her crazy, until all she could do to get away from it was to die. She didn't have cancer. She stayed out of the public eye all year because she was particularly vulnerable to Intrusions, and they tore her apart. And they only got worse after she Named me, and I wasn't there to pick up the torch from her. So one night she went out onto the High Level Bridge and she jumped."

I can't look away from Victoria's pupils. They're like dry wells, sucking me down into the depths with her.

"I felt her die," she says. "I was sitting in my office at work, on the other side of the world, and then I was her. I'd been having Intrusions since she Named me, but they were just minor things like smelling cookies baking or hearing a song playing in the other room. My first full-scale Intrusion was her suicide. I died with her, jumping off that bridge. And then we died again. And again. And again. And I felt it. Over and over. It haunted me in my dreams. It tore into me when I was awake. She killed herself—I killed myself—a hundred times. I died speaking my own name. Her last word, begging me to come home. A thousand times."

Victoria shudders. But she pushes through, desperate to exorcise this ghost.

"I came back to Edmonton so that I could apologize to Shishira's mother," she says. "And then I did my duty as Melting Queen. I didn't want to be around anyone, so I just planted elm trees by the thousands. It's a pathetic memorial to the seventeen-year-old life I ended, but at least it made Edmonton a tiny bit better. And every time I see an elm tree, I remember her. And every time I plant something new, and help something grow, I pray that it will restore some kind of natural balance against the life I snuffed out. But I know it never will."

She lets out a long breath. Her eyes are dry—as if she's already shed all the tears she ever had to cry, and now can't make any more—but she rubs the backs of her hands against them anyways.

"It's a sacrifice, to be the Melting Queen," she says. "It's not fun. You have Intrusions tearing you apart. Some of them are painful, and dark, and frightening. Some of them make you run for your life in terror. But even the nice memories are difficult, lifting you out of yourself and then slamming you back down. You bring things back with you. You're assaulted with dozens of horrible stories every day from people who expect you to make them better. No matter what you do, some people will hate you. But you have to do it, once you're Named. You owe it to your sisters who've gone before you."

She digs her fingers deep into the soil, carving out another hole.

"I hope you don't have many Intrusions, River. Some Melting Queens don't have any. Some Melting Queens are like Shishira, and have Intrusions every day. Every one of us is different. But we're all connected."

I see the pain in her thin face and I understand. Here she is, clutching at my skirts. This is her confession.

"It wasn't your fault," I say. "You couldn't have known what would happen. I'm sure she wouldn't have killed herself if there hadn't been other things going on in her life, some other reason."

Victoria shakes her head.

"I wish I could believe that was true. It's not. But thanks for saying it."

She plants another marigold, then looks over at me.

"I think you're going to be a perfectly suitable Melting Queen, River Runson."

9

A flourishing throne in full bloom

The next week is a whirlwind of activity. I'm cloistered in the Melting Queen offices, working with Kaseema to prepare for my coronation. There are sacred words to memorize, logistical details to finalize, and protocols to internalize. All of the regular staff have gone, disappeared like Birch and the ECHO board members, so it's just Kaseema and Odessa and Sander and me. I'm worried that Birch and ECHO will return at any moment, and I become even more worried when they fail to reappear. I ask Kaseema what they're up to and if she's heard anything from Birch, but she waves off the question.

"I'll deal with that. You have more important things to focus on right now."

Odessa and Sander stay close to my side throughout my training, keeping me company and giving me moral support. Every night we sleep over at Odessa's house, and she talks me into staying in Edmonton all over again. It's good to have my allies around me.

Sander knows exactly what I'm supposed to do in the coronation ceremony, and he coaches me through each step. He continues to watch me like a research subject, peppering me with facts about my predecessors like he's trying to spark another Intrusion. But my week is mercifully free of any other episodes. I know that while Odessa and I are sleeping Sander is poring over every scrap of writing about the Melting Queens. But he can't find anything written about the Intrusions, and to compensate he throws himself into teaching me every detail of the coronation ceremony and its significance. Kaseema seems equally impressed and exasperated by his enthusiasm, but with all of the regular ECHO staff gone, I'm sure Sander Fray and his superfandom are a welcome addition.

Odessa couldn't care less about the traditions of the Melting Queen. She places herself in charge of my wardrobe, a decision Kaseema resists until I speak in my friend's favour. Kaseema's absolute faith in me is somewhat terrifying. I've never had someone be automatically loyal and attentive to my every need before. It makes me want to not disappoint her. But I still feel energized by embracing some of Odessa's non-traditional ideas.

The Melting Queen always wears a green gown at her coronation and a pink gown on Melting Day, just as May Winter did a hundred years ago. But Odessa has other ideas. She builds a gown out of glass and mirror—a thousand shards all glinting in the sunlight, showing the viewer little pieces of my naked skin beneath the dress along with little fragments of themselves. From my knees down, the pieces of glass and mirror grow larger, pointing out in all directions like jagged shards of ice. I'm like a pillar of the High Level Bridge, collecting all the mounded icebergs which get shoved up on its skirts by the inexorable force of the river. A sheer green scarf is arranged across my bare shoulders—the only touch of colour, the northern lights shimmering above it all. I study myself in the mirror. There I am. River Runson. Melting Queen 115. Edmonton embodied.

Odessa weaves my Tymoshenko Crown each day, and the looping braid becomes a fiery redheaded halo which makes me feel powerful. She applies small touches of makeup along my jaw and around my eyes. I warn her not to bury my features and cover up my real face. I'm not some obnoxious drag queen like Magpie. I just shine a light on it in the right way.

By the end of the week, the three of them have got me as ready as I'm ever going to be. They make me go over my words one more time, rehearse the physical steps in the giant ECHO boardroom, and before I know it I'm standing in a large tent in Coronation Park—backstage, listening to the drone of the vast crowd outside.

"What does it look like out there?" I ask as Sander pops his head through the tent flaps to check on us, like he's been doing every five minutes.

"Everyone is really eager," he says. "The park is completely full."

Coronation Park is the most important place in Edmonton. The site of the first Melting Day, it sits right next to the river. Over the years the park has gotten smaller and smaller as commercial development in the river valley eats into it. But at its heart, the Spring Throne remains undisturbed.

According to Sander, the Spring Throne grew up out of the ground at the moment May Winter was crowned as the first Melting Queen. The branches wove themselves together to make a seat, shot up in straight lines to form a tall majestic backing, and burst into bloom across the throne's wide back—a mantle of pink wildflowers to welcome the new queen. There are archival photos showing the Spring Throne in full bloom, but for at least sixty years no flower has sprouted from its branches. Some people say that only a truly perfect Melting Queen will make it bloom again, and inherit May Winter's legacy, and perform grand miracles like the Melting Queens of yore.

The Spring Throne stands on top of a small hill at the east edge of the park. There are no signs warning off trespassers—Coronation Park belongs to everyone— but no one has ever sat on the throne except a Melting Queen. Like so little else in Edmonton, the Spring Throne is sacred. When May Winter first sat the throne, the sun roared over the horizon behind her and blinded her astonished, adoring Edmontonians. Just as it should in about fifteen minutes.

I go up to the tent flaps and peek through a slim crack.

The trees along the edges of the park are leafless, but they've been adorned with white fairy lights that shine down on the crowd. Paper lanterns are strung between them, green and pink, the royal colours of the Melting Queen.

A hush falls over the crowd as the lightshow begins.

"From the beginning," a deep voice rumbles, "we have come again and again to this gathering place, this valley, this bend in the river."

I watch the silk screens which have been suspended behind the Spring Throne. Everything is backwards, but I can see what's being projected on the other side: teepees popping up along the river bank, bison charging across the prairies, canoes being paddled upstream by sharp-nosed, stony-faced men with bare chests.

"We grew in number, and gathered from all corners of the earth. We learned to live together, no matter our differences."

European settlers march westwards across the screen, leading oxen by the ear, towing everything they own in a wagon. The Indigenous people fade quietly and conveniently off the far side of the screen. The walls of the first Fort Edmonton spring up, and Mounties ride out from it, towards the audience.

"We were always a transient city. A gateway. A boomtown. People came, and left again. Shallow roots were pulled up before they could grow and thrive."

People decked out in shabby Klondike prospector's gear appear, along with oil sands workers, both eager to move north and make their fortunes before returning to the East.

"Through time, the face of our valley changed. We built and rebuilt and made a home for ourselves."

The teepees reappear, then the fort, then Edwardian brick buildings, followed by brutalist concrete blocks and glittering glass spires. They mound up on top of each other and jumble together, along with some recognizable buildings like the Legislature and the Stalk.

"And through it all, from the birth of the city to this day, through storms and crises, through sun and shine, one woman has watched over us. One woman has united us, has defended us from the dark and cold, has shown us to ourselves."

The faces of one hundred and thirteen women flicker by in rapid succession, giant faces which fill the screen. Each one has a number underneath, from 1 - May Winter, to 29 - Saoirse Beltane, to 58 - Vivian Tegler. Certain Melting Queens are greeted with applause and cheers, others met with silence. We run through all of them, all the way up to 113 - Louise Morrison, and then finally Alice Songhua, Melting Queen 114.

She's supposed to emerge beneath the screen. That's how it always goes. But Alice Songhua still hasn't been found, by Kaseema or anyone. So the list skips back, to the Melting Queen who was missing from the parade of faces, though nobody seemed to notice. Melting Queen 92 steps out from behind the Spring Throne.

"Edmonton!" cries Victoria Goulburn. "Tonight we crown our Melting Queen!"

The crowd roars with joy, but there's definitely an undertone of confusion—a feeling of "Who is this woman and where is Alice Songhua?" I hope it goes well for Victoria. It took a lot of persuading to get her to do it, but in the end she agreed. And Sander said that there is a precedent. Shishira Sarasvati was not there to crown Victoria herself, so her predecessor Mia Paraná did it instead.

I stand there quietly for a moment, listening to the distant echo of Victoria's voice. I feel a wave of anxiety pass through me, a twist of familiar panic, like I'm running for my life.

"I don't think I can do this," I say.

Odessa is right there at my side.

"Yes you can. Yes you can, River."

She takes my hand.

"I know you have doubts, but everyone has doubts. You think I'm so decisive and certain about everything? I have doubts all the time."

"But you are decisive and certain about everything."

She puts my hand on her abdomen.

"This was the last day I could get an abortion. This was the day I had to decide whether to actually go through with this crazy plan of mine. But I'm going to see it through. Once you start something you should finish it. You should trust that Past You was wise when they put you on this path, and trust that Future You will be resourceful and resilient enough to work it out, no matter what happens, no matter what name you take."

Her stomach is warm and I feel the small swell of her belly. For a moment I even think I might feel a kick, but that's probably just my imagination.

"You're right," I say. "I've been running and running all winter. Walking in circles and getting nowhere. It's time for me to stop."

Sander pops his head through the tent flaps again.

"It's time."

My friends usher me to the ramp which leads up the back of the hill. I can hear the sound of a million strangers on the other side. I crush Odessa's fingers but she doesn't say anything. Each breath feels shallower than the last. My hands are numb and freezing. A gauze has descended over my ears. But I hear Victoria speak those four symmetrical syllables, and my feet carry me up and out into the lights.

As I step into the glare, I feel a million sets of eyes feasting on my face—the whole city, come out to see the new Melting Queen. A sea of glittering eyes in the dark, reflecting the green and pink lanterns. My dazzling dress creaks as I make my way towards Victoria, who holds the emerald crown on a white cushion in her hands.

Silence. No cheering. No jeering. Nothing.

I walk past the Spring Throne, draw level with Victoria. We've run through the ritual over and over and I'm grateful for Kaseema's insistence that we rehearse it to death now that I can walk through this on autopilot.

Victoria invites me to be the new Melting Queen. I assent by bending down and allowing her to place the crown on my head. I straighten up and she approaches me for the crucial symbolic moment, the point of communication where one's reign ends and another's begins.

As her face draws nearer, I notice that Victoria's lips are dry and cracked. I wish I had some lip balm to offer her.

She kisses me, the lightest of kisses. It feels like solid air pressing against my lips. She pulls her face away from mine, keeping her back to the crowd, giving us this silent private moment together in front of a million people. I can see concern hiding deep in the dark dry wells of her pupils, behind a veneer of reassurance and pride. She gives me the smallest of nods, then turns to face the crowd.

"Edmonton!" she cries, taking my hand and lifting both our arms into the air in a victorious salute. "I give you your Melting Queen!"

Silence. No applause. All I hear is my heart thundering in my chest. The crown is heavy, and my neck starts to ache from the weight of that huge emerald. My lips are still burning from Victoria's kiss, but otherwise I feel no different.

Say something. Anyone. Anything. Shout a slur. Start a cheer. Even a single hollow clap. But they just stare at me.

A cold breeze tries to tear the northern lights from my shoulders. I have to pee.

Victoria lets our arms drop and gives me hand a squeeze before she backs away from me, leaving me alone at centre stage. I look out at the crowd, singling out individual faces. A chubby man in an Oilers jersey. An old woman who rubs her dripping nose with a balled-up tissue from her cardigan pocket. A guy with comically raised eyebrows and wide eyes. A girl who's blushing the blush that I can't because all the blood has drained from my head. A child perched on its father's shoulders, looking around at everyone else and then up at the sky, bored by the proceedings. I take a deep breath.

"Edmonton!" I proclaim. "Brothers and sisters! And others," I add in a mumble. I imagine Sander biting his tongue at that. I'm not supposed to deviate from the sacred text, not even by a single word. "It is with great joy and humility that I accept this responsibility. I..."

Their lips are pressed together anxiously. Their brows are knit. They all seem concerned and sad. They all just watch me. Tense. Awkward. Uncomfortable. *Silent.*

"I come before you as a daughter and a sister and a friend."

I see several eyebrows go up at this statement.

"Tonight, in the sight of you, my city, I am not just a woman—"

A loud shout issues from somewhere in the crowd. No words, just a long angry boo which fills up Coronation Park and then dies out. People look around to see who shouted, but nobody can seem to locate him. They settle their eyes back on me, and I feel the increased skepticism and judgement in their gazes. I swallow against my dry throat, and continue.

"I am not just a woman..."

I hear the man's shout still ringing in my ears. I feel the next line rising in my mind, and I know I'm supposed to tell them that *I am not just a woman, I am the emblem of us all, I am the vessel of our renewal.* I feel dizzy. I feel the saliva in my mouth turn sour like I'm going to vomit. I feel something rumble inside me, as if that one jeering cry has triggered an avalanche.

"You know what?"

The faces perk up. Everyone looks up from their smartphone screens, where they've all been recording this awkward travesty.

"No. This isn't right."

I see their eyes swell. This is not in the text.

"Do you think I don't know what you're all thinking?"

I step forward and the crowd shrinks away from me. I feel a swell of confidence, and a smile spreads across my face. Their fear makes me feel powerful.

"I am not *just* a woman," I say. "Obviously. I know that. I'm not pretending otherwise."

The crowd reels back a little further, stunned. I feel all the anxiety and shame and panic that have been lurking in me burn away, erupting in a bright flash of rebellious joy.

"I'm not a woman at all. I'm not a daughter. Or a sister. Or a queen. I'm not a king either. Or a son. Or a man. I'm nothing. I'm no one."

I tear off the emerald crown and hold it in my shaking hands.

"I won't be May Winter. I won't be Alice Songhua. I can't be your picture-perfect queen. Your latest goddess. I can't be a beauty pageant princess or a proud civic booster. But I can do something else. Something that nobody else has done before: I can tell you the truth."

The crowd begins to recover from its initial shock. People start yelling, booing, making rude and violent gestures at me. I don't care. I can't stop myself. It feels so good, like tearing off a scab, itching a scratch until it's gloriously raw.

"And do you know what the truth is, Edmonton? The truth is that you're not that great. You think all these projects will make you better, but they won't. You think all these women stroking your ego make you special, but they don't. You think a single day of whimsy and freedom once a year makes you wacky and colourful and open-minded? You're lying to yourself. You're nothing special. You're not important. You're just a grey, bland, boring city full of tired, timid, small-minded people. And if you think that I'm going to keep playing along, to keep pretending that you're the greatest city on earth, think again. I'm River Runson. I'm genderfluid. And I'm not going to let you get away with these lies anymore."

I drop the crown, turn my back on the wailing crowd, and march off the hill. I go past the withered throne, past the horrified Sander and the elated Odessa, past the tent, out of the park, down to edge of the swiftly flowing river. I look out on my namesake, running on fast and free. The roar of the crowd is deafening, buzzing, hysterical. Good. Let them howl.

The queen is dead. Long live the queen.

{10}

A gathering of worthy petitioners

"MELTING QUEEN MELTDOWN," declares the *Edmonton Bulletin*. My face appears on every newspaper, every broadcast, every social media feed in the city. Battles rage on TV panels and Twitter threads, Edmontonians debating everything from my gender to my body to my perversion of tradition. I'm an abomination, come to destroy a sacred institution. I'm a misogynist, muscling my way in on women's territory. I'm a breath of fresh air after a century of treacly garbage. I'm a monster. I'm a brat. I'm a rebel. I'm a hero. I'm a man. I'm a woman. I'm a threat.

I try to go home, but from down the block I see a pack of reporters camped out in front of my door, circling like hungry coyotes. The city has been set on fire by my tirade, and I can't hide away. Protesters and counter-protesters picket in front of the Stalk. Kastevoros Birch and ECHO officially denounce me, fire Kaseema, and kick her out of the Office of the Melting Queen. We relocate to Odessa's house and make do with what we have.

Odessa is thrilled by my performance and the ensuing scandal. Sander is sullen and moody with me for making a mockery of his great mythology. But Kaseema is a rock.

"You've made things more difficult for yourself," she says. "But if we abandoned every Melting Queen at the slightest impropriety we'd never make it through to spring."

She looks at Sander and he nods reluctantly.

"There have been worse coronations," he admits. "Fran Fletcher spat on her predecessor and punted the emerald crown into the crowd. It was missing for a month."

"Exactly," says Kaseema. "So let's get to work." She starts performing some finger gymnastics on her tablet. "It's time for the next step."

The beginning of every Melting Queen's tenure, explains Kaseema Noor, is marked by a gathering of petitioners. They come to convince the new figurehead to be their champion for the following year. Every Melting Queen has a project. In 1908, Aurelia Green presided over the official opening of the University of Alberta. In 1960, Astrid Knudson got the Queen Elizabeth Planetarium built, sharing her love of the cosmos with Edmontonians of all ages. In 1999, Karen Mackenzie, a bartender at the popular Jasper Ave nightclub Phrique, celebrated the turn of the millennium by organizing the biggest fireworks display in Edmonton's history.

According to Sander Fray, nothing has ever come with the position of Melting Queen except a ceremonial crown and a small team of advisors. There's no salary, no residence, no clearly defined agenda or set of duties. The Melting Queen is given nothing except a voice—a platform to advocate for whatever issues are important to her. And so, of course, she attracts hundreds of organizations and businesses, all desperate to bask in the warm glow of her limelight.

The Melting Queen's Picnic is their chance to persuade her to send a little love their way. I ask whether anyone will want the endorsement of a crazy, loose-cannon queen like me. Kaseema assures me that the petitioners will still come. Even if I'm damaged goods. Even if my reputation isn't good-as-gold. I'm still a cash cow they're all eager to milk. And a queen who can command headlines is the kind of queen they want, no matter how I get myself on the front page.

So, two days after the coronation, I climb on board *The Edmonton Queen* with Sander, Kaseema, and a crowd of about a hundred people. They bought tickets for the boat ride down to the Melting Queen's Picnic months ago, so it's a real mixed bag. Some of them are moderates who are willing to overlook my incendiary coronation. Some of them are radicals like Odessa. Some of them are just curious to see me in person. But the riverboat isn't full. Some of those who had tickets clearly stayed home in protest.

We set off on a slow chug upriver. The Melting Queen's Picnic, Sander tells me as we cruise, always takes place on Big Island—a land mass which sits an hour upstream by paddle steamer. Despite the name, it isn't actually an island, having been reabsorbed into the riverbank several decades ago. The weather is nice and the ride is smooth and leisurely, with the riverboat's paddlewheel chopping through the shallow, jasper-green water. All the ice is gone by now and the air is tolerably warm, but I still see no signs of greenery on the riverbank. My fault, the Cultists say. I never sat on the Spring Throne. I don't have a uterus. I did everything wrong.

I stand at the railing and watch the riverbank slide by, enjoying how the spring breeze plays with the evergreen trees. Suddenly, I feel a shiver of fear rip through me. I feel tree branches slapping against my face, and hear men's voices howling over my shoulder. I clutch the rail, overcome by dizziness and nausea for a second before these foreign feelings all evaporate.

Sander is by my side in an instant, wide eyes all over me.

"Is it happening? Are you going to have an Intrusion?"

"I don't know, Sander. I really hope not."

He must hear the irritation in my voice, because he shrinks back, looks down at the river dejectedly. I feel guilty.

"It's not always a big, out-of-body thing," I say. He perks back up, instantly back in research mode. "Sometimes I just have random sensory experiences, like smelling pine needles or hearing a song that nobody else can hear or tasting a really strong flavour of saskatoons in my mouth. Sometimes it's more like ideas that randomly pop into my head, stuff I've never learned on my own, like the melting point of sulphur or the capitals of South America or the name Albert Herring."

"Who's Albert Herring?"

"I don't know. Nobody. That's what I'm saying. I just have random memories that aren't my own, bubbling up to the surface of my mind."

"It sounds incredible," says Sander, staring at me with awe.

"If it never happens again it will be too soon," I say. "How much longer till we get to Big Island?"

"Not much longer. Are you excited to hear the pitches for your project?"

"If anyone shows up," I say, gesturing around the half-empty deck.

"They'll show up," says Sander. "Who wouldn't want to meet a history-making Melting Queen like you? I bet there will be huge crowds!"

When we arrive at Big Island, Sander is proven right—though perhaps not in the way he expected. *The Edmonton Queen* is met with a huge group of protestors holding up signs and banners:

Not MY Melting Queen!

#DamTheRiver

Melting QUEEN, not Melting QUEER

They boo at me as I walk down the gangplank onto the dead grass. Across from them, a smaller counter-protest has formed. They don't have any signs, but they're chanting "I don't care if She's a He, River is the Queen for Me!" City police hold back both sides, keeping them away from me and from each other. The pro-testors outnumber the supporters by at least two to one, but I hold my head high as Kaseema leads me through the crowd. I smile and wave at my supporters, and turn my back on the protestors, trying not to listen to the insults they hurl my way.

I'm led to the centre of the island, where a remarkable sight sits in a huge grassy expanse surrounded by small poplars. An old riverboat, the *City of Edmonton*, was beached on the island decades ago and is being slowly consumed by the ground. The sun shines down as Kaseema leads me through the ruins of the ship, into a large room with a wood-planked floor. At the end of this slightly slanted grand audience hall sits another throne, though nowhere near as fancy as the Spring Throne. It's really just a carved wooden bench on a raised platform, with several chairs and couches arranged in front of it.

Kaseema gestures for me to sit, then brings me some peach tea and pomegranate macarons. There's already a huge pile of gifts waiting for me, offerings and bribes by groups trying to curry favour. Sander settles into a seat near the gift table—which is heaped with all kinds of food, from potluck-style casseroles to expensive bottles of wine—and loads up three plates, blending borscht and blueberries and bulgogi with blatant disregard for flavour. He's still in his recovery-from-hibernation phase, and I swear he gobbles down a couple plastic forks while he eats. Odessa is nowhere to be seen—she said she'd drive down and meet us here, but she seemed preoccu-pied. It's not unlike her to flake out on things at the last minute.

Kaseema stands before my throne, holding her trusty tablet.

"We have quite a schedule to get through," she says. "Seven hundred and eighty petitioners have registered for an audience with you."

"Well, we'd better get started," I say, already shifting on the uncomfortable wooden throne. Kaseema nods and goes to the door.

Over the next ten hours, I meet with dozens of organizations and hear their pitches for why I should give them heavily publicized endorsements or spearhead their initiatives.

SPYGLASS (the Society for Promoting Youth Games, Leisure, And Summer Sports) urges me to push for more recreational facilities.

EOS (the Edmonton Organic Society) wants me to advocate for a ban on all pesticides and genetically modified food in the city.

PURGE (the People's Urban Reform Group of Edmonton) asks that I endorse their plan to build a hugely expensive sky train around the city perimeter.

The representatives from CURVED (Citizens United for River Valley Environmental Defence) don't seem to want anything, but shout at Kaseema and me for five minutes about how bad the salt fall on Melting Day was for the environment.

RAMROD (Rural Albertans Managing Responsible Oil Development) promises to fund any initiative or project I take on—provided I sign a pledge that I won't be as anti-prosperity as some of my predecessors.

The extremely large delegation from PAPRIKA (People Against Potholes Ruining the Integrity of Key Avenues) asks that I criticize city council for not spending enough on road maintenance. When they leave, Kaseema tells me that they're one of the most powerful lobbying groups in the city. Apparently if I don't do at least one anti-pothole event, I'll lose what little support I have.

I'm surprised to see a former Melting Queen amongst the petitioners. Iris Zambezi—a big Black butch lesbian whose head practically scrapes the ceiling—was the first out Melting Queen when she was crowned in 2004, on the 100th anniversary of the first Melting Day. Her signature initiative was to popularize Edmonton's Pride Parade, at a time when Mayor Bill Smith and Premier Ralph Klein refused to attend and were attacking LGBTQ rights. She's here today representing BUGLE (Bisexuals United with Gays and Lesbians of Edmonton).

"I knew this day would come," she says with a huge smile as she strides across the room. "It's been lonely being the only openly queer Melting Queen. But here you are at last."

"Here I am," I say. "I mean, I'm not sure if I'd really call myself queer, but here I am."

Her eyes narrow. Her exuberance evaporates.

"Of course you're queer," she says, crossing her muscular arms. "You're gender-fluid. You said it yourself. It's your responsibility to stand up, and be counted, and be a symbol of our community."

"What community is that?" I ask, turned off immediately by her aggressiveness. "I'm not a bisexual united with gays and lesbians. I don't even think I count as being transgender. I'm just me. I don't feel comfortable being the symbol of any community."

She lets out a long blast of air through her nose, like an inflamed dragon. She's a huge, tall, formidable woman. She could snap me like a dry twig if she wanted to.

"I think we got off on the wrong foot here," she says after a moment. "Let's start over."

"Okay. I'm sorry. What exactly do you want?"

"I want you to be the grand marshal of this year's Pride Parade."

I shift on my wooden throne.

"I don't think that's really for me," I say.

Iris Zambezi grinds her teeth audibly.

"You know, I've met hundreds of young gay men just like you—oh I know that's not what you are, but that's where I always hear this bullshit. They all say 'Oh Pride isn't for me, it doesn't represent me, I'm not that kind of gay guy.' They all think they're different from the rest of us, that they're not part of our community, that being queer is 'just a part of who I am, it doesn't define me.' And sure, yes, of course it's not everything you are, nobody said that. I get it, you've got your rights, everybody treats you like you're a normal heterosexual human, like you're almost their equal. But not everybody gets those rights. And until they do, you'd better fucking show up. You'd better fucking do your duty to the community that won you your freedom to be a whiny little asshole."

"Maybe people would be more willing to come to your parade if you didn't try to guilt them into it like this!" I cry. "And maybe people would feel more comfortable coming to Pride if you didn't have an orgy in the streets!"

Iris looks at me with cold fury. My eyes start to water, but I force myself to face down the heat of her stare.

"Have you ever been to Pride?" She throws each word in my face.

I don't answer. Brock never wanted to go. He always said exactly what she just said.

"That's what I thought," snarls Iris. "So don't you dare fucking echo all these straight lies about Pride. We march in a parade to honour our ancestors, who fought for our rights. We march to send up a signal to all our brothers and sisters—and others, yes, just like you said—around the world, that we are with them, that they are not alone, that they can find a home with us. Not just for the queers in Africa of the Middle East or the Caribbean, but for the kids in rural Alberta, in Canadian suburbs, whose parents throw them out into the street. Pride lets them know that they're not alone. Pride saves lives. And people like *you*, who buy into the straight lies, who don't do your part, who give in to the *shame* inside yourselves, are putting those lives at risk."

Her fuming rage ignites my own. I feel the fury boiling beneath her skin, the rage and the resentment and the pain underneath it all, and it fans the flames of my own anger.

"What's your problem?" I snap at her. "Do you really think shouting at me like this is going to convince me to lead your parade?"

She laughs in my face.

"Oh I'm done trying to convince you. Clearly you've made up your mind about what I am and what Pride is. Yes, Pride is a party. But Pride is still a protest. Or did you not see the dozens of people picketing against you out there?"

I stand up and my throne falls over behind me.

"I see them, and I'm going to keep ignoring them! I'm going to keep being myself, and reject these boxes that they—and you—want to put me in."

She shakes her head, her lip curled in disgust.

"I hope you'll soon *remember* what those of us who came before you experienced," she says as she turns to leave the ship. "Maybe that will help remind you of what you're fighting for. Of what you owe to *your* community."

Iris Zambezi stomps down the length of the audience chamber, the old ship shaking with every step. Kaseema sets my throne back on its feet and I sit down, shaking as much as the derelict riverboat. I take a deep breath and try to regain my composure.

"Was she always that angry?" I ask.

Kaseema's face is inscrutable.

"She was my first Melting Queen," she says. "It was never easy for her."

I look at Sander. He crunches awkwardly on some carrots that he's brought in a sandwich bag from home. The parade of petitioners resumes.

Businesses shower me with gifts—dresses and coats, cosmetics and accessories, food and wine—hoping I'll wear or consume their products in public, or come to their establishments with a bunch of media in tow. Concerned citizens read me statistics and tell me stories about drunk driving and teen pregnancy and the old derelict house on their block. One guy even plays me a song on a mandolin.

I hear them out, nodding along and showing as much polite interest as I can. But none of these people look me in the eye. None of them seem comfortable being in the same room as me. And they all seem to have a sense of entitlement about them. As if, since I'm a defective Melting Queen, I'm lucky that they're even here agreeing to work with me. That they'd risk alienating people by having me as their mascot. As if I should pick them because they're generous enough not to tell me, at least to my face, that I'm a freak. I know I'm supposed to give them some bland encouragements, praise how admirable their ideas are and tell them how happy I would be if we got to work together over the coming year. But I'm just as bad at faking my enthusiasm as I was at following the proper steps in the coronation.

These projects and initiatives are important, sure. But what would any of them really accomplish? Edmonton might pay a little more attention to one issue or another for a year, but then everything will go back to normal. What even were the projects of the Melting Queens ten years ago? Apart from the two people in the room with me, nobody can remember. Like Odessa says, there can be more transformative change than this.

By the time the sun starts to set, we've finished only half of the groups on Kaseema's list.

"I can't do any more of this," I say. "I physically can't. Sander, bring me some tea and cakes. I feel weak."

My thin friend won't meet my eyes as he brings me a cup of tea.

"There weren't that many cakes," he says innocently. "But I put some extra honey in this."

He places the cup on the table beside me and then Kaseema looms over his shoulder, tablet in hand.

"Please no. No more."

"There's just one more that you can't ignore," she says, staring down at me. "They won't take no for an answer."

I sit up against the throne and take a sip of tea.

"I'm sure that whoever it is can wait for next year."

"It's your mother."

I choke on my tea and start coughing roughly and before I know it Madeleine Truman is striding through the dilapidated ship. She's a solid, red-cheeked woman with short brown hair and thick legs. I scramble to my feet as she approaches.

"Oh Adam," she says, and before I can stop it she's collapsing forward onto me, sobbing and hugging me tight.

I stand there, mortified, stiff as a plank. It's been ten years or more since my mother gave me a hug. I've never seen her cry.

She pulls away from me and stares up into my face.

"I can't believe it's true."

She buries her face in my chest and squeezes her arms around me. I'm still so thin and she's too strong and it hurts. I slither out of her arms and step back. My mother stands there, holding both hands up to her mouth, shedding big theatrical tears and watching me.

The sight of her here is so surreal that it completely consumed my attention. But now I notice that someone else entered the ship behind her. Brock Stark stands at the end of the long hall, glowing like a marble statue in the golden light of dusk.

"What are you doing here?"

At least he has the decency to look ashamed of himself.

"Your mom asked me to come," he says. "I tried calling her after you disappeared, but I just heard back from her after the coronation."

My mother dabs at her eyes with a handkerchief.

"You're a good boy, Brock. You did your best."

She turns back to me.

"I couldn't believe what I heard when I got home. You abandoned your fraternity brothers? You dropped out of school? I was so worried."

"I'm sure you were fine."

Last fall, Candace Khan, the telegenic leader of the newly created Lodgepole Party, destroyed the forty-six-year-old Conservative government dynasty. My mother went from being a promising Legislature backbencher with Cabinet potential to losing her seat by a sixty-percent margin. She flew off to Palm Springs to lick her wounds all winter and plan for the previously unthinkable—a life after politics. But now here she is, sharpening her claws and getting ready to sink them back into me.

"I'm here for you now," she says, taking a step towards me. "When I first heard you were the Melting Queen, up there wearing a dress, I didn't know what to think. Part of me thought that this was just a phase, like when you asked us to call you 'Atom' in junior high. But Adam or River or whatever you want to be, I support you. I understand."

I back away from her as far as I can, pressing up against the old wooden walls of the paddle steamer.

"Stay away from me. Please just go."

Madeleine stays where she is but she reaches out her hands beseechingly.

"Honey, I love you. I just want to be here to support you. I will be by your side for as long as you need me."

"What, so you can use me as a prop for your comeback campaign? No thank you."

Her face slides into a wounded pout. She's always been good at manufacturing the right emotions, but they always appear just a millisecond too late.

"That was unkind," she says. But I can hear the machines behind her face whirring. I've figured out her obvious strategy already.

"Give us a chance," says Brock Stark. "We all miss you, Adam. River, I mean. Sorry."

"You miss Adam. You don't know River."

"We could get to know you. If you let us. We could be your brothers again."

I look at Brock's shining white teeth and glittering gold hair and earnest green eyes.

"I believe you. More than her. I know you want to be my friend. But every time I look at you it reminds me of a past life. A life that no longer belongs to me. And I can't go back to that."

"I'm sorry, River. I just want to know what we did wrong. What I can do to make things right again."

"Nothing. You were the best friend Adam Truman could've asked for."

Brock shakes his head and trudges out the door. My mother is more determined.

"Your father and your brother and sister are all very concerned about you," she says.

"I doubt that very much."

"Is it so bad if I want to stand up and say that I'm proud of my transgender son or daughter or whatever you are? That I love you and support you? Is it so bad for me to stand by your side, in solidarity with you?"

"I know you. This isn't about me. This is about you. That's what it's always been."

My mother glances at Kaseema and Sander, clearly uncomfortable with me airing our dirty laundry in front of strangers. But I'm too tired to play the perfect son in our little Truman Show anymore.

"Okay," says Madeleine. "You need space. I understand."

"Stop saying that. You don't."

She walks towards the door, then pauses and turns back.

"I'm here whenever you need me, sweetie. And I'll be an advocate for you, no matter what people say. Don't worry about that."

I say nothing, watch her go. When she finally leaves the room, I look to Sander.

"Typical," he says.

Sander's always understood my relationship with my family in a way that none of my other friends could. His parents adopted his little brother Alex because they didn't want to gamble that their next kid would be as defective as the first and hibernate every winter. Sander was actually born asleep (we celebrate his half-birthday in June, because he's always asleep in December) and he still lives with his reluctant parents. They took him to Hawaii one year, before the First Snow fell, to see if he would fall asleep even far away from Edmonton. He failed this test, and so they decided to effectively replace him with a normal child.

"Yeah," I say. "Well. Hopefully that's the last of her."

"I doubt it," says Sander with a wry smile.

"Me too," I sigh. I turn to Kaseema. "What's next?"

The Melting Queen's Ball marks the end of the Picnic, a masquerade and feast under the night sky. Odessa still isn't here, so I have to try to make myself look as good as she can make me look. After I've changed into a three-piece suit with a mirror-encrusted carnival mask, Kaseema leads me outside onto the dancing green (I guess it should be called a dancing beige, because the grass is completely dead), which stretches out before the prow of the *City of Edmonton*. The grand lawn is once again strung with pink and green lights, which shine down onto the hundreds of assembled guests. Tables are spread all around the field, where the petitioners can eat and network and scheme.

Everyone applauds as I walk across the lawn, still eager to win my favour. Except, of course, the protestors, who continue to chant and boo from the police cordon at the edge of the great lawn. I'm led to a podium and I give a boring two-minute pre-written speech (Kaseema is taking no chances) about how excellent all of their proposals are, and how overwhelmed I feel by the array of choices in front of me.

After I sit down, a string quartet starts playing and the grand banquet begins. I make it through three courses of stilted conversation with the few city councillors that I'm sat beside (the mayor didn't come to lead me in the first dance of the ball, which is another tradition I'm fine with breaking) before I excuse myself. I head over to the park building with the bathrooms, and see a woman going into the ladies' room. I hesitate a moment outside the doors, then follow her inside. Her eyes widen as she sees me in the mirror, then she seals herself into a stall. I pick one at the other end, leaving a two-stall buffer between us.

When I exit my stall, the other woman is still in hers. I take a while washing my hands to see if she'll come out and acknowledge me. I half-expect her to emerge, eager for this one-on-one opportunity to convince me of her cause. But she stays put, afraid to face me. Or maybe she just doesn't have a lot of fibre in her diet.

I spend a few minutes standing beside the sink as the air dryer coughs gently on my hands. I'm just about to wipe them down on my pants when the door opens and Odessa Steps enters. She's wearing a full regalia Royal Canadian Air Force uniform and her heels click.

"Hey!" I say. "Thank god you're here. Where have you been all day?"

Odessa shrugs. She seems distracted.

"I was taking some self-portraits for a performance piece. I'm going to print them on little circles of paper—you know, the kind you get from a hole punch—and scatter them across the city from Top of the Stalk. Sander will know which day of the year is the windiest."

"I wish you would've been here," I say. "You could've made things less boring."

"I have my own stuff to do, you know. I can't always just be standing in the wings cheering you on."

Her tone is frosty. Of course she's feeling a little neglected. She's used to being the star.

"I'm sorry if I've sidelined you," I say. "Anyways, I'm glad you could make it."

Odessa starts washing her hands thoroughly.

"It seems like a fun event. I haven't been to a masquerade since I was in Venice. I met this guy who brought me to an underground Vivaldi party, where everyone was dressed as one of the four seasons. He gave me flowers to put in my hair and I was Summer."

"That sounds incredible," I sigh, imagining Odessa covered in a thousand pigeons in St. Mark's Square. "Hands clean enough?"

Odessa's still scrubbing energetically. She reddens a little then turns off the taps, avoiding my gaze in the mirror.

"Did you decide on a project for the year?" she asks.

"Not yet. Any ideas?"

"Oh I'm overflowing with ideas, of course. And why pick just one? That's the whole problem."

She doesn't even bother to try the air dryer, preferring to wipe her hands on her trousers. She pulls out her own bright red carnival mask and I help her tie it on.

We make our way back to the ball, where we find that the tables are being cleared away. When the dancefloor is clear, Odessa offers me her hand and steers me across the lawn. It's fun surrendering to the suggestions of her touch—sometimes firm, mostly gentle. After a while I spot Sander sitting at a table with Kaseema and make my way over to them.

"...but why is it such a big secret?" Sander is saying. "It only makes me revere the Melting Queen even more. If people knew about the Intrusions—"

"River!" exclaims Kaseema. She turns immediately to Sander. "Could you get me another drink?"

"Of course!" says Sander, eyes agleam. He gets up from his chair. "Gin and tonic?"

Kaseema lifts her empty glass agreeably. As soon as Sander's gone she leans in.

"Your friend is very knowledgeable," she says. "But it's kind of exhausting."

"You don't have to tell me that," I say, and we share a smile. Kaseema's the best.

A figure plunks down in the seat beside mine, wearing a frayed black cocktail dress and no mask at all, although her makeup is caked on dramatically—blue and white stripes shooting back from the corners of her eyes, to match the streaks in her sleek black hair.

"I don't like your friend."

Magpie cradles a champagne flute and glares through the throng at Odessa, who's smoking a cigarette by the riverboat's prow.

"She thinks she's so eccentric and interesting but she's totally fake. I caught her in a lie about having read *The Second Sex*. All style and no substance. Trying to be everything to everyone. She's a liar."

"That's worth a lot, coming from you."

"Trust me, she's a bad person. The kind of person who pretends to be an alcoholic because she thinks it's glamorous. Or pretends to have depression because she thinks it's romantic."

I don't say anything, but I'm grudgingly impressed by Magpie's perceptiveness. Odessa has done both of those things.

"Excuse me," says Kaseema, looking at Magpie with a surprising amount of distaste on her face, "but we're having a private conversation and—"

"So what did I miss?" says Sander, settling on Kaseema's other side and sliding a drink in front of her. "It's something to do with the Intrusions, isn't it? No? Give me a hint."

Magpie looks at the two of them with total disinterest and stands.

"Come on, River. I need to talk to you."

"It seems everyone does."

Kaseema looks at me for a moment like she's going to beg me to take her with us, but then she turns dutifully back to Sander as Magpie pulls me away.

"You really are stalking me, aren't you?" I ask as we go around the perimeter of the dancing lawn.

"I thought you'd miss me," she says.

"Considering you left me unconscious in a public park, I don't see how you could've thought that for a minute."

"I didn't know what was happening and it freaked me out," she shrugs. "You're looking much better, I might add."

"Are you trying to flatter me? Because it's not working."

"Well, I had to try."

She leads me over towards the riverbank, where a crumbling stone promenade looks out on the waters. We walk along the broken flagstones, beneath bare branches.

"What did you want to talk to me about?"

Magpie leans against the stone balustrade that looks down over the river.

"Oh nothing really. I just thought you wanted to get away from your little entourage, so I provided an excuse. Look, the ice is all gone. Wait. Is there someone down there? There is! Look! Someone is skipping stones on the river."

I come up beside her and place a hand on the stone railing. I look down at the trees beside the riverbank, rustling in an evening breeze. I feel a spark of panic arc through me like chain lightning. I look at Magpie. She raises her eyebrows.

"You gonna pass out on me again?"

"I swear this is all your fault. It happens most often when you're around. You're a witch, aren't you?"

A wave of dizziness washes over me, an undertow pulling me away from my own body. And then I blink, and everything has changed.

The old man sits beneath a display case with a leafy green dress in it. A gentle mist rains down on the gown, supposedly keeping it fresh after all these decades. Even from here I can tell that those leaves are fake. Nothing could've survived for ninety years.

"Now, Mrs. Pass-qua-most-toast," says Kastevoros Birch, a holy-shit expression on his face after all those syllables.

"Paskwamostos. Ms."

"Is that Greek?" says one of the identical old white men beside Birch. "It sounds Greek."

"Cree."

"Well it's all Greek to me," he says. All the other men and women laugh along with him. They all have uncomplicated names like McDougall and Ritchie and Oliver.

"It says here that you're recently divorced," says Birch. The others cluck their tongues, sigh in regret.

"I am."

Birch takes another piece of paper out from his big file. I don't know why they even bothered calling me here. They know everything already. They've already made up their minds.

"Why did your husband file for divorce?"

Birch taps his pen against the paper.

"Doesn't it say right there in that file?"

"It says that he was the one who initiated your separation. But not why he wanted to divorce you. So? What did you do?"

I meet his stare.

"That's personal."

Birch sighs, and a woman beside him takes up the interrogation.

"We need a stable, gentle Melting Queen," she says. "After your predecessor's war on religion, we need a true, compassionate mother to knit our city back together again. Please don't take this the wrong way, but I'm afraid she may have Named you as one last act of defiance against us. Normally the Melting Queen respects our input. But respect is something that Oswin Thompson knows nothing about."

"All she did was convince the government not to fund Catholic schools anymore. Seems fair to me. We don't fund any other religious schools."

"That's not the point," says another man down the table. "Did you go to a Catholic school?"

"Yes."

"See, well, then you understand. This is a matter of conscience. Of religious freedom. We should be free to choose where our children go to school. Not have some activist Melting Queen make that choice for us."

"My parents weren't given a choice," I say.

The fifteen white people in front of me seem both ashamed and irritated. As if I'm being rude by bringing it up.

"Yes. Well. We all know that's very tragic," says Birch. "But we can't rewrite the past, can we? All we can do is make a better future together. And having a strong Melting Queen is crucial, especially considering recent events. The Great Tornado killed dozens. Then Mr. Gretzky abandoned us. Now Mrs. Thompson has torn our city apart with this issue. Spirits are low. The Melting Queen has her work cut out for her."

"I have an idea," I say. "I know what we can do to make things better."

"Traditionally, the Melting Queen chooses her project from the petitions at the Melting Queen's Picnic," says Birch.

"I don't need to do that. I know exactly what I want to do. We need to build a fountain. A beautiful, giant fountain. A gathering place where people can come. Soak their feet. Be at peace."

The ECHO people look at me like I'm nuts. Birch turns to another page in his file.

"We'll discuss your project later," he says. "There are more important things to worry about." He circles something with his pen, then looks at me over the top of his glasses.

"You have no children."

"No."

"Why not?"

"The same reason I have no husband," I say. "None of your goddamn business."

A willowy woman at the end of the table blinks in shock.

"But you can have children, correct? I don't mean to be indelicate, but you are capable of having children, aren't you?"

I look from old white face to old white face. They can't think I'm that stupid.

"Why are you asking me all these goddamn questions? If you already know, then why are you wasting my goddamn time?"

"Mrs. Paskwamostos—"

"No. I can't have children. Not since I was eleven. Not since they called me a moron and cut out my ovaries. Is that what you wanted to hear?"

The ECHO people are utterly silent. Birch's face is grey.

"This is a disaster," he says. "This will not stand."

The old man's eyes are swimming with tears, as if he's heartbroken that he has to tell me I'm unfit to wear the crown. Of course all his identical cronies are looking so sad, so upset. We're sorry. We're sorry that you can't have kids. We're sorry that they did this to you. But most of all we're sorry that you're ugly, and dumb, and dirty. We're so sorry. Everyone's sorry. What a sorry life you've had.

"We're sorry," says another old woman, cracking under the pressure of silence. She's thin as a sheet of loose leaf. I could crumple her into a ball and throw her away with one hand. But she's sitting behind a desk. She's got a pen and a stack of important papers. No touching her.

"It really isn't your fault," says an old man with well-manicured fingers. "We see that."

"But Oswin Thompson pulled a horrible prank on you," says Birch. "There's no reason for you to be burdened with this responsibility. If only you could—"

His lips keep moving but suddenly everything is silent. I speak but I can't hear myself. I look out the window and I see snow on the ground, then flowers blooming, then leaves falling from the trees.

"River."

A face hovers over mine, some girl with black and blue hair and crazy makeup. She wears a thin necklace with a little gold cage dangling from it. Inside its bars, an evil black stone stares out at me.

"I didn't leave this time. I think I should get some points for that."

She sniffs and rubs her nose with the back of her hand.

"Who are you?" I ask.

She raises her eyebrows.

"I'm River Runson," she says.

"No," I frown, coming back to myself. "*I'm* River Runson. You're René Royaume. You're Magpie."

"Well, it was worth a shot," she says with a shrug.

I sit up and Magpie passes me a chipped mug filled with cold tea.

"Where are we?"

We're in a nondescript spare bedroom. Paint-by-numbers prairie landscapes cover the walls. The bedspread I'm lying on looks knitted by hand. Everything is clean but impersonal.

"We're at Clodagh's house," says Magpie. "She was the one skipping stones, down on the riverbank. We carried you to her car after you passed out. She explained what was happening and it seemed like the best thing to do. Kidnapping's not normally my thing, but you are a queen. There's probably a good ransom in it."

"Who?"

"Clodagh Pasta-something. Nice lady. Big. Said she was the Melting Queen once. Do you think you can get up? Clodagh's cooking us a midnight snack."

My stomach gurgles and Magpie cackles. I get up off the bed, follow her down the hallway to the kitchen. The decor reminds me of Odessa's house—everything is old and well cared for, although here there are no expensive trinkets from around the world.

The kitchen has an avocado-green refrigerator and Formica countertops. A mountain of a woman stands at the stove. She glances up as I walk in.

"You."

The depressed travel agent who taped up my boots grunts in recognition. She turns over a slice of bacon and it sizzles in the pan.

"Sit down," she says.

I go to the kitchen table with Magpie.

"I used your postcards," I say to the travel agent. "I made them into a dress on Melting Day."

"It was pretty awesome," says Magpie.

"I'm glad you used them for something," says the travel agent. Two slices of toast pop up and she fishes them out of the toaster with a fork.

"Well I know your name," she says, "but you don't know mine."

"Clodagh," I say. "Clodagh Paskwamostos. Melting Queen 88. 1991."

She cuts a tomato and doesn't look at me.

"What did you see?" she asks.

"The ECHO people were trying to convince me to step aside. Convince you, I mean."

Clodagh comes over to the table. She sets down our sandwiches, pours us fresh mugs of tea and sits down at the end, her chair creaking.

"I always really wanted bacon every time I had an Intrusion. No idea why. Just a craving."

We set to work on our bacon and tomato sandwiches, which are crunchy and salty and immensely satisfying. I wait for Clodagh to say something, but she just chews. I glance at Magpie, who's using a diabetic test strip to check her blood sugar level.

"You wanted to build a fountain," I say, remembering the Intrusion in bits and pieces as the memory is absorbed into mine.

"Yes," says Clodagh self-consciously, eating her sandwich, not meeting my eyes.

"But they didn't let you."

Her face is faded and haggard and paunchy. I can tell that she's become good at guarding it, at holding her muscles in one configuration so nobody can know what she's feeling. But I can see by the bunching-up of the wrinkles around her eyes that she's crestfallen. I've dredged something up.

"I'm sorry," I mumble, and sip my bitter tea. She served it black, without any milk or sugar. I take another crunchy bite of my sandwich.

Clodagh clears her throat and takes a long gulp of her own tea.

"I was sterilized when I was eleven," she says. "I was Cree and Irish. A half-breed. A mongrel. Mixed race, I guess I'm supposed to say now. They didn't approve of mixed races then. Plus I was officially declared a moron. Too stupid to reproduce. I would've contaminated the gene pool."

She uses the crust of her bread to wipe up the bacon grease on her plate.

"I wanted to build a fountain," she says. "But then these fancy young lawyers came to me. They wanted to make a name for themselves, launch a class-action lawsuit against the government for the Alberta Eugenics Board. The province sterilized almost three thousand people, you know. People like me. Certified morons."

She finishes her sandwich and takes a deep gulp of tea, even though it's still hot enough to scald my tongue.

"No one told me that my fountain idea was stupid," she says. "Not outright. But I knew it was a pointless project compared to what they wanted to do. I was just a plumber with a dumb dream. I had a responsibility to represent all those other victims, they said. So I became their face. The sterile Melting Queen, even if Birch never wanted me. He thought that I'd make it so spring never came. But it did. We won the case. I got 700k—350 for each ovary, I joked, no one laughed—and an official apology. And that was that."

The room falls silent. Clodagh takes another gulp of tea. Magpie twirls her stone-cage in her hand.

"Iris Zambezi came to the Melting Queen's Picnic and told me I had a duty to march in the Pride Parade," I say.

"People love telling other people what to do," says Clodagh. "And it's always easier to let other people make your choices for you."

She picks up her plate and goes over to the sink and rinses it off.

"Wait, so I get the rest of the story, but why a fountain?" asks Magpie.

"When I was little, in my first foster home, I saw this one movie I really liked. *Roman Holiday*. I was obsessed with it. I even got a poster from it—well, a magazine cover that I stuck up on the wall—and I learned all about Audrey Hepburn. I wanted to cut my hair like she did but they wouldn't let me, so I did it myself and got in trouble. Anyways, I always thought Rome would be the best city in the world to live in. That's why I used my ovary money to start a travel agency. But then, I never got around to going."

I study this husky old woman, whose skin I've been in. She's so strong, but so tired. She could probably lift a car over her head, but it takes just as much effort for her to get up in the morning. She used to want things.

"What were you doing at the masquerade?" I ask.

Clodagh turns off the water but doesn't turn to face us.

"When I saw you on the news, I thought it was a sign or something." She comes over to the table and sits back down. "I've wanted to go for years. To make my own petition. I even made up a name for myself, a dumb acronym like everyone uses. FLOE. The Fountain Lovers of Edmonton. Although that's just me, as far as I know. Anyways, I didn't get in to see you. Not that I was surprised."

"You still want to build a fountain."

Clodagh sighs.

"You should get some sleep," she says. "It's past two."

"I'm not sleepy, I have chronic insomnia," says Magpie proudly. "And I want to watch *Roman Holiday*."

"Well, I suppose we could," says Clodagh. "I have it around here somewhere."

We go into the family room and Clodagh opens up a cupboard full of VHS tapes. She can't find *Roman Holiday* so we settle for *La Dolce Vita* instead. Magpie laughs and claps as Marcello traipses around Rome. She doesn't touch her stone once. Clodagh watches her with satisfaction.

I keep almost drifting off to sleep, but then thunder rumbles in the sky.

"There's going to be a storm," says Clodagh.

On screen, Sylvia shouts for Marcello and splashes through the Trevi Fountain. The thunder builds.

"Listen," says Sylvia as the roar of the Trevi Fountain fades away and Rome is frozen in the light of dawn. They wade out of the fountain and the TV snaps to black. The power is out.

Magpie stands up and takes both of our hands.

"Come on," she says.

She leads us out into Clodagh's back yard and stands in the rushing wind, waiting for the storm to arrive. Soon, the sky splits open and water pours down onto the city. I smile up into the night sky, feeling the cold raindrops strike my cheeks. The first true spring rain, come to wash away the lingering shadows of winter.

{11}

Resurrected by the rains

The storm continues all night and all day and all night. The rain washes away all the salt and dirt and grit and grime and grey hues of winter. The earth opens, drinking up the water with greedy thirst. And then, at last, the summer sun comes out.

The next day, budding greenery blooms everywhere. Flowers burst open. Grass spears up out of damp soil. Leaves hang thick and succulent on groaning branches. The sun blares down on everything, soaking into the dirt. And I start to feel alive again, at last.

I'm going to build a fountain. Not for Edmonton. Not for a million ungrateful citizens. Not for me or my legacy or the glory of the Melting Queen. I'm going to build a fountain for Clodagh Paskwamostos. I don't care about embodying the spirit of the city or changing Edmonton forever. I'm just going to make one person happy.

It's hard to put exactly what I feel about Clodagh into words. I've never had such a strong, instantaneous connection with another person before. When I'm around her, despite all her gruff and awkward aloofness, I feel happy. I feel safe. I feel like I'm at home. And I also feel what she feels, still, after all these years. I feel aching, chronic pain. I feel world-weary cynicism. I feel a tiny flame of hope that a lifetime of winters hasn't been able to snuff out. She needs me. She deserves this.

98

And I'm going to do everything I can to fan that flame into a roaring fire, and bring Clodagh Paskwamostos back to life.

The day that Edmonton begins to bloom, I introduce Clodagh to my little team. We tell Kaseema and Sander and Odessa about our project, the long-overdue fountain that will make one tiny piece of Edmonton as beautiful as Rome.

Kaseema instantly starts drawing up timelines and plans, budgets and charts, reaching out to landscape design companies, researching everything she can learn about fountains. In one afternoon I see that Kaseema Noor *is* the Office of the Melting Queen. ECHO and Kastevoros Birch and all the glitz and grandeur of the Stalk are just the fancy packaging. She's a one-woman organization, doing the work of a dozen people. She's how a Melting Queen can demand a bridge be built in May and have it finished by April. I wouldn't be surprised to see her with grout and trowel, building the fountain brick by brick if she had to.

Once he works up the courage to talk to Clodagh, Sander starts getting as excited by the fountain as she is. At first I cringe as I watch him ply her with questions about Intrusions and her famous court case. Her answers are sharp monosyllabic bullets, when she bothers to answer at all. But then he asks her about fountains, and Clodagh's stony silence crumbles. She can talk for hours about her peculiar obsession, and Sander is an enthusiastic listener. He asks intelligent questions, and she instantly takes a liking to him.

Odessa is another story. Shortly after Clodagh and I announce our plan, she says she has to go for a walk and leaves her house in a huff. Everyone is so engaged, either in planning or in conversation, that they don't seem to notice that something's wrong. But I follow her outside, onto the back patio where I helped her smash bottles only a few weeks ago.

"What's wrong?"

She turns to face me. I'm surprised to see so much anger in her grey eyes.

"Is this really what you want to do?" she asks. "Yet another spirit-boosting project?"

"I don't care about boosting Edmonton's spirits. I'm doing this for Clodagh."

"You're going to be just like all the others, then. Think of what you said at your coronation! You aren't going to be a cardboard cut-out Melting Queen. You need to tackle issues that matter. You need to make real, challenging changes. Push people! Resist! Make them uncomfortable. Turn over the table."

"I don't know if I can do that. I don't think that any Melting Queen could do that. All I know is that I'm excited by this idea, more than I've been about anything in years. I feel like I'm finally coming back to life. Please don't be mad at me. I wish I could be the radical queen that you imagine. But I'm not you."

Odessa's face hardens. She pulls out her car keys.

"No," she says. "You're not me. I thought you were going to be different. I thought you were going to be better than this."

"You don't understand," I say. "I felt what she felt. *I was her.* I need to do this. She needs this."

"Whatever," she says, walking past me towards her giant copper Chrysler. "I'm going for a drive. Have fun with your new friend. I hope she's worth it."

I watch her drive away and listen to the roar of her engine down the block. I stand on the back patio for a few minutes, waiting for Odessa to come back, like she always does whenever we have an argument and her dramatic sensibilities take over. But she's gone for real this time, and all I can do is go back inside to the others. Nobody seems to notice that anything is different.

I settle down with the three of them and start laying out plans for the next steps of our project. We need to choose a site for the fountain, come up with a design, work with the city planning department to stay within the bylaws. We need to find the money to build it and promote it across the city, at the countless events I'm supposed to attend. And even though I'm reluctant to admit it, Kaseema eventually brings up the inevitable: I need to go out and meet the people. Talk to them one on one. Hear their stories. Try my best to turn enemies into allies, or we'll never build this fountain.

So I force myself to face my fears and walk through the city in endless circles, having conversations. I live through the same scene a thousand times. A person recognizes me, sneers at me, comes up to spit at my feet or shout in my face. Then, before they know what's happening, they're spilling their deepest secrets out—their doubts and their woes and their desires and their sins.

"I'm sorry," they sob into my shoulder.

"I forgive you," I say, feeling my warmth reanimate their cold bones. Feeling their coldness seep into me.

It feels like everyone hates me until they talk to me. All they can see is a man in a dress. 'Genderfluid' and 'nonbinary' mean nothing to them, especially when I'm not demonstrating perfect gender equilibrium every day. They see my painted lips and my dark stubble, my free-flowing hair and my sharply cut tie, my lace-up skirt and my button-down shirt and they shrink away. Then they feel the inexorable pull, like the force of gravity, drawing them in to clutch at my skirts and whisper in my ear.

A big muscular guy in an oil-stained jean jacket comes up to me, and I think he's going to bash my head in. Instead he just sits beside me on a bus bench, sweating and not meeting my eyes, and tells me about his breasts. It's a condition called gynecomastia that he's had since puberty. He binds them down with a stretchy tube of fabric. He's afraid to go to the gym or to a swimming pool or anywhere with a locker room. He's afraid of bringing a woman home. He's afraid of going to the doctor to get surgery to cut them off. He says he thinks I have bigger balls than he does, and he wishes he could be as brave as me.

A four-year-old runs over and asks me, "Are you a boy or a girl?"

"No," I say. "I'm not. I used to be a boy but I grew out of it."

"Oh, okay," he says. Then he tells me his favourite colour is pink even though he's a boy, because he likes the watermelon scent of the pink marker. I agree that the artificial watermelon smell is awesome and the boys and girls who tease him about it are small-minded bumheads with no imagination. His mother comes over and pulls him away from me. She slaps his hand down when he waves goodbye.

An old man has a stroke at the grocery store, and I hold his hand as we wait for the ambulance. He keeps trying to talk, whispering slurred words that I can't understand. I keep telling him that I won't leave, I'll stay right here, he's going to be okay. He dies before the ambulance arrives.

Sometimes they come to me with great news—I just got in to vet school! I just got an STI test and I'm all clear! I just released my first album!—and they search my eyes for a mother's approval. But these interactions are rare. Mostly they tell me stories of anxiety or insecurity or persecution or shame. I had no idea there were this many people with this many problems in Edmonton. I had no idea that the misery I felt all winter ran so deep, was so widespread across the population. Everyone is miserable all the time. Everyone is pretending they're fine, hiding their pain, ashamed of what they feel. All I can do is listen to their stories and try to comfort them. I don't know if I'm really helping them. But still they come.

It's draining, listening to story after story. I want to lock myself away from them and never hear another sad story in my life. I look at myself in the mirror and see the weight of their collected gloom etched into my face, the burden I've absorbed to lighten their loads. Odessa is barely around anymore, so I have to learn my own makeup tricks and cover up my haggard features by myself. I have a few tantrums, grumbling to Clodagh and Kaseema about how unfair it is that I have to listen to all these secrets and miseries, take on all these troubles and worries. They both humour me, telling me to take breaks if I get too worn out, treating me with far more patience than I deserve.

But even if I stay in my room, the powers of the Melting Queen won't let me be. I'm having more and more Intrusions. Sometimes I'm being crowned Melting Queen or leading a grand celebration. Sometimes I'm doing something mundane like painting a wall or mowing my lawn. Sometimes I get to experience the joys of having a female body, like the time I was stuck having menstrual cramps for six horrible hours. On rare and glorious occasions, I even jump back into a Melting Queen who's asleep, and when I come back to myself I feel incredibly refreshed and rested.

There's only one memory that I've experienced more than once: running through the woods in the middle of the night, fleeing in terror. Whenever it comes I grit my teeth and close my eyes and pray for it to end. I trip over a stray branch, I go flying through the air, and I'm thrown into another Intrusion—safer, blander, where my heart can stop hammering and my blind panic can fade away. But no matter how much I try to avoid it, this dark memory keeps coming back. I have no idea what it is or when it is or whose it is. I don't want to know. All I know is that I have to stay away from it.

I complain. I whine. But in the end, I have a job to do. These are my duties. This is what I signed up for when I decided not to run away to Phoenix with Odessa. I keep walking. And meeting people. And listening.

But eventually it's time for the people of Edmonton to listen to us. Over the past few weeks, Kaseema has drawn up a plan of action, but we still have a lot of decisions to make. Where should we build our fountain? What materials will it be made of? How will we fund its construction and upkeep? What should we do with any money people throw into it?

We decided that we should get regular Edmontonians to help us answer these questions. We want everyone to contribute to this project—dreaming it up, having their say, donating as much as they can. So Kaseema organizes a public forum, a meeting in Sundial Park, one of Edmonton's greatest Melting Queen projects.

In 2006, Ananke Cosmopoulos (Melting Queen 103) successfully campaigned to turn the derelict site of an old meatpacking plant into a unique and spectacular park. For years after the plant was torn down, its giant brick smokestack stood at the centre of a barren dirt landscape beside Fort Road on the city's northeast side. Ananke persuaded the city to repurpose the land, maintaining the smokestack and using it as the central needle in a giant sundial.

Hundreds of people turn up and spread out their picnic blankets on the lush green lawn of the circular park. The media shows up too, and a handful of protestors, who've lost a bit of steam now that the inevitability of my reign has set in. The smokestack's long shadow falls across picnickers gathered around the Hour of the Rooster statue. Clodagh stands in front of the smokestack, facing out on the crowd, brimming over with passion. After so many weeks of interacting with the public, I'm very happy to cede the spotlight to my friend.

"Fountains," she says, "have been the beating hearts of cities for millennia. They used to provide clean drinking water to the people, maintaining the health of the body. But they also bring beauty to public spaces, nourishing a city's soul."

Her eyes shimmer like coins under rippling water. She's been reinvigorated by our joint project. She's a different person than the one I met in that travel agency all those aeons ago on the last day of winter.

"Fountains are places where people give voice to their deepest desires," says Clodagh. "What do we all do at a fountain? We toss in a penny and pray for a blessing. A fountain holds the memory of a thousand whispered wishes. In its waters, the pooled secrets of an entire city circulate."

Clodagh draws the eyes of every person present. She has them completely in her grasp. She takes a sip of water from a glass bottle and holds it up for all to see.

"The waters of our fountains are the waters of the river. Our river is in our blood. We suck up its water and pump it through a huge network of pipes, buried deep beneath our feet, insulated against the cold. You probably don't think about it when you turn on a tap, flush a toilet, draw a bath, or take a drink. But this water is river water. It's been carved up into your own personal tributaries and distributaries. There are vertical rivers channelled up and down skyscrapers, and horizontal ones running back and forth across bridges. The river runs through this city in a million little rivulets. In the winter it runs on beneath the ice, just like it runs beneath the surface of our own skins, circulating through us."

Clodagh shares a radiant smile with the picnickers.

"A grand, cascading, monumental fountain may not seem like the most urgent of projects. There are always people to feed. Children to save. Potholes to fill. But it's something Edmonton needs. Something that will make our city better. An oasis of peace in these times of constant stress."

I look out at the crowd and see hundreds of individual faces. Crowds can never be singular entities for me anymore. There's a white woman with a shaved head and a dozen piercings. A group of Sikh men in green turbans. A young family with kids lying on the grass, looking at the clouds. Protestors, as always, gathered at the edge of the park.

Kaseema has organized a roving microphone, so people can put up their hands and ask a question or make a comment. The first person to speak is an old man in a grey coat.

"This is a stupid waste of money," he says. "We need to spend money on fixing our roads, not building expensive and pointless fountains."

"Thank you for sharing your point of view," says Clodagh, showing what I think is an impressive amount of restraint.

"I've always wanted to go to Rome and see the fountains," says an old lady with a sun hat covered in a strawberry print. "Or at least to Kansas City, the Fountain Capital of the Midwest. I think this sounds just divine."

"I think you should resign as Melting Queen," says a woman with wiry red hair. "I'm not an intolerant person, but I think that this whole genderfluid thing is just an excuse for a man to muscle his way into a sacred women's tradition."

"I agree with that lady who just spoke," says a young man with a British accent. "There are two genders, male and female. You're clearly just a man who likes to wear women's clothing and makeup sometimes. And sure, if that's what you want to do, whatever. But that doesn't make you another gender, and it shouldn't make you Melting Queen."

"I like the idea of having a fountain," says a young man with a little black dog. "But I don't want it to be downtown. People downtown get everything. You should build it in a new neighbourhood and make it a real destination where people want to go."

"I think it's fine that you identify as whatever gender you want," says a girl with a prosthetic arm. "What it means to be a man or a woman changes all the time throughout history anyways, and like everything else we do gender is just a big incompetent mess of made-up bullshit that we think is important, and human civilization is going to collapse soon anyways because of climate change. So do whatever you want and enjoy your life while you still can. Oh and the fountain idea seems cool. Go for it."

"I think building a fountain is a bad idea in a city that's frozen for half the year," says a woman with a sunburn. "Let's build a big teepee where we can have sweats down in the river valley instead."

"I'm not opposed to this fountain," says a man bouncing a baby on his knee. "But I think that you shouldn't've said those nasty things about Edmonton at your coronation. I think you should apologize."

"I don't think you have anything to apologize for," says a woman with mermaid tattoos on her arms. "What you said about Edmonton is so true. It's a breath of fresh air to have a Melting King. And if you think that this fountain is the best way to fix Edmonton, then I'm all for it."

The conversation continues like this for an hour, everybody sharing their ideas and opinions, about the fountain and about me. I'm surprised that most people seem on board with our project. But I suppose that the people who gathered for our announcement were already inclined to support us.

Kaseema announces the launch of our website, where we'll hopefully get more feedback from Edmontonians and keep everyone updated on the process. Clodagh and I spend the rest of the afternoon meeting with individual picnickers, hearing ideas, taking photos, and in my case listening to whispered confessions. It drains me, but I finally have the energy for it. This project has brought me back to life as much as it has for Clodagh. For the first time in months, I want something. Even if it's just this one small thing, for just this one person. I have a vision of the future where I exist and where the world is a little bit better—and it's *my* vision, not an Intrusion from someone else's life. And that keeps me strong, and makes me happier than I've been in a long time.

Over the next few days, we see results pouring in on our site. Lots of it is abuse and threats that people are too cowardly to make in person. But some of it contains interesting ideas and suggestions. Based on one of them, we decide to do a comprehensive review of Edmonton's existing fountains and document this journey on our site to build enthusiasm.

We float in the reflecting pool in front of the Legislature. We feed magpies beside the Ortona Memorial Fountain in Giovanni Caboto Park. We watch kids splashing under the water arches in front of City Hall. We picnic beneath the rusting iron sculpture fountains at the University of Alberta. We pour laundry detergent into the fountain in Alexander Circle Park and watch the suds build up in delicate mounds. We take a paddleboat in lazy circles around the jet d'eau in Rundle Park. We speak with people everywhere, trying to convince them of our cause.

Drawing upon the ideas on our website, we draft a series of sketches with our fountain designers, trying to create our masterpiece. Many of our imaginary fountains can freeze in the winter into skating ponds, like the fountain at City Hall. One of them involves damming up Mill Creek and reshaping it into a series of cascading pools. One of them is not so much a fountain as a structure of mist-gates. One of them is an Edmonton cliché: a giant glass pyramid that people can walk into, with water constantly running down its sloped sides.

I like all of these ideas, but it feels as if something big is still missing. When that hidden detail reveals itself, then the rest of the design will come.

Which is why I go to West Edmonton Mall, to scrape the bottom of the barrel for creative possibilities. We left mall fountains off our original list. But the mega-mall has its share of water features, and its massive indoor waterpark is itself a testament to the powerful allure of aquascapes.

West Edmonton Mall has been Edmonton's dubious claim to fame for forty years. The sprawling consumerist temple takes up two dozen city blocks, making it North America's largest mall. In addition to its thousand stores, it also features a full-size replica of the *Santa Maria*; a revolving array of exotic animals; an indoor theme-park where several people died on a roller coaster in 1986; a white marble statue of Augustus Caesar which presides over the largest food court; and dozens of people who've memorized the floorplan of this enormous building so thoroughly that they can live illegally in its hidden service corridors, without fear of ever being caught by the private army of security guards who seek to evict them.

I walk through the crowd, trying to ignore the noise and brightness and focus on the feeling of the space, the ideas that it inspires. The mall is designed to be deliberately disorienting, to trap you inside so that you spend more money like at a casino. I weave around distracted shoppers who stare into their phones and swat away their children, past the aggressive kiosk vendors who try to sell me remote control drones, past the old brown women who sweep up trash.

In the middle of one of the bubbling fountains that separates the two walking lanes from each other is an enormous bronze whale. It's been here since I was a kid, one of the hundred random features of this hodgepodge mall. I've always enjoyed walking down into its belly. I peek into its mouth to check if anyone is sitting on the bench at the end.

The whale is vacant, so I step down into its belly and escape the din of the retail floor. I settle onto the bronze bench—worn down into ridges and polished to a gleam by a hundred thousand bums—and watch the shoppers milling past. They seem far away, at the end of a long tunnel. None of them sees me down here, which is just fine by me. A red light in the roof of the whale's mouth makes everything inside glow. I close my eyes and listen to the sound of my breathing echoing through the bronze cavern, along with the tinkling of the fountains outside. Clodagh's right. I feel impossibly peaceful in the midst of all this chaos.

"So who's stalking who, really?" calls a voice, breaking into my meditation. I open my eyes and see René Royaume standing at the top of the steps in silhouette.

"Who's stalking whom," I correct. René clomps down into the whale. He's wearing a Miles Hortons apron and visor. His hair is in a bun, and he has dark circles under his eyes that no makeup can hide.

"Did you get fired again?"

"No," he glowers. "I'm on my break."

He plops down beside me.

"I wonder how many people come in here and don't make out," he says, running his hand over the names and heart-ringed initials which have been carved into the walls (along with several phone numbers).

"That's kind of a lazy chat-up line," I say. He rewards me with another scowl.

"You're not my type," he says. He holds up a paper bag.

"What's this?"

"Milestones," he says. "Want one?" He shakes the bag of doughnut holes.

"I don't know. Is your own little poison stone crouched in there somewhere?"

"Don't make fun of my mental illness," he says bluntly. "And I'm not telling you if it's in there. You'll never know unless you reach inside."

I take the bait, pull out a Milestone, take a bite. Dark chocolate with pomegranate jelly.

"Yum. So you work at West Edmonton Mall now?"

"Ugh I know, rub it in. I hate this place."

"It's not so bad," I say. René inspires the devil's advocate in me.

"It's awful," he whines. "It's the worst place in the city."

"You have to admit that it's kind of impressive. At least from an organizational standpoint."

"Yeah, in the way that factory farming is impressive from an organizational standpoint. In the way that the Holocaust was impressive from an organizational standpoint."

"Wow, are you sure you want to make that comparison?"

"I think that it conveys how strongly I'm disgusted by this mall. People boast about the fact that even though we lost the title of World's Largest Mall to China, we still have the World's Largest Parking Lot here. That's all you need to know about Edmonton."

"I don't know. It's good for people to be proud of something. We've got to work with what we've got. Maybe Edmonton isn't so bad after all."

"Oh god, you've really drunk the Kool-Aid. Next thing I know you're gonna be telling me how Edmonton is really Canada's hidden gem, a diamond in the rough, a dirty geode that sparkles on the inside. BARF."

René snorts at his own mockery and then slides down the back of the whale's mouth until he's practically horizontal on the bench, his legs sticking out in front of us. He tilts his face up to look at mine. I look pointedly out the whale's mouth.

"Shouldn't you get back to work?"

"I can be late. What are they going to do, fire me?"

"Uh yeah, they could."

"Then I'll get another job."

"How many jobs have you had?"

"I don't know. Who has time to remember those sorts of statistics?"

I study René's face in the red glow. The way he's sitting gives him three chins, and his dark eyes look extremely sleepy.

"What do you want from me, René Royaume? Seriously. Why do we keep running into each other everywhere?"

He shrugs.

"It must be destiny. Which I'm cool with. You're an interesting supporting character in the story of my life. Eddie Redmayne can play you in the movie adaptation."

"I think I'm more of a Tilda Swinton."

"Ha! You wish. Anyways, we should officially be friends."

"I have enough friends."

"Oh yeah, the nerd and the liar. Where were they when you had your seizures?"

"I'll remind you that your own record is only one for two on that count."

"Well, I'm improving."

"Yeah, good for you."

René falls silent. I watch the shoppers ambling by with their plastic bags swinging from their arms. After a while I notice René staring up at me.

"What?"

"Nothing," he sighs. "I have to get back to work."

He shimmies to his feet.

"Walk me back," he says.

"I think I'll stay."

"It'll do you good to get out of this whale," he says, offering his hand.

"I love this whale. I've always loved this whale."

"Oh god," he laughs. "You're really beyond hope, aren't you? I don't know why I bother."

I grumble and clamber to my feet, stooped over in the whale's belly.

"Wow, you are unfortunately tall," says René.

"I'm not tall, you're just short."

"I'm not short, I'm just very far away."

I roll my eyes and laugh as I follow him back up into the lanes of shoppers. He leads me through the mall, past the *Santa Maria* and the decommissioned submarines, past the New Orleans-style Bourbon Street, past the waterpark and the Ice Palace skating rink.

I shiver. Even up on the second level I feel a chill from the ice below. Maybe we shouldn't have a fountain that freezes. Skating is all well and good, but what everyone really wants in the winter is to be warmed up.

"I'm super bored," says René as we enter the Miles Hortons, which overlooks the skating rink. I'm surprised that it's completely empty, considering that there are apparently forty thousand people in the mall at any given time. "If you promise to stick around and chat until my shift is done I'll make you The Great One for free."

"What's The Great One?"

"It's our legendary, off-the-menu Miles Hortons drink. It's like a double-double but it's nine creams-nine sugars. Get it? After Wayne Gretzky. Number 99."

"That sounds horrifying. I think I'll pass."

"Your loss. I drink one every day."

René struts across the café and goes behind the counter. I sit down in the middle of the empty coffee shop and look up at the TV screen hanging on the far wall. Kastevoros Birch's face is on it. He's being interviewed by Rosemary Silt on *EdmonTonight*.

"—unprecedented, yes, but not unforeseen," Birch is saying.

He pauses dramatically, flips open a leather folder. Rosemary Silt sits across the table from him, food conspicuously absent from her wide desk.

"I have here an original copy of the Melting Day Proclamation, the founding document of the Old Lore, set forth by the eight thousand citizens of Edmonton on March 20th, 1904. The first Melting Day."

Birch removes the yellowed paper from its plastic sheath and stretches it out towards Rosemary. The host reaches out her hands and Birch hesitates, drawing it back.

"This is one of only three surviving copies."

"I'll be careful," says Rosemary in an irritated tone. I cheer her on for this rare moment of emotion. Normally she's a master of the poker face.

"As you can see," carries on Birch, "one of the most famous articles of the Old Lore is written right at the top. Number three, which creates the position of Melting Queen."

He reads it out as the camera zooms in on the paper.

ARTICLE III.

And on that glorious day—that splendid, shining, singular moment of the year—the people of Edmonton shall be led by One Woman. A daughter of the city, the mother of its people, the Melting Queen shall embody the spirit of the city, proclaim our victory over the Long Winter, and lead a Parade of Revellers, who dance with joy to see a shattered river.

"And if you'll look farther down the page, I'm sure you'll take an interest in Article Six," says Birch. "You'll notice the incredibly harsh wording, and the fact that it is the only article which our forefathers saw fit to exclaim, and not just state."

ARTICLE VI.

Woe to the woman who, once Named, refuses to heed the call of service to her city! Woe to Edmonton should she deny her sacred duty! She shall be Melting Queen, and nothing in Heaven or Earth shall prevent it. For once one is Named, she cannot be changed. She who flees the call incurs a curse on our city. Let history forget her name. Let her memory be damned.

Birch recites these articles from memory, drilling his eyes into the camera, cheeks flushed like a brimstone preacher. He turns to Rosemary and continues in a calm and condescending voice. "But I want you to look at Article Number 15."

Rosemary tracks her eyes over the blank space at the end of the long page, then flips it over to find another item in bright black ink.

"Read it," whispers Birch.

Rosemary looks at her guest for a tense second, then turns her eyes back to the page and speaks.

ARTICLE XV.
And last of all, should a Melting Queen be Absolutely Unable to fulfill her Sacred Trust, the Good People of Edmonton shall be called upon to appoint Another to serve in her place.

She trails off, realizes what she's said, jerks her head up at Birch.

"Go on." The old man smiles like a wolf.

Rosemary frowns down at the page. Speaking softly, she finishes reading Article 15.

And should this Sad Event occur, a General Consensus shall be required among Edmontonians, so that she who is Late-Named, like every Melting Queen from First to Last, shall surely embody the Spirit of Spring.

I'm frozen. I look over at René, who frowns at the TV.

"If someone is totally unsuited to serve as Melting Queen, then they must go," says Birch. "Clearly River Runson—or, to use *his* real name, Adam Truman—meets this criterion. It is up to Edmonton to choose an appropriate replacement. Luckily, we've already found a suitable woman for the job."

Birch's smile broadens. He looks directly into the camera, his face looming over us. We're silent, tense, waiting, wondering how it can get any worse.

"We humbly submit this wonderful candidate for your consideration, Edmonton. All that remains is for the referendum we're circulating to pass—as I'm sure it will—and then she will be Queen. It may be premature to say it, but here she is: please welcome this year's *true* Melting Queen, Olechka Stepanchuk!"

No.

No. No no this isn't happening this isn't real. This isn't possible.

Odessa comes out and sits next to Birch. She's wearing a modest pink dress which shows her baby bump and a platinum blonde wig woven in a Tymoshenko Crown. Her tattoos have been covered with makeup. Her smile is radiant.

"Olechka is a kindergarten teacher," says Birch. "She's been very active in her local community for years, and is about to welcome her first child."

Rosemary seems just as wrong-footed as the rest of us. But she gathers her wits far quicker than I can. She asks Odessa some questions about her work and her life, and I can only stare at my friend. Why are you doing this? Is this a joke? Is there going to be some subversive turnaround, some prank to embarrass Birch?

But she just sits there, smiling, talking about being an expectant mother and how excited she is to fill Edmonton with new life and joy.

Soon, Rosemary recovers from her shock and realizes that she let Kastevoros Birch and Odessa Steps hijack her show. She interrupts Odessa.

"So let me get this straight: River Runson has agreed to step aside and name Olechka Stepanchuk in their place?"

Odessa nods sympathetically, knits her brow. Her voice is buttery soft.

"Adam Truman is going through a lot of soul-searching right now, and this is the worst possible time to have such an enormous responsibility thrust upon him. He's not able to—"

There's a crackle of static and the screen sizzles to black. I look around and see that René is standing behind me, pointing a remote at the TV.

"What are you doing? Put it back on!"

"No," he says.

"Put it back on. I need to see." My voice trembles. "I need to see when she embarrasses Birch. It's a joke. Don't you understand? It's a piece of her performance artwork. She's mocking them, we just haven't got to the big reveal yet. Put it back on!"

René shakes his head. I lunge at him, try to claw the remote out of his hands.

"Put it back on you asshole! We'll miss it!"

"River."

"PUT IT BACK ON! WHAT ARE YOU DOING? GIVE ME THE FUCKING REMOTE!"

I almost twist the remote from René's hands. He snatches it back from me, throws it down and it shatters on the floor.

"WHY DID YOU DO THAT?"

"River, listen. I'm sorry. I know she's your friend but she's—"

"She's pulling a prank. It has to be a prank. It's artwork, that's her thing. She's crazy and unexpected sometimes but she's my friend. She wouldn't. She wouldn't. She'd never do it."

René comes towards me, arms spread, and I feel the familiar panic shoot up my neck from the base of my spine. I stumble back. No. This isn't happening. It's a prank. He'll see.

I race through the mall, pushing through the crowd, ignoring the gazes of a hundred people who probably want to come and fill me up with more misery. My mind is spinning in circles. I can't control my thoughts. But my feet carry me back to a safe place.

Down in the whale, in the dim red light, I feel the tears starting to flow. I haven't cried in so long. In six months, or six years, or more. I never let myself cry. I never let myself really feel anything. But now the dam breaks. *She betrayed you. For fame. For nothing. For a moment in the limelight.* My tears leave stinging tracks on my face and my sobs echo through the whale and there's no Melting Queen to come and comfort me.

{12}

The Melting Queen
shall brook no rival

"Anechka, she always has many stories to tell."

Ludlow Spetnik sips his tea and looks off into the distance across the dining hall, staring into the thick fog of his memories. I focus my eyes over his shoulder, at the sliding doors which lead out to the care home's parking lot.

"Brilliant stories, crazy stories from my Anechka! Impossible stories. But they have truth, this I know. I doubt her, I think 'surely this one is too much to be believed!' And sure enough I find some proof that shows it is so."

He looks down at his hands and toys with the monogrammed handkerchief in his lap. He becomes absorbed in working his fingers over the tiny pink roses sewn into the cloth.

"And they were always true?" I ask, repeating myself for the tenth or eleventh time. We've cycled through the same conversation so many times that I know exactly what I have to say. He looks up at me, seems surprised to see a person sitting here across from him.

"Anechka's stories?" I prompt.

His face lights up and he gives a dry chuckle. His laugh ignites a series of coughs. "You say Anechka! To you she is Anna. To me she is Anechka."

"But Anna told stories," I continue.

"Anna, yes. Anechka, she told the most amazing stories. Places she goes and peoples she meets and dangers she finds her ways out of, always. And all the fellows she goes with! They call her Anechka, Anyutka."

He chuckles, looks down and sees the mug of tea in his hand, takes a sip.

"I never call her *my* Anechka," he says. "I never say, 'look here, I own this Anna.' We never marry—marriage no good for Anechka. So I never say 'you are mine, doll.'"

He grins at me as if this is the most topical cultural reference, sure to impress. I can't help but crack up at his awful attempt at some sort of Humphrey-Bogart-in-*Casablanca*, 1940s American accent. The skin arounds his eyes crinkles with joy at my laughter and I feel a pang of guilt. I didn't expect to like him so much.

"Maybe this is why she stays with me until the end, and not with any others. I think sometimes, 'Ludlow, maybe there are no others, and she tells you stories to make you jealous!'"

He lifts his eyebrows and gives me a wide-eyed grin.

"Even if there were no others, they were real to her," he says. "And they became real to me too. She tells me about this Jack, the Painter, and comes back with portraits he makes for her. And this Joe, the Dentist, who likes that she bites him as they make love."

He settles a weighty gaze on me. He doesn't blink.

"And then there is me. Nothing special about Ludlow. But I think I am Ludlow the Listener. Maybe she tells the others all her stories too. But I don't think this is so."

He finishes his tea and looks at my face for a minute, frowning. I can never hide the masculinity of my features, nor do I fully want to, and today they are festooned with feminine flourishes, a sculpted eyebrow and a painted lip. I've unwoven my hair crown, and it tumbles around my shoulders. I wonder if Odessa's grandfather thinks I'm a man or a woman.

But Ludlow Spetnik is probably just trying to remember if he knows me or not.

"Maybe there were no others," he repeats, looking down at the table. "Maybe she believes in them but they aren't real, and she convinces me because she is convinced."

He looks up at me again and the dark cloud blows away off his face. He smiles.

"But it does not matter. I love her and her stories. I let her go away and I hope she comes back and she does, always. I forgive her when she hurts me. That's when you know you love: when you forgive anything."

The sliding doors open and I hold my breath. But it's only an elderly woman returning from the farmers' market, pushing a walker with bundles of leeks and chives in its basket.

"No," I say, waiting for Odessa to appear. "Sometimes you can love someone and still not be able to forgive them."

"I think your mind, it will change when you have love," says the old man, struggling to rip open the plastic seal on his butterscotch pudding. "When you find one who is worth love, then you will forgive them anything."

I take the butterscotch pudding and open it for him. The door slides open again and I turn my eyes expectantly to the entrance. I've been sitting here all morning, having the same few conversations over and over with this old man, waiting for Odessa to get here and see me with her grandfather. She'll freeze, and she'll feel fear, and she'll feel violated. She'll understand how *I* felt when she chose the spotlight over our friendship. I'm not proud of myself for stooping to her level, but it's the only way I can think to get through to her. I have intruded on her safe ground, interfered with the one person she might actually care about. And just for a second, before our inevitable confrontation, her face will show a real emotion, not a manufactured one.

Over the past week, Odessa has become the Queen of Lies. Immediately after Birch's grand announcement, ECHO flooded the city with images of their usurper Melting Queen. Her smiling face is everywhere: beaming from billboards, flashing her perfect white teeth on the front page of the *Bulletin*, smirking on the sides of buses and taxis.

ECHO publishes ludicrous facts about her accomplishments. She's donated no less than three kidneys to dying children. She rescued a two-legged dog from drowning in the river. She pulled a pregnant woman from a burning car.

Even worse are their propaganda videos, which play at every commercial break and bounce around social media ceaselessly. Odessa speaks sanctimoniously into the camera, unspooling lie upon lie. She builds up an immaculate image of herself as the perfect Melting Queen and me as the defective, offensive parody.

"I'm a fifth-generation Edmontonian, born and raised," she says, standing between two actors who've been hired to play her parents. "My mother is a nurse and my father works for an oil sands developer."

"We're expecting our first child," she says, standing in the arms of a handsome young man who's been hired to play her husband. "I know it's cliché, but we had the classic high-school-sweethearts story."

"I'm proud of my Ukrainian heritage," she says, standing in front of a billowing blue-and-yellow flag. "My ancestors were farmers, and lived off the land of Alberta."

"Adam Truman wants to spend millions of taxpayer dollars building a pointless fountain," she says, standing in front of the Legislature fountains. "He thinks that Edmonton needs to copy Rome or Paris in order to be a great city." The images of falling water are intercut with slow-motion footage of my meltdown at the coronation, tinted red. The attack ad is almost comically bad, almost a parody of itself. But judging by the comments, people are lapping it up.

"I think that Edmonton needs to be a great version of Edmonton, not a poor copy of any other city," says Odessa, wearing an orange safety vest and helping a construction crew fill in some potholes. "I'm proud to be an Edmontonian, and I'll be proud to raise my children here."

"I'm honoured to carry on the tradition of brave women who served this city," she says, walking along the hall of Melting Queen portraits. "Women who carved out a place for the female voice in a man's world, who weren't afraid to do what is right rather than what is popular, who heard the cries of their people and offered their firm but gentle support in a way that only a mother can."

She stands before the Spring Throne, surrounded by a group of women with a rainbow of skin tones. The casual viewer, unversed in local history, would probably assume that these actors are the former Melting Queens. Odessa holds a random baby in her arms, and her cheeks burn with passion as her eyes bore into the camera.

"Never Send a Man to do a Woman's Job," she says with melodramatic flair.

#NeverSendAMan hovers on the screen for a few seconds, followed by "Vote Yes on August 31." The video has been shared over 15,000 times.

The city has been split in two. A great divide. Everyone is picking a side. No one seems to have officially organized it, but the two rival factions have each claimed one of the Melting Queen's colours, dividing into the Pinks and the Greens. Odessa's supporters wear pink in an explicit celebration of her gender. My supporters are little green thorns in the rose-choked landscape, with felt patches on their arms and brave hearts.

The Greens still come up and talk to me, seeking comfort, sharing their stories. But now the Pinks are here to shout them down, threaten me with violence. I thought things were getting better. For the shortest of periods, it felt like Edmonton was ready to give a great collective shrug to the issue of my gender identity. But my detractors were just lurking in the shadows, waiting for a figurehead to rally around. Now, their anger has been legitimized. They know they'll be shamed by the politically correct, ivory tower, outraged-by-everything brigade. But they have strength in numbers now, and they feel comfortable claiming the moral high ground.

The people who come up to me offering support and seeking solace find themselves surrounded by jeering crowds. Some are driven by a primal urge to defend me, and fight off my enemies. I try to defuse dozens of fights, but I always end up having to flee the scene to escape escalating violence. After a couple days, I stop going out. It's not worth risking people's safety. Better to be out of sight, even if I can't be out of mind.

I thought that Kaseema might jump ship, abandon me for Odessa. My rival is the ideal Melting Queen: pregnant, popular, perfect with crowds. But Kaseema stays by my side with Clodagh, immediately organizing a counter-campaign.

We move our base of operations into Clodagh's house, and Kaseema starts recruiting volunteers to campaign for me. They scurry around, making signs and pamphlets and phone calls, stopping me every so often to give me a hug or a word of encouragement—which inevitably leads to me comforting them in the spare bedroom while they sob out their miseries.

Clodagh has been fighting valiantly to continue work on the fountain, but nobody seems to care about our glorious project anymore. Not when Odessa is everywhere, drawing attention to a thousand injustices: the women's shelter that had its funding slashed; the families whose children are getting sick from industrial pesticides; the workers who've been laid off following the candy factory closure while the CEO got a $20 million bonus. She's on the front lines, fighting for the people, and everyone is slowly but surely falling in love with her brave words and beautiful face.

But it's not her face that I see come through the care home's doors, breaking me out of my thoughts. Now that Sander Fray has woken up to the world and eaten half the city, he's full of vitality and vigour. I haven't seen him since we moved to Clodagh's house. I wonder if he's tracked me down, come to make peace in our triad. If he thinks he's here to engineer a reconciliation, he's in for a letdown.

"What are you doing here?" he asks, eyes shining. Much like Edmonton, Sander has been fully restored to the radiant beauty of his summer self.

"What are *you* doing here?" I snap. He shrinks back and I feel instantly guilty. He's not Odessa. I shouldn't treat him like this just because he's my closest substitute for her. I sigh and shake my head and run my fingers through my limp orange hair.

"I'm sorry, Sander. I'm here to confront Odessa and force her to tell me the truth after all these lies. She's done some insane things in the past—like that time she broke her rib when that giant vulva sculpture she was building out of porn magazines in Churchill Square collapsed on top of her, or all those times she was arrested for public nudity during her Asking For It project—but this is on a whole other level. This isn't something that we're going to rescue her from. This isn't something she can just walk away from."

"I'm on your side," says Sander. "I can understand why part of her thinks this is a good idea, but I know that she's going to regret this. I tried to talk to her, but she won't answer my calls. I left her a bunch of voicemails, though."

"It looks like she's found herself some new friends," I say bitterly.

Ludlow Spetnik twists around in his wheelchair and looks up at Sander.

"Who is this bright boy? Come sit here and I will make us tea."

Sander hesitates a moment, then takes the chair beside Ludlow Spetnik, who shoves a plate of biscuits towards him.

"I don't think you fully understand her motives," says Sander, beginning what I'm sure will be a long apologist essay explaining Odessa's choices. But he doesn't get a chance to continue, because the next thing I know, Odessa Steps enters and breezes up to the table.

"Hello Papa," she coos as she drapes her hands across her grandfather's shoulders and leans down and kisses his cheek. She doesn't seem at all scared or shamed or threatened by me.

"Ah, Alina!"

Ludlow Spetnik raises his hand and pats Odessa's. She gives him a warm smile which only brightens when she turns her gaze on me.

"You are done your lunch, yes?" she says to her grandfather.

"I am talking with this strange lady," whispers Ludlow loudly, gesturing at me. "I am telling her stories of your Mama."

"He's been telling me about your grandmother," I say. "Apparently she made up countless lies about herself. I guess it runs in the family."

Odessa laughs as she sits in the remaining chair.

"Papa," she says through her wide smile, "this one used to be my good friend, but now we are in a fight. They have something I want. They had a chance to do something great, but they threw it all away. So now I have to take up the torch, and do what they failed to do."

Ludlow looks between me and his granddaughter, his bushy white eyebrows drawn in concern.

"If she is friend, you two, you must not be fighting. You share."

"What if it's not something that can be shared, Papa?"

"Then one of you will have it and one of you will not have it. The one who cares more for her friend will let her friend have it. She will be happy for her friend! This is a true friend who does this."

I skewer Odessa with my most disgusted look.

"Even your own grandfather tells you to drop this. To stop all your lies."

She gives me an infuriating, patronizing smile.

"Ugh, lighten up, River. Of course I'm telling lies! I love lying. You know this. I do it all the time. So does everyone. So do you. Lies are how we create our identities. We're all just playing characters, putting on masks and projecting certain images of ourselves into the world. You're just playing River Runson, and he's just playing Sander Fray, and now I'm playing Olechka Stepanchuk."

She leans forward, invading my personal space. I can feel her body heat and smell the scent of her grandfather's musty cologne. Her grey eyes drill into mine. Her platinum blonde wig is aggressively bright. She smirks as if we're sharing an inside joke.

"Olechka's pretty horrible, isn't she? I mean it's fun to play the most stereotypical Edmontonian possible—especially because most people are idiots and don't realize that I'm making fun of their bullshit—but I'm still horrified. I didn't think I had it in me to be the darling of these paleoconservatives. Believe me, I regret having to act like such a transphobe. It disgusts me. But if this is what I have to do to make some real changes to this shitheap of a city, then that's what I'll do. I'll play Birch's game for as long as I have to—he really hates you, I think he offered me the job just to spite you—because in the end the people of Edmonton deserve a Melting Queen who challenges the established order and fixes real problems, not just yet another figurehead who works on some decorative project."

"This isn't about Edmonton," I say. "This is about *you*, just like it's always been. You don't care about 'the people' at all. You don't have any empathy."

"Oh come on River," she rolls her eyes. "You know just as well as I do that you shouldn't be the Melting Queen. You didn't even want this job! And when someone shows up who actually wants to do this, then you have a change of heart? I'm giving you an out. I'm doing what you've wanted me to do from the start. That's why you came to me first, and not Sander or anyone else. You know that *I* should do this, that *I* need this, and that you need to give it up."

A deeply concerned, sympathetic smile replaces the humour on Odessa's face. Her emotions seem so manufactured, just like my mother's always are. Was Odessa always this fake? Was she always putting on an act, trying to manipulate her audience? I don't know how I never saw it before.

"I don't want to humiliate you," she says, knitting her brows in a practised way that makes me want to rip her wig off. "I know it's hard for you to believe, but I *am* really disgusted by some of the things that I have to say about you as I play Olechka Stepanchuk. It would be better for you to just step gracefully aside and not get in the way. Honestly, I think this is what's best for both of us. We both know I'm going to beat you if we ever get to a vote."

"I don't know how I was ever friends with you," I say. "That's how bad this is. I look at you and I can't even see a trace of that person I used to like."

Odessa glances at her grandfather, who has rediscovered his butterscotch pudding and is wiping a dab of it off his vest.

"So your plan was to come here and ambush me?" she says. "Which would make me realize the error of my ways?'

Odessa is smiling wide again, as if this is all some big joke. I realize that I'm never going to get through to her by arguing with her. She thrives off confrontation.

I take a deep breath and set my hands down on the tabletop. I look into Odessa's eyes and feel my cheeks heat up as I force myself to say it.

"You know I've always envied you. You know that, right?"

It makes me ashamed to admit it. But this is my confession, to this false Melting Queen.

"I always wanted your life. To be as bold and fearless and shameless as you, to travel the world like you do. But now the tables have finally turned and I'm the one who has something and you're the one who's jealous. I have one good thing. I didn't like it at first. I didn't want it. But now I know that it's what I have to do. For Clodagh. It's important to me. And as soon as you saw that, you decided to take it from me. Because I have to be your little audience and that's all I'm allowed to be."

I look at Sander, whose eyes flick nervously between me and Odessa.

"That was always the unspoken agreement between the three of us, wasn't it? Sander and I would be your perfect audience and applaud you, and you would be the dazzling spectacle. You'd do dangerous, impressive things and we would gasp with delight and save you when you got in trouble. No matter how many other people got hurt, we would always be safe. We were always exempt from the chaos, shielded from the bomb we helped set off. But not anymore."

I look down at the table, shake my head in frustration.

"You have everything, Odessa. Everything. Why do you have to have this too?"

Odessa stares at me for a long time, smile frozen on her face. Then she turns and takes a napkin and wets it with her tongue and wipes at the pudding stain on her grandfather's sweater.

"Alright," she says. "Fine. You're right. I'm being really shitty to you. I'm letting these old conservative people tell me what to do. I'm opportunistic. I'm exploiting the situation to my own ends, and ultimately all I want is publicity and attention. I'm a terrible person. Is that what you want me to say?"

Sander looks back and forth between us, holding his breath, a biscuit held forgotten in his fingers. I can tell that he's hoping we're on the cusp of a ceasefire.

"No," I say. "I don't want you to say something just because you think I want to hear it. I want you to tell the truth. I want some honesty for once."

I look at Ludlow Spetnik, Odessa's only point of vulnerability. He's been picking at the scab on the back of his hand, totally engrossed, ignoring all of us.

"Why don't you tell *him* what you've been telling everyone? About your loving parents and your gorgeous husband. About your sudden love for Edmonton—a place you never seemed to give a shit about before last week."

Odessa's smile has hardened on her face. She's adopting it as a defensive posture now, clinging to her "I'm-above-all-this" humour. But I can tell I'm finally getting through to her.

"Lie to him," I say. "Lie to his face."

Odessa's rigid smirk remains, but she blinks a few times as she looks at her grandfather.

"But I do lie to him," she says. "I *have* to lie to him." Her voice cracks and she looks away. She pauses, takes a breath, then forces a smile and looks back at Ludlow Spetnik.

"Gido," she says, placing her hand gently over her grandfather's. "The nurse said you should not scratch at that. Or it will never get well."

"Ah, Alina!" Ludlow looks up and smiles at Odessa, then glances at Sander and I. "These people, they are friends of yours?"

"No, Gido. They used to be but not anymore."

"Why you say 'Gido?'" he asks, grinning bemusedly. "Your Gido, he is not living through the dark time you know. He is still in Ukrayina, beneath the ground."

"No, Gido. That was Alina's grandfather. I am Alina's daughter. So you are my Gido. You are my grandfather."

Ludlow frowns at Odessa, wets his chapped lips with his tongue, stares at her for several long seconds.

"You are not Alina?" he says, his voice laced with doubt.

"No, Gido. I am Odessa," she says. "Alina was my mother. You are my Gido."

She pats her grandfather's hand reassuringly, but he draws it back from her, frowning in confusion.

"Where is Alina? *You* are Alina. I know you, I know your face. My dochka. My Alinushka."

"No Gido," repeats Odessa, softly but firmly. "I am Odessa. Alina was my mother."

"You are not Alina? Where is Alina?"

"Alina is dead Gido," says Odessa. "We buried her. Beneath the ground. You just don't remember."

Ludlow stares at his granddaughter with disbelief written across his face. Then his sagging skin crumples and he lets out a low groan and looks down at the table.

Odessa turns back to me, and this time she doesn't bother to hide her pain and sadness.

"I am my mother," she says. "When I am here, I am Alina. Because he doesn't know who I am. He doesn't remember that I was ever born."

She turns back to her grandfather, who's rubbing his dribbling nose with the back of his hand. She pulls his handkerchief out of his breast pocket and offers it to him.

"So I lie," she says quietly, turning back to me. "Because otherwise I have to have this conversation every time, a dozen times. And hurt him every time."

Her eyes shimmer with tears and she wipes them away angrily.

"So don't say that I don't have any empathy. That I don't care about my family. Because I do. And don't say that I have everything and you have nothing. Because you have a family, you have a whole community of your university friends, even if you've chosen to cast them all aside. This is all the family I have. I do everything I can to keep it safe, but I know that any day I'm going to see the nursing home number on my phone, and they're going to tell me that I don't have a family anymore."

Our eyes meet and I see her in there for the first time, huddling behind her bravado. I know she's surprised too—she didn't ever want to show that to anyone and here it is. I open my mouth but I don't know what to say. I feel my hand sliding across the table towards her.

Her pupils swell and consume me and everything is blackness.

All the grown-ups look angry. I stand in front of them on the hill and they look at me like I did something bad. I know they're supposed to put the flowers on my head soon and I'm supposed to sit on that old tree stump. But they all look so mean. So angry.

I'm scared. I want to go back to mummy but I'm not supposed to. I'm supposed to say some special words but I don't remember what they are.

One of the grown-ups shouts something, and then they're turning their backs one by one. They're not leaving the park, they're just standing there. Facing away from me. Because I'm the wrong one. I shouldn't be here. I made a mess of everything.

I feel a wave of nausea strike me and I see Sander Fray's face looming over mine. I'm mesmerized by the blackness of his eyes and the yellow shirt he's wearing and the painful brightness of the ceiling light. I've never noticed the details of Sander's face like this: the tiny blackheads that pepper his nose, the chip in one tooth, the couple stray hairs that he failed to shave off at the corner of his mouth.

"What happened?" he asks. "Who were you?"

I look around me. I'm lying in a hospital bed.

"Where am I? How long was I out? Where's Odessa? Where's her grandfather?"

"You're still at the nursing home. We had to move you."

"And Odessa?"

"She's gone. Ludlow is back in his room. But Isobel let us stay here until you woke up."

"What are you talking about? Who's Isobel?"

Sander looks toward the armchair in the corner, where what I thought was an old orange blanket is thrown across the faded flower-print brocade. But now I see that my eyes lied to me. It's an old woman, as tiny and thin as anyone I've ever seen.

"You asked me why I was here," says Sander. "I came here to visit her. River Runson, meet Isobel Fraser. Melting Queen number eight."

The old woman raises a couple fingers in greeting. She looks like E.T.

"I've been hearing a lot about you," she says. Her voice is thin and strained, but she sounds happy. "I never thought you'd come to see me."

I prop myself up against the headboard, and Sander sits back down on the end of the bed.

"I've been coming to visit Isobel since I decided to write a book about the Melting Queens and their Intrusions," he says. "There are countless stories about the Melting Queens performing miracles: summoning rains in times of drought, turning back crop-destroying hail storms, bringing dead people back to life. ECHO and Birch want everyone to think that the Melting Queen is magical, a goddess in human form. So why does nobody know about the Intrusions? It's a whole chapter of our history that's been covered up. And I'm going to find out why. I'm interviewing every Melting Queen who's still alive. People deserve to know the truth. If ECHO won't tell this story, then I will."

Sander looks to Isobel, who squints at us through her thick glasses.

"Isobel has been helping me. She's kept an eye on all the Melting Queens over the years, and she's almost as old as the tradition itself. She just turned one hundred and ten. We celebrated her birthday last Wednesday."

"It was lovely," says Isobel. "The cake was heavenly. They say I'm not supposed to have so much sugar. But I say: 'I'm a hundred and ten, I can eat whatever I want.' And Sander brought me this wonderful gift, here, let me show you."

Isobel reaches for a photo album on the table beside her, but it's too heavy for her to lift. Sander hops up and opens the album for her, placing it in her lap so she can flip through its pages. Isobel looks up at Sander with such palpable affection, and I feel a pang of bittersweet happiness for both of them.

"Come and see," says Isobel, so I get up off the bed and perch on her chair's armrest.

"Sander took all my old photos and organized them. I just had them in drawers and in boxes, I never took the time to arrange them all nicely like this. Look, there's me when I was crowned as Melting Queen."

She's standing on the hill in Coronation Park, a shy-looking girl in blurry black-and-white.

"Isobel was Named when she was four years old," says Sander.

"I was you," I say. "Just now, when I had the Intrusion. It was your coronation. Everyone turned their backs on you."

"They hated me at first," says Isobel. "They all said I would lead the city to its doom. Because I was from the wrong side of the river."

"What does that mean?"

"Edmonton used to be two cities," says Sander. "The City of Edmonton was on the north side of the river and the City of Strathcona was on the south side."

Isobel laughs creakily.

"Everybody in Edmonton was so angry," she says. "Melting Day was their tradition. Not ours. We could come across the river and celebrate, just like the people who started coming up from Calgary. But we were visitors. We were guests. We weren't part of their sacred tribe."

She touches the old photo of herself, in her coronation best.

"My project was to unite Edmonton and Strathcona into one. We had a referendum, which everybody thought we would lose because everyone was so furious."

She turns over the page and I see another photo of her, noticeably bigger, riding a horse down Jasper Avenue.

"But we won. And then we weren't two cities anymore. We were one city, with a river running through it."

She brushes her fingers across a couple other photos on the page, a man and a woman who I assume are her parents, then sighs and closes the photo album. Sander helps her lift it up and put it back on the table. I go back to Isobel's bed and sit down on the end, watching as Sander brings the old Melting Queen another blanket.

Just like with Victoria and Iris and Clodagh, I can feel my connection to Isobel. As she moves her frail arms and slowly pulls the blanket up over herself, I feel it covering me too. Sitting on the edge of the bed, I feel as small and light as a feather, as if a strong gust of wind could blow me away. And, just like the others, I feel the weariness, the deep-seated fatigue.

"What did you do after you were Melting Queen?" I ask. "What was your life like?"

"Oh," says Isobel, "it wasn't a special life. I went to school, I was a secretary for a while, then I got married and had a family."

She places her hand back on the photo album but doesn't open it.

"I had some problems with my health," she says after a moment. "Well, I guess nowadays you'd say, I had some problems with depression. I wasn't a good wife. I wasn't a good mother. I did my best, but it wasn't good enough."

"I'm sure that's not true," I say. "And I'm sure your family loves you, no matter what. They probably told you as much at your birthday last week, right?"

Isobel sighs and looks out the window.

"All of them are dead," she says. "My husband, my children, my granddaughter. They all died, and I just kept living. I'm the only one left."

"I'm sorry," I say, not knowing what else to say.

"You know, before Sander came, no one had been to visit me in twenty-three years."

Isobel smiles sadly at Sander. He takes her hand in his and gives it a gentle squeeze. It feels like a deep, loving hug from an old friend you haven't seen in years.

"It makes no sense to me that Birch and ECHO would just abandon Isobel here," he says. "She's such a valuable source of information. She remembers everything. But nobody has ever come to ask her anything."

"Until you," says Isobel, smiling at Sander. She looks at me. "And you're the first Melting Queen who's visited me since Alma Lake, back in the early '50s. I've been watching the Melting Queens for a hundred years, but I've only met five."

"Victoria Goulburn told me that none of the Melting Queens would ever agree to a reunion, because our connection made things too uncomfortable," I say.

"That may be true," says Isobel. "But there's more to it than that, isn't there?"

"What do you mean?"

She looks at me like she's peering into my soul.

"There's something rotten at the heart of Melting Day," she says. "I don't know what it is, but I've been watching the Queens for a hundred years, and I've seen it over and over. Being the Melting Queen changes you, makes you less than you were before."

I feel the hairs rise along the back of my neck, a familiar sense of panic swelling up in me from somewhere deep below the surface. Sander nods in grim agreement with Isobel.

"I've been visiting the Melting Queens one after another," he says, "interviewing them and learning about their lives. I've met divorced Melting Queens and depressed Melting Queens and even one homeless Melting Queen. Some of them go on to brighter and better things after their terms are done. But most of them retreat from public life and struggle to recover from the intense psychological double whammy of Intrusions and Confessions."

"I don't want to blame being Melting Queen for every problem I had," says Isobel. "But not a day goes by where I don't wonder what my life would've been had I not been Named. Whether I would've had a normal, happy life. And I had it quite easy as Melting Queen. Edmonton didn't like me at first, but by the end of my term everyone was on my side. That hasn't been true for everyone."

Sander picks up Isobel's photo album and walks over to the bed. He sits next to me and flips to the back of the album, where the photos give way to newspaper clippings.

"I always thought I knew a lot about the Melting Queens," he says. "But I never realized how many of them were so unpopular in their own times. The official story of the Melting Queen is that she's our city's first lady, our universal mother, beloved by all. But so many of them have been 'wrong' in some way or other."

He points to a photo of a young Asian woman.

"May Abashiri was wrong because she was Japanese," he says. "She was born in Edmonton but she moved to the west coast when she was little. They had to go get her from an internment camp in Lethbridge when she was Named. And that was in 1945. Four months before the bombs."

He flips the page and points to another photo, an unsmiling queen.

"Jolene James was wrong because she was Indigenous, an 'Indian' Melting Queen. She didn't even get to have a signature initiative, because her whole term was dominated by the question of whether she should be allowed to stay on as Melting Queen."

Another, a queen I recognize.

"Iris Zambezi was wrong because she was a lesbian—and not just a lesbian, a big Black butch lesbian, barely even a woman at all."

He turns to look at me, a sombre expression on his face.

"Every first is fought," he says. "Every time a Melting Queen is something new—Irish, Indigenous, from Strathcona, whatever—everyone freaks out about it. What's happening now with you and Odessa isn't something new or exceptional. It's the norm."

I take the photo album from Sander, flip through its pages, see the parade of misfit Melting Queens amongst their more-acceptable sisters.

"Some of these Queens might have ruffled feathers," I say. "And I'm not saying that racism or homophobia aren't a big deal. But none of them were wrong like I'm wrong. Even if they were Black or Japanese or gay, they were all still women."

Isobel lifts her old, gnarled hand, beckoning me over.

"Come here," she says.

I put the photo album on the bed and walk over to her, stand beside her chair.

"Come closer," she says.

I kneel beside her chair, so that she can look down into my face. She reaches out and brushes my hair back from my face, touches my skin, traces the lines of my masculine jaw and my feminine eyebrow.

"I'd never heard of genderfluid before you came along," she says, pronouncing the word carefully. "I didn't get it at first. I just thought you were a young man who wanted to explore his feminine side. But I talked about it with Sander, and now I understand better. There are probably hundreds of people having conversations like Sander and me, because of you. It might not seem like it now, but you are changing things. Maybe by the end of the year, people will change their minds about you."

"Or maybe they'll all just vote for Odessa," I say.

"Maybe," says Sander. "But you can't just give up on yourself. To be honest, I didn't really understand when you first told us you didn't feel like a man anymore. I wanted to be a good friend and support you, but part of me just didn't get it. I read all the Wikipedia pages about being genderfluid and nonbinary, but those didn't help either. But then, as I was talking with Isobel about it, I realized that I *do* understand."

He stands up, goes over to Isobel's bookshelf and picks up a dust-capped globe.

"You know about the Demilitarized Zone in Korea, right? The DMZ?"

I nod as he brings the globe over and sets it on the floor in front of us.

"When my grandparents left Busan with my mom during the war, they made a promise. They wouldn't return home until their country was whole again. Not artificially divided into two. But unified. One Korea."

Sander scratches at the little Korean peninsula on the globe, as if he could erase the heavily guarded border with a swipe of his finger.

"I can only imagine what you're going through, River. But to me it seems like a reunification. We split our species into two genders, two completely opposite halves. They're not at war, but there is a DMZ dividing them. It's invisible, but it's just as heavily guarded, in its own way. We're just as upset by people going across it."

He spins the globe and an ice cap of dust disintegrates.

"I've never really talked about this with you and Odessa," he says, "but some days I feel really white. Really assimilated into my dad's Euro-Canadian culture. But most days I'm reminded of the fact that I'm also Asian—whether it's a white person complimenting my English or other Asians asking me what my real name is. But then, I'm also reminded that I'm not really Asian enough. I don't speak Korean very well, and my mom would kill me for saying this, but I don't really like her kimchi."

He smiles at me.

"So I guess what I'm saying is, at a certain level, I get you. I don't know what it feels like to be genderfluid. But I know what it's like to flow between two categories, depending on how you feel or who you're with. And if other people think about it, they'll realize that they probably feel the same way in some area of their lives. They probably understand better than they think they do."

I look between Sander and Isobel, this unlikely team that's knitting together an alternate history of the Melting Queens. I don't know how they found each other, but I'm happy for them. I wish I could share their optimism.

"I hope you're right," I say. "I hope I'll be an Isobel Fraser, and not a Jolene James. But I guess we'll just have to wait and see."

A chime rings out through the loudspeaker in the corner of Isobel's room.

"That's the bell for dinner," says Isobel. She presses a button and her chair starts lifting her slowly to her feet. "Will you stay and eat with us?"

"I don't think so," I say. "I think I need to get going. But thank you."

Sander takes Isobel's hand and helps her take a shaky step forward. He fetches her walker and we head downstairs to the dining hall.

"You're sure you can't stay?" asks Isobel as Sander goes to claim a table.

"No," I say. "I need to get back to Clodagh's house. But thank you, for everything."

I bend over and give her a light, careful hug.

"Please come again," she mumbles into my ear. "Whenever you can. Please don't forget about me."

"I won't," I say as I pull away. "I promise."

When I get back to Clodagh's, Kaseema is waiting for me, tablet in hand. Without her quiet managerial efficiency, this whole venture would have imploded long ago. She seems not even a little bit stressed as she delegates and organizes.

"Rosemary Silt wants to sit down with you and Odessa," she says.

"Why?"

"I guess because it will make great television. But from our point of view, it will allow you to address the lies Odessa has been spreading. Convince the people that she is false."

"A debate? This isn't a political campaign."

"It is," says Kaseema. "I think this is a good chance to clear up any misinformation."

"Fine."

She nods and makes a note. She's wearing a green hijab which brings out some pale green flecks in her eyes.

"Is there something else, Kaseema?"

"Literally dozens of things," she says, deadpan. "But I can take care of them."

I nod, and she goes to the door.

"Kaseema."

She looks back.

"What will happen if everyone votes against me?"

She looks me in the eye. She's steady and cool as always.

"Something bad will happen. Then everyone will realize they made a mistake. And then you'll forgive them."

13

Howling winds lay waste to a thriving city

Over the next week, Odessa's attacks intensify. She continues to revel in the spotlight and call me a confused young man. She continues to winkingly agree with her supporters who say I'm a disgusting monster, even if she herself is the picture of tolerance. She continues to build up her mythology, concocting the confection of the perfect Melting Queen.

It seems to me that we should be able to find traces of Odessa Steps online and prove that Olechka Stepanchuk is a fabrication. But ECHO must have a diligent digital team, because we can't prove the existence of Odessa Steps any more than we can disprove Olechka's fake backstory. Odessa always looked down on any kind of recordings or social media, preaching the value of live bodies in real spaces and the ephemeral nature of performance. But she still should have some kind of digital footprint.

Sander could probably help us, but he's busy digging into the murky past of the Melting Queens with Isobel. Kaseema is computer savvy, but she's organizing dozens of volunteers to go out and speak to people on my behalf and help with our campaign. They're both fine. I don't worry about them.

But Clodagh has returned to her old self. To her mind, the fountain is dead, eclipsed by something more dire, just like it was thirty years ago. She lurks in her room, never coming out, even when I try to convince her it's going well, even when Kaseema tries to give her updates on our project.

Hundreds of people are donating small sums of money on our Fountain Lovers of Edmonton website. We only have a few thousand dollars at this point, but the messages of support and optimism keep trickling in. The fountain has become a symbol of my fight to remain as the Melting Queen, and although my small core of supporters is being shouted down left and right by fans of the surging Olechka, they're still quietly donating.

As much as I want to forget about the whole distracting sideshow of Odessa and focus on the fountain, I need Clodagh to take the lead on that while I fend off this challenge. I keep trying to rouse her from her funk, but after a while the battle takes precedence over the war.

"I need you to find someone for me," I tell Kaseema the day before my Great Debate with Odessa.

"Name them," she says.

"His name is René Royaume, but he also goes by Magpie. He leads a troupe of drag queens. I need them to make me magnificent."

In no time at all, Magpie flaps into our little base of operations, followed by Mary Cone and Cherry Poppins. They're all in their masculine civvies, so I guess I should call them René and Andrés and Carl.

"Thank god you finally called me!" squawks René the moment he traipses into the room. "It was torture seeing what that bitch did to your eyebrows."

René and Andrés and Carl work through the night. They scurry around me like magical mice, painting faces over mine and then peeling them away until I'm a genderfluid goddess. I am myself. I'm not hiding who I am. But I'm also majestic in a way that I've never been before. My genderfluidity doesn't flow between male and female so much as it does between "both" and "neither." René and the drag queens sharpen my cheekbones to hard-edged swords. They plump up my lips and make my eyes swell to deep freezing glacial pools. I'm masculine and feminine and neutral at the same time, like an iron-faced statue on top of a victory column, a national icon or a herald angel.

"No matter what happens, Odessa won't look half as good as I do," I tell my drag queen posse. "Thank you."

"Have you thought about what she's going to say?" asks René. "How she's going to attack you? How you're going to respond?"

"She's going to keep calling me a man," I say. "She's going to keep trying to confuse people about what I am, even though she's the one who called me genderfluid in the first place. She's the one who recognized what I am and helped me find the words to express myself."

René looks at me in the mirror, unwinds the braids in my hair so that strands spill out in loose tumbling spirals.

"No," he says. "You found yourself on your own. You named yourself. Just like me."

"Well not really like you," I say. "I'm not a drag queen."

"I didn't mean Magpie," he says. "I meant René Royaume."

He comes around in front of my chair.

"I wasn't always René," he says. "My mother named me Angélique, when I was born. I spent ten awful years as Angélique, until I had the courage to tell her that I was a boy. And then I had to tell her that I was a gay man. And then I had to tell her that I was a drag queen. It was very confusing for everyone. '*Mais ma belle, pourquoi pas rester une fille si tu veux porter des robes?*' she asked me. 'Because I'm not a girl,' I said. 'But I am a queen.'"

He brushes an eyelash off my cheek.

"It's really not that difficult to accept people who are different from you," he says. "All you have to do is shrug your shoulders and say 'Oh, okay, cool, whatever.' I do it every day, for all the assholes I have to talk to. It's actually way more work to get into big arguments and be an asshole. But people freak out about people who blur gender lines—whether you're genderfluid or a trans gay male drag icon like me—because they think we're special snowflakes making this shit up for attention."

He blows the eyelash off his finger and comes back around the chair to work on my hair.

"You're not going to convince any of those people with rational arguments about equality or justice. So don't waste your time on them. Don't put any energy into arguing about what you are. Just be who you are, and the people who actually deserve to know you will accept you."

"Did your mother accept you, in the end?"

René pauses a moment, then meets my eyes in the mirror.

"I showed my mother my stone, so that she would understand what trying to be a girl for her was doing to me. She held it in her hand, and she screamed and screamed. It was hurting her, and she begged me to make it stop. To help her. But I didn't want to. Hearing her scream gave me so much joy—to know that, just for a few moments, she was feeling what I felt every second of every day. Hearing her in pain made me *happy*. And that scared me more than anything. The next day I left home. We haven't spoken since."

René goes back to brushing my hair, mechanically moving the brush while he stares through my head, off into some vast internal distance.

"Do you want to see your mother again?"

He breaks out of his trance, gives me a bitter smile.

"Never," he spits. "I know that's not the answer anyone wants to hear. Everybody loves a story of time healing all wounds and families coming back together. But sometimes people don't deserve another chance."

Andrés puts a reassuring hand on René's shoulder, and the drag queens share a look. In that one glance, I can see the years of history they've lived together, the strength they've given each other in dark times.

"The world is full of cruel, stupid people," says René. "All we can do is not be one of them."

René finishes up my hair and adds some final touches to my makeup. Andrés and Carl make some last-minute adjustments to my outfit. It's a simple green smock, a couple of white flowers in my hair. A little while later, Kaseema says it's time to go. I knock on Clodagh's bedroom door and tell her where I'm going. She doesn't make a sound in return.

Odessa sits across from me, showing not a hint of the real person I saw for a moment at the nursing home. That's all buried beneath a shiny immaculate veneer. She's wearing her blonde wig, a pink dress, and a teeth-aching smile.

"Good evening," says Rosemary Silt into the camera's leering black eye. Our host is a bubbly, peppy Black woman whose constant on-air feasting has done nothing to detract from her obvious physical fitness. "Welcome to a very special edition of our program. Tonight our guests need no introduction. River Runson—"

I see Odessa's tight smile across the table from me. She's been soundbitingly consistent in her use of my former name.

"—was Named Melting Queen only a short time ago, but in that time you've managed to make quite an impression."

I can only imagine what graphics are accompanying my face on screen.

"And Olechka Stepanchuk—"

Odessa smiles glowingly into the camera, places a hand on her baby bump.

"—has been teaching kindergarten for years, but only recently have you caught our attention with your bold and controversial campaign to claim Edmonton's most cherished title."

"I'm happy to be here, Rosemary."

Odessa's voice is colourful and light.

"Thank you for having me," I say in my dry-mouthed baritone.

"Well, before it gets cold we had better tuck in," says Rosemary, gesturing at the dinner before us.

"Thanks, it looks delicious," says Odessa. "I'm famished—I'm eating for two after all."

"You've outdone yourself," I interject. Kaseema's voice rings in my ears: *Don't let her talk about her baby. Don't let her dictate the terms of the conversation.* The table groans with an enormous feast.

"Don't you recognize it?" asks Rosemary.

"Of course," says Odessa. "These are all the dishes from *The Melting Queen's Cookbook*." She gives me a smile and raises her eyebrows and assumes the tone with which one would lecture a child. "In 1952, Alma Lake collected the favourite recipes of her predecessors."

Advantage Odessa. Damn you Sander if it was you who told her that. I dish myself out a helping of saskatoon berry pie as Rosemary attacks a turkey with an electric carving knife.

"So," says our host, "there have been some heated words on either side of this issue. I invited you here tonight for a casual chat, so our viewers can really get to know both of you."

I take a deep breath and swallow the rich saskatoon jelly that dissolves on my tongue. I take a sip of water and stare into the camera lens.

"I have a very simple reason why I'm here," I say slowly. "This person sitting across from me—Odessa Steps, as she used to call herself—was one of my best friends. One of my only friends. And in the midst of the most difficult time of my life, when I was trying to figure out how to be true to myself, when I got thrust into the public eye in a way I didn't expect, she betrayed me. She went behind my back and decided to prey on this situation. And now she's saying vicious things about me every day, and spreading incredible lies about herself. And it terrifies me to think that anyone believes her and supports her. But clearly some people do. So all I can say is that I'm very sad to have lost a friend, and hurt to learn that she doesn't care about me like I thought she did."

Rosemary turns her eyes on Odessa, eager to see her response.

"I don't know why this man and his friends keep insisting that we know each other," she says, faux-flustered. "I don't know him and I don't have anything against him. I just want to be a good ambassador for my city. I just want to be the woman we need right now."

I can't help but roll my eyes.

"So you love Edmonton, do you? That's why you want to do this? You feel a responsibility as a citizen?"

Odessa nods proudly, opens her mouth to spew forth more manufactured saccharine propaganda.

"That's a load of crap," I cut her off before she can begin. I can imagine the wince on Sander's face but I can't stop myself. "You don't love Edmonton at all, Odessa. You're barely even an Edmontonian. You leave every winter! You're not an Edmontonian if you don't go through the worst half of the year."

Odessa is smiling in the most irritating way imaginable, acting like she's above it all, humouring my tantrum.

"Setting aside the fact that that is totally false," she says in an infinitely reasonable adult-voice, "there are many thousands of great citizens who journey south every winter. To say that they are somehow less Edmontonian is utterly ridiculous."

"So that's false? You don't leave every winter?"

"No, not at all. Apart from a few vacations to Mexico and Hawaii, I've always been here working all winter."

She lies with such conviction that even I have a lurking doubt. I'm struck with an image of Odessa that's totally different from the one I've known. What if she doesn't fly away at the First Snow? What if she pretends to have a glamorous lifestyle but really she just takes a taxi to the airport, watches the planes take off, and goes to a different part of the city where she lives alone all winter? She doesn't go out much in case she might run into someone. She sends her grandfather stock postcards and she almost convinces herself that she's having adventures.

I meet her eyes across the table. This is all a possibility. Maybe her name really is Olechka Stepanchuk. Maybe she really does have a husband and parents. Maybe she dreams of a life that's not her own, and gets to live it in the few moments when she convinces two gullible chumps that she's an exceptional person who goes on extraordinary adventures.

She's a talented liar. If she can make me have doubts, it's no wonder that she's suckered in everyone else.

"I really don't know what you're talking about, Adam."

Her voice is soft, with only a hard serrated edge on the final word to cut into me.

"My name is River now," I say. "The name you choose is a promise you make to yourself. You told me that. Back when you were still my friend. Not an opportunistic bigot."

Odessa sighs with frustration.

"Okay, I'm sorry, but I'm getting real tired of being called a bigot. I am not a bigot. I'm not a hateful person just because I refuse to indulge your little fantasy."

"It's not a fantasy. This is who I am."

Odessa turns to Rosemary, trying to recruit her support.

"This is what happens when you live in a bubble where everyone is so paranoid of being called privileged that they accept every bizarre trend."

"I don't live in a bubble," I say. "And I'm not following a trend. I'm just trying to be truthful about how I feel."

I look into the camera, try to imagine a sympathetic viewer. I think of René. I feel the muscles in my face relaxing, and I picture him sitting down at the bottom of the whale, turning his stone over and over in his small hands. I look down at my own hands, man hands whose nails have been painted dark forest green by the drag queens.

"I'm not asking for special treatment," I say. "I'm only asking to be recognized for who I am and treated with respect. I know it's hard for people to understand what genderfluid means or even believe that it exists. But I'm just asking you to trust me, and trust that I know myself. That I was male for a long time, until I couldn't be anymore. That masculinity became a millstone around my neck, dragging me down, and I had to cut myself free. That this is me being honest with you about who I am. I'm not trying to hide the truth anymore, or disfigure myself to fit into an easy category. It's messy, yes. Some days I feel ashamed, and I have to remind myself that I'm carrying a lifetime of rocks on my back—a lifetime of being trained to be male and to hide my emotions and to cut off whole parts of myself. The only thing I know is that I'll only be at peace with myself if I always tell the truth."

Odessa raises her eyebrows and stabs at some tourtière on her plate.

"That was a very moving speech," she says. "But I can't let you get away with framing this situation in those terms. Because all you're trying to do is make me the villain and make yourself the victim. And it's more complicated than that."

"No, it's really not. I'm asking to be treated with dignity and you're refusing. You're trying to stir up hate against me just because I'm not something that's convenient and readily understood."

"You're not a hero, Mr. Truman. You're not leading some brave crusade against the final frontier of discrimination. You're not standing up all alone in the face of oppression. You're just *following a fad*."

She turns her appealing eye on Rosemary again, waving a hand in my direction.

"We live in a culture that's so saturated with guilt, so overwhelmed by navel-gazing conversations about privilege and identity politics. It's trendy to identify with some marginalized group, just so that you can claim victimhood too and don't have to think of yourself as an oppressor."

She brings her gaze back to bear on my face. She seems genuinely angry.

"You're not genderfluid, *Adam*. You're more like trenderfluid."

I laugh out loud at the obviousness of her hashtag-baiting, and she barrels on.

"You're just jumping on the bandwagon. You can paint your nails and grow your hair and wear a skirt like any punk-rock rebellious teen, but you're not a woman. You don't know what it's like to be a woman in a man's world. You're comfortable in your male body. Which means you can't be the Melting Queen."

"It's strange that you know how it feels to be me better than I do," I say, tripping over my dry tongue. "Sure, yes, binary gender exists here, now, in our culture. But it's not eternal and unchanging, and it's not the natural order of things. There have been hundreds of different genders in different cultures throughout history, and now our culture is just starting to recognize that. I'm not a man. I'm not a woman. I'm something else, sometimes more and sometimes less, and that's okay. People are confused by that, I get it. But it's really not that complicated. There are more than five senses. There are more than four elements. There are more than three states of matter. So why can't there be more than two genders? People like me are like proprioception, or neptunium, or Fermionic condensate—maybe you didn't learn about us in kindergarten, maybe you didn't know about us until very recently, but we've existed for thousands of years. So *you*, Odessa, don't get to tell me that I'm just some confused kid following a trend."

Odessa puts her hands down on the table on either side of her plate, as if she might launch herself across at me any moment and tear out my throat with her teeth.

"I know the theory," she growls. "There's a difference between sex and gender. And there's a difference between how you identify inside and how you present your gender on the outside. And what it boils down to is that someone like you—a straight, white, able-bodied, upper-class *man*—can have a male body, and wear masculine clothes, and enjoy all the privileges of being classed as masculine, and then whine about how he's being discriminated against because we're not recognizing his 'true self.' Your 'gender identity' is located deep within your own mind, which is convenient because otherwise we would have no way of knowing about it. And as a feminist, as a woman who lives in this world—the world where women are hurt, brutalized, controlled by men—I am absolutely insulted by you claiming to experience one tiny fraction of what I experience. And by assuming you can come in and take this one little slice of women's history in my city and say you get to control it too."

"Why don't we talk about something other than gender?" interrupts Rosemary, no doubt sensing that the audience's patience for this topic has long ago been exhausted.

Odessa blinks rapidly and forces a smile to bloom on her face. I'm sure she never intended to sound so alienatingly angry as that.

"Yes. Of course. I'm sorry that I let my passion run away with me."

"River," says Rosemary as she dabs at the corner of her mouth with a serviette, "tell us more about this fountain."

I turn and stare into the mesmerizing black abyss of the camera lens. I see my reflection, all distorted and misshapen in its convex circle.

"I chose to work with the Fountain Lovers of Edmonton this year because I don't think that things should stay the same forever. I know I was rude at the coronation. I apologize for that. But I stand by what I said. Edmonton is an ugly city. Which is why Clodagh Paskwamostos and I want to make it better."

Odessa smiles a genuine smile of triumph, no doubt celebrating how I'm dooming myself with honesty.

"I completely disagree with you. I think Edmonton is a fantastic city. Yes, we have work to do. We need to make things better for the poorest and most vulnerable among us. But Edmontonians are generous. And spending time on a frivolous fountain is a complete waste of money when there are serious issues we need to resolve as a community."

"Well, Olechka," says Rosemary, patting her own food baby contentedly and pushing her plate away, "you've already taken on a lot of different initiatives for yourself. But what do you have planned as your own big signature project, should you succeed in your mission to replace River?"

In the one-second pause before she starts speaking, I feel a shadow of panic in the air and I realize that Odessa has nothing. Her handlers have spent all this time building up the image of The Perfect Edmontonian—Beautiful Mother, Devoted Wife, Responsible Citizen—that they've totally neglected to set any real goals.

Of course, Odessa is able to improvise some bullshit about how public consultation is the most important thing, and she'll follow the general will of all Edmontonians and truly embody the spirit of the city. But Rosemary has a pinched, disappointed look on her face, and I can tell that Odessa senses the shift of power. I try to cut in and speak more about the fountain, but Odessa barrels on, choosing to follow a reliable course of debate.

"It's going to be difficult to hold down a job and raise a family and be a Melting Queen at the same time. But thousands of Edmonton women do difficult things like this every day. And I'm lucky that Noah has been very supportive as well."

"Who is Noah?" I say, frustrated by this transparent ploy. "Who *is* that!?"

"My husband," she says, setting a hand to her heart, which also coincidentally shows off her modest wedding band. "My best friend," she mewls, giving a tiny wave to the camera which makes me livid.

"Oh my god," I groan. I'm rocked by a geyser of anger, which bursts out from some deep primal level of my being. I can't take any more of this bullshit. "You don't have a husband, Odessa! Your whole story is a sham!"

She gives me a humouring smirk.

"Really, Adam, these accusations are getting desperate. I've been married for two years. All my friends and family and coworkers can tell you that. And *you're* going around accusing *me* of lying? Please. I'm not the one making up a fake name for myself and chasing down the spotlight like some attention-starved drag queen."

"Yes you are!" I shout at her, practically tearing out my hair in frustration. "Everything you're saying is a lie! Everything about you is fake! You're just a heartless narcissist who flies away every winter and abandons your so-called friends here to freeze!"

I slam my hand down on the tabletop and our plates shake.

"I *stay here*, Odessa, in this frozen wasteland. *I* endure. *I'm* a survivor!"

Odessa laughs in my face.

"So what?" she says. "So does everybody else. That doesn't make you special. It doesn't make you 'a survivor.' It doesn't make you strong. It just makes you a typical Edmontonian."

Her words cut into me like a knife, slicing into the deepest part of me. I didn't think it could get any worse. But now I see it, in her icy grey eyes. She never loved me. She never cared about me. Not even a little bit. It was all a lie, from the beginning, just like everything else.

The geyser of anger boils over, exploding into a supervolcano of rage. I leap from my chair and reach across the table. I rip off her wig, exposing her baldness for all the world to see.

"This is a wig! Your story is fake. Your family is fake. Everything you've ever said is a lie. You're probably not even pregnant, you psychopath!"

I'm standing across the table from her, holding the wig dangling from my hand. Rosemary watches me, eyes wide. Odessa looks down into her lap. The studio is silent. I feel a cold sheet of water crashing over me, like I'm falling through the ice again.

Odessa looks up after a moment. Big fat glistening ornamental tears are sliding down her cheeks.

"I didn't want to talk about this," she croaks. "I didn't want people to think I was weak, and couldn't finish out the year if they chose to put their faith in me."

Her voice wavers and she has to choke back tears. She hides her face in her hands as her breaths hitch, shaking her shoulders.

"I was diagnosed with cancer right after I learned I was pregnant. I hope I will survive by the time my daughter is born. But they can't say."

She glares up at me.

"So yes, I'm wearing a wig. I'm wearing makeup, so I don't look as sick as I am."

She wipes her hands across her tear-tracked face, smearing her mascara extravagantly. Rosemary, the camera operators, everyone at home wait with bated breath to hear what she will say next.

"I just want my little girl to look back and see a mum who looked happy and healthy. Who could leave her a legacy to be proud of."

Rosemary passes Odessa a box of tissue which she dives into. The cameras go on rolling. The interview might go on and I might recover some face.

But I know it deep down in my gut. I just lost.

After, at Clodagh's house, I lock myself away and try to understand what happened. *She beat you, that's all. She provoked you, and you rose to her bait. You fell into her trap.* For once I actually wish for an Intrusion to come whisk me away, drop me into some other life where I can forget my troubles. But no trip back in time is forthcoming.

Even my most ardent defenders are hard pressed to support me now. Odessa launches ad after ad, showing my face contorted with rage as I rip the wig off her head—the face of male power committing violence against a defenceless woman. She stops wearing the wig, and pledges to stop wearing makeup so people can see that she's not ashamed of her sickness. Her bruises and lesions are painted on.

I try going out the next day. People on the streets are just as hostile as before, only now no one will step forward to defend me. No matter what mystical influence I might hold as the Melting Queen, it only goes so far. I see no Greens at all, just a sea of angry Pink.

So I squirrel myself away in Clodagh's spare bedroom, just like Clodagh herself. Two defeated queens. I can't make her dream come true anyway, so what's the point of trying to win this contest? It's easier just to sleep, and get up to go pee, and watch the water flow through the toilet and the sink and think about the waters in the river and the glorious fountain that'll never be built and go back to sleep where at least I can dream that it's real.

How long does life carry on like this? A day? A week? A month? Does it matter? Kaseema keeps pestering me, knocking on my door just like I used to knock on Clodagh's door. René says mean things that are probably meant to provoke me into action. But I don't care. Odessa won. A vote will only be a formality at this point. And besides, she's doing good works for Edmonton. She's helping the homeless and feeding the poor. She's shining a light on injustice and fixing potholes. She deserves to be the Melting Queen.

"River."

Kaseema is at my door again. Never gives up. It's annoying.

"Go away."

I roll over in bed, wrap myself more snuggly under the covers.

"There's someone here to see you."

"I don't care. If it's my mom again you're fired."

"It's not your mother. It's Alice Songhua."

The 114th Melting Queen sits in Clodagh's front room with Sander and René. It's weird seeing her up close, with all the pageantry of Melting Day stripped away. She looks severely normal, if a bit tired. Though not as tired as me.

When she sees me standing in the doorway, she stands up and walks over to me.

"River. It's good to finally meet you."

She folds me into a one-sided hug that lasts for a few awkward seconds. She pulls back and looks up into my face.

"What are you doing here?" I ask numbly. I hardly care at this point, but it seems like the right thing to ask. She leads me to the couch.

"It was finally time for me to come home. I'm sorry that I abandoned you. But I had to get out of Edmonton for a while."

"Okay. That's nice. But you're too late. I'm not the Melting Queen anymore."

"Don't say that," she says. "Of course you are. And I'm here to help you. I just needed some time away, to recharge and to find myself again. And I'll be honest," she says, looking down at her hands. "I was scared."

"Alice was telling us how she just got back from Maui," says René.

"I needed to be in the sun for a while," says Alice. "And I couldn't stand the sight of another Edmonton face."

I shake my head to clear it. They're all looking at me expectantly.

"But I don't understand," I say. "Why are you here now? What do you want from me?"

Alice looks around the room, her eyes lingering on Kaseema for a moment before she looks back at me.

"I left the day that I Named you, River Runson. I went straight to the airport and got on a plane and didn't look back. I was finished with it all."

"Why?"

"Because I was finally free. Because I hated Birch and I hated ECHO and I hated every minute of being Melting Queen. I hated the Intrusions ripping me into pieces. I hated the groups constantly pestering me for my support. And the people. I hated the people most of all. How they came and demanded my time and told me their stories. How I could feel myself becoming a worse, weaker person after every encounter, taking on their problems and their little pieces of poison. No one should have to endure that. No one. Never again."

"Then why did you Name me? If you knew it was so terrible. Why did you Name me!?"

My voice breaks. It's a question that's been haunting me for months. I didn't realize how much it hurt that I'd never had the chance to ask it.

"They gave me a list of five names to choose from," says Alice Songhua. "They sang me songs about how great each one of these women would be for Edmonton. And I smiled and nodded, just like I'd learned to do all year. I asked to see the leaves from May Winter's statue, but Birch said not to worry myself about all that. They'd already done all that work for me, and sorted out the cream of the crop for me to choose from."

Alice Songhua looks up at my executive assistant, whose tablet is forgotten in the crook of her arm. She's hanging off Alice's every word.

"Kaseema helped me. She's loyal to the Melting Queen, not to Birch or ECHO or anyone else. She brought them to me. I sifted through the thousands of leaves, ran them through the computer, waiting to see what the CIRCLE directory would spit out. I was going to find someone so terrible that they would end the whole thing. Or at least embarrass them beyond belief. But then I found you, River Runson. The directory listed your birthday as September 21st, 2018. I thought it was a glitch or something. But there was no other information, no height or weight or occupation or gender."

The 114th Melting Queen stares straight into my eyes.

"I Named you because I thought you didn't exist. I thought I'd be the end. The last Melting Queen. So no woman would have to suffer through it again."

Kaseema clears her throat.

"You were unhappy all that time?" she asks Alice.

"I'm sorry, Kaseema. I know you care about the Melting Queen. You practically *are* the Melting Queen. But you don't know how it feels. Day after day. Week after week. It wears you down and breaks you."

"She's right," says Sander, then pinkens at the attention when we all look at him. "I've interviewed forty-three Melting Queens. Some of them are doing better than others, but all of them say pretty much the same thing. Being the Melting Queen drained them of something vital. They've never felt the same since they took off the crown. They've never been as energetic or as happy."

"But why was my name there at all?" I ask Alice. "I didn't stick a leaf on the statue."

"I did," says René. He smirks at me unapologetically. "Right after we met. Right after you named yourself."

"Why?" I ask, too tired to be angry.

"Do you really have to ask that? Because I hoped you would be Named! I knew you'd be a great Melting Queen."

I look around at all of them, these friends and supporters and manipulators.

"But I'm not a great Melting Queen. Odessa's right. I never wanted this. I'm not suited for it like she is."

"If she wins then Birch wins," says Alice. "And if Birch wins then it'll just keep going, year after year, queen after queen. Edmonton will just keep eating them alive, chewing them up and spitting them out and forgetting about them the moment that everyone has a fresh new queen to use."

"But if I win, then what? Everyone hates me. I won't accomplish anything. I can't even build a little fountain for my friend."

"Good thing you don't have to do it alone then."

Everyone's eyes flick to the doorway. Clodagh Paskwamostos stands there in a rumpled sweater, finally out of her hibernation.

I'm off the couch before I know it, wrapping my arms around her stiff awkward body just like Alice did to me a moment ago.

"You're back."

"I didn't go anywhere," she says. She gives me a terse hug, then lifts me away from her and sets me aside as if I'm a straw doll.

"It's impossible to sleep with all you out here shouting. You're terrible guests. But I'm being a terrible host. Who wants tea?"

Clodagh doesn't even bother counting hands, just shuffles into the kitchen to put the kettle on. She emerges a moment later with a tray full of mismatched mugs and coasters.

"I'm sorry," she mutters as she sets them down. "I haven't been my best."

"That's okay," I say.

"No. It's not. I'm not giving up on you. And neither are you."

"But Odessa's better at this than me. She's won already."

"So what? You're the Melting Queen. She's not. And you've got a fountain to build."

Clodagh's speckled brown eyes are fixed on mine. I feel her quiet confidence in me. She still needs this. She still needs me to be strong. And not just her, all of them. Victoria and Isobel and Alice too. There's still work to be done.

"Kaseema?"

I turn to my loyal advisor, the truest devotee of the Melting Queen.

"Do you still have the number for Iris Zambezi?"

14

The beating heart of her proud city

Whyte Avenue is a chaos of colour. A cracked-open kaleidoscope, spilling out its glorious gems into the world. Beads and feathers, glue and glitter, body paint and wigs explode in a rainbow collage. Music crashes up and down the street, various floats competing to drown each other out with their preferred diva.

The sun beats down on the assembled floats, burning the plentiful expanses of bare skin. Parade organizers flit around like hummingbirds sipping the sap from exotic flowers, trying to get everything in place before we go prancing down the street.

There are a hundred different floats, and I spot a dozen familiar faces. Candace Khan and all the other Lodgepole Party MLAs have a line of gleaming classic convertibles and several tons of candy to rain down on the people. The Conservative rump caucus has their own sad float—including my mother, whose requests to march with me were deftly deflected by Kaseema. There are representatives of all the organizations who came to the Melting Queen's Picnic, from SPYGLASS in their sports gear to CURVED with their eco-justice banners to PAPRIKA, who are dressed as construction workers with Madonna cone-boobs made out of orange traffic pylons.

And then there's me, standing beside the flower-choked float which will lead the parade. I'm surrounded by my team, as well as Iris Zambezi and some of her deputies, the festival's main organizers.

"How many people do you think will come today?" I ask as Magpie puts some finishing touches on my dress with a soldering iron.

"Estimates range from thirty to thirty-five thousand people," says Kaseema, stepping neatly aside as sparks fly off my skirt and skitter over the street.

It's more supporters than I expected. At least some people have forgiven me for my eruption on Odessa. Or else they never bought her act in the first place.

"How many of those are protestors?" asks Clodagh.

Iris gives us a sober stare. She's tall and regal in a beautiful purple gown.

"There will always be protestors," she says. "It wasn't so long ago that there were more protesters than people in the parade. For those of us old enough to remember, it's nothing new."

I give her what I hope is a brave, compatriotic nod. Iris was quick to anger, but also quick to forgive. As soon as Kaseema called, she agreed to slot me in, despite the protests of some of her lieutenants.

In many ways I still feel like I'm not supposed to be here. Like I'm too queer to be the Melting Queen but not queer enough to be in this parade. Too trans to be a frat brother but not trans enough to call myself trans. I suppose that feeling will never go away, especially when I have people like Olechka Stepanchuk almost convincing me that what I am is an offensive parody.

I cast my eyes around the busy street again. Despite the fact that almost everyone I know is here, there is one notable absence.

"Have you seen Odessa? Is she here?"

"Yes, she's here," says Iris. "We didn't allow her or ECHO to march in the parade, but we can't stop them from organizing their own side event. I think it would be best if you two stayed away from one another."

"I'm not going to fight her. Don't worry."

Magpie shuts the valve on her gas canister and lifts her welder's mask and grins up at me.

"I think we're all good," she says, eyeing her handiwork with satisfaction. "Give us a spin and show it off."

I twirl around on the pavement and hear the leaves of my skirt clank against each other. Magpie didn't have much time to design my outfit, but she came up with something brilliant at the last minute. Since I'm in a war for my title, she said, I might as well wear some armour. She showed me some sketches and now here I am standing in this contraption: hair wrapped in a high bun, my crown woven in, a tight green silk corset which leaves my shoulders bare. And hanging from my waist, a skirt made of metal—sheets of emerald green armour, glittering like a dragon's scales, pocked with rivets. I'm also reclaiming the colour that Odessa stole from me—the superstructure of the dress supports a long pink cape.

The skirt's weight drags down on my hips, but the ensemble is so striking that I can bear the temporary discomfort. I look into the amused faces of Clodagh and Kaseema and Iris.

"Flashy," says Clodagh.

"You're a warrior," says Magpie, clapping her hands. She gathers up her stuff.

"Now I need to go put the finishing touches on myself," she says, adjusting her bright red dress and straightening out the white infinity symbol which loops around her foam breasts. "Can't keep my adoring audience waiting."

I lean down for a hug and a kiss on the cheek then she rushes off into the crowd. I catch the eye of a person with swirling Van Gogh stars painted all over their body and we smile and nod, admiring each other's colourfulness.

Beside Iris Zambezi stands Clodagh Paskwamostos, wearing an ultramarine blue pantsuit that she keeps readjusting on her large frame. Alice Songhua wears a blazing scarlet summer dress. Isobel Fraser is stooped over the handles of her motorized scooter, wearing an orange vest covered in various buttons. And Victoria Goulburn has a long canary yellow coat with a marigold in its lapel.

I will not be the grand marshal of this parade. We will line up, all six of us, and lead this carnival procession together: Alice in red, Isobel in orange, Victoria in yellow, River in green, Clodagh in blue, and Iris in purple. A show of force from the true Melting Queens, who embodied the spirit of the city.

"Are we ready to go?" I ask Iris.

"On your signal," she says.

"Then what are we waiting for?"

I join hands with Clodagh to my left and Victoria to my right. The line of Melting Queens marches around the corner, hand-in-hand (or hand in electric scooter handle, in Isobel's case) and we greet the cheering and jeering crowds. Confetti pours down from the rooftops. Speakers on the float behind us belt out a rousing pop anthem. The people in the crowd dance along and people from the group behind us bequeath them with Mardi Gras beads.

I feel my back straighten, my shoulders open. I imagine the emerald on my crown sparkling in the sunlight. I allow myself to feel majestic, and I smile freely at the crowd. The cheers drown out the jeers as we five generations of Melting Queens lift our hands into the air.

I lean my head towards Clodagh as we pass by her travel agency, which has since become a bubble tea shop.

"I'm glad I met you," I say. "I'm lucky that my bootlaces exploded where they did."

She blushes and shrugs her shoulders.

"I'm glad I met you too."

I feel Victoria squeeze my hand and I look at her.

"Look who it is," she says, nodding her head at the sidewalk. At first I don't know what she's talking about, but then I see a reporter and a cameraperson interviewing Kastevoros Birch.

"Let's not let him spoil our day," I say.

I resist the urge to make a face at the camera as we pass by. Soon I'm distracted by the joy of the crowd, and all thoughts of Birch and ECHO and this stupid referendum leave my mind. All along the parade route, a miracle is happening. The protestors are being shoved to the back of the sidewalks, sidelined and ignored by the joyous celebrants. The Greens have prevailed, at least on this day. Everyone is smiling and dancing, waving and jumping and kissing. Proud and happy. Not afraid. Not ashamed.

People scream and cheer and applaud when they see us coming, and the parade is slowed several times as we pause to take pictures with people—young gay couples and their adorable babies, drag queens who are far more glamorous and beautiful than any biological woman, a group of Muslim women in rainbow burqas.

As the music crashes back off the buildings, I feel like I'm relaxing and enjoying myself for the first time in months. They might not all accept me, they might not be able to come out and show their support every day, but I've got an army in my corner.

The parade weaves its way down Walterdale Hill, across the new bridge beside Café Fiume, and eventually spills out into Coronation Park. The party continues for the rest of the day and into the evening. From time to time I glance up at the Spring Throne, there on the hill, still showing no signs of life. It makes me uneasy for some reason, like a predator crouching in our midst that no one else can see. Kaseema suggests that I sit in my royal seat and receive the thousands of revellers, but instead I walk amongst the crowd, taking pictures and sharing hugs. The sun takes forever to sink below the horizon, one of those never-ending Edmonton evenings of high summer.

After a full day of drinks and performances (Magpie and Mary and Cherry take the stage, dazzling the crowd as much as they did on Melting Day), I feel the need to get away from the crush of people. As night falls, I leave the party, telling Clodagh that I'll meet them all back at her house.

I walk down to the river's edge, dip my fingers in the cool water. I take a deep breath, and say a silent promise to Clodagh that I will finish this fight and get her fountain built.

"River?"

He says the word uncertainly, testing its shape with his teeth and lips. I turn and see Brock Stark standing on the upper bank, rainbow streaks painted on his face and carnival beads hanging around his neck.

"You came to Pride," I say.

"I wanted to support you," he says. He comes down the bank, to the water's edge.

"Are you having fun?" I ask.

"Yeah," he says. "It's not what I thought it would be."

He takes off his sandal, dips his toes into the water.

"I watched you on *EdmonTonight*," he says after a moment.

"Oh god. I'm sorry."

"For what? I thought you were really brave."

He takes off the other sandal and puts both feet in the water, leaving wet footprints on the silty sand. I look at our blurry reflections in the smooth water, mirror images of each other once again. We glance up at each other at the same moment.

"All the Dixies have your back, by the way," he says. "We're all going to vote for you."

"Thanks," I say. "I wish you didn't have to, but thank you."

He mushes his feet into the muddy riverbank, stirring up clouds of silt which billow through the water and cover up our reflections.

"Do you think you could come for a movie night some time?" he asks. "All the guys miss having you around."

I meet his eye. He flashes me the crooked smile that I've seen a thousand times—his only asymmetric feature, which somehow only makes him more physically perfect. Even in my magnificent battlegown, I am still dowdy and derelict next to him. I can't stop comparing myself to him, no matter how badly I want to.

"I'm sorry Brock. I'm not quite ready for that yet."

"But you will be? Some day?"

"I don't know."

A couple of guys walk by on the path above us and Brock looks back at the party. He watches them go along the path, hand in hand, then turns back to me.

"I understand how you feel, you know. Before I came out, there were so many days where I thought about doing what you did, just running away. But you accepted me, like I knew you would, and so did all the other brothers."

I sigh.

"I'm not a brother, though. Our situations aren't the same."

"Maybe not," he admits. "But still, you shouldn't've just ghosted me."

He fixes me with a stare and I see the intermingled anger and sadness on his face.

"You hurt me," he says. "After everything we've been through together, you didn't trust that I would support you."

"I'm sorry," I say. "I don't have a good answer for you. I just did what I felt like I had to do."

"Why? Why did you feel that way? Why couldn't you trust me?"

I kneel down next to the water, dig a pure white stone out of the silt.

"One day last fall—a normal, boring day where nothing out of the ordinary happened—I was walking back to my locker in the U of A change room when I glanced in a mirror and didn't recognize myself. I saw the same face I'd seen thousands of times. The same body, the same eyes. But it was a stranger."

I turn the stone over and over in my fingers, let the current wash away the muck until it shines like the moon.

"It's hard to describe exactly how it felt. It lasted for only a second, and then things went back to normal. But it didn't go away for good. I kept feeling it, randomly, no matter what I was doing—during gym sessions with you, movie night with the Dixies at our frat house, in the middle of my urban economics lecture. I'd look around and feel completely disoriented, like I'd been dropped into someone else's life."

I lift the stone out of the water, hold it in my palm, feel it getting heavier as I tell my story.

"Eventually, I just started feeling it all the time, from the moment I woke up to the moment I went to sleep. Everything felt fake. I just felt... wrong, somehow. My clothes didn't fit me, and I didn't like any of them. I hated my apartment and its spotless white surfaces. I was bored in all my classes, and couldn't remember why I'd decided to do urban planning—I couldn't bring myself to care about area structure plans and development bylaws. I went to parties with the Dixies and met new people and told them who I was and what I did, and all of it felt like some rote script I had memorized. I told the same story about myself for so long that eventually it just became a pattern of words that I repeated, and the words themselves had no meaning. I was just going through the motions, playing this character called Adam Truman, hoping that nobody would notice that I'd become completely hollow."

The icy white radiance of the stone begins to fade, greying like a sun-damaged photo.

"One day—the day that the First Snow fell—I looked in the mirror and saw no trace of myself left in my eyes. I could normally force myself to recognize my reflection if I stared long enough. But as much as I tried, I couldn't connect to what I was seeing. I finally accepted what I'd been feeling for months—I needed to leave, to start over, to become someone else. And so I dropped out of all my classes. I abandoned my apartment and found a little hole in Chinatown for next to nothing. I went to sleep, and when I woke up, Edmonton was covered in a thick layer of ice and snow."

I clench my fist around the stone, then throw it as far as I can out into the river. It plunks into the shallow water and the current swiftly obliterates its ripples.

I turn to look at Brock.

"I'm sorry I cut you out of my life. That was cruel. I just felt like I needed to make a clean break, but I should've thought about your feelings too."

Brock smiles again, then reaches out and puts his hand on my shoulder.

"You did what you had to do. But that doesn't mean that we can't still be friends."

He senses my tension, my hesitancy.

"You're a Dixie, River. You pledged for life. You don't have to be my brother. But you'll always be my sibling."

I look at him for a moment, then return his crooked smile. He was right, all those weeks ago. He won't give up on me.

A new song comes on up at the party lawn and a thousand people scream with joy. Brock takes his hand off my shoulder and looks up the riverbank.

"Want to head back up to the party?" he asks.

I look back out at the river, its mirror-smooth waters racing on to the sea.

"No," I say. "I think I'll stay here for a while."

Brock hesitates a moment, then nods.

"Okay. Well, I hope you have a good night. I'll see you around, River."

He says my name with confidence and clarity.

"Yes," I say. "You will."

As the stars come out, I walk along the river trails, smiling at all the couples who are kissing and giggling in the woods around me. I leave downtown, and venture out onto an old footbridge. Its wooden railings are a vandal's mosaic. I spot an ambivalent statement about the city. Someone carved "Edmonton Sucks" into the wood, which someone amended by carving "Edmonton Rocks" right over it, or maybe vice versa. The result is the ambivalent phrase "Edmonton Socks," which seems about right.

I walk along the river path. The sky is cloudless. The moon is a perfect circle. I can't shake the smile on my face—the feeling that no matter what happens with Odessa, everything is going to turn out okay. I am the Melting Queen.

After a while, my feet carry me to the High Level Bridge, lit up as a strobing rainbow of light for Pride. I lean on the rail and look down at the shallow, ice-free river below—the swiftly flowing waters, the tree-lined riverbanks. The wind makes the leaves rustle, and for the briefest of moments I feel the familiar panic swell up in me. But just as soon as it rises, it subsides. I take a deep breath of warm, fragrant summer night air and I feel fine. I haven't had the dark forest memory for weeks. I've escaped its pull, just like I've escaped my defeatism against Odessa and the despair of winter.

I feel the sturdy metal railing in front of me and give thanks for its solidity. I can't believe I once considered throwing myself off this bridge. Everything has changed so much in so little time. I look out at my city below, the horizon far off in the distance. Maybe I'll see the sun rise soon, after this short summer night. Maybe I'll get out of this city soon. Maybe I'll stay.

"Hey."

I turn around. There are two men behind me, soaked with rainbow light. A couple of musclebound fitness gays.

"Hi," I smile at them. "Happy Pride."

They both scowl at me. I feel a tingle run up my spine.

"I know you, don't I?" asks one of them.

I shake my head silently, hoping that this big tough guy is just going to spill his guts to me and cry at my skirts, confess some hidden misery. I look both ways along the bridge, but there's no one else here. I could walk away, but they'd catch up to me easily. I feel a shiver of familiar panic, only now it's not some unknown men chasing me through the woods. Now the men are right in front of me.

"Yeah, you're that Melting Queen, aren't you?" says his buddy. His tone is light, comical, like he's telling a joke. He has a big smile on his face.

I shake my head again. I take a step forward and the first one steps slightly to the side, blocking the path.

"Saw you attack that hot cancer mom," he says, slathering his gaze all over my body. "Dude, that is fucked up. Never seen a Melting Queen so angry before. Never seen one that's a man before either though, eh?"

"That's not a man," corrects his friend, cuffing him on the shoulder. "He's trans-gendered, right? Trying to be a woman."

His friend looks me up and down in mock surprise.

"Well he's not doing a great job of it, is he?"

He comes towards me and I step back. The guy stumbles. They're drunk. I could definitely outrun them, though not in this heavy battlegown. But before I even try to launch myself away, the guy darts up to me and slings his arm around my shoulder. He reeks of booze. He marches me towards his friend.

"If you want to be a girl, you gotta have more makeup," he slurs. "You gotta smell nice and shit. What's that thing they say girls smell like?"

"Sugar and spice," says his friend, who sticks his hands in his pockets and watches me. "Sugar and spice and everything nice."

This is insane. I can't believe they're quoting nursery rhymes at me. I think I can break out of the guy's grasp if I do it fast enough. If I elbow him in the chest maybe. I tense up and he tightens his arm around my shoulders.

"Nah, come on man. Don't do that. We're friends, aren't we? We're just having a good time tonight."

"Please let me go," I say. My voice is low, too low. The guy laughs.

"You're funny. You're a funny faggot. We're just playing. We're just hanging out. Relax man."

His friend watches the whole time. I relax my body and then twist my shoulder out of his hand, use my momentum to bury my fist in his chest. It hits him like he's a cement wall, he doesn't even react. He uses my own motion to wrap his arms around me so he's holding me from behind.

"See, what I don't understand," he slurs, unleashing a blast of horrible breath from over my shoulder. "What I don't understand is why a guy would wanna cut his dick off. That's fucked up. You're fucked up, man."

He tightens his grip around my body, crushing me in a hug. His friend comes toward me.

"You cut your dick off yet? You sure don't look like it."

"Maybe we should check and see," says the guy who's holding me.

"Maybe we should help you out, if you want your dick cut off so bad," says the other guy quietly. The one who's holding me releases his grip a little.

"That's fucked up," he says. "I don't wanna do that shit. What the fuck man?"

I wrench myself out of his arms and try to dodge past the other guy but he catches me.

"Let me go! Help me!"

I scream at a car that goes by on the bridge deck, but it doesn't stop.

"Nah man you're fine," he says. "We're just playing," he says to the other guy.

"So, you want to see what's under that dress? You wearing panties under there honey?" says the guy who's holding me, which makes the other one laugh. If he was put out by his friend's suggestion before, now he's back on board. He comes at me, grasps my shoulders. I whip out my leg and bring up one of the metal panels on my dress, right into his shin.

"Fuck!" He falls, clutching his leg. "What the fuck d'you do that for you little cunt? I told you we were just playing, but if you want to be a little bitch then we can fucking do this."

The one holding me smacks the side of my head and I see stars.

"You said you wanted everyone to call you River, right?" he growls in my ear. "Maybe you'd like us to put you in the river. Is that what you'd like?"

He throws me toward the railing and I scrape my hands on the concrete path. The shifting rainbow hues of the bridge lights slide over my skin and scramble my brain as I try to focus. I try to run but he kicks me in the side and I roll over. I scream for help but if there are any more cars they don't stop either. If there are any people on the bridge they don't hear. He walks towards me, grinning. His friend is leaning against the railing, holding his shin.

"You're disgusting," he says. "I fucking hate even having to touch you."

He pulls me up off the concrete, slides my body up the side of the rail. I swing my hand toward his face and he catches it and laughs thickly.

"Nice try faggot," he says. "But too late. You're fucking dead."

His friend with the hurt leg says *hey, maybe we should talk about this, what are you doing, stop*! But he lifts me up and tips me over the rail.

{15}

Her time has come and gone

I slip on dead leaves and slick stones as I run through the forest. Branches slap at me and I put my arms up to shield my face. The dry wood and sharp thorns leave scratches in my skin, but that's nothing compared to what will happen if they catch me.

The men holler and shriek and crash through the brush behind me. Their laughter and howling cries create chilling harmonies with the sounds of revelry from up the hill. If anyone hears them, they'll no doubt be mistaken for joyous celebrants, just letting off some steam. But I know better. I've been here before, so many times before, and I know that their intentions are not innocent.

I skid on a patch of mud-coated ice, far from melted, and I almost crash to the ground. I'm able to recover my balance at the last second, but my heart hammers explosively beneath my breast. One misstep and they'll catch me. One mistake and they'll tear me apart like wolves.

I was so stupid. I got careless. And now all I can do is flee this city, just like the last, and the one before that.

I glance behind me. I can't see any of them, but I see the trees rustling and hear their shouts.

I look forward just in time to see the branch, lying across the forest floor, the perfect height to catch my foot.

I crash to the ground, slam onto rocks and twigs and roots which punch me in the gut and tear at my clothes. And then I feel their hands on me.

As with all of my Intrusions, I'm thrown back into myself in a disorienting heap. I open my eyes frantically and see a bright light shining down from the ceiling. No, not the ceiling. The sky. The sun.

Fresh, lemon-yellow light streams down through a canopy of lush green leaves, dancing in the wind far above my head. I'm lying on impossibly soft grass, spread beneath a tall tree. I usually have a piercing headache after an Intrusion, but now I feel fine. Actually, I feel relaxed, serene, like I'm stretched out in bed on a lazy Sunday afternoon. I feel the tension in my muscles releasing. I let out a long, satisfying sigh, purging the stale air from the bottom of my lungs. I feel my body melting into the huge, solid earth beneath me, drawing strength from its massive living energy. I roll onto my stomach, through soft and fragrant clover, and push myself up to my feet. And then I see where I am.

The wind collides with my back, propelling me violently towards the edge of the tower. The city is miles beneath me, stretching to the horizon, pulling me towards the precipice.

I throw myself to the ground, sliding across the Top of the Stalk's slick green grass until I crash into a small railing right on the lip of the abyss. I stare down the edge of the Stalk and my mind screams in panic.

What the fuck is happening? This is wrong, this is all wrong.

I stare in terror over the edge and see a city I don't recognize. Edmonton is tearing itself apart. The Legislature dome collapses, only to pop up again several miles away. The Muttart pyramids pile on top of each other before City Hall rises up like a new mountain and pushes them aside. I can only watch in mute horror, clinging to the railing for dear life as the city shudders and folds in on itself and smashes itself to dust. Edwardian brick disappears, twenty-first century glass and steel rising in its place, only to be overcome by Brutalist concrete bunkers and squat postwar bungalows and buffalo-hide teepees. All the Edmontons it's ever been crash into each other, flickering in and out of existence like a patchwork kingdom of historical eras.

This isn't real. This can't be real. You're still having an Intrusion.

The tower quivers and groans and I can only pray that it won't collapse into the chaos below. The wind howls in my ears, shoving me forward, prying at my numb fingers, trying to tumble me over the edge. I close my eyes and force myself to take a breath.

"This isn't a memory," I say aloud. "This is something else. This is just a dream. And it's going to stop *right now*."

"If only it had been that easy," says a voice from above.

I tear my eyes open, twist around, and see her standing over me, looking out on the city. Her straight black hair is unmoved by the wind. She's young, barely out of her teens, but her eyes are old as earth. She gazes down at me with a defeated, exhausted look on her face.

"Why do you keep running?" she asks.

"Running? What do you mean? Where am I? Who are you?"

She looks back out at the landscape, watches the city eviscerate itself.

"You keep holding yourself back," she says. "You know what you have to do. You know what you have to face. But you're afraid. You refuse to remember."

"All I remember is falling," I say, looking over the edge and feeling a fresh wave of vertigo crashing over me. "There were men... They attacked me. They threw me off the bridge!"

I feel myself plummeting through the air all over again. I squeeze my eyes shut and grasp the railing tighter.

"Oh god," I groan. "Oh my god. I died. I'm dead."

"No," she says. "You're alive. You're still fighting it. You're still resisting."

"What are you talking about? Who are you? This is insane. I'm not resisting anything."

She looks down at me again, this time with a snarl of anger and disgust.

"Get up," she says.

She bends down and yanks me off the roof like I weigh nothing. The wind pulls at my clothes, but it doesn't push me over when she lets me go.

"Look," she says.

She juts her chin at the cityscape below. The High Level Bridge shoots up out of the ground vertically, rivalling the Stalk for height. The twisting hedges of the Infinite Maze overcome the big concrete blocks of West Edmonton Mall, digesting it until it's nothing but dirt.

"This is you," she says. "This is what's happening to you. And it will only get worse if you don't stop running from it."

I pull away from her, walk back from the edge.

"I don't know what you're talking about," I say. "I'm not running from anything. What kind of fucked-up Intrusion is this? Who even are you? Answer me!"

She starts to follow me, but then she stops suddenly. She shudders and staggers closer to the edge. Her face begins to change, just like the city below us. Her brown skin lightens. Her hair shoots back into her head. She shrinks until she's shorter than my waist. She transforms into Isobel Fraser, a four-year-old Melting Queen quivering on the precipice.

"We all knew," says Isobel. "We've all seen glimpses. We've all felt it, deep down. But none of us have faced it, save one."

"What are you talking about? Get back from the edge!"

Isobel grabs her stomach, doubles over in pain. Her face changes again, darkening and widening as her body swells like a helium balloon. Clodagh Paskwamostos towers over me, panting and grinding her teeth as Edmonton dissolves behind her.

"She felt it like we all felt it," gasps Clodagh. "She ran from it like we all run from it. But she was the only one who couldn't run fast enough."

"WHO?" I cry, stepping toward Clodagh as she teeters on the edge.

She cries out and her features twist back into their first form, the girl with the young face and the old eyes.

"You know who I am," says Shishira Sarasvati, and she falls backwards off the tower.

I rush to the edge, but Shishira is gone. The city below has stopped shifting, but it hasn't gone back to normal. The dust has settled, the constant shuffling has ended, and Edmonton has been reorganized. All the city's landmarks have been rearranged, scattered across a strange new map. The Stalk stands at the centre of a big circular metropolis, the needle at the heart of a great sundial. Twelve huge canals cut through the city, full of sparkling green water, all leading here. The Stalk is on an island, surrounded by a lake whose waters are dazzlingly silver and bright.

I stare out at the new city, watching the shadows of clouds spread across the landscape like oil stains on a map. I wait for this bizarre Intrusion to end, to jolt me back to reality like all the others. But nothing happens. I'm still here.

The wind has died down, and I walk across the park, lie down in the place where I first woke up. I close my eyes. I take deep breaths. I count to a hundred in my head. But nothing works. I'm stuck here, alone, in this nothing-place with no escape.

I stand up.

"Hey!" I shout at the sky. "Let me out of here!"

I look around, but Shishira is nowhere to be found. I walk around the park again and find a doorway to some emergency stairs. They lead me down into the Office of the Melting Queen. I walk along the long, curved hallway and see a hundred grand oil portraits, with Chinese dragons and Pride parades and dark forests. A hundred Melting Queens, and every one of them has Shishira's face.

"You know what you have to do."

Her voice whispers in my ear, but when I whip my head around the hallway is empty.

"Where are you? Let me out!"

"It's finally time for someone else," she says, "to see what I have seen. To be who I have been."

The forest floor is wet and cold. Meltwater soaks through my clothes, just as cold seeps into my skin and muscle and bone.

I feel their hands all over me. They tear at my clothes, pull my hair, turn me over so I'm facing the sky. I shut my eyes tight, twist my face away. I don't want to see them, don't want to see myself reflected in their vicious eyes.

"No!" I cry. "Please stop! Please."

"Stop resisting it," says Shishira. She sits in the middle of Churchill Square, under the great copper statue of May Winter. Its burnished leaves are falling off, one at a time, leaving a dull steel skeleton exposed. Shishira doesn't seem bothered by the clanking pieces of metal falling around her. She's drawing infinite circles in the air with pink spraypaint. They hang in front of her unnaturally, spirals of neon-bright pigment.

"Stop running from it," she says. "You have to know the truth."

"I have no idea what you're talking about," I say. "All I know is that you've trapped me here. Let me go. Let me out of this place!"

Shishira winces and clutches her belly. She throws the can of spraypaint away and it clatters across the abandoned, windswept square.

"Maybe there's only one way," she groans. "Maybe if you feel what I felt, then you'll understand."

"Feel what? What are you talking about?"

"I gave birth to myself," she says. "Every day. And in that pain, I remembered what my mother forgot. I skipped back even further, from one memory to another, to an even deeper pain. It was stronger than any other Intrusion, magnified and concentrated beyond comprehension, a double refraction that split me to pieces. I experienced what no one else has experienced: I had a memory within a memory. I was myself. I was my mother. And I was another."

Shishira's belly swells and she grits her teeth.

"I remembered the truth that my mother had lived, that all our sisters have known but none have let themselves believe."

"I don't know any truth," I say. "I don't know what you're talking about. I don't want to know. Just let me go!"

"I tried to run," she says. "I tried to hide. But there's no escaping the undertow, once it catches hold of you."

The earth starts to rumble. The wind starts to blow. The ground buckles and cracks, huge crevasses opening up. The last leaf falls off the statue, and May Winter tumbles backwards into the earth.

"Give in," says Shishira.

"No!" I shout, scrambling back from the edge of the chasm.

The wind howls, stirring up dust around us. Pieces of the sky shatter like a glass globe, falling to earth around us. Shishira stands amidst the chaos, unscathed.

"Give in!" she cries again. "You have no choice. You can remember. Or you can die."

I meet her eye, stand my ground, and the world collapses around us.

"PUSH!"

The voice booms in my ear like an atomic blast. Pain erupts through my body, setting me on fire.

"Come on Vasanta! You're almost there! PUSH!"

A bright round light shines down from the cracked ceiling above. There are shadows moving above me, people looking down, telling me to breathe, telling me it'll all be over soon.

I blink and the world snaps around me, throwing me from a warm, soft hospital bed onto the cold hard frozen dirt of the forest floor.

The full moon shines down from the night sky above. The men are shadows, plumes of warm breath in the cold night air.

"This is what you get for coming to our town and trying to bring your filth here."

He slaps me across the face. My ears ring. My skin sings.

I'm lying in a hospital bed.

No.

I'm lying on the forest floor.

No.

I'm doing both at once. I'm being split in two by a pain unlike anything I've ever felt.

"Come on, Vasanta, come on. That was almost it. You're so close, you have no idea how close you are."

"I can't," I gasp. "I can't."

"Yes you can! Keep going, come on. One last big push, that's all, that's all you need."

Their feet smash against my side, into my ribs, knocking the wind out of me. I gasp for air and beg them to stop but they can't hear me, no one can hear me. I struggle against them but they're too strong, too determined to hurt me. Two of them hold my thrashing legs down and another draws his foot back.

He kicks me between the legs, igniting pain like I've never known before. Pain that splits me in two.

The pain splits me in two. I can't do this. I can't take this anymore.

"Push, Vasanta!"

My breathing quickens, my heart hammers. I feel the pain exploding and I push, I push, I squeeze as hard as I can and I try to relax even though it's impossible. The pain obliterates everything, I feel my body breaking down.

The men hit me. Across the face, across the chest. They kick me in the side. They rip out part of my hair and howl to the moon. I scream and I scream but no one can hear me. No one is coming to save me.

I hear the screams. The choking, gasping wail. The slap on the back, a kiss on my hair. An arm wraps around my shoulders. I'm on the verge of passing out. One thought rings through my mind like the clear peal of a bell. One question I must know before I go. The only thing that matters.

"What is it?" I croak.

"It's... It's a girl."

{16}

A shattered river

"Adam."

A stern-faced woman leans over me.

"He's awake. Get the doctor."

She looks at the man next to her. He folds up his newspaper and leaves the room.

Something is wrong. I lift my hand to my head and feel scratchy stubble where my smooth silky hair used to be.

"We had to cut it off," says the woman. I have a strong image of her wielding shears greedily, hacking off my golden hair with glee. Or is it black as coal? Or is it red like cedar?

"What did you do?" I rasp out.

"Don't try to talk," she says. She pats her finger on my dry, cracked lips.

"Where am I?"

"In the hospital. You've been unconscious for almost two weeks! We were so worried. They found you on the riverbank. They said you had no brain activity! Your father almost suggested... but no, I would never let them do that."

The woman brushes an imaginary tear away with quick, violent swipes.

"Who are you?" I ask.

The door opens and a man with a newspaper comes in, followed by a doctor in a white coat and a blue turban.

"He just asked me who I am," whispers the woman. "He doesn't remember!"

The doctor comes to my bedside.

"Hello," he says amiably. "I'm Doctor Kanwari."

"Hello," I say. "I'm—"

I open my mouth to tell him my name, but I don't know what it is. It's like reaching on top of the armoire for a hatbox you know is always there, but your fingers only pull down dust. I grasp desperately for my name. For any name. But nothing comes.

There are three people in this small room watching me. One of them holds a clipboard in his hands, so he must be important. He clicks his pen.

"I'm going to ask you a few questions, okay Adam?"

"Okay," I respond. The name feels wrong, but I don't correct him. What's my name? Victoria? Isobel? Alice? Iris? Names bloom and wilt in my head in rapid succession. I feel a rush of joy at each one before I realize it's wrong and I crash back down into uncertainty.

"Can you tell me the last thing you remember?"

A hundred images speed through my mind, like I'm stopped at a railway crossing with a train rattling past. Each train car houses a big screen, playing a different movie. All of the movies are about me, but they all star different actresses. I can't focus on any of them. It makes me nauseated to try.

"The only way to make it stop is to go where you don't want to go."

I twist my head around and see her there, leaning against the wall in the far corner by the door, dressed all in black like an evil spirit.

"*You* can stop this! *You're* doing this!"

"You were almost there," says Shishira. "Just give in. It's all you have to do."

"I don't have to do anything."

"It won't stop until you remember," she says. "It's happening to you like it happened to me. You're falling to pieces. You're losing yourself."

"Adam! Who are you talking to?"

Hands on my shoulders, spinning me around. Mean buzz of ceiling fluorescents. Fingers digging into me.

"Get off me! This is outrageous!" I shout at the woman who placed her beefy red hands on my body. "Don't you know who I am!?"

I can't believe these people! Kitty and Joan and the other ladies at the yacht club are going to be so superior when they see me knocked off my perch like this. The thought of their smug, gloating faces makes me sick to my stomach.

The Pakistani reaches out his hand and I jerk my arm away from him.

"Don't touch me! What kind of hospital is this, anyways? I'd like to speak to a qualified doctor, at least. Not someone who ought to be cleaning the floors."

"Adam!" The woman swats my shoulder with her hand and I slap it away, incredulous that I should be assaulted in this way.

"How *dare* you, madam? That's *Mrs. Sable* to you. Just wait until my husband hears about this. He'll have *your* sham licence revoked," I spit at the so-called doctor, "and he'll destroy *your* reputations, whoever you are." I curl my lip at this low-class man and woman. "He's a very prominent attorney, I'll have you know."

The sham doctor gets off my bed and I breathe a sigh of relief—honestly, you can never know what that type might do to you. The three of them have a whispered consultation in the corner and then turn back to me.

"Mrs. Sable," begins the fraud. "Can you tell us—"

The dragon dances along the street. Ten thousand lanterns float in the sky. According to legend, we light lanterns to fool the Jade Emperor. He'll look from high above and see that the city is already on fire, and so we'll be spared his wrath.

I smile at the crowd and see Birch's old face looking on with satisfaction. Yeah. Enjoy it while you can, old man. In a couple months you won't be smiling quite so much.

I don't like to look in the mirror. When I do, it's not me I see looking back. Some stranger. Tall. Mannish. With an angular jawline and fiery red hair cropped short. I move my arm up and down, and the simulacrum moves its arm as well.

"River."

A Muslim woman in a green head scarf appears in the mirror behind me. I turn around and see her standing there awkwardly, in the middle of a shabbily decorated living room.

"What river?"

The woman glances at the young, thin, anxious-looking Asian man sitting on the couch, surrounded by piles and piles of books.

"These Intrusions aren't just pulling River away from themselves anymore," he says. "They're taking over River's identity in the present. I've heard that sometimes a Melting Queen will bring something back with her—she'll take a couple seconds to remember who exactly she is, until her mind digests the foreign memories and stabilizes—but nothing like this. It's like a hundred and fifteen people are all competing for one body."

"Evelyn and I have a very close relationship," I tell my advisors. "I'm sorry that people refuse to understand that, but I will not send him away. It's no one else's business but our own."

The woman looks at me with the same frightened, confused expression I've seen a thousand times.

"It's okay, Vivian." The young Asian man stands up, pats my hand. "We won't make you send him away."

He looks at the woman in the green head scarf beside him.

"Vivian Tegler," he says in an undertone, "1962. She declared her twin brother Evelyn as her co-Melting Queen. Everyone thought they were lovers."

"And is she here now? Or is it just River?"

The man shrugs.

"I don't know," he says. "But I've noticed a pattern."

He stares into my eyes, searching for something.

"River seems to be moving backwards. They're jumping around, all over the place, but their Intrusions are getting further and further back in time."

"So maybe once River experiences them all, then everything will be fine?"

The man shakes his head.

"I don't know," he says. "But it needs to happen soon."

He squeezes my hand. His voice is pleading, imploring.

"I don't know if you can hear me or understand me, River. But you need to come back. Odessa is beating us. She stopped her campaign for a few days, condemned the attack on you. But now you're gone. Nobody has seen you. They're going to pick her by default if you don't come back to us. We missed Klondike Days. We missed Heritage Days. We missed Folk Fest and Taste of Edmonton and the Dragon Boat Festival. We even missed the Fringe. The Fringe, River! No Melting Queen has missed the Fringe since Breanne Breg launched it in 1982. You need to be seen in public."

"We can't just throw River to the wolves," says the woman. "Everyone has a cell phone. Imagine what they could post if something bad happens. Going out in public is a very bad idea. Don't you think, River?"

"What's a cell phone?" I ask, intrigued. They shake their heads and don't answer me. Quite rude, I should say.

I notice that my fingernails are bitten down to the quick. That's a filthy habit that I've never had. It was always my sister who couldn't control her slovenly impulses. I look around for my purse, to take out my nail file, but I must've set it down somewhere. I glance in the mirror and feel my blood run cold.

She's behind me, staring at me from the edge of the room like a cobweb in the corner.

"Stop fighting it," says Shishira. "It's only getting worse."

"Because of you!" I shout, whipping around to face her. "Why are you doing this to me?"

"River!"

Sander and Kaseema look back and forth between me and the corner, horrified. "Who are you talking to?"

I recognize both of them, but the thrill is eclipsed by my fury with Shishira.

"She's still here, Sander. She won't go away, no matter what I do."

I can feel the current trying to pull me back under, trying to suck me back down into the whirlpool of memories. I try to hold on to the shreds of my identity, gasping for air.

"Your friends can't help you," says Shishira. "Only you can make it stop."

I feel the panic racing up my spine, that implacable terror that sets my nerves ablaze. I feel an echo of pain, the wind knocked out of me by a phantom blow to my stomach.

"No!" I shout, staring down Shishira as Kaseema and Sander gape at me. "No, I won't."

"Then it will never stop."

"River!"

Sander grabs me by the shoulders, forces me to meet his eyes.

"Who are you talking to?"

"She won't leave me alone. She's the one doing this."

"Who?"

"Shishira."

We march along Whyte Avenue, a rainbow-clad regiment of queer soldiers. Protestors line the sidewalks, chanting the same hateful slogans I've heard since I was young. I've always been too butch to hide what I am, and people have always felt the need to tell me exactly what they think of me. They might think they're tearing me down, but they've made me stronger than anyone else. I'll fight every single one of them, if I have to.

I look to my right, and see Kaseema holding the sign we made together, demanding marriage equality. I see the fear in her young face, and I feel my heart swell with love and gratitude. That bastard Birch told her not to come. Her mother told her that they wouldn't let her back into her mosque. But she's here. For me.

We face down the protestors together, hold our heads high, and march on.

Rain runs down the car window, splitting apart and rolling together in runnels. I watch the water, mesmerized as it converges and diverges endlessly.

"River."

I turn and see a gigantic woman, sitting beside me in the driver's seat. Her tired face has seen better days. Her black hair is greying. Her black eyes are surrounded by crow's feet. Her brown skin hangs loose on her face.

I look past her, out the window, and see a very average house on a very average street.

"Where are we? What are we doing here?"

"We're here to see Vasanta Sarasvati. Your friend Sander said that she's the only one who could help. She's been through all this before, with her daughter. Come on, we're late."

I follow the woman—*Clare? Cashla? Caragh?*—up the front walk. The door opens for us, and a round brown woman stands in the entranceway.

"Come in, come in," she says. "Get out of the rain."

I recognize her from my memories. But the Vasanta Sarasvati I remembered was younger, smaller and more vibrant. This one looks like a cruel caricature of her former self, like a faded and distorted old photo. She's put on a lot of weight, but not in that warm, plump way of a mom who always bakes every weekend or a grandma who always has chocolates in her purse or an auntie who always has one glass of wine too many at dinner. Instead she looks like a supermarket strawberry, swollen with water until it's bloated and flavourless. She doesn't look at home in her body, and she moves like she's still not used to it. When I look at her, I can see her old face buried under the new one, like an ancient temple half-submerged in sand.

"I made us some tea and sandwiches," she mumbles as I slip out of my shoes in her front hallway. "I hope you like smoked salmon."

"I'm sorry," I say, "but I'm a vegetarian."

"Don't worry," grunts the big mountain of a woman beside me, rolling her eyes. "You won't be in a few minutes."

We follow Vasanta into her front room and sit down on her couch. She serves us our tea and sandwiches and then sits down in the chair facing us. I look out the window behind her and watch the rain pelting the street. It must have been hot out earlier, because the black asphalt is steaming. I try to enjoy this rare moment of tranquility, as the winds which have been pulling me apart die down and I can just sit in silence.

After a few moments, I notice Vasanta watching me intently.

"What?"

"Nothing," she says, blushing and looking away. "I just... I wondered if you'd seen her again. Sander Fray said, on the phone... Never mind..."

She picks up a sandwich and takes a small bite. I notice that there's one in front of me too, and I have a taste. It's delicious, with crunchy cucumber and crisp chives and buttery smooth smoked salmon. My favourite.

"We're hoping you can help us," says Clodagh, whose name I can finally remember. "It's been hard to piece together, but we think the same thing is happening to River that happened to your daughter. They're having so many Intrusions that they're fragmenting and forgetting who they are."

Vasanta glances at the wall, where a bunch of Shishira's old school photos are hung.

"I wish I could help you," she says. "But I don't think I can. I spoke to your friend Sander for a long time for his book, and I told him everything I know. I told him about my time as the Melting Queen, and I told him about Shishira. How I went to the statue with her and stuck up her leaf. How I coached her through the coronation. How she... how she died."

She takes a sip of her tea and her cup clatters against the saucer.

"I'm sorry," she says, not looking at us. "I thought I could do this but I don't think I can."

She meets my eye, and I see every day of the past two decades strung around her neck like ten thousand tiny millstones.

"I couldn't help her," she says, shaking her head back and forth. "I can't help you either."

Vasanta starts to stand up, mumbling that she's sorry, that we should go.

"I keep seeing her," I say.

Vasanta stops. She looks at me, devastated and jealous and desperate to hear more.

"I keep seeing her, in front of me, talking back to me, like none of the other Melting Queens. I've never had another Intrusion like that."

"What does she say?" asks Vasanta, sinking back down into her chair. "What does she look like? Is she okay?"

"She tells me I have to remember," I say.

"Remember what?"

Vasanta is on the edge of her chair. The wind gusts and raindrops speckle the window. The trees across the street bend in the gale.

"Something bad. Something buried, deep down. I've been seeing it since I was first Named as the Melting Queen: I'm running through the trees, desperate to get away from someone. And then they catch me."

I look between Vasanta and Clodagh, and I see the recognition on their faces.

"She said that everybody knows," I say, "but nobody lets themselves know. She's the only one who saw it all, who felt it all."

Neither of them will meet my eye, and I can tell they're feeling what I've felt since the beginning: a frantic, primal aversion. An overwhelming urge to run, to avoid, to forget.

"It's true, isn't it? You've all felt it, and you've all run from it."

Vasanta holds her head in her hands.

"Do you think... do you think she's still in there somehow?" she asks. "Connected to the Melting Queens somehow, through your memories?"

She looks at me, eyes glistening.

"I don't know," I say.

Vasanta looks back at the school photos on her wall. Shishira's smiling faces watch over us.

"Alright," she says. "Alright. Come with me."

She leads us down the beige hallway, towards the back of the house. The drabness of the walls seems to pull all the colour out of my clothes. I start to feel numb, sleepy. The dull decor is exhausting me. But then we come to a room which vibrates with colour.

The bedroom's walls are covered in all types of art—chalk pastels and oil, acrylic and charcoal—in every shade of the rainbow. None of it is a masterwork, or even very good at all. But there are strong colours and clear scenes in each piece. Wheat fields. Snowy prairies. Foothills. Mountains. The sky. The sea. Stars and nebulas, office towers and interchanges. Rivers.

"This was Shishira's room," says Vasanta. "Over that last year, the only thing that brought her peace was to paint and draw and make art. But even that wasn't enough, in the end."

She touches one of the paintings, a landscape drenched in honey-yellow sunlight.

"She had so many painful Intrusions. She saw so many dreadful, horrible things. So I told her to focus on the most beautiful thing she'd seen every time, and she would reproduce it from memory as soon as she came back to herself. No matter who she was, no matter how much she forgot herself, she would always grab for her paints and chalk and pencils."

She runs her fingers over a turquoise blue lake, smiling the tiniest of smiles, a weak little light on her face.

"At first they were all colourful pictures like these," she says. "But then they changed. She changed."

She walks over to a dresser, opens a drawer, and lifts out a stack of papers with visible effort, as if they weigh a ton. She sets them down carefully on the bed.

The topmost piece of paper is almost completely black, a shadowy vortex of trees in dark charcoal. Vasanta flips to the next, and the next, through a dozen paintings and sketches and drawings. It's all forest, dark and terrifying, with visible gouges in paint and pencil where Shishira tried to exorcise the memory onto the canvas.

I shiver.

"She kept trying to tell me something, but I didn't understand what it was," says Vasanta. "All I had were these."

She touches one of the dark artworks tentatively yet reverently, a keepsake that she clearly hates but could never bring herself to throw out.

"She tried to tell me what was really happening. That there was something more, something even worse than the pain of giving birth to herself every day. But every time she started talking about it, she was thrown back into the darkness, and it would be days before I could get her to remember who she was."

Vasanta looks up at us. Her eyes are exhausted, haunted, underlined by dark circles.

"So I told her not to talk about it. I told her to try to forget it, to avoid it. It was the only thing I could think to say. Kastevoros Birch agreed."

"Birch?" Clodagh spits his name. "He knew about all this?"

"He tried to help," says Vasanta. "He was here all the time, talking to Shishira about it. But he didn't know any more than we did about what this meant, where these memories came from. He just said Shishira should try to avoid talking or thinking about it as much as possible."

Vasanta looks at the head of the bed and I know she's remembering Shishira there, watching helplessly as her daughter thrashes about fitfully, fighting to survive a memory of unparalleled pain.

"It didn't work," she says. "The harder she tried to avoid it, the more often it happened. She fought against it for so long, longer than I ever could have. I told her that she just had to wait until the next Melting Queen was crowned, and then she'd be okay. But after she Named Victoria Goulburn, she still kept having Intrusions. It even got worse. And so..."

She looks down at the dark drawings, the poison at the heart of her daughter's sickness.

"I don't blame Victoria Goulburn," she says. "It wasn't her fault. It was mine."

"That's not true," I say. "You know that's not true."

Vasanta looks up at me, and in the corner of her eye I can see the formidable foe I'm up against, the voice in her head which for two decades has whispered this narrative in her ear.

"It is true," says Vasanta. "I pushed her into being the Melting Queen and it killed her. It's that simple. Her mind was torn apart. She had this dark memory, and it only got worse after she tried to avoid it. And the worst part is..."

She covers her face with her hand, filled with shame at her confession.

"The worst part is that I *did* know what she was talking about. You were right. I had seen the woods. I had felt myself running, long ago when I was the Melting Queen. But I never let myself face it. I locked up those memories so tight, so deep inside myself, that even when my own daughter was being tortured I wouldn't let myself remember. Not even to save her."

Vasanta Sarasvati lays a hand on the pillow beside her. For a second, I see her as she was twenty-four years ago—not the faded remnant of today, but a desperate, loving mother, powerless to help her child. Memories from Shishira swirl through my mind, and I feel Vasanta laying a damp cloth on my hot forehead. I hear her whispering in my ear, telling me that she's right here and she won't leave my side.

"Birch made us say it was cancer," she says. "We couldn't have a Melting Queen who killed herself. But she did. She snuck out one night and she... she jumped off the bridge. Because of me. Because I couldn't face it."

She stares through the bed, through the pile of dark drawings, through the earth itself, numb and empty.

"It wasn't your fault," I say. "She didn't kill herself because of you."

Vasanta looks at me for a long minute. Now I can see two voices, one begging her to believe me and the other, long-dominant voice convincing her that she was to blame. She sighs and looks down at the drawings.

"I'm sorry," she mumbles. "I can't fix you. I couldn't fix her when her mind broke. We can't fix anyone. All we can do is live our lives and try to forget."

I look at this woman, crumpled and worn out and broken, trapped in this house with nothing but painful memories to keep her company. I think of Victoria, suffering the same fate for the same reasons, blaming herself for Shishira's death. I think of Iris, trying to burn up her pain with righteous anger, and Isobel, locked away in a nursing home with no visitors, and Alice, so consumed with bitterness that she'd take a hammer to her legacy. I think of Clodagh, shuttering her travel agency, watching her dreams melt away one by one, making bacon sandwiches for one and watching old movies in her shabby old house. And finally, I understand.

"No," I say.

I reach out and put my hand on Vasanta's shoulder. She looks at me hopelessly. The evil voice, as always, has won.

"No," I say again. "We have to remember."

I take Clodagh's hand in mine. She has an awkward look on her face, but she gives my hand a gentle squeeze.

I look around Shishira's room: the explosion of colours, the dark pit of images at the centre of the room, trying to pull the three of us down into the abyss.

I look at the corner and see Shishira standing there, watching us, a hint of hope in her ancient eyes for the first time.

"Okay," I say to her. "Okay. I'm ready."

I take a deep breath. I close my eyes. I let myself fall backwards, into the storm.

{17}

That glorious day

"May!"

A big burly bearded man is coming toward me, swaying unevenly as he crosses the sloping lawn. He holds a bottle loosely in his hand.

"Mr. Moon," I say cautiously. I look over his shoulder at the bonfires where everyone is gathered. I'm suddenly very aware that I'm alone over here at the food tent. I see the way his eyes rove over me and I pull my shawl tighter around my shoulders. I should never have worn this blouse. It reveals too little and too much.

"Do you want some pie?" I ask him. His tongue hangs out of his mouth like a hound's.

"Oh no," he shakes his head. "Just came over to say hello. What's all this Mr. Moon? That's Bill to you! Mr. Moon makes me sound like an old man, heh heh!"

He wiggles his eyebrows at me, with that theatrical flair that's made his vaudeville shows the most popular acts in town. I give him a polite smile.

"Bet you've got all the boys chasing after you, don't you? Hank Sheer's boys, and those McClaskey twins. Wild young lads, but growing into stout-hearted men."

He beams blearily, proud of his city's young sons. I don't know who any of those boys are, but I can imagine them. Ready to inherit the earth from their fathers. I feel my eyebrow twitch but I know I can't let anything show on my face.

"No," I say sweetly. "No boys for me, Mr. Moon. I'm just focusing on working. Mrs. Rutherford has been so kind."

"Is that so?" he says. "You're just the perfect girl, aren't you?"

He looks me up and down.

"You know," he says, "some people are saying we should get a pretty girl to give a speech, some kind of May Queen. I heard they were writing a whole fancy proclamation to celebrate the spring. Maybe you're just the girl to be that Queen, Miss May, and read out that proclamation in front of everyone. Would you like that?"

His speech is slurred but his eyes are sober, too sober.

"I wouldn't really know how to make a speech," I say. "I'm sure you'll find someone else who's much better than me."

He says nothing, just leers at me, tugging at my shawl with his eyes.

"Here, have some pie," I say to cut the tension. I pass him a plate with a thick wedge, bursting with saskatoons which tumble out and roll across the plate.

He takes it into his big hairy hands. His fingers close over mine as I pass him a fork. I jerk my hand back. Mr. Moon frowns. He scoops up a big bite of pie and slides it between his lips, never taking his eyes off mine.

"Mnph," he groans, "that's just perfect. D'you make this?"

"No, Mrs. Morris did."

"Course she did. Darn fine pies, that woman makes. Nothing beats her saskatoon pie. You oughta ask her to teach you how to make pies this good. Then you'd have all them young men around your finger. More than a pretty girl like you already does, anyways."

He gives me a wink, licks his fork. A dribble of saskatoon jelly is stuck in his beard.

His eyes glow with a mischievous hostility that makes me nervous. He sets down his plate on the table beside us, uses a dirty finger to wipe up the remaining pie filling. He sticks his finger in his mouth and frowns at me as he pulls it out with a wet pop.

"You know, some people get mighty curious when a pretty young girl don't give the time of day to any fine young man. Some people talk about that."

I feel a blush rising up my neck, feel my heart quicken. I try to breathe normally.

"I... I don't know what you mean." I try to keep my voice level, polite.

Mr. Moon comes towards me and I move around to the other side of the table, inside the tent. I start cutting more pieces of pie and placing them on plates. I glance up at him to see his eyes fixed intently on me.

"I should bring some of this over to the party," I say, picking up two of the plates. He steps sideways and blocks my way.

"Excuse me."

I go to walk around him and he steps in my way again. He speaks softly, reaches out and hesitates a moment before putting his hand down on my shoulder like a caring father.

"I saw something queer in the fall, down at Mill Creek."

His voice is just shy of a whisper, barely audible above the hoots and hollering of the party across the lawn. I look down at the pieces of pie I'm holding.

"You know," he says, "where those boys dam up the stream and make a pool? They're gonna be doing that any day now that the snow is melting. I saw something mighty peculiar down there in the fall. Can you guess what it was I might've seen?"

I force myself to meet his eyes. I try not to look frightened, even though he can probably feel me shaking.

"You didn't see anything, Mr. Moon. You're drunk. Let me go or I'll scream."

His eyes bore into mine. Then a bright smile breaks open across his face and he squeezes my shoulder. His voice is cheerful, but I hear the threat in it.

"I know what I saw, Miss Winter."

I relax my shoulder and twist out of his grasp. He stumbles forward and I duck past him. I walk quickly towards the bonfires, towards the massive crowd of people who've come out to celebrate the end of winter.

"I'll be seeing you, May Winter!" he calls after me. He says my name like it's a joke.

I find two eager recipients for the plates of pie, and then I try to enjoy the party. The festivities are taking place on a wide, slanted lawn on the side of a hill. Down below I can see the river, aflood with little icebergs. Up the hill the palisades of Fort Edmonton loom.

I join one circle around a bonfire where someone is playing a fiddle and some people my age are dancing in time. I accept an offer from a boy and as we spin around I keep my hips held well back even though he's trying to press up against me.

But then I realize that everyone is too drunk to care, and mine is the least of the evening's transgressions. I see a priest off his rocker, swigging from a bottle of communion wine, laughing bearishly and slurring in French with some burly men who are smacking wooden spoons against their naked thighs. Respectable ladies lift their skirts, pulling bottles of amber liqueur from their garters and pinching each other's pale peach skin. A redcoat is telling a grisly murder story to a group of elderly women around a fire, gnashing his teeth and titillating them with the details. Two of the fine young men Mr. Moon mentioned make eyes at each other from across a bonfire, then sneak off down the hill into the moonlit forest by the river. I even see some of the Cree and the Blackfoot sitting together at their own fires nearby, telling stories and acting out myths.

All throughout the night I keep feeling my neck tingle and turning around to see Mr. Moon watching me. He's talking with a group of men who all look like him: the town fathers, the stout-hearted men. They puff away lustily at thick cigars and slap each other on the back. I try not to let our encounter earlier bother me. Whatever he saw in the Mill Creek ravine, there's nothing I can do about it now. If they find out, I'll just have to leave town again. Like in Regina. And Winnipeg. And Toronto.

I can't seem to shake the sour feeling from my stomach though. No matter where I wander through the mass of people, there isn't a bonfire where I want to stay. I look down at the river valley, darker than I've ever seen it, and feel something pulling me there. Maybe that's how I'll celebrate the ice breaking: alone in the dark. Or maybe

I'll come across the two boys I saw earlier, and find some allies who know how to keep secrets like mine.

I slip away from the revelries and pick my way down the slope, through the woods. The ground is a slippery brown mush—last autumn's dead leaves dissolving in the spring meltwater. I breathe in the crisp air and tie my shawl tighter around myself. I feel myself smiling, my spirits lifting in spite of my knotted worries. It was a long winter. The longest I've ever lived through. But now it's over. And everyone is so relieved, they've all gone a little wild.

I make my way carefully through the trees, right down to the water's edge. I crouch on the riverbank and look upstream, watch all the little pieces of ice flowing smoothly and silently towards me. I stick my hand into the water and the cold bites at my skin. Bringing a handful up to my mouth, I drink it in. Thin tendrils of cold spread through me like roots burrowing into the earth. I stand up straight and look down at my reflection in the river. If I didn't know the truth, I would never guess that I'm anything other than what I say I am.

I let out a long sigh. I feel my body releasing some of the tension that's been built up for months and months. For years. A gnarled, twisted mass of anxiety, curled around a truth I can never share with anyone. Maybe I'm not one for big parties, but I've got to admit that everybody is onto something. It feels good to celebrate the spring like this. To curse the winter. To say goodbye to the past.

I'm about to bend down and take another sip of water when two hands grab my shoulders, jerking me away from the river. I collapse backwards and find myself in the lap of Mr. Moon. I try to break free but his grip tightens.

"Careful now!" he laughs. "You almost fell in! Good thing I was here to save you."

"I was fine! Let me go!"

"It's okay, I got you. I got you."

I squirm against his powerful grasp. I gag on the reek of whiskey which pours from his mouth. I let my body go limp, then thrust up against his arms with full force. But he's wise to this trick.

"Hoowee!" cries a voice behind us. "You sure were right Bill! That's one crazy girl!"

I hear a chorus of laughter and I realize to my horror that other men are standing on the bank behind us.

"I saw what you were doing down near that creek," Bill Moon slurs into my ear. His hot humid breath soaks the side of my face, reeking of rancid saskatoons. I try to turn away as far as I can.

"You like coming down here near the rivers and creeks, don't you? You like swimming late at night, when you think nobody will see. Somebody's got a big secret that you don't want anyone to know... well, it's not that big of a secret."

The men behind us laugh. I feel my body grow cold, drain of all its heat, tense up. Bill Moon relaxes the tiniest bit. I explode forwards, sink my teeth into his hairy arm.

Bill Moon howls and I snake out of his arms and I'm running, running away from the men, running through the forest. They're howling, they're following me, I pant and taste the blood and spit it out and it runs down my chin.

"HELP ME! SOMEONE HELP!"

I crash through the trees, hopefully towards the party. Hopefully someone will hear me: the boys in the woods, or someone relieving themselves, or someone, anyone, please.

The branches keep hitting me in the face so I raise my arms in front of me. The dry wood and sharp thorns leave deep scratches on my arms, but I barely feel them.

I turn around, see the trees rustling behind me as the men follow.

"YOU CAN'T RUN FOREVER!" bellows Moon. "WE'RE GOING TO CATCH YOU!"

I turn back just in time to see the branch under my foot, tripping me, sending me crashing to the ground.

Their hands are on me instantly, tearing my shawl off my shoulders and throwing it into the trees.

"Let's see what you really got up under those skirts of yours," a voice growls. It could be Bill Moon, it could be any of the others.

Rough hands rip at my dress, pulling it up. I try to squirm free but they're too strong. I feel my bare legs exposed to the air, my belly pressing down into the cold slimy mush, prickled by pine needles. I shut my eyes as tight as they'll go. They rip my dress all the way off, until I'm naked as the day I was born. The huge rough hands turn me over so I'm facing the sky.

I shut my eyes tight, twist my face away. I don't want to see them, don't want to see myself reflected in their vicious eyes.

"No!" I cry. "Please stop! Please."

The men just stare at me for a few seconds. I cover myself with my hands but they have seen my secret, fully exposed. Bill Moon crouches down next to me.

"We know who you are, Albert Herring. We've heard all about you, from folks back in Regina. This is what you get for coming to our town and trying to bring your filth here."

He slaps me across the face. I feel the sting, feel my skin sing. He hits me again— once, twice, over and over. Then the others fall on me, hitting me and kicking me and pushing me and shouting at me.

Their feet smash against my side, into my ribs, knocking the wind out of me. I gasp for air and beg them to stop but they can't hear me, no one can hear me. I struggle against them but they're too strong, too determined to hurt me. Two of them hold my thrashing legs down and another draws his foot back.

He kicks me between the legs, igniting pain like I've never known before. Pain that splits me in two.

The men hit me. Across the face, across the chest. They kick me in the side. They kick me between my legs. They rip out part of my hair and howl to the moon. I scream and I scream but no one can hear. No one is coming to save me.

And then it stops. I keep my eyes closed. I hear them talking nearby, but I don't know what they're saying. I open my eyes after what feels like hours and I see the stars swirling through the night sky. I can't move. Every part of my broken body screams.

The men stop talking and come back over to me. They pull me up by my hair and I'm too numb to even worry anymore. Just let it stop now. Let it be done, all of it.

"We have a job for you, milady."

Some man's voice. Bill Moon. I don't know. They're all just rough hands, beards, sneers.

"We need a special lady. A woman to be our queen. That's what you want, isn't it?"

They drag me up the hill to a tent. One of them scrubs roughly at my face, pulls my hair back and ties it. The remnants of my dress hang in tatters off my body, dead mushy brown leaves stuck all over me, barely covering me. I stand there mutely. I can't move on my own.

They bend my fingers around a little bouquet of broken branches. They lead me outside the tent and onto a small hill, in front of a huge crowd.

"Ladies and gentlemen!" bellows Bill Moon. He waves his arms extravagantly and then he almost falls over. His arms pinwheel until his thick calloused hand grabs onto my bare arm and he steadies himself with a chuckle.

"The good people of Edmonton have drafted a Proclamation! You have convened a council of Edmontonians and created a Proclamation! You have declared this day, when the ice breaks up on the river and we come together as a city to celebrate spring-time shoulder to shoulder, a civic holiday forevermore! May Day! The Day of the Great Breakup! The Day the River Runs Free! Melting Day!"

The crowd cheers at every word. Bill Moon smiles at me, basking in the joy of the city.

"And, in thanks, we humble gentlemen have found you a Melting Queen!

Bill Moon lifts up my hand and the crowd erupts into laughter. There's a bright flash as someone takes our picture. Dozens of people raise their glasses and bottles in a mocking toast to my health.

"Beautiful, isn't she?" He laughs along with them. "A proper lady, a good daughter of Edmonton, rosy-cheeked and stout-hearted."

Mr. Moon leers at me, hiccups jovially.

"Give a twirl for your adoring people, my queen!"

The crowd roars with laughter as he spins me about, crushing my fingers in his.

"This lovely lady has agreed to embody the spirit of the spring," bellows Moon. "We need never fear winter again, for we are safe in her warm bosom."

The crowd weeps with laughter. I stand there in front of everyone I know, the whole city come out to celebrate. Do they recognize me? Do they understand that I was briefly one of them? Or do they just see a drunk fool, a man in a dress putting on a show for them?

They cheer and laugh and hug each other. None of them seems to notice the way I'm bent over, covered in mud and dead leaves, tears streaming down my cheeks. None of them seems to notice the red marks on my skin, already blackening into bruises. Or maybe they do notice. Maybe they do know who I am. Maybe they understand exactly what they're doing.

"Our queen deserves a crown!" yells Moon.

A pair of rough hands comes down on my shoulders and I smell whiskey breath once more. I'm frozen, I can't run, I can't cry out to the people that these men have hurt me. No one cares. They cheer them on as they lower a circle of muddy, strung-together leaves onto my head.

"Our queen deserves a throne!"

Moon shoves me down onto an old tree stump nearby and bows mockingly in front of me. He turns to the crowd.

"Well? Bow to your queen, Edmonton!"

The crowd howls with delight and bows, shouting out mocking congratulations.

"To your majesty's health!" screams one taunting voice.

"Long live the queen!" jeers another.

The men and women in the crowd try to outdo each other's bows, bending lower and lower, cackling at each other's false prostrations.

"Give us a blessing, your majesty!" shouts one man.

"Grant us gifts with your feminine charms!"

"Give us a speech!"

"Dance for us!"

"Show us your womanly talents!"

I sit there shivering in the dark, waiting for it to be over, wishing I was anyone but who I am. Bill Moon yanks me to my feet and leads me in a dance, pulling my ragdoll body across the lawn as a band strikes up a tune. Soon the whole crowd is dancing, laughing about the hysterical spectacle Bill Moon has conjured up for them.

Moon sits me back down on the stump and I hold my rags around myself, trying to find the power to move, to leave this place. No one is looking at me—they've forgotten me here, they're done with their toy. I could sneak away so easily, if only I could bring myself to stand up. But I feel such intense pain inside of me, as if every bit of me is broken and can never be made whole again. I can't move. All I can do is sit and watch as they dance.

The party goes on—I don't know how long, it could be hours or minutes, it could be two songs or twenty—and they start coming up to me. One by one. Sheepishly. Guiltily. Glancing warily at the revellers around them, in case they should be seen talking to the freak. Someone drapes a blanket loosely around my shoulders. Someone wipes the mud off my face with their handkerchief. They all apologize for what they've done: We're sorry, May. We're sorry, Albert. We're sorry, whoever you are. Whatever you are. We do not love you, but we are not cruel.

But you were cruel, I think. You are cruel. You are a cruel city.

Each of them melts away into the night, unburdened by their confessions, absolved of their responsibility. The aching pain inside me starts to disappear. It doesn't hurt anymore. I feel numb, hollow, lighter than air.

The world spins before me and I feel my balance give way. I collapse onto the cold dead grass, but nobody notices. I lie in a pile of dead leaves, beside the dead stump, listening to the hum of the party, looking up at the sky. I see the aurora dancing, peaceful and sad above us all.

The aurora fades as my eyes flicker closed, and then the world is dark.

{18}

Let history forget her name

They arrive one by one, ringing Clodagh's doorbell and stepping warily into her house. They file into her back garden, sitting on a multitude of folding chairs that Kaseema scrounged from somewhere and arranged in the closest approximation to a circle that she could manage.

I look around the circle and I see so many familiar faces. The Melting Queens, united for the first time. Only sixty or so are still alive, and Sander has interviewed them all. While I've been fighting Odessa, and then fighting my own memories, he's been quietly building up friendships, recording their versions of events for his book. Some of them had vowed to never attend any kind of reunion. Some of them have publicly endorsed Odessa. But they all came when Sander asked them to.

They're all different than they were in my memories. Most of them are visibly older. Greyer. Thinner and less substantial. Even the young ones have Shishira's old eyes, eyes that have seen too much. They're uncomfortable with this meeting and they're uncertain about me and they're unconvinced that they should stay. But they're here. And that's what counts.

"You've all come here because of Sander Fray," I say, standing before them. I nod to Sander, who watches from Clodagh's back doorstep, standing beyond the circle with Kaseema and René.

"He's writing a true history of the Melting Queens, and all of you have told him *your* truths, so he can share them with everyone. I hope you'll help me do the same."

"I heard you had a nervous breakdown," says Ananke Cosmopoulos, the architect of Sundial Park.

"I think you all know better than to believe that," I say. "After I was attacked, I was overwhelmed by Intrusions. I was torn apart. I didn't even remember who I was most of the time. And when I did, I could feel memories raging at the edge of my mind—*your* memories."

I lock eyes with Doreen Spurlong, who founded the Edmonton International Cat Festival, and remember coming home to find Catsy Cline dead on the bathroom floor.

I look at Eliza Lake, the deafblind Melting Queen who helped establish 911 emergency services in Edmonton, and remember the indescribable panic I felt when I was dropped into her life and lost my sight and hearing.

"I remember being all of you," I say, "and all the others too. How many lifetimes did I live, lost in those memories? One minute I was Oriana Kuruliak in 1959, inventing a new Ukrainian dance named after a whirlwind. The next I was Katherine Held mourning my father and Karen Mackenzie watching the Millennium fireworks and Giselle Schaft looking on with satisfaction as old buildings were torn down to make way for something new."

I meet the eye of the queens I mention, and I know they feel the connection we share. Out the corner of my eye, I can see the others too, the ones who've passed away, standing silently behind us, around the outside of circle. They will always be a part of me now.

"I lived it all," I say. "I saw it all. I flickered through a hundred and fourteen years of our history, out of order. I jumped across years and decades. But I worked my way steadily back, to the beginning, to the night when this all started."

A gentle breeze plays with Clodagh's windchime. A cloud moves in front of the sun. The Melting Queens listen to me, feeling our connection growing stronger by the second.

"All my life I heard that the Melting Queen was magic. But I never saw any magic. I heard that the Melting Queen could perform miracles. But I never saw any miracles. All I saw was a bunch of women cutting ribbons and kissing babies, with a bunch of goddess mythology glazed overtop to make things seem more mystical."

I look at Victoria and Alice, Iris and Isobel and Clodagh. I feel my connection to them the deepest, these abandoned queens that I have befriended. They look at me with love, giving me the strength to tell this story.

"I never heard about Intrusions," I say. "And I didn't understand why not, because they prove the magic of the Melting Queen more than anything else. Why not tell everyone that the Melting Queens are all connected, that we can remember our whole history, going all the way back?"

I look at Vasanta. She gives me a small, sad nod.

"Because there's a secret. There's something that Birch doesn't want anybody to know. Something that he learned long ago, and has been fighting to hide ever since. Something that he saw as a threat to his grand mythology."

"What are you talking about?" says Oswin Thompson, who led the campaign to make publicly funded education completely secular. "Get to the point."

Some other queens grumble their agreement. I take a breath. It still hurts to think about it, to cast my mind back to that night. But I have to make them remember.

"The point is that we're all living in the shadow of May Winter," I say. "She was the perfect Melting Queen, the mother goddess that nobody else can ever live up to, the ideal woman. Edmonton always wants us to be her, reincarnated. But none of you has ever been May Winter, have you?"

I look at Tanya Schmetterling, who tried to replace Christmas with a Saturnalia Festival.

I look at Zophia Volga, who tried to create a Great Edmonton Movie and ended up with a four-hour-long cinematic monstrosity, ridiculed for its ludicrousness and adored for its ambition.

I look at Philippa Scalderson, who revolutionized Edmonton's waste management system and introduced the blue bin recycling program.

All of them shake their heads, as I knew they would.

"That's not true," I say. "You have all been May Winter. You've run from it, and made yourself forget it. But you all felt it. Every one of you."

"I think I'd remember the honour of being the first Melting Queen," says Tiller Sable with a laugh. A bunch of the queens beside her titter along. She's already built a little clique around herself of queens who I know prefer Odessa.

I stare her down, not angry that she supports my rival, just sad that this has to happen.

"You do remember," I say quietly. "You remember fear. You remember running through the forest. You remember the men chasing you."

Tiller Sable blanches, and I see the panic tear across her face as her memory cracks open like a rotten egg, filling her with its noxious stench. A shiver goes around the circle of queens. I see all of them going through the same process. The dam bursts at the back of their minds, flooding them with the fear and the shame and the pain. They might not have seen it all. They might not have gone through it all, all the way to the end. But they can all feel it.

"I don't know if it was destiny for me to become the Melting Queen," I say, looking at Alice and René, who share a guilty glance at each other.

"I don't know if it was fate for me to have been thrown off a bridge and into the memories of Shishira Sarasvati," I say, looking at Vasanta, who gives me a watery smile.

"But I do know that it was my choice to bring you all here, so we could face this truth together. They didn't Name her to praise her. They did it to shame her. They did it because they were afraid of her, and disgusted by her, and wanted to put her in her place. They did it because May Winter was born as Albert Herring, and they hated everything about her."

The queens aren't shocked. They're not surprised. They know, deep down, that I'm telling the truth. They can feel it, in their own memories.

"They didn't believe in any of the magic they pretended she had. It was all a joke. A mockery. But then, against all odds, it became real. They unburdened themselves of their guilt. They confessed their sins. They felt lighter, and she felt heavier. And then, after all they'd done to her, she died."

I feel myself shaking with rage, wishing I could reach back through history and destroy everyone who hurt her.

"They murdered her," I say through clenched teeth. "And now we pretend that they revered her."

I feel the wave of disgust that's sweeping through the circle of Melting Queens— the anger and the pain and the horror that they all feel. We feel it together, as if we're a single entity.

"May Winter deserves justice," I say. "The truth has been buried beneath a mountain of lies, a grand mythology that erased the real person and replaced her with a fantasy. Kastevoros Birch has done everything in his power to cover up the truth, and now we have to expose it. We have to tell the story of May Winter, and tell the story of Albert Herring."

Ananke Cosmopoulos leans back in her chair.

"So May Winter was a man," she says, hardly believing her own words.

"No," says Iris, shaking her head, eyes wide from the memory that's still freshly rekindled in her mind. "May Winter was a woman. A brave, strong, transgender woman. She might have been born as Albert Herring. But she chose her own name."

Iris looks at me, pride in her eyes, and I feel the strength of her unconquerable will flowing into me.

"It's time for everyone to remember," I say. "For Edmonton to remember who we are, and face our true history."

"You've probably all heard that, after River disappeared, Kastevoros Birch cancelled the referendum and declared Olechka Stepanchuk Melting Queen by acclamation," says Kaseema. "They're having a coronation ceremony for her next week."

"We'll go there," I say. "And force Edmonton to confront the truth."

"Why should anyone believe us?" says Oswin Thompson. "We're just a bunch of washed-up old Melting Queens."

"They'll believe it because it's true," I say. "They'll believe it because I'll show them who we really are, and remind them of the power that they've given us. And they'll believe it because we have proof."

I look at Sander and Kaseema, and my two faithful friends step forward.

"It was there, in the ECHO archives, all along," says Kaseema. "I worked there for fourteen years, and still they never granted me access."

"I've requested access to their archives for years," says Sander. "But ECHO doesn't open their archives to accredited historians, let alone PhD candidates. And now we know why."

He holds up a photograph for all the Queens to see. I don't have to look at it to know what it is—May, her dress in tatters, covered in leaves and mud, her face swollen and bruised, standing beside the smiling man who murdered her. I look away. I don't want to see it. Neither do any of the Melting Queens, but they can't help but stare at this final, damning evidence.

"After River told us what happened, we knew what we had to do," says Sander. "We broke into the ECHO archives in the middle of the night, under their noses, and found more than we ever imagined. Not just this photo. There are diary entries from witnesses, newspaper clippings... an autopsy report." He gulps, then his face darkens with anger. "They kept all of this, from everyone. They never thought anyone would find it, or hold them accountable. It's hard to grasp the scale of their arrogance."

"I still had building access," says Kaseema. "We practically walked inside. They didn't even have an alarm on the main archive vault."

She looks out at the Melting Queens, her life's work, and shakes her head bitterly.

"Kastevoros and ECHO need to answer for this," she says. "They've run the show for too long. They've used all of you. I should've done something about all this years ago. I'm sorry."

"Don't apologize for *them*," says Iris, staring at Kaseema like a protective older sister. "Don't you ever blame yourself for this. They're the ones who kept this whole sick tradition going year after year, even though they knew the truth. They're the ones who are going to pay for this."

She looks to me, gives me her full support.

"Burn it to the ground, River."

I return her angry smile, then look out at the rest of the Queens.

"It's not just about what they did to May Winter," I say. "It's what they did to us too. This vicious tradition started with her, and the pain has been echoing down ever since. You've all been scattered around, dealing with the aftermath of all these Intrusions and Confessions on your own. Your minds were put through the wringer. You were forced to absorb all of Edmonton's negativity. And then you were disposed of and replaced."

I look at René, whose black-white-and-blue hair tumbles down around his shoulders. I feel the power running through me, the power of a hundred and fourteen women, the power they never knew they had.

"Come here," I say.

He hesitates a moment, then walks across the circle, to my side.

"Hold out your hand," I say.

He pauses again, then does as I tell him. I unfold his fingers and see his black stone sitting there in the middle of his warm palm. I pluck it off his hand.

A shiver rips through my body. The kidney-shaped stone is colder than a chunk of ice. It presses down into my hand, heavy as a boulder a hundred times its size. I feel its malice, as if I've woken it from its slumber and now it will destroy me.

I can feel its truth better than I could ever see it. It's not a solid, smooth stone like I've always imagined. It has tiny fissures all across its surface. This is not one simple thing, his externalized tumour. It's not an ultra-dense singularity, sucking in all light and energy. It's not smooth or perfect. It doesn't have a pure, single kernel at its core. It's an accumulation of tiny particles all accreted together. Every dark feeling, every poisonous thought that's ever coursed through René Royaume. He made them into little black flakes, infinitesimally small, and forced them all together in a structure that's as powerful as it is fragile. This is a sootstone.

I hold up the stone for all my sisters to see.

"This is what we are. This is what they made May Winter become. This is what they made us become. We are an externalized tumour. We are a sootstone—a tool that Edmonton uses for purging its darkness. The Melting Queen is powerful, but she is also disempowered. She's a dirty rag that they use, to clean up their stains before they throw it away. But not anymore."

I close my fist around the stone. For all its ultimate fragility, I know that no matter how hard I squeeze I won't be able to make the sootstone crumble. So instead I cradle it in my hand, wrapped around it with gentle strength. I lift my fist to my face and release a long breath through my fingers, to warm this shard of ice.

I feel myself draining out the sootstone. I feel myself disrupting its clenched fury. Before our eyes, the stone in my hand begins to glow. I open my fist and there it sits, radiant. Light seeps back out of its blackness, until it forms a brilliant point, brighter than the sun. The luminosity flares for a moment, then dies instantly. René snatches up the stone. It's perfectly clear, a chunk of pure glass.

"We are powerful," I tell my sisters. "They mocked her. But they also gave her power. They killed her. But they made us strong enough to avenge her."

I look at all my sister's faces, the exhausted eyes, the sunken cheeks and frown lines.

"I will not Name another Melting Queen. I will not force another woman to endure this. When the ice breaks, and the river runs on again, the city will not have another disposable goddess to worship then throw away. Instead, people will drain their darkness into another sootstone, larger and more powerful than any ever made in Edmonton. They'll learn to purge themselves of their own darkness. They'll learn to cope without a Melting Queen."

"How?" asks Alice.

I look at Clodagh and smile.

"I'm going to build a fountain."

{19}

The fiery sun of summer returns, to free us from our winter prison

The birthing dome is made of green glass, a fragile mosaic of smashed Canada Dry bottles. Its giant curve swells into the sky, reminiscent of a pregnant belly. She built it in the most obvious place, right next to the river, in the heart of Coronation Park.

Good.

The crowd parts for us as we enter the park. Some give me dirty looks, but I'm used to that by now. Mostly they just look stunned. I was supposed to be dead, or comatose, or just conveniently out of the picture.

Or maybe their eyes are so wide because of the women behind me, who walk and roll along in my wake—all these old broken dolls they'd stuck back up on the shelf, come back to remind them of their existence. The Melting Queens wear a rainbow of colours, but I am all in green: forest and fern, olive and mint, shamrock and emerald

181

and honeydew. My dress is stitched together from the Coronation gowns of my sisters—donated to my cause, torn apart into patches of silk and lace and cotton, sewn together into a giant patchwork of foliage. I sit atop the big blue horse, Poseidon, as many queens have done before me as they ushered in the spring. My long green train trails off Poseidon's rump, flowing down the street behind us, supported by the nearest of my sisters.

The crowd might be dazzled by us. But we do little to impress the old man who stands at the entrance to the birthing dome. Kastevoros Birch crosses his arms and pierces me with cold, sharp eyes as I lead the parade of Melting Queens through the crowd, to his door.

"Step aside," I cry from atop Poseidon, hoping that my voice will carry throughout the park, over the heads of a thousand people.

"Never," says Birch. "You have no place here. You are unimportant."

"I am important. I'm River Runson. I am the Melting Queen."

"You're Adam Truman."

"No. I'm not. I'm Clodagh Paskwamostos. I'm Shishira Sarasvati. I'm May Winter."

The old man darts his eyes at my champions, who stand proudly at my back.

"You've embarrassed yourself enough, young man. You've brought shame on our traditions and yourself. You will never sit the Spring Throne. Go home."

I look him right in his eyes.

"You're right," I say.

I turn my back on him and face out at the crowd. They'd gathered around Odessa's dome for a murky, glass-obscured view of her birth performance. But I have stolen the show.

"I will never sit the Spring Throne. Nor will Odessa Steps. Nor will anyone, ever again."

I look back at Birch, fuming noxiously beside the great extravagance of his pretender queen.

"Your traditions are over. Your lies are over. We've learned your secret, Kastevoros Birch. I've seen it. We've all seen it. And now it's time for everyone to know it."

I ride Poseidon through the crowd, people melting away from us like ice in the rays of the sun. We go up the little hill, so everyone can see me.

"I have been away too long," I cry out. "Too long, lost to myself. Too long, haunted by a memory too horrible to contemplate. I resisted it. I ran from it, just like every Melting Queen before me. I fell to pieces. I lived a hundred lives. I jumped back in time, through the memories of all my sisters."

The crowd watches reverently as the Melting Queens follow me up the hill, forming a circle around me and the Spring Throne. I look down at its gnarled roots and twisted branches and I grimace, remembering her. Remembering that night.

"We are all connected," I say. "All of us Melting Queens. We draw strength from each other, and we feel each other's suffering. I felt the suffering of Albert Herring."

Kastevoros Birch gives out a choked wheeze. But he can't stop me.

"Albert Herring," I repeat. "That was the name May Winter was born with, before she named herself. She wasn't a goddess and she wasn't a fertile mother and she wasn't a legend in her own time. She was beaten, and ridiculed, and humiliated. She was shamed, and used, and abandoned. She was mocked. She was degraded. She was murdered."

I look out over the crowd, all of them standing here in the very place where she was tormented.

"The good people of Edmonton celebrated that first Melting Day by murdering a woman. Every year, we repeat the lie that conceals their crime. Every year, we sacrifice another woman to this sacred institution—another woman to criticize, to use up, and then to discard. This has been our tradition for too long. It ends today."

Clodagh helps me dismount the great blue horse, and we face the crowd together. The eyes of a thousand strangers drink in the spectacle.

"Our traditions are evil."

I look at my sisters, who've been made to bear the weight of their city, then suffer in silence for the rest of their lives.

"Our history is a lie."

I put my hand on the arm of the Spring Throne, which still hasn't flowered.

"And this? This is just a dead stump."

I nod to Magpie and Alice, who come forward with the gas can. Magpie throws the fuel across the Spring Throne's withered branches, atop its wooden seat. Alice hands me the box of matches.

"Stop this!" yells Kastevoros. "Stop him now!"

Some people in the crowd respond to the old man's cries, and strong men start pushing forward, towards my circle of Melting Queens. But they're too late. I strike a match, and throw it on the chair.

The Spring Throne erupts in a ball of fire. It twists and contorts itself like a living creature as its bent boughs begin to burn. The crowd shrinks back from the heat, shields their eyes from the unnaturally bright light. I face them fearlessly, the fire at my back.

"EDMONTON!"

I speak with a hundred and fifteen voices, all woven together like a rope made of sound, a chorus of queens from first to last. The words boom out of my mouth, reverberating across the river valley in powerful harmony. Odessa's birthing dome trembles against the power of my voice—all our voices, finally speaking as one.

"Ladies and gentlemen and others! Hence forth you shall have no Melting Queen to trouble and to torment. No one will ever again be made to wear a false crown or sit a dead throne."

The crowed watches me with awe, and I know they can feel my words echoing through their flesh and bones as much as I can. Birch's mad shrieks are overcome, drowned out by the voices of all the women he sought to silence and control. The

Melting Queens stare at me with pride, lending me their voices, feeling the same euphoria that I feel.

"I am the Melting Queen," I say. "The last Melting Queen. I burn down this tradition to build a new one in its place. We won't have a throne, or a crown, or a mother goddess. We won't have parades and pageants and projects. We won't have me, or Shishira Sarasvati, or Albert Herring, or anyone else trying and failing to be May Winter. We'll just have a fountain."

I reach out and put my hand on the burning throne. I give it a shove, and it collapses in on itself. The flames continue to consume the wreckage as I walk down the hill, through the line of Melting Queens, to the birthing dome's entrance. The old man stands there, shaking, silenced. I stand before him, above him, my Melting Queens all around him.

"I say again, Kastevoros Birch. Step aside."

The old man chews wordlessly on the air for a moment, then steps aside. I walk past him, into the birthing dome, into the greatest performance of Odessa Steps.

Under the oculus, in a perfect circle of sunlight, my former friend lies on the grass. She's naked, puffing and panting, red-faced, clutching at her swollen belly. Her muscles are all clenched tight. Her whole body is contorted. The day has come. Her child is ready to be born.

Aside from Odessa, there are only a few people—doctors, nurses, midwives—in the birthing dome. They've been watching me as much as they could through the distorting glass, and as I approach Odessa they gape at me. I kneel down on the grass next to her, take her hand in mine. She looks up at me, squeezes my hand with all her strength.

"That was... a performance," she says, struggling to squeeze out the words as well.

"So is this," I say. "But now you need to go to a hospital."

"No... I want to... Here."

"It's over."

"Still. Please."

I look into her pale grey eyes and see her stubbornness, undimmed.

"Fine. But I'm not leaving until you're okay."

She studies my face, and I don't have a clue what she's thinking, but eventually she nods.

"Good," I say. "Now take a deep breath. And *push*."

{20}

A city unlike any other

Edmonton is not as I dreamed it.

Standing at the Top of the Stalk, looking down on my city, I don't see a chaotic nightmare dreamscape tearing itself apart or a perfectly organized circle of canals. It's just a city, sprawling out over the prairies, growing in all directions.

People are like cities. You might have a perfect plan for them, a grand vision, an exact idea of how they should develop. But really they just get slowly built up day by day, week by week, month by month. A thousand small decisions accumulate, and before you know it you've got a big scattered mess, with beautiful things and ugly things and strange things all crowded together, side by side.

I am not the River Runson I imagined I would be. I'm not happy all the time and full of boundless energy. I'm not a brand new person, completely free of the past. But I am still magnificent.

I'm dressed in a copper-scale gown, gleaming like the rising sun. I asked Magpie to make me one final Melting Queen dress, and she didn't disappoint. We melted down May Winter's statue—tore down the lie of the First Melting Queen and turned her image into the final extravagance of the Last. I feel the weight of the thousand copper leaves and think about the cost of these traditions.

After Kaseema reclaimed the Office of the Melting Queen, I asked for the green leaf dress in the lobby to be taken down and burned. I don't know who made it or when, but the lies are over now, as is the pageantry. Today will be the last grand celebration, and I mean to go out in style.

I reach up and run my fingers through my long red hair. The magic of the Melting Queens has granted me this one final indulgence, to regrow my pride and joy in six short weeks. I unravel my fiery crown and the wind catches my hair, unfurling it like a victory banner over a conquered city.

When I exit the Stalk and walk through the busy streets, hundreds of costumed revellers approach me. I stop to share a photo or a hug, to answer questions or to listen to a few final confessions. The streets are full of celebrants, but it's not Melting Day. It's Hallowe'en, and the First Snow is falling over Edmonton.

I spend my day walking through the city—from the Sky Harbour Gardens to Sundial Park to Churchill Square to Whyte Avenue. As the sun begins to set, I walk down into the valley, out across the Walterdale Bridge. I glance into Café Fiume as I tread the boardwalk, and our eyes meet. She stares at me for a moment, then lifts her hand in a tiny wave. Her baby is in a carrier on the chair next to her, sound asleep. I hesitate only a moment before continuing down the boardwalk to the café's door.

"Hi," says Odessa as I sit down.

"Hi."

"Nice costume."

"Thanks. I'm being May Winter for Hallowe'en. Where's yours?"

She nods at the baby.

"I'm being a mother this year."

"How's that treating you?"

"It's the hardest thing I've ever done," she says. "It's the hardest thing I've had to make interesting for myself. I'm tired, and cranky, and sore everywhere, and my breasts are aching all the time, you've no idea."

"Actually, I do."

She smiles tightly.

"Yeah, I guess you do, don't you?"

We sit in silence for a bit. The baby gurgles and twists in the carrier, but keeps sleeping. I look up and see little rivers flowing off the glass bridge, snowflakes melting as they hit the glass roof.

"So I guess you're headed off then. Baby in tow. Unless this means you're going to stay."

Odessa shakes her head immediately, reaches out to slip the pacifier back into the baby's mouth.

"No, we're gonna go."

"Where?"

She looks up at me.

"I don't know. Somewhere warm. Somewhere far away."

She leans back in her chair and finishes her coffee. I look over her shoulder, up the riverbank at the familiar skyline. My feet start itching to move again.

"Well, I suppose I should be on my way," I say, pushing my chair back and standing. "Goodbye, Odessa."

She grabs my wrist.

"I don't want to be Odessa Steps anymore," she says quietly. "Or Olechka Stepanchuk. They're both done now, I think. I'm entering an abyss of identity for a while. Like you described, the last time we were here. I'm on the ocean floor."

She looks at her child with a mixture of hope and terror in her eyes. Then she squares her jaw and turns back to me.

"I'm scared to do this alone," she says. "Even though I know that I can."

"I know you'll do fine," I say. "Your kid will be amazing and brilliant and so weird."

She laughs, then her face becomes set and serious.

"I'm sorry for the things I said about you. I'm so sorry, for everything."

I sigh. Once I imagined that hearing that would make me feel so much better. I shrug.

"It's water under the bridge," I say quietly.

We both look down at the dark grey waters sliding by beneath us. My attention is drawn into their mesmerizing current for a while.

"Will you come back in the spring?" I ask casually.

"I don't know," she says. "I used to come back every year because of my grandfather. But he died during the summer."

"I'm sorry," I say.

"It's okay. This baby is alive. Ludlow Spetnik is dead. This isn't home anymore."

"You still have friends here," I say. She seems about to respond when the server comes up with her bill. The baby stirs and squawks at the noise.

"Ooh," says the server, "hello little baby. You're adorable! Is it a boy or a girl?"

The woman who is no longer Odessa Steps looks up at me.

"I don't know," she tells the waiter. "They haven't told me who they are yet."

I leave the café with a smile on my face.

The snow is neither crescendoing nor fading in fervour. But the sky is darkening. It's getting dark so early lately.

As I go up the other side of the riverbank, I hear music blaring through the city. The party must be well underway. When I reach Jasper Avenue at the top of the hill, I find a dizzying array of people dancing, drinking, and making merry. The snow doesn't stop, but evaporates before it reaches us. Here we are, the people of Edmonton, burning bright in the night.

There are familiar faces in the crowd. Sander's wearing a Mountie uniform that I'm sure he'll be spending the next six months in, yawning constantly as the snow swirls down around his felt hat. He's surrounded by Melting Queens, celebrating the completion of his book. *The Melting Queens of Edmonton: A True History* comes out next spring. Thousands of people have already pre-ordered a copy.

Kaseema is holding court with the Melting Queens, dressed as Lady Olenna Tyrell from *Game of Thrones*. Alice Songhua is doing her best Anne of Green Gables, and Isobel Fraser has covered up her scooter with cardboard and become Thomas the Tank Engine. Victoria Goulburn is rather unimaginatively dressed as a ghost, but Iris Zambezi makes up for it with her incredible confection of a costume, a mounded rainbow kaleidoscope that cascades off her in all directions.

"What're you looking for?" says René, slipping through a grove of people and appearing in front of me. He's dressed as a kangaroo, his hand in his pouch, no doubt turning his sootstone over and over.

"Where's Clodagh?"

René smiles.

"Come on."

He grabs me with his non-preoccupied hand and tugs me through the crowds, which extend down several side streets, through several alleyways. The festivities are almost on the scale of Melting Day. My troublemaker friend leads me down some grubby alleyways and through some microparks and parking lots.

"I know where you're taking me."

"No you don't. Shut up, it's a surprise. Close your eyes."

I do as I'm told until René positions my body and tells me to open my eyes.

The Winter Fountain sits in the heart of a hole that used to be a hill. We tore out the roots of the Spring Throne and built this giant sootstone out of a hundred different types of stone: marble and granite and sandstone, basalt and limestone and slate, everything. People will come here, summer or winter, to soak their feet and their bodies, to relax, and to let go of the darkness inside themselves.

The fountain is really a hundred and fifteen fountains, all woven into each other. The walls of the fountain, sunk into the earth, will flow with water from the base of a hundred and fifteen columns, each one holding a statue that represents some aspect of a Melting Queen's reign. None of them have been installed yet, but we have plans for many of them already, dragons and elm trees and bridges.

Steps and ramps lead down from ground level into the fountain's heart, where a huge circular reflecting pool sits empty. Beside it stands Clodagh, dressed as Audrey Hepburn from *Roman Holiday*, a little Vespa parked beside her.

René starts down into the lower fountain, and after a moment I follow. Clodagh turns and greets us.

"Can you believe all this?" she asks giddily. "In what, six weeks!?"

"It was the last command of the Melting Queen," I say. "Kaseema has been working day and night."

Clodagh beams.

"Hold out your hand," says René. I obey, and he pulls his hand out of his kangaroo pouch and holds it over mine. I can't help but tense up, waiting for the sootstone even though I've already drained it dry. He opens his fingers and a shiny penny falls onto my palm. René grins.

"See, it is a surprise."

I inspect the coin. Maple leaf. 2018. The profile of the Queen. But I see that René has scratched out "Elizabeth II" and written "River Runson" in tiny letters.

"Throw it in," says René. "Make a wish."

"It's bad luck to throw a coin in a dry fountain. Everyone knows that."

"Of course they do," says Clodagh. "Which is why we'd never ask you to."

"You mean...?"

I look between them, and Clodagh grins. She lifts her phone to her mouth.

"Turn it on."

Water begins to leap forth from the base of each of the pillars. We stand there, watching, mesmerized as the water fills the reflecting pool and starts to cascade over the sides. Hot water, water that steams in the cold autumn air. The Winter Fountain. Edmonton's first hot spring, where people can come to thaw out their cold bones in the long dark season. I listen to the rush of the cascade, smell the fragrant steam of hot water waking up cold stone, feel the heat emanating from the pool.

"River."

René looks at me, gestures impatiently at the coin in my hands.

I look into his dark magpie eyes, which always seem to mock me but also let me in on the joke. I look over his shoulder at the glowing lights of downtown Edmonton, snow falling softly from high above. I look at Clodagh, whose joy lights up her face like a blazing sunrise.

I smile, close my eyes, and make a wish.

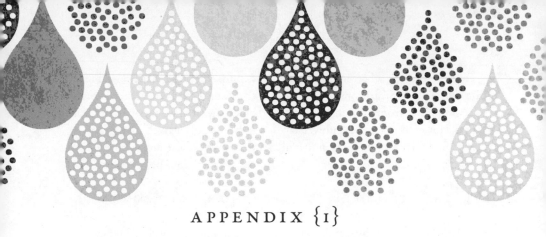

List of Melting Queens

The Melting Queen is a work of fiction, but many real women have made important contributions to Edmonton. A number of them are included in this list of former Melting Queens, to honour their legacies and to thank them for the vital role they've played in building our city. Their names are italicized in the list below.

1 | MAY WINTER

The First Melting Queen brought Edmonton together to celebrate the end of winter and inaugurate the Melting Day tradition.

2 | LOUISA CAROLINE LORNE

Louisa Lorne organized festivities to mark the creation of the Province of Alberta—and the selection of Edmonton as the new province's capital city—on 1 September 1905.

3 | ORGANZA GRANT

Organza Grant was the first Melting Queen who truly had a signature initiative rather than just presiding over festivals and ceremonies. Many Edmontonians lived in tents in the river valley in this era (including the Grant family) and Organza worked with the City to create a sanitation initiative to protect these citizens from typhoid and other diseases.

4 | *ROSETTA GRAYDON*

During her tenure, Rosetta Graydon founded the Edmonton SPCA and Humane Society, advocating especially for the ethical treatment of horses, which were a key component of local life in 1907 Edmonton.

5 | AURELIA GREEN

Aurelia Green pushed for the University of Alberta to be built in Edmonton—and not in Calgary, as had previously been suggested. Ultimately, a compromise was achieved by locating the university in Strathcona, directly across the river from Edmonton. Aurelia formally opened the university for its first forty-five students in the fall of 1908.

6 | PEARL FLINDERS

Pearl Flinders was hit by scandal when, two months after her coronation, she was found to have been having an affair with a married man. She was not able to recover from the social fallout and spent the rest of her term in isolation.

7 | *ADA MAGRATH*

One of Edmonton's most prominent socialites, Ada Magrath helped organize and develop the YWCA in Edmonton, assisting single women who arrived by train in the booming city and who had no permanent place to live.

8 | ISOBEL FRASER

Only four years old and from the city of Strathcona, Isobel Fraser was an incredibly controversial choice when she was Named. Her term saw a referendum to unite the two cities, with majorities on both sides of the river voting to merge—largely because the unity committee used the adorable and precocious four-year-old as its figurehead.

9 | *ANNIE MAY JACKSON*

The first female police officer in the British Empire, Annie May Jackson was deputized as a Special Constable with the Edmonton Police Force shortly before her tenure. She used her position to help newly arrived immigrant women avoid the men who tried to recruit them into prostitution.

10 | BRIDGET BOWER

Partnering with the still hugely popular Isobel Fraser, Bridget Bower organized a gigantic summer festival to celebrate the completion of the High Level Bridge, Edmonton's most iconic landmark, which joined the two cities together.

11 | ERNESTINA LAKE

A poet and member of the wealthy Lake Family, Ernestina Lake helped promote recruitment for the 49th Battalion (Edmonton Regiment) of the Canadian Expeditionary Forces.

12 | ALOISE PENNANT

Aloise Pennant was the first Melting Queen to outright refuse the call to serve her city. She faced such intense criticism for this choice that her family was forced to leave Edmonton. Massive floods during the summer of 1915 were subsequently blamed on her absence.

13 | *DR. GENEVA MISENER*

The U of A's first female professor, Dr. Geneva Misener led the Edmonton Equal Suffrage League, pushing the provincial government to give women the vote (although the Voting Rights

Act only extended the franchise to
white women; Indigenous women did
not get the vote until 1965).

14 | MARIGOLD HUMBER

Marigold Humber's brother, husband,
and two sons were all killed in the Great
War. She organized convalescent homes
for wounded and traumatized soldiers,
and is regarded as one of the most
admired Melting Queens in Edmonton
history.

15 | MIRANDA MEDWAY

Miranda Medway carried on the work
of her predecessor and had a close
relationship with her. Her term saw the
end of the Great War and the Armistice
ceremonies. She was instrumental in
maintaining calm and educating the
public on quarantine practices during
the 1918-19 flu outbreak, which killed
over 600 Edmontonians.

16 | ISABELLE CONNELLY

Alberta's first licensed female embalmer
and owner of a family funeral home,
Isabelle Connelly had a tough act
to follow with her two immensely
popular predecessors. She sought to
demystify the process of death and start
a social conversation about mortality
and mourning, but in many ways she
was ahead of her time and her death-
positivity failed to gain traction with
Edmontonians.

17 | GLADYS REEVES

The first woman in Western Canada
to own a photography studio, Gladys
Reeves' signature initiative was creating
the Edmonton Face Book—a photo
archive of all 61,045 citizens going
about their everyday lives in 1920
Edmonton.

18 | ELLA MAY WALKER

Musician, artist, author, historian, and
deeply involved Edmonton advocate,
Ella May Walker (who created her
own middle name as a child, using her
birth month as another name because
she felt cheated by not having been
given one) had a finger in every pie and
an iron in every fire. She encouraged
Edmontonians to paint, write, play
music, and create art about their city.

19 | CLARABELLE MERSEY

Head of the Radical Women's Labour
League, Clarabelle Mersey represented
a generational shift for the Office of
the Melting Queen. She advocated
for prisoners' rights, old-age pensions,
equal pay for women, and access to
birth-control information—provoking
the ire of older Melting Queens, who
openly opposed such radical reforms.

20 | MARITSA SAVA

Maritsa Sava chaired the Moderation
League of Alberta and successfully
campaigned to repeal the province-wide
prohibition on alcohol, which had been
in place since 1916.

21 | MAUDE BOWMAN

Maude Bowman founded the Edmonton Museum of Arts, the precursor to the present-day Art Gallery of Alberta. She partnered with the Edmonton Art Club to encourage citizens to paint their city *en plein air*.

22 | JOSEPHINE NELSON

A deeply religious Melting Queen, Josephine Nelson was at first convinced that the Intrusions she experienced and the power she held over Edmontonians were the result of demonic possession. After several months of mental anguish and public meltdowns, she instead became convinced that she was gifted with angelic powers after she saved a drowning child by parting the waters of the river. She refused to give up her position on the following Melting Day and was ultimately committed to a provincial institution.

23 | JANE MURCHISON

Jane Murchison was actively involved in the politics of the United Farm Women of Alberta, and used her tenure as Melting Queen to campaign for the UFA in the 1926 Alberta election. This overt politicization of the Melting Queen role provoked a huge backlash against Murchison, and established the convention that Melting Queens—even if they were political—would always be above partisanship.

24 | LENA PASKAROFF

In 1927, the Blatchford Field became the first licensed sky harbour in Canada. Lena Paskaroff promoted the aviation industry and Edmonton's position as the "Gateway to the North," holding an air circus and free flying lessons.

25 | ELIZABETH MURRAY

Elizabeth Murray was a fantastically wealthy widow who suffered from major depression. During her tenure, she slowly recovered from her mental health problems by engaging with her community. She spent all of her money on lavish community events, bringing in performers from around the world and feeding everyone who came. She died six months after her term ended, reportedly very happy.

26 | JOY BROWN

A close friend and ally of the Famous Five (the five Alberta women who fought for women to be deemed as legal persons under Canadian law), Joy Brown presided over the celebrations on 18 October 1929 when the U.K. Privy Council ruled that women are indeed persons and entitled to the same legal rights and privileges of men.

27 | MARIANNE MOSELLE

The first French-Canadian Melting Queen, Marianne Moselle's family fled into Edmonton when her father had to give up the family farm to their creditors at the start of the Great Depression. She helped organize donation drives for food and clothing for people in similar circumstances to hers.

28 | MARGARET MACBURNEY (VASHERESSE)

Margaret MacBurney was the longest-playing and highest-scoring member of the Edmonton Grads basketball team—one of the most successful sports teams of all time, who won 502 of their 522 games between 1915-1940. Margaret promoted girls' participation in competitive sports and achieved a world record during her tenure by sinking sixty-one free shots in a row during an exhibition period.

29 | SAOIRSE BELTANE

Saoirse Beltane helped organize the 1932 Christmas Hunger March, which brought 12,000 unemployed Edmontonians together to demand government action at the height of the Depression. The march was broken up by police in Market Square, who assaulted the assembled farmers and workers with truncheons and arrested forty protestors—including the Melting Queen—on charges of trying to overthrow the government. The Trial of the Melting Queen created huge sympathy for the labour movement. After her acquittal, Saoirse spent the rest of her term criticizing the government and pushing for more social reforms.

30 | DOLLY FREEMAN

Dolly Freeman was a psychic and seer who was able to tell Edmontonians their futures by reading tea leaves, crystal balls, and palms. She used her clairvoyance to help people regain hope in the depths of the Depression, showing them a light at the end of the tunnel and a future worth living for.

31 | ALICE MARGARET MARSHALL

A columnist at the *Edmonton Bulletin*, Alice Margaret Marshall organized the Sunshine Fund to provide needy families with Christmas dinners and gifts. She continued to organize the Sunshine Fund after her term was over.

32 | BEATRICE CARMICHAEL

The Grand Dame of Edmonton opera, Beatrice Carmichael founded the Edmonton Civic Opera Company during her term and promoted the fine art of opera in the city.

33 | GRACE DOBIE

Grace Dobie became "interim" head of the Edmonton Public Library for three years after the resignation of Edmonton's first Chief Librarian. She promoted literacy and literature in Edmonton during the lean years of the Great Depression.

34 | GIOVANNA TEVERE

In 1937, the provincial government of Premier William Aberhart passed the *Accurate News and Information Act*, an extremely controversial piece of legislation that required newspapers to print official "clarifications" to stories the government didn't like and forced journalists to name their sources. Giovanna Tevere led the resistance against the bill, which has since gone down in infamy as an assault against freedom of the press.

35 | HILWIE HAMDON

Edmonton's first Muslim Melting Queen, Lebanese-Canadian Hilwie Hamdon campaigned tirelessly to raise money to build a mosque in Edmonton. With support from Edmontonians of all faiths, the Al Rashid Mosque—the first mosque in Canada—opened during her tenure.

36 | JOLENE JAMES

The first Indigenous Melting Queen helped Johnny Callihoo and other band leaders with treaty status organize the Indian Association of Alberta. Her reign was initially opposed by the majority of Edmontonians, who saw her reign as a continued corruption of the purity of the Melting Queen tradition— *first an Italian, then a Lebanese woman, now an Indian!* But Jolene's controversy was overshadowed by the outbreak of WW2, and her protests against the internment of Italian and German Edmontonians went unheeded.

37 | GERTRUDE POOLE

A prominent community member of numerous clubs and societies, Gertrude Poole opened up her home to a group of forty women who knitted and sewed clothing for the Red Cross to aid in the wartime relief efforts.

38 | MARGARET CRANG

Formerly the youngest person to ever serve on Edmonton's city council (1933-37), Margaret Crang was an ardent anti-fascist and pacifist. She led demonstrations against Nazi Germany, sharing information about the Holocaust and demanding that Allied forces focus on ending the genocide.

39 | OPAL PEARSON

Opal Pearson was the second Melting Queen who outright refused to serve. The apocalyptic snowstorm in the winter of 1942, which smothered Edmonton with more snow than it had ever seen before, was subsequently blamed on her absence.

40 | VELVA THOMPSON

Velva Thompson successfully challenged the Edmonton Public School Board's policy of terminating female teachers' employment contracts after they got married. She refused to resign her position and helped push forward Edmonton's opinion on women in the workplace.

41 | *EDA OWEN*

After accurately predicting Melting Day every spring for twenty-two years, Canada's first female professional meteorologist had long been tipped as a potential Melting Queen. She used her position to educate Edmontonians about the emerging science of meteorology and the importance of good data.

42 | MAY ABASHIRI

May Abashiri was born in Edmonton in 1925 before her family moved across the mountains to British Columbia. When she was Named, she had to be retrieved from a Japanese internment camp in Lethbridge. Her appointment divided the city like no other Queen before her, with many Edmontonians demanding a replacement be Named instead and accusing May of being an enemy spy. Ultimately, May tried to remind Edmontonians about the shared humanity of their enemies and their responsibilities as victors in the war. She created a rock garden and a peace monument in Coronation Park following the atomic bombings.

43 | *JUNE SHEPPARD*

A journalist and radio broadcaster, June Sheppard is widely regarded as one of the most well-read Melting Queens in Edmonton history. She inaugurated the Great Debates, an annual festival which brings two panels head-to-head to argue controversial topics of the day— like whether the use nuclear weapons against civilians is ever morally justified.

44 | GISELLE SCHAFT

On 13 February 1947, the Leduc No. 1 well struck oil. Giselle Schaft was one of the thousands of young immigrants who rushed to Edmonton to share in the plunder. She was Named as Melting Queen after only one week in Edmonton, and spent her term exploring her new city and sharing her discoveries with other newly arrived citizens. She also organized a campaign to name the marigold as Edmonton's official flower.

45 | ATHENA ALMOND

At the Melting Queen's Picnic in 1948, Athena Almond agreed to take on every single initiative that was proposed by her petitioners. She soon discovered how much of a mistake this was, and after failing in her attempts to be everything to everyone for several months, she finally just helped construct more playgrounds for Edmonton children.

46 | *FAITH CLIFTON*

Faith Clifton opened the Canadian National Institute for the Blind and focused on making Edmonton more inclusive for citizens with physical impairments.

47 | *PONCELLA BEAUCHAMP*

Poncella Beauchamp was born on the High Level Bridge on Melting Day in 1935. When she was a child, she and her brother had to live at an orphanage while their mother worked, so her signature initiative was focused on creating day care spaces to help working mothers.

48 | FRAN FLETCHER

Although she did not refuse to serve, Fran Fletcher effectively ignored all the duties of the Melting Queen and made a mockery of the events she did attend.

49 | ALMA LAKE

The first Melting Queen to make a deliberate attempt at a reunion, Alma Lake visited many of her predecessors and learned about their experiences and Intrusions. She failed to achieve the grand reunion she desired, but she created *The Melting Queen's Cookbook* as a tribute to the four dozen queens before her.

50 | KATHERINE HELD

A history student at the University of Alberta, Katherine Held had many personal problems when her father died during her term, but she also helped inform the public during a polio epidemic that affected 319 citizens and killed sixteen.

51 | ELSIE PARK GOWAN

Acclaimed Edmonton actor and director Elsie Park Gowan wrote a play for Edmonton's Golden Jubilee (titled *Who Builds a City*) that traced the community's fifty-year growth through the story of one family.

52 | DR. ANNE ANDERSON

Dr. Anne Anderson created a 38,000-word Cree-English translation dictionary, the first of its kind, and fought to preserve Indigenous language, religion, and social practices during an era of cultural genocide.

53 | WINNIFRED STEWART

Winnifred Stewart's son Parker was born with a developmental disability, and she refused to give up on him when the education system (not to mention society at large) didn't believe that he could achieve anything. She founded the Edmonton Association for the Mentally Retarded, creating an educational program that achieved a level of development that was previously considered impossible. During her tenure, she helped thousands of Edmonton families access the educational resources they needed and thrive despite the stigma against developmental disabilities.

54 | NENA TIMPERLEY

An immigrant from England, Nena Timperley worked for the Red Cross in Edmonton and, along with organizing cultural events, inaugurated the city's first blood bank.

55 | PHOEBE MCCULLOUGH

A member of the Deaf Detection and Development Committee, Phoebe McCullough helped direct resources to services for hearing-impaired

Edmontonians. She also organized sign language classes for citizens.

56 | ORIANA KURULIAK

Oriana Kuruliak helped found Edmonton's Ukrainian Shumka dancing group, promoting her home country's culture and heritage through a whirlwind of motion.

57 | ASTRID KNUDSON

When Astrid Knudson was five years old, she was hit in the head by a meteorite fragment that lodged itself in her temporal lobe. This injury sparked her interest in the universe and led her to become an astronomer. In 1960, the space-obsessed Melting Queen opened the Queen Elizabeth Planetarium and provided telescopes to communities across the city, educating Edmonton about its place in the universe.

58 | DR. RUTH CARSE

After a storied dancing career in Toronto and New York, Dr. Ruth Carse returned to Edmonton and founded the Alberta Ballet, promoting the art of dance in the city.

59 | VIVIAN TEGLER (AND EVELYN TEGLER)

Vivian Tegler had a controversial relationship with her twin brother, Evelyn, with many rumouring that they were lovers and others suggesting he was a corrupting homosexual influence on her after she declared him her co-

Melting Queen. Vivian spent more time hosting fancy cocktail parties than doing community work, and, as such, she has no widely recognized signature accomplishment.

60 | ZOIE GARDNER

Zoie Gardner was Edmonton's foster mother par excellence. Over the course of her life—starting when she was only nineteen years old—she took over one hundred children into her home and continued to care for many of those with developmental disabilities into their forties. The model Melting Queen, Zoie never expected recognition or praise and used her position to humbly advocate for Edmonton's orphans and homeless children. Thanks to her efforts, hundreds of children were adopted into caring households.

61 | DOREEN MCLEOD RYAN

An award-winning speed skater, Doreen McLeod Ryan was warned against continuing her sport because it would negatively impact her ability to have children. She ignored this advice, gave birth to three children, competed in two Olympics, and spent her time as Melting Queen encouraging girls to get involved in competitive sports.

62 | MARGARET CHAPELLE

Margaret Chapelle was an artist and social activist. During her tenure, she fought against the City's plan to build a freeway through the Mackinnon Ravine—even going so far as to lie down in front of a bulldozer to halt construction.

63 | TANYA SCHMETTERLING

A devout atheist, Tanya Schmetterling tried to educate Edmontonians about the Roman origins of Christmas and attempted to replace Christmas with a Saturnalia festival. To no one's surprise, her efforts were an abysmal failure and she provoked a huge backlash from both Christian communities and the general population, which painted her as a Grinch trying to steal Christmas.

64 | GLORIA TREMBLAY

Gloria Tremblay's signature initiative was largely decided before she was ever Named. As Canada's centennial year, 1967 saw celebrations across the country—including those presided over by that year's Melting Queen in Edmonton.

65 | ESTHER MATCHAM

Having recently moved to Edmonton from Winnipeg, which hosted a Christmas lights competition, Esther Matcham organized the first Candy Cane Lane in her neighbourhood, establishing a Yuletide tradition that continues to this day.

66 | ELIZA LAKE

The only deafblind person to have been Named as Melting Queen, Eliza Lake helped educate Edmonton about the unique experiences and the struggles of her community. She also promoted the establishment of 911 emergency services, making Edmonton the first Canadian city to have a 911 system.

67 | JESSICA HANNA

Jessica Hanna focused her reign on helping women who were experiencing domestic violence. She formed the Women In Need (WIN) House and the Women's Emergency Shelters.

68 | DR. LILA FAHLMAN

Dr. Lila Fahlman was a teacher and community activist who saved Rutherford House from being demolished (which earned her major respect from ECHO) and who led the Canadian Council of Muslim Women. She worked to integrate Muslim education into Edmonton Public Schools and fought for interfaith dialogue and respect.

69 | TILLER SABLE

Tiller Sable had lobbied to become the Melting Queen for three years, and is largely seen to have bought the position with a $500,000 donation to the Edmonton Civic Heritage Organization (ECHO). After attaining the position, she was largely an indifferent figurehead, refusing to attend most community events. Her one nominal accomplishment was the establishment of the Edmonton Yacht Club, an exclusive group for wealthy citizens interested in mooring their pleasure craft on the river.

70 | JENNY SHIRT-MARGETTS

Jenny Shirt-Margetts helped found the Alberta chapter of Indian Rights for Indian Women and was an early advocate for Cree language education. She founded the Awasis educational programs in Edmonton schools to help a new generation of Cree youth regain their language and culture.

71 | HELEN LAROSE

A consummate history buff, Helen LaRose devoted her term to educating the public about Edmonton's history. Her crowning accomplishment was the creation of the Edmonton Municipal Archives.

72 | ELLY DE JONGH

Elly de Jongh was a founding member of SPARE (the Society for the Protection of Architectural Resources in Edmonton) and fought to preserve the city's built heritage in a time when Edmonton was keen on knocking things down.

73 | PATRICIA CULLEY

An amateur botanist and high school biology teacher, Patricia Culley suffered from major Seasonal Affective Disorder every winter and longed to escape to a rainforest oasis in the coldest months. She achieved this wish by opening the Muttart Conservatory in the river valley.

74 | VASANTA SARASVATI

Vasanta Sarasvati, the city's first Indian Melting Queen, created the Edmonton Heritage Days festival to celebrate the diversity of all peoples in the city. The second-most attended festival in the city (exceeded only by the Fringe), Heritage Days brings everyone together to feast on the food and song of a hundred nations.

75 | PAULINE POSKAIAO

Pauline Poskaiao created the Edmonton river valley parks system, which chained together all the disparate pockets of green into the largest continuous urban park in North America. She also helped forge the city's Green Ribbon Policy, which states that no commercial development may occur in the valley (although this policy has been increasingly ignored in recent years).

76 | JANET HUGHES

During her reign, Janet Hughes helped found the Edmonton Food Bank, redistributing surplus food from grocery stores and local growers to hungry citizens.

77 | OLIVE TELLFORD

Olive Tellford ushered in Alberta's 75th anniversary by inaugurating the Great Divide waterfall—taller than Niagara Falls, cascading off the side of the High Level Bridge, and ultimately shut down in 2009 when Environment Canada pointed out that dumping thousands of gallons of chlorinated tap water into the river was not a good idea.

78 | DAWN PLATTE

Music-lover and picnic-blanket enthusiast Dawn Platte organized Edmonton's first Folk Fest in the river valley during her reign in 1981. It has since become a mainstay of Edmonton's summer festival lineup.

79 | BREANNE BREG

Following the warm reception of her predecessor's initiative, Breanne Breg decided that she would also launch a festival. Just like the Folk Fest, Edmonton's Fringe Theatre Festival was an immediate success, and has since become the largest Fringe in the world outside of Edinburgh, gathering hundreds of thousands of people in Old Strathcona every August to see over 200 shows.

80 | ANTONIA SEPÚLVEDA

A Chilean refugee and community activist, Antonia Sepúlveda helped popularize the Hispanoamerica radio program and the Nosotros TV channel. Her cultural events to promote Latin American food and music were popular, but her frank discussion of racism in Edmonton met with less enthusiasm from the city's dominant white population.

81 | DR. MARGARET ANN ARMOUR

A chemistry professor at the University of Alberta, Dr. Margaret Ann Armour had long noted the lack of female students in her faculty. When she became Melting Queen, she founded WISEST—Women in Scholarship, Engineering, Science, and Technology— to encourage women to pursue careers in STEM fields.

82 | NELLIE MILDRED CARLSON

A Cree woman living on Treaty Six territory, Nellie Mildred Carlson lost her status when she married a Métis man. She used her position as Melting Queen to fight against this injustice, having long been involved in the Indian Rights for Indian Women movement. Her phones were tapped and she faced numerous threats, but nevertheless she persisted and ultimately succeeded in changing federal law so that Indigenous women would not lose their treaty rights by marriage.

83 | RACHEL KASTERMAN

From a labour activist family, Rachel Kasterman became the voice of the workers during the Gainers Meatpacking Plant strike. The increasingly violent strike gripped Edmonton over the summer and fall of 1986, as the company owner, Peter Pocklington, brought in scabs, called the strikers terrorists, and refused to negotiate with their union. The tension culminated in an assassination attempt against the Melting Queen—which both sides blamed on the other—who was shot in the chest and spent three days in surgery. The ensuing vigil ended the strike, leading to a new deal between the workers and the management. The defiant Rachel Kasterman continued to insist that the compromise was a bad deal for the workers.

84 | INVIDIA STRAUM

After witnessing the attempted assassination on Rachel Kasterman, Invidia Straum refused the call when she was Named. A devastating tornado hit Edmonton in August, killing twenty-seven people and destroying millions of dollars' worth of property. The natural disaster confirmed the narrative that absent Melting Queens cause devastation for the city, and Invidia Straum was widely blamed for the destruction.

85 | PHILIPPA SCALDERSON

Philippa Scalderson revolutionized Edmonton's Waste Management system by introducing the blue bin program and educating the public about recycling. Edmonton's recycling efforts boomed, with a 95% diversion rate of solid waste in 1988-89 (though this has since fallen).

86 | MARGARET "PEGGY" O'CONNOR FARNELL

Peggy Farnell was both a reference librarian and an intelligence agent for the British Secret Service during her long career prior to becoming the Melting Queen. Her tenure as Melting Queen focused on promoting the unique identities of Edmonton's 375 neighbourhoods, starting with her home of Old Glenora and featuring a new neighbourhood every day for a year.

87 | OSWIN THOMPSON

Oswin Thompson divided the city by calling for the government to suspend all funds to the Catholic school board. By a very slim margin, she successfully persuaded Edmontonians that funding Catholic schools—while not funding special schools for any other religion—was discriminatory. The province mandated instead that world religion classes must be taught in all public schools.

88 | CLODAGH PASKWAMOSTOS

Clodagh Paskwamostos wanted to build a monumental fountain in the heart of Edmonton, a gathering place where people could make wishes and relax in the sun. Instead, she became the reluctant face of the Alberta Eugenics Board class-action lawsuit against the government.

89 | DR. ANNE BURROWS

Dr. Anne Burrows became blind at six years old, but she did not let this impairment get in the way of her dream to pursue music. She studied at the Royal College of Music in London and became an exceptional piano teacher. Her reign focused on spreading her love of music throughout the city and providing services to blind Edmontonians.

90 | MIA PARANÁ

Mia Paraná's multiple initiatives focused on sustainability and overconsumption of energy. She established the hugely successful Lights Out Edmonton Earth Hour event during the 1993 Perseids meteor shower, which continues to this day with a 99% participation rate.

91 | SHISHIRA SARASVATI

Seventeen-year-old Shishira Sarasvati faced huge expectations when she was Named. Not only was she the first daughter of a Melting Queen to be Named, she had also been born during her mother's term. Despite these expectations, she became overwhelmed by intrusive memories and backed away from public life. She found solace painting and drawing her visions, but ultimately the memories shredded her mind and she killed herself by jumping off the High Level Bridge.

92 | VICTORIA GOULBURN

Victoria Goulburn blamed herself for Shishira Sarasvati's death, and saw her term as penance. She planted elm trees all around Edmonton, causing the city to have the highest concentration of urban elm trees anywhere in the world.

93 | *LUCIENNE MEEK*

The "Mother Theresa of Boyle Street," Lucienne Meek created the Mamaokiskatema Society to further Cree culture and advocate for homeless Edmontonians.

94 | EMILY THOMPSON (ALMOST GLORIA HOLE)

When Lucienne Meek went rogue and vowed to Name drag queen Gloria Hole (the alter-ego of local author, historian, and queer rights activist Darrin Hagen), ECHO intervened and pre-emptively announced Emily Thompson as Melting Queen. Emily protected homeless children by fundraising for Youth Emergency Shelters and shining a light on the violence faced by children in Edmonton.

95 | *DORIS BADIR*

Throughout her career, Doris Badir worked for the United Nations and for numerous universities in Canada. Having witnessed extreme poverty around the world, she was a tireless advocate for providing the necessary resources to help lift women and children out of poverty in Edmonton.

96 | KAREN MACKENZIE

A DJ and bartender at Phrique, Jasper Avenue's most popular and notorious nightclub, Karen Mackenzie's signature initiative was creating the largest New Year's Eve celebrations in Edmonton's history to mark the turn of the millennium. The fireworks show alone lasted over an hour.

97 | *DR. PHYLLIS CARDINAL*

Author and educator Dr. Phyllis Cardinal founded the Amiskwaciy Academy, a high school for Indigenous students which preserves First Nations culture and oral traditions.

98 | ZOPHIA VOLGA

A film and television arts student at NAIT, Zophia Volga aspired to create a Great Edmonton Movie in the vein of Elsie Park Gowan's *Who Builds a City*. She brought in dozens of scriptwriters, consulted with hundreds of historians and community members, and featured thousands of everyday Edmontonians as actors and extras in the feature film. The four-hour-long movie that resulted, titled *53/113*, is regarded as an overly ambitious mess that nonetheless highlights some of Edmonton's charms.

99 | *BARB TARBOX*

Barb Tarbox was an anti-smoking activist who spoke to thousands of young Edmontonians about the dangers of cigarettes even as she was dying of lung and brain cancer. She visited hundreds of schools, and died days after crowning Theresa Darling as the 100th Melting Queen.

100 | THERESA DARLING

The one hundredth Melting Queen tried to create a reunion of Melting Queens, but almost all of her predecessors refused to participate in any commemorative event. Instead, Theresa Darling promoted the 2003 Heritage Classic hockey game and celebrated each major festival by honouring the Melting Queen that

started it. She presided over the 100th Melting Day in 2004.

101 | IRIS ZAMBEZI

The first out lesbian Melting Queen, Iris Zambezi advocated for Edmonton's LGBTQ community and pushed major public figures to attend the Pride Parade in an especially controversial era. The Alberta government was blocking same-sex marriage and threatening to invoke the Notwithstanding Clause again (as it had in 2000), and Iris challenged Premier Ralph Klein and Mayor Bill Smith to join her or stand on the wrong side of history.

102 | ROSA ACICULARA

Much like Gloria Tremblay in 1967, Rosa Aciculara's signature initiative was decided long before she was Named. She organized centennial celebrations for the province of Alberta, including the royal visit of Queen Elizabeth II.

103 | ANANKE COSMOPOULOS

An urban planner with the City of Edmonton, Ananke Cosmopoulos used her newfound celebrity to push for a project she had long dreamed about: transforming the barren industrial lands beside Fort Road into a park. Ultimately, Sundial Park used the surviving smokestack from a former meatpacking plant as the needle in a giant sundial garden.

104 | APRIL TREMOR

An aspiring fashion designer, April Tremor helped found Western Canada Fashion Week in Edmonton and encouraged citizens to develop bolder and more individual styles. She also organized clothing drives for needy families.

105 | KATHY KIFTS

In 2008, the population of metro Edmonton surpassed one million people for the first time, making it the furthest north metropolis in North America. Kathy Kifts advocated for the merger of all the surrounding satellite communities into a gigantic super-city. Although she attracted some support, her idea ultimately fizzled out.

106 | INGA CAUSEWAY

A chef at The Silver Spoon, Edmonton's finest restaurant, Inga Causeway promoted the Taste of Edmonton festival for its 25th anniversary and raised money to help poor families go to Edmonton restaurants and experience various international cuisines.

107 | JENNIFER FINLAY

The first truly social media savvy Melting Queen, Jennifer Finlay popularized the mainstream use of #YEG and encouraged citizens to share photos of their city's hidden beauty. She also spoke at Edmonton schools about the psychological dangers of consuming mass amounts of curated photos and the inevitable feelings of inadequacy that result from this new culture of treacherous images.

108 | LENTE VAN DEN BERG

An enthusiastic cyclist, Lente van den Berg advocated for the construction of bike lanes throughout downtown Edmonton and criticized the city's reliance on cars. She ran afoul of PAPRIKA (People Against Potholes Ruining the Integrity of Key Avenues) when she suggested that all of Edmonton's streets should be torn up and replaced by public transit lines and bike lanes. Her reign was a lukewarm success, but she did manage to get 5,000 people to participate in a winter cycle through the river valley.

109 | DOREEN SPURLONG

Doreen Spurlong founded the Edmonton International Cat Festival to celebrate the city's feline population. Her own cats—all twenty-nine of them—became local celebrities in their own right and inspired dozens of fake Twitter accounts.

110 | AUTUMN KAGERA

Autumn Kagera fled to Edmonton as a refugee from Uganda during the 2011 East African Drought. She focused her term on water conservation and founded Glacier Day, an event which honoured the Saskatchewan Glacier that feeds the river and sustains Edmonton.

111 | SUMMER JOHNSON

Figure skater and ice dancer Summer Johnson worked with landscape architect Matt Gibbs to create the Freezeway—a 20 km skating loop that wraps around downtown Edmonton like a shivering white halo, rivalling the Rideau Canal.

112 | TEGAN STORNOWAY

Tegan Stornoway transformed the derelict Edmonton City Centre Sky Harbour—a huge plot of land in the heart of the city, which had previously prevented any construction over 40 storeys high— into the Sky Harbour Gardens, a huge urban park. She also planted the Infinite Maze, Canada's largest labyrinth, at the centre of the gardens.

113 | LOUISE MORRISON

Louise Morrison created Citizen Identity Registration Cards for Living in Edmonton (CIRCLE), which centralized public services (library, transit services, public Wi-Fi, fitness centres, etc.) under one system and created a central municipal directory.

114 | ALICE SONGHUA

Alice Songhua popularized the Chinese community's Lunar New Year celebrations, ringing in the Year of the Dog in February 2018.

115 | RIVER RUNSON

The Last Melting Queen. Created the Winter Fountain to honour the memories of their foresisters and replace the need for a Melting Queen forevermore.

APPENDIX {2}

The Melting Day Proclamation

ARTICLE I.

AFTER A LONG WINTER, when darkness reigns and dawn surrenders to the night, when **howling winds lay waste to a thriving city**, when ice and snow entomb our verdant valley, the people of Edmonton cry out for the salvation of spring. And on that triumphant day when the ice breaks up on the river, when our city wakes from its slumber, when **the fiery sun of summer returns, to free us from our winter prison**, the people of Edmonton shall gather by the riverside and celebrate Melting Day.

ARTICLE II.

The Day of the Sun, **the first day of spring**, the victory of sunshine over shadow, Melting Day shall be the festival of all peoples. The prince and the pauper, the radish and the rose, the saint and the savage shall join hands and celebrate their liberation from the tyranny of winter, an unlikely family, united by a shared trauma.

ARTICLE III.

And on **that glorious day**—that splendid, shining, singular moment of the year—the people of Edmonton shall be led by One Woman. A daughter of the city, the mother of its people, the Melting Queen shall embody the spirit of the city, proclaim our victory over the Long Winter, and lead a Parade of Revellers, who dance with joy to see **a shattered river**.

ARTICLE IV.

As day turns to night, **as sundown claims the melting city**, the people of Edmonton shall be free to indulge their wildest whims and appetites, their fancies and delights. As dawn decorates the city with light, we shall assemble before our Melting Queen, and she will Pardon us for all our sins and transgressions.

ARTICLE V.

The great carnival shall end only when the people have been assured that their grand tradition shall continue through the ages. As the embodiment of the general will of the people, **the Melting Queen shall Name a successor** to her Sacred Charge. The Melting Queen shall be free to choose any daughter of Edmonton to carry on her hallowed duty.

ARTICLE VI.

Woe to the woman who, once Named, refuses to heed the call of service to her city! Woe to Edmonton should she deny her sacred duty! She *shall* be Melting Queen, and **nothing in Heaven or Earth shall prevent it**. For once one is Named, she cannot be changed. She who flees the call incurs a curse on our city. **Let history forget her name**. Let her memory be damned.

ARTICLE VII.

When the river flows swift and free of ice, the Melting Queen shall crown her new sister. The new Melting Queen shall assume her rightful seat, **a flourishing throne in full bloom**, and summer shall truly begin.

ARTICLE VIII.

The blossoming city shall truly have cause to rejoice. For a true Melting Queen shall restore the natural world to its grand, majestic splendour. The city shall burst into full flower, **resurrected by the rains** of spring, and the people of Edmonton shall exult in the purity of their Melting Queen. She shall be **the beating heart of her proud city**.

ARTICLE IX.

As summer gives way to fall, as crisp autumn leaves are dampened by the First Snow, the people of Edmonton need not despair. The Melting Queen shall uphold the joyous spirit of Melting Day over the next Long Winter. She will light the way through the darkness, a fiery beacon in the night. She shall provide a warm bosom against the cold winds, **a lush oasis in a desert of ice and snow**.

ARTICLE X.

Should the Melting Queen so desire, she may endeavour to undertake a Grand Project as a key strategy in the battle against the manifold miseries of winter. To assist the Melting Queen in her Good Works, she shall be attended by advisors who convene **a gathering of worthy petitioners**. From amongst these meritorious supplications, the Melting Queen shall select an initiative, to warm the hearts of her people in the depths of the Long Winter.

ARTICLE XI.

The Melting Queen must be **endowed with a marvellous vision** for her city. She shall only be released from her duty when she fulfills this vision and crowns her successor.

ARTICLE XII.

Though she is Edmonton's perfect mother, though she is beloved of the people, no Melting Queen shall serve her city for more than one year. **Her time has come and gone**, and she must clear the way for her successor to join our city's great sisterhood.

ARTICLE XIII.

The Melting Queen shall brook no rival. All festivities, all revelries, all celebrations shall be organized under her auspices. Edmonton shall not permit any Other, man or woman, to usurp her sacred place at the head of our city.

ARTICLE XIV.

And finally, we lucky few, the people of Edmonton, must remember our Melting Queens and honour their devotion to our city. For we are **far from the world, here at this bend in the river**. We shall not appear in the pages of the great histories of man. We must treasure this obscurity, and love our traditions, and rejoice that we are **a city unlike any other**. And in return, our eternal mother, with her infinite grace, shall bring us springtime forevermore...

Note: the following Article was inserted by Kastevoros Birch shortly after River Runson became the Melting Queen.

ARTICLE XV.

And last of all, should a Melting Queen be Absolutely Unable to fulfill her Sacred Trust, the Good People of Edmonton shall be called upon to appoint Another to serve in her place. And should this Sad Event occur, a General Consensus shall be required among Edmontonians, so that she who is Late-Named, like every Melting Queen from First to Last, shall surely embody the Spirit of Spring.

Acknowledgements

I would like to thank the following people for their help and encouragement while writing this book:

First, I'd like to thank Thomas Wharton, my first and last editor, who helped me begin the journey of writing my first novel and who was there at the end when I needed to make sure that every last word sings.

Next, thank you to Mark Witzaney for having the patience to read a 240,000-word first draft and for pointing out that I'd accidentally written two novels which were hopelessly entangled with each other.

Thank you to Ruth DyckFehderau, for reading the 140,000-word second draft and for giving me the exact same feedback. Sometimes you need to hear it twice before you believe it.

Thank you to Kimmy Beach, for helping me disentangle my two novels, write my third draft, and lay the foundation for a book called *The Melting Queen*.

Thank you to Natalie Cook and the Writers' Guild of Alberta Mentorship Program for introducing me to Kimmy Beach and giving me the opportunity to reshape my manuscript.

I'd like to thank Daphne Read for reading every draft I sent her and for providing me with continuous feedback and moral support throughout this lengthy process.

I'd like to thank Norma Dunning for her advice and encouragement, not only with this novel but with many short stories way back in my very first writing class. We made it, Norma! Seriously, buy her book, it's amazing.

I'd like to thank Danielle Fuechtmann, who has not only read multiple drafts and been the perfect sounding board for countless ideas, but also provided me with emotional support during the hundreds of times I doubted myself and this book.

I'd like to thank Kyla Hewson, for asking questions that nobody else ever thinks to ask and for helping me bring this book across the finish line.

I'd like to thank Matt Bowes, Claire Kelly, and everyone at NeWest Press for taking a chance on this book and agreeing to publish a parallel-universe, magic realist, alternate history, genderfluid Edmonton fantasia. Fingers crossed guys.

I'd like to thank my family—my parents, my aunt, and my sister—for always encouraging me and for never making me feel like I was wasting my time by pursuing an artistic passion.

And finally I'd like to thank Edmonton. It's easy to hate your hometown when all you read in books and see on screen are images of New York and Paris and London. It's easy to hear, and believe, and uncritically reproduce the narratives that you live in a boring, grey, boiler room of a city. But any city can be grand and colourful and magical, if you just look around. All you need is an open mind, a curious spirit, and a little imagination. Dozens of authors have written books and stories and poems set in Edmonton. I'm proud to be one of them.

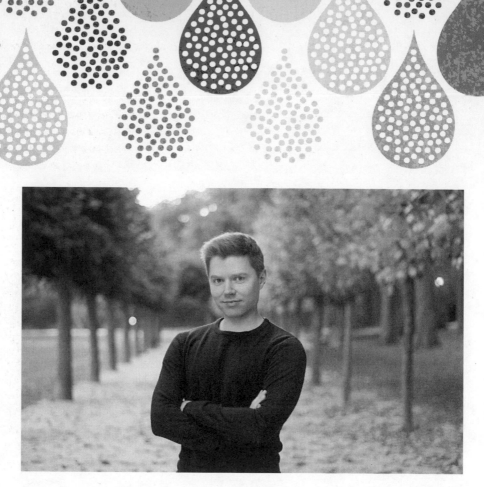

Bruce Cinnamon was born in Edmonton and grew up just downstream in Fort Saskatchewan, along the banks of the North Saskatchewan River. He holds a BA in English and Creative Writing from the University of Alberta and a Master of Global Affairs from the University of Toronto. His favourite authors and literary influences include Garth Nix, Haruki Murakami, Jorge Luis Borges, Rachel Carson, Thomas King, Tomson Highway, and Italo Calvino. *The Melting Queen* is his first novel.